CW00968766

Fantasy Books by B. V. Larson

THE HAVEN SERIES
Volume I: Haven Magic
*(First three books: Amber Magic, Sky Magic,
Shadow Magic)*
Volume II: Dark Magic
*(Books 4 thru 6: Dragon Magic, Blood Magic,
Death Magic)*
Volume III: Dream Magic (Series finish)

Visit BVLarson.com for more information.

HAVEN MAGIC
Haven Series VOLUME I
by
B. V. Larson

*This book contains the complete, reworked
versions of books 1 thru 3 of the Haven Series.*

ISBN-13: 978-1499564624
ISBN-10: 1499564627
BISAC: Fiction / Fantasy / Epic

Book I: AMBER MAGIC

Chapter One
The Deepwood

Twrog was a Deepwood Giant of middling size. He had fingers as thick as tree branches, huge flapping ears and teeth like walnuts. Being no more than two centuries of age, he was young and inexperienced for a member of his lonely race. He had wandered the murky depths of the forest along the River Haven's western border all his life. Normally, he kept away from the humans who lived in the Haven and the Fae who danced upon their mounds. Today however, two strangers had entered his territory.

The first creature claimed he had come to warn him about the second. This being was a member of the Wild Hunt, a dead-thing known as Voynod. Among the Wild Huntsmen, Voynod ranked high. He was often called the Dark Bard, which Twrog gathered was due to his playing of music and his odd costume of rancid, black cloth. Twrog cared little about rank and status, being a solitary creature. The Wild Huntsmen were dead-things, and Twrog knew better than to trust the Dead. They were tricky—even trickier than humans that still drew breath. Normally, Twrog would have doubted the Dark Bard's word. No one trusted one of the Dead without good cause. But he had seen the human invader Voynod spoke of with his own eyes, wandering among the birch and ash trunks of the Deepwood as if he owned the place.

"Imagine," said the Bard, leaning forward in his saddle. Ancient leather creaked with the movement. "Imagine the unmitigated *gall* the man must have to come here into your lands."

Twrog shied away from Voynod slightly. He did not like the smell of dead-things. This one was so ancient it no longer had an odor of decay, but the musty smells of the long-dead still disturbed the giant's sensitive nose.

"Is not right," said Twrog thickly. He was not good at speech. The bulging muscles that clung to his jawbone were meant for cracking bones and sucking out marrow, not forming fancy sounds.

"No!" agreed the Bard. "Not right at all!" Voynod's horse, which was as dead as its rider, stepped closer as if knowing what its master wanted. Twrog's eyes strayed to the horse, and his face twitched in disgust. Skin, flesh and hair covered most of it, but here and there the gray-white of a bone could be seen. The horse's eyes were tiny lavender flames.

"This man ignores the Pact that keeps his own people safe," continued the Bard. "Just the very fact the human breathes your forest air befouls it. His presence despoils this sanctuary of natural beauty."

The Bard's melodic words conjured an image in Twrog's large, slow brain. To the Deepwood giant the River Folk intrusion seemed monumentally unfair. The puny humans insisted on maintaining their Pact with the Faerie, the Dead and other creatures like Twrog, forbidding all but humans entry into the Haven. At the same time however, they felt they could cross the borders into other folk's territory at will. To add insult to injury, the human was a hunter seeking wild boars, which were a major part of Twrog's diet this time of year. He could not spare a single pig.

The forest around the two beings was unusually hushed. A tall ash tree loomed over Twrog and Voynod, but the rest of the region was populated by lowland oaks. The giant was squatting, as was his nature, upon a boggy spot of ground. A single fungus thrust up in front of his feet, but he had been careful not to touch it. The mushroom was known to the River Folk as a *maiden's veil* due to the fungus' odd golden shroud which grew to encircle the central horn of white. Twrog's name for the mushroom was *stinkhorn*, as the growths made an

3

unpleasant smell when trod upon. Maiden's veil or stinkhorn—whatever the name, this variety often sprouted half a foot in height in a single night.

"The River Folk have their river," said Voynod intently. "They have their boats and their fields, but that isn't enough for them, is it?"

Twrog blinked up at the dead-thing on its horse, uncertain as to the correct answer. He did not like the Bard, but he did not fear him, either. He had an attitude toward the Dead that was rather like a farmer's attitude toward large spiders in the barn. They were disgusting and to be avoided whenever possible—but they were not to be feared.

Staring at the Bard, Twrog thought of the wonderful smells the river man was emitting from his rucksack. Far from ruining the forest, to the giant it was as if the hunter spread perfume with every step. Twrog's mouth dripped with saliva. He eyed the Bard dully, forgetting he had been asked a question at all.

Voynod rolled his eyes quickly, then bent conspiratorially close. "What I want to know, noble giant, is this: what are you going to do about it?"

"Huh?"

"What are you going to do about this creature that parades itself in your woods?" Voynod demanded.

The giant had first scented the human the day before, but it was not the stink of the hunter's small clay pipe or his flagon of ale that had caught Twrog's attention. Rather, it was a *new* scent, a meaty scent that he could not quite place. Twrog knew every wild flavor of game in the forest and every fish in the river. He could identify every fowl as it was roasted, but this odor was slightly different. If he had to gamble, he'd say it was pig, but there were other smells as well, mixed in with the typical musky scent of a boar.

Although he could not identify the scent that so flavored the air, it was definitely mouthwatering. He decided to track the hunter, even as the man tracked wild boars along the gloomy forest trails.

"What are you going to do?" pressed the Bard.

4

"I'm going to eat it," Twrog said, thinking about whatever the human was carrying. He desperately wanted to know what made such wonderful flavors in the air.

The Dark Bard cocked his head, and then nodded slowly in approval. "I suppose that will do," he said.

* * *

Today Arlon of the Thunderfoot clan wore his hunting outfit: a homespun tunic of wool, poorly-dyed and stained to a splotchy brown. He liked the tunic, believing it made it harder for animals to see him. He gripped a crossbow in both hands, the iron prod of which had been carefully scraped and oiled until it was free of rust.

When he had first entered the Deepwood three days earlier, the banks of the Berrywine River had been overgrown with a profusion of marsh violets and bog asphodel. As he'd tied his boat to a tree and headed inland, he'd spotted a variety of birds, including three buzzards and a rare red kite flying overhead. All that changed as he delved more deeply into the forest. The birds had quieted, and those that still sang were distant and forlorn. The canopy of leaves overhead thickened until only snatches of blue-white sky could be seen.

Arlon was not afraid—not exactly. He'd been in the Deepwood before on dares as a teen and on occasional expeditions since then to chop down a hardwood tree or to hunt for birds' eggs. Like most River Folk he didn't *fear* the Deepwood, but he was wary of it. Strange events occurred out here beyond the borders of the Haven. Odd beings lived and danced beneath these trees at will. There was no rule of law with them—the peace treaty known as the Pact did not extend to this quiet sea of green leaves.

He had to question the wisdom of coming to this place alone. Arlon was no foolish youngster. At forty-two, he was an experienced woodsman from the west shore town of Hamlet. Arlon had rarely ventured into the Deepwood along the western bank of the Berrywine, even though it was close to his home. He'd spent many nights of his life in the forests of the east bank, in the region known as the Haven Wood, which was inside the borders of the Haven and quite safe for River Folk. The Deepwood that bordered the fields outside Hamlet was a different matter entirely.

Arlon knew the venture was something for a younger man to undertake, but hadn't been able to refuse Molly's offer back home in Hamlet. She'd told him she would marry the man who first brought her fresh boar meat for her birthday dinner—and he'd taken the invitation seriously. His own wife Dera had passed on some winters back leaving him with no children. He didn't think he would get too many more invitations to share a bed with someone like Molly. She was ten years younger than he and strong, with three daughters of her own in need of feeding. Her husband had been lost to Merlings last spring, and like all couples who meet one another after having lost their mates, the two had felt an instant kinship.

"Is this an open invitation, then?" he'd asked her in a voice that was regrettably gruff. He could not help but wonder how many other suitors had been told to prove themselves in this fashion.

"Absolutely," she'd said, throwing her nose high in the air. "Anyone who brings me a fresh boar steak for my birthday dinner—hunted down by his own mettle, mind you—will be given my hand."

Arlon had made a sour face. He'd been on the verge of making a nasty comment when Molly had touched his arm gently and smiled. "The trouble for all the rest," she said quietly, "is that you are the only one that I've told about the contest."

Arlon had blinked, and his frown had melted and transformed into a smile. A contest with only himself as a contestant? He ought to be able to win *that*.

Molly had provided him with a cured ham for his journey. He had looked at the ham in surprise. If she already had a ham hock, why did he have to bring her a wild pig for her birthday? He did not question her, however. Perhaps this bit of irony was part of the test. He gazed into her eyes, ignoring the fine lines of care and age that circled them. He saw in her face the beauty she once was. He wanted her, and so he took the ham and the sack and set off to prove himself to her. He was no drunken lout, no matter what had been whispered around the taverns since Dera's death. He would win this new woman—by bringing her six boars, if that's what she wanted. His only hope was that he could find a small, young pig. Boars were dense of meat and thick of bone. They were notoriously difficult to carry out of the forest. Perhaps, he thought, this was part of the test. Did he have enough strength and manhood left to provide what his woman needed? He vowed to prove to her that he did.

With less than a week to go before Molly's birthday, Arlon had decided to hunt in the Deepwood rather than the relatively tame Haven Wood. He knew the boars weren't due to be in rut until the winter and now they would be fat and plentiful after a long summer of feasting on truffles in the forest loam. The piglets would be the easiest to find and shoot with his crossbow. They would be the lightest and easiest to dress and carry out of the forest, too. Boars were rare in the Haven Wood in this season, usually hunted out by the end of summer. But in the Deepwood, where few hunters dared to travel, he hoped to easily find wild pigs. His plan was simple: he would bring one down and take it back to his boat which waited on the shoreline several miles to the east.

And so three days later, he found himself wandering the unfamiliar trails of the Deepwood, where the young boars were thick this year by all reports. He wasn't happy with his mission by this time, and each step farther into the gloomy trees left him wishing he'd been tasked with slaying a Merling along the wilder parts of the Berrywine River instead.

He'd taken his rowboat, loaded it with arms and provisions, then paddled to a spot along the shore where game was known to be plentiful in years past. He'd tied the boat on the shore and pressed ahead into the green quiet of the Deepwood. A feeling of unease had grown upon him, hour by hour, as he walked the forest trails. Each mile he traveled away from the protected borders of the Haven weighed upon his mind. He expected the cat-like leer of a goblin behind the next trunk—or worse, the pipes of an elf playing in solitude atop a tree. None of the River Folk ever felt completely safe in the Deepwood. Everyone knew that its apparent tranquility was deceptive. The quiet trees masked a hundred unknowable sins.

There had been nothing substantial to spook him, however. It was only a feeling of foreboding. He constantly discounted the sensation, telling himself it was the natural fear all his people felt when they found themselves far from the roaring Berrywine for long. His bigger worry was the growing cold, especially at night. It was unseasonably bitter in the evenings now for autumn. Three nights he'd spent in the Deepwood, and each night had been colder than the last. He thought it might snow soon if matters didn't improve.

Following the trails fruitlessly until late afternoon, Arlon found a glade at long last and crept up to the limits of the tree cover. There, in a sun-drenched open area of the forest was a welcome sight. It was a salt-lick, a naturally occurring spot in the land where animals gathered to consume revealed minerals. Harsh weather had probably opened up this glade—perhaps lightning had struck here, knocking down the trees. Whatever the cause, this spot had exposed stones which were rich in calcium and salts. The animals needed these minerals and they would come here often to find them.

No less than three pigs were in sight at the salt-lick. Two were sows, their big ears twitching and their bellies distended by months of eating tubers and grubs. The last of them was a young boar. His hair was so short Arlon could see through it to the brown skin underneath. The thin coat and small size indicated youth. Arlon could not believe his good fortune. He smiled hugely, and lifted his crossbow.

With sudden dismay, he realized it was not loaded. He shook his head at himself. Here it was, the moment of truth, and he was not thinking! It was quite normal to carry the crossbow unloaded. It would weaken the iron prod to keep it loaded all day. But he should have been loading it the moment he saw the salt-lick, before he had even spotted the first pig. Surely, he had only a minute or two before the pigs picked up his scent and fled.

Slowly, quietly, Arlon put the crossbow down nose-first into the brush at his feet. He put his foot into the stirrup and drew back on the string. He struggled to bend the prod and latch the string in the trigger mechanism. Doing it quietly made the process all the harder.

He thought later it was the tiny *click* of the trigger mechanism that gave him away. Whatever the case, he heard the animals shuffle, then rustle among the bushes circling the open glade. With a hissing curse, he rammed a bolt into the slot, brought the crossbow to his shoulder and pulled the trigger.

A bolt went streaking through the air. It should have struck nothing. It should have missed and vanished into the forest, forcing him to purchase a new bolt from the grinning fletchers back in Hamlet. But the bolt flew true. It struck the young boar in the shoulder and the shock knocked the animal down momentarily. The pig scrambled back up and fled, but it was grievously injured.

Arlon, disbelieving of his good fortune, whooped and charged out of his hiding place. He ran after the pig as it limped for the trees. With a blood trail to follow and an injury that would slow it further with every step, the young boar was as good as his.

Arlon could already see himself, in his mind's eye, giving the pig to Molly. She would be impressed! What woman could not be? She had set a task and this man who everyone called washed-up—a Thunderfoot clansman people whispered had turned into a worthless drunk—this man had met her challenge.

As Arlon chased down the pig, he thought this might well be the best day of his life. It was certainly the first truly good day since Dera had up and died on him.

* * *

Twrog was a masterful hunter. He knew men were difficult to hunt—they were tricky and smart. They must be handled differently than the usual beasts that lived among the trees. Men who heard a giant crashing after them would run into a thicket or fight with sharp weapons. Twrog had no more desire to be cut than anyone else did. So he hunted the man who had dared invade his forest with great care.

The giant had not simply followed at a safe distance. He knew every trail in the forest, and had blazed many of them himself. Instead of following the trail, he proceeded through the trees a hundred paces off, following the course of the trail as if it were a wary beast itself. He did not travel too fast, nor to slow, but he came to the glade and the salt-lick just before Arlon did. He knew the spot well. Often, he lured game here and bashed them with his lucky club.

From a hidden shadowy region under a group of three large rowan trees, Twrog watched the salt-lick. He hunkered down and waited downwind of the pigs. The human stupidly followed the game trail directly to the salt lick. Twrog could tell from this fact alone that he was inexperienced. One had to pay great attention to the winds when hunting—as much attention to it as the animals did. If they scented you, man or giant, you would go hungry that night. And Twrog hated trying to fall asleep on an empty, growling stomach.

Twrog watched the man reach the far side of the glade and pause there, finally noticing the pigs that milled in the open. Stupid *and* blind, this one was. He grinned, but managed to stifle the rumbling laugh that wanted to exit his flaring lips.

Then he watched as Arlon shouldered his crossbow as if to shoot. Twrog tensed. The pigs had not yet scented the hunter. Was he perhaps not as foolish as he seemed? But then he did not shoot, and Twrog knew the truth. He had forgotten to load his cumbersome weapon. Twrog sniffed quietly. Men always built things that were overly complex and took time to make ready. Twrog's club never needed to be loaded.

The pigs became restless. Twrog's grin returned. He considered a booming shout that would send them all running. That would be quite a surprise for the invader! But he held back. The man had his crossbow loaded now, and Twrog had no desire to feel its sting. Let the man fire at the pigs. Let the river man do the shooting—Twrog would do the eating, later.

Twrog rose from his squatting position into a ready crouch. He carefully shouldered his stout oak club, the thickness and weight of which was greater than the fattest man in the Haven. It was a good club, and had always brought him luck. Privately he thought it was magical. Flittering Faerie might scoff and

10

twitter at the idea, but Twrog was convinced. Today, he suspected he would prove once again his club was special. Today, he would crush a man down with it until his blood and bones were driven into the black earth of the Deepwood.

The man fired his crossbow too late. The pigs were already running. But, to Twrog's surprise, he saw one of the pigs stumble and go down. The young boar had been struck in the shoulder. The man whooped and raced forward to follow the wounded animal.

Twrog's flapping lips flared wide. His gnarled, stinking teeth were yellow and riddled with decay. He could not believe this insult. This human was not to be tolerated, killing Twrog's game in his part of the forest. If this intrusion went unchecked, there might be a dozen of them next year with a dozen yapping dogs leading the way.

Twrog burst out of cover and rushed after the man and the wounded boar. His club rode his shoulder, his fingers wrapped tightly around it. So intent was the human on chasing down his wounded boar that he didn't seem to notice the giant that trailed him. Twrog controlled his pace. Rather than crashing through the brush, he moved as quietly as he was able, keeping up with the man's rush without having to break into a thundering trot. He moved with care, ducking under branches rather than smashing them aside and paying attention to where his broad, hairy feet came down. It would not do to alert the human now. The joke would be all the sweeter if the river man's fate arrived as an utter surprise.

* * *

When Arlon caught up with the small, young boar a feeling of triumph surged through him. He had done it! He had brought down a wild boar in the forests—in the Deepwood no less—and he would take the carcass back to Hamlet. He would present it to Molly with a ribbon as red as the blood that flowed from its shoulder. A ribbon which he would wrap all the way around the beast. She would be pleased and surprised. He had no doubt she would cook it for him. He imagined himself

11

pridefully cutting into the prize in front of her three daughters. Before the first bite was served and swallowed, he would propose. How could a good widow do anything but accept his offer? For the first time since Dera had passed on, he felt truly whole inside.

Arlon's pleasant moment was short-lived, however. He stooped over the fallen boar, examining it as it twitched in a pile of dead leaves, when something caused the back of his neck to tingle. He had a sensation of foreboding. He turned and felt the hot wash of a vast creature's breath full upon his face. The giant must have been standing there, holding its breath, waiting for him to notice it.

It was huge. Standing as tall as a farmhouse chimney, it must have weighed as much as any three horses in the Haven put together. On its shoulder rode a surprisingly thick club, a branch that was as big around as a tree trunk. The bark of the tree the club had been torn from still clung to it—rough oak bark it was, black and gnarled.

Arlon did not scream, nor did he stammer and plead. He simply turned and ran for the thickest copse of trees in sight. With a great, warbling cry, the giant gave chase. The ground shook now with crashing footsteps. Arlon could not imagine how this creature could have snuck up on him. It must have followed while he was hot on the trail of the boar, laughing all the while.

Arlon was no soldier and he did not carry a sword. He did have a long knife, however, with which he'd planned to use to dress the boar. He pulled the blade from its sheath on his belt as he ran.

He never made it to the safety of the thick grove of trees. He heard a thrumming sound behind him as if something huge moved through the air. The club swept him up from behind, like a matron's broom catching up with a fleeing cat. Unlike a broom, however, the club crushed his legs, breaking them both in several places. Arlon was uplifted and thrown, tumbling head over heels into the trunk of an ash tree. He sagged down on the thick roots and leaves at the bottom of the trunk, a broken tangle of limbs. He lay stunned as the giant approached.

The giant wore a broad, imbecilic grin on its face. He made a great honking sound, a heavy laugh that would haunt Arlon's dying thoughts.

"Is not right!" said Twrog, shaking his club at Arlon.

Arlon stared back in shock and incomprehension. He felt the giant's thick fingers, probing into his rucksack. The monster removed the ham hock Molly had given him and gnawed at the meat with obvious relish.

What was not right? Arlon thought. He pondered the giant's words vaguely as he lost consciousness.

* * *

Arlon awakened once more before he died. A strange figure stood upon a horse and bent low over him. The creature was dressed in rancid black cloth and none of its features could be seen. In the night, the outline of the figure glowed slightly. Arlon knew the being must be one of the Fae, or some other creature of darkness.

"Help me," Arlon said in a voice that was barely above a whisper.

The figure made a soft sound of dismissal. It ignored Arlon and continued dipping something down toward him. Arlon tried to move, but was unable to operate his broken body.

"Will you not aid a fallen man?" Arlon asked.

The unseen figure chuckled. It was an evil sound, and upon hearing it Arlon abandoned all hope of rescue.

"It is *thee*, who shall be helping *me*, this eve!" said the figure. It leaned down from its saddle and commenced working again.

Arlon, his mind fuzzy with the nearness of death, tried to puzzle out what the creature was doing. As far as he could tell, it used a goblet to gather the blood that ran from his wounded body. The goblet was small, silver and ornately decorated. The silver shone in the moonlight, although moonlight shouldn't have been able to penetrate the thick canopy of the forest above.

13

Thinking of Molly, Arlon smiled weakly. She would have been so pleased to have tasted the boar. The creature, never leaving its horse's back, bent far down to scoop with the goblet. The edge of the goblet thumped against each of Arlon's stacked ribs as it was dragged over them. The being whistled a soft piper's tune as it worked. Arlon thought it was a wonderful sound. The creature was musical and mysterious.

But why does it fill a silver goblet with my blood? Arlon died while wondering about the Dark Bard's true purpose.

Chapter Two
The Berrywine River

The final reddening rays of sunlight streamed down from the heavens to touch mountains, sea, leafy treetops and thatched roofs. Near the western border of the River Haven, at the foot of the Black Mountains, the dying light illuminated a rain cloud. Silvery-gray droplets fell from the cloud's belly and shimmered into arcs of crimson, orange, amber, green, blue and violet. Together, the arcs formed a brilliant rainbow. Everyone in the Haven who saw it knew that somewhere, at the impossible foot of the rainbow, danced a ring of the elusive Faerie.

To the east of the rainbow lay the Berrywine River. There the sunlight fell upon the backs of Brand Rabing and his older brother Jak. The warmth of the sun was slight, but it felt good on Brand's bare head and helped keep him from shivering beneath his cloak of gray, homespun wool. Brand glanced to the west and shivered at the sight of the rainbow. Its presence chilled him anew. For the River Folk rainbows were bad omens indeed, not due to superstition, but rather due to the beings that gathered promptly when rainbows appeared. He hunched over his pole and worked harder.

Brand and Jak were speaking little now, saving their energies for punting the loaded skiff quickly to safety before the light failed completely. They had gotten a late start, and the trip had taken most of the afternoon. The short mast at the center of the skiff was unadorned by a sail as the wind was blowing upriver and into their faces. They had only the current and the power of their limbs to move them downstream.

Jak was three years older, but Brand was taller. They didn't bear much family resemblance, Jak being blond and brown-eyed, while Brand was dark-haired with eyes like clear blue water. Both, however, had well-muscled shoulders from long years of battling the river's currents and eddies. They wore tunics of buckskin, the wet sleeves and leggings of which were stained nearly black by the splashing water.

Brand blinked at his brother for a moment, reminded of first his father and then his mother, both dead these last seven years. In years past, they had all traveled to Riverton for the offering as a family. Now only the two brothers were left to farm the family Isle and transport their bounty to the Faerie.

Their hardwood poles glinted wetly. A dragonfly landed on the tip of Brand's pole, making him smile and pause briefly before it flittered away with a shimmering movement of its translucent wings.

They rounded the last of the Thorn Rocks and entered the deep, slow-moving eddies on the far side. Brand thrust his pole down to where his hands touched the inky river in order to reach the bottom. Soon, they were able to do little more than drift between the spots where they knew the bottom was in range of their long poles.

So busy were the two young men with their task that at first Brand missed the movement of a shadow in the white-barked birch trees on the west side of the river. The second time, however, the water seemed disturbed, and he looked up. What he saw amongst the trees left him gaping.

The shadowy figure of a man on horseback stood there—at least it was man-shaped—but obscured somewhat by the long afternoon shadows of the trees. His surprise was not in the sight so much, although it was strange to see a man in the River Haven clad all in black and staring silently, but rather in the feeling that overcame him. Later, he could only describe it as dread—the feeling of a cornered rabbit that turns to face the fox's teeth. Instinctively, he hunkered down, losing his grip momentarily on his pole as fear numbed his fingers.

16

He saw a silvery glint of something in the shadow's hands. Something long and bright.

"You're losing your pole!" shouted Jak, turning back to see what the matter was.

Sure enough, it had slipped completely from his hands and was drifting away. Brand made a grab for it, caught it, and nearly fell in as the skiff wallowed with the sudden movement. After a precarious moment, he regained his feet, saved by years of boating experience. He turned back to the shore, ignoring Jak's perplexed frown.

"What's gotten into..." began Jak, but he halted, following Brand's wide-eyed stare.

They looked together at the trees along the western shore. There was nothing there.

"What was it?" hissed Jak, stowing his pole and unlashing the crossbow. "Was it a Merling?"

Brand shook his head. "It's gone."

"That's the edge of the Deepwood and the Deepwood is full of Merling dens. It probably slipped into the water. You get the boathook. If I see its froggy eyes pop up, I'll chance a shot at it," said Jak, hurriedly putting his foot into the stirrup of his crossbow and cocking it.

"No, no Merling..." said Brand. "It was a man—maybe." He quickly described what he had seen, leaving out only his feeling of cold dread.

Jak stared at him for a long moment, and Brand feared that even his brother was not going to believe him. It did seem very odd, even to him. But finally, Jak nodded, placing a bolt into the slot of the crossbow.

"It's been a strange autumn," was all that he said.

They watched the water and the trees for a time, but nothing else happened.

"We must get our offering to Riverton before dark," said Jak when it seemed clear that the shadowy figure would not return. "The Harvest Moon is almost full tonight."

Brand quietly agreed.

They spent the rest of the trip tensely watching the western shore. The river moved below them, carrying the skiff rapidly downstream in the narrow portions, barely creeping or swirling backward in the wide slow parts. They knew every mile of the river, every deep, backwashing eddy and pole-catching snag. More importantly, since the river changed somewhat with the seasons and the years, they knew how to tell a new snag just by the way the current wavered as the water passed over it. Like all the folk that lived in the River Haven, they felt most at home when near running water, or preferably *on* running water.

Feeling the chill breath of the night that lay ahead, Brand half wished he had worn his newest thigh-high boots, dreading the intrusion of river water and squishy delta mud when they had to wrestle the cargo up to the docks. These older boots were no longer thigh-high as he had grown so greatly this past year. He had not yet been able to bring himself to wear his new boots on the river, wanting both to keep them clean and new, and at the same time wanting to savor the comfortable softness of the old ones.

Autumn had come early this year, very early. It seemed that winter was already on its way, hard on autumn's heels. The Black Mountains to the east and the higher peaks of Snowdonia to the north were already dusted with caps of snow. Hail had damaged much of the crops, ending hopes of a good harvest. Worse still, there had been many signs that things were not right in the River Haven. Rainbows occurred almost daily, earning frowns and concerned looks cast over hunched shoulders. Reports of wolves, Merlings and worse things had become commonplace. All over the Haven, from the High Marshes to the Glasswater Lake delta, came word of things appearing from the forests and mountains, and even out of the Berrywine River itself. Fisherman and hunters made sure they were home by dark, and the shepherds hurried their flocks into their pens early each evening. Up on the Isle of Harling, as far up the river as Haven folk ever ventured, a hill giant was said to have wrecked a farm with his two great fists. Many scoffed, though all were given to glancing back at the trail behind.

Brand stared down at the crossbow and the boathook that lay atop the skiff's netted cargo of broadleaf melons and berrywine casks. He wondered if a single steel-tipped bolt could stop a hill giant. When he looked up, his brother Jak was eyeing him sidelong.

Jak huffed at him then and he was reminded that he wasn't punting, nor was he watching for trouble as was his assigned task. Worse, they were close to the Talon Rapids, where the going became the toughest. Blushing, he put his back into it and turned to watch the shores again. Jak returned to his work in the prow, shaking his head.

Both heaved a sigh of relief when they rounded the final bend into the wide slow section of the river that surrounded Stone Island. In the blue-white twilight, Stone Island was an impressive sight. On three sides the island rose up on cliffs of hard granite, twenty to fifty feet high in most places. Atop this gray wall perched a hilly land of forests and glens. The fourth side, the eastern side, dipped down to the water and cradled a lagoon and the village of Riverton. Chosen long ago as a good site for a community as it was well-protected from storms and floods, Riverton had been the prosperous center of the Haven for as long as anyone could remember.

* * *

Darkness fell swiftly as they drifted toward the island. The first anchored buoy clanged its bell in greeting and they exchanged smiles. Their faces were now illuminated only by the light of the lantern that swung from the mast. They let the current take them now, lifting their poles from the water and saving their energies for the final push to the village docks at Riverton. Both were tired, a bit shivery, and glad the journey was almost at an end. It seemed to Brand that their home island was further away from Riverton this autumn than ever before.

Tonight, Stone Island was a towering shadow of blackness. Only the twinkling lights from the outlying houses that were sprinkled along the cliffs and the warm diffuse glow that came from Riverton relieved the darkness. It wasn't long before the skiff slipped into the lagoon and nudged up against the docks. Brand and Jak were lucky; there was plenty of space at the high public docks. There was no need to jump down into the cold squelching mud of the river to pull the skiff up to shore. A lone cart waited for them at the docks. A chestnut carthorse stood,

19

tail flipping. The cart's driver climbed down from the board and held aloft a heavy brass lantern in greeting.

"Hey there, Corbin!" shouted Brand to the driver. "Give us a hand, man!"

With deliberate steps that suggested bulk, the man approached. Brand noted that the man had the hood of his cloak pulled up and that the lantern failed to penetrate the gloom within. He frowned. Was this truly his cousin, Corbin Rabing? Or was it someone good at imitating his slow, stumping gait? Thoughts of the shadowy horseman back on the river sprang to mind.

"What's wrong with you, Brand?" asked Jak. He was a bit short-tempered after the three hour journey. "Take this cask, will you?"

Brand clambered up onto the dock and took the proffered cask. He set it down on the creaking boards while still eyeing the approaching figure. Then he shook his head, chiding himself. Of course it was Corbin. No shadow man could walk like that.

Corbin stepped closer and threw back the hood of his cloak. "It's a cold one tonight, isn't it? It took you gentlemen quite some time to get here. Couldn't use the sails?" he asked. His wide face split with a smile that showed his strong white teeth. "Good to see you, in any case." He was the same age as Brand, both of them being about twenty, but looked older with his heavy reddish beard and big-boned shoulders. Corbin was as wide as Brand was tall. As was often the case with young hard-working men, there was no fat on either of them.

Brand grabbed Corbin's free hand and shook it. He couldn't help but feel relieved. "Good to see you too, my cousin."

Jak, standing in the skiff, was looking up at them with his fists on his hips. He said nothing, but Brand could tell what he was thinking: *You've been acting jumpy all day, ever since...*there was no need to finish the thought.

With renewed energy, Brand jumped back into the skiff and began handing up the cargo with Jak. Corbin stacked the casks two at a time and piled the melons beside them with easy, deliberate movements.

Soon they were finished unloading, and after securing the skiff for the night they carried the cargo to the cart and loaded it. Lastly, they tossed up their rucksacks with their fresh clothes and gear. "I wish that Tator would come out on the dock," said Jak. "Although I can't say that I blame him for being skittish about the water."

The chestnut carthorse tossed his head, perhaps recognizing his name. Corbin patted him as he loaded two more broadleaf melons. "Tator knows what's best for him," he said gently. "And falling into the lagoon ain't it."

While Jak climbed up onto the board next to the driver's seat and Brand tried to get comfortable perched on the wine casks, Corbin fed Tator an apple from his pocket. Then he heaved himself into the driver's seat and they set off. The horse pulled the cart slowly but gamely up the hill toward Riverton.

The first houses they passed were mounted on spindly-looking stilts. Neither the stilts nor the rickety houses themselves appeared to be in the best of repair. Most of these belonged to the less reputable clans among the Riverton folk, which meant the Hoots, who were the most numerous, as well as the Silures and the Fobs. They inhabited the dock region primarily because the land was cheap, as no one else wanted to live on stilts that may or may not hold up in the yearly floods. It was even cheaper if one simply squatted on the land and built a shack there, which was what many of them did. Brand always disliked the first part of the road up from the docks as it wound through this section of town. It was no fun passing beneath the sour eyes of the Hoots and the Silures who had made a family tradition of sitting out on the raised porches of their shacks in the evenings. There they would sit, some rocking, most smoking long-stemmed clay pipes, all with a large corked jug of fruit wine at their feet.

Years ago, when Jak and Brand had been children and their parents had still lived, the Silures had tried to take Rabing Isle from them with an ancient writ of inheritance. The writ, supposedly discovered among the effects of old man Tad Silure, had turned out to be a forgery. The entire Silure clan, as well as the Hoots, who counted the Silures as close kinsfolk due to excessive intermarriage between the two clans, had never forgotten the loss of Rabing Isle, which they still regarded as rightfully theirs. Brand looked at the others on the driver's board, and noted their determined postures. They leaned forward, hunching over without glancing from side to side. He could imagine the grim look of distaste on their faces. No one in the Rabing Clan would give a Silure or a Hoot the time of day. The Fobs alone were decent dock-dwellers, a cut above the grasping Hoots and Silures.

"I can only imagine the offering that this lot has come up with for the Feast," muttered Jak back over his shoulder to Brand. "Probably a barrel of last month's salmon garnished with old man Tad Silure's shoelaces."

Corbin and Brand said nothing in return, but they did exchange a glance. Jak had never forgiven the Silures or the Hoots, and persisted in the claim that they had had a hand in the odd boating accident that had left his parents missing and presumably eaten by Merlings.

Slightly higher up the hill they passed the tannery and the slaughterhouse. Brand turned a wistful eye to the rambling old house that stood near the tannery. A single candle burned in an upstairs window. Brand wondered if it was Telyn's room.

Jak nudged Corbin, and it was a moment before Brand noticed that they were both eyeing him and grinning. "You sure are sweet on that Fob girl, aren't you Brand?" chuckled Jak.

Corbin laughed and slapped the reins lightly on Tator's back, as the horse had begun to slow, sensing their distraction. Brand felt his cheeks flush and grimaced at the melons.

"Scraper, isn't that what they call her?" asked Jak.

Brand frowned at him. "Her name's Telyn."

Jak nodded, saying nothing more. Corbin began humming a little tavern song about the lord who loved the pig farmer's daughter. Brand sighed, and they both grinned at him.

"I think she's a fine girl, Brand," said Jak quietly.

Corbin cleared his throat; a mannerism that Brand knew was his mild form of apology. Nothing more was said of it, but Brand continued to watch the lonely candle in the window until they had left it beyond a bend in the road.

After a time the rutted road left the docks and the shacks behind and Riverton proper began. Here the houses were larger and more pleasantly lit up. Sounds of merry-making came from beneath several of the thatched roofs. Smoke curled into the night sky and the scent of burning pine and frying trout filled the streets. Brand and Jak both found their mouths watering. It had been many hours since lunch.

Corbin, never one to travel far between meals himself, sensed their mood. "The Harvest Moon won't come for a few more nights. We needn't take the offering all the way to the Faerie mound tonight. Let's go by Froghollow and see if my mother has some of her stew and cornbread left over."

Brand perked up visibly. His eyes pleaded with Jak.

"Well," said Jak after a moment of thoughtful chin rubbing. "If you think we can get to the common by tomorrow afternoon...."

"There isn't a doubt of it!" said Brand.

Jak nodded. "I would certainly hate to miss out on any of Aunt Suzenna's cornbread muffins."

"Nor her stew, either," added Brand, delighted. At his age, skipping a meal, especially supper, seemed an almost criminal act. And for a fact, there was no better cook in the clan than Aunt Suzenna. Even old Gram Rabing's legendary cooking had been surpassed years ago.

"Good then, it's decided," Corbin said. He made a comfortable readjustment of his bulk on the sagging driver's board. "Quite possibly, I could do with a bite myself."

Jak laughed out loud at this, poking Corbin in his thick ribs. "Thin as a rail you are, boy. Famished!"

Corbin took all this good-naturedly. When they came to the fork that led to Froghollow, Corbin let Tator turn toward home. Knowing he was headed for fresh straw and a good brushing, the colt picked up the pace, almost trotting as they left Riverton and entered the forest.

Chapter Three
Froghollow

The night was moonless and still. A tranquil farmhouse squatted under a dark sky near the cliffs overlooking the Berrywine River. A soft orange light glowed from the windows.

A tiny manling parted the leafy hedge with delicate, thin-boned hands. Dando of the Wee Folk watched the farmhouse and barnyard for several minutes, but there was no sign of the River Folk or their beasts. He leered hungrily at his goal: a small clay pot set out upon the back porch that brimmed with fresh, creamy milk.

A dark, overly-long tongue snaked out, swept across Dando's lipless mouth and snapped back from whence it had come.

Crouching for the sprint, the tiny thief pushed his cap down squarely upon his head and gripped his walking stick. He burst from the cover of the hedge and dashed across the barnyard. His coattails fluttered as he ran. He shoved his face into the pot and greedily slurped up the feast, pausing only for quick wheezes of breath. Although the clay pot was nearly as big as he was, the milk was gone in a trice.

Face dripping and belly distended, he cast about for more solid fare. His candle-stick nose wrinkled and twitched in the evening air. He caught an enticing scent—that of fresh fur, fresh life, fresh *meat*.

Bounding from the porch, he followed the scent to the barn, where cows lowed fearfully at his approach. An old carthorse nickered and kicked once in its stall.

A pile of loose straw obscured a wooden crate. From inside came mewling sounds. Grinning at his good fortune, the manling dug furtively at the straw and poked his face inside. Six gray-furred kittens squirmed deliciously. Their eyes were not yet open. The manling grinned more widely.

Some moments later, a great ruckus brought Aunt Suzenna to the back porch. She noted the absent milk.

The screeching sounds from the barn continued. She called to her husband over her shoulder, "Mama-cat has caught something in the barn!"

The screeching and commotion grew in intensity.

"Here, puss, puss," Suzenna called, looking with concern toward the dark hulking building.

Suddenly, a tiny figure bounded out into the yard. It wore clothes like a man but was no bigger than a doll. It took incredible leaps, despite its swollen belly, each stride carrying it a dozen feet or more. Right behind it was Mama-cat, ears flat, eyes blazing.

The chase went around the farmhouse once and then off into the woods.

"Wee Folk!" gasped Suzenna, eyes wide with wonder and fear. Trembling, she looked in on the newborn kittens in the barn. She counted all six, although she had to scoop up two of them and put them back in their wooden crate. She stepped back into the house and pulled the door shut.

Soon after that, the shutters slammed and the house fell dark. None inside dared speak above a whisper until they were sure the manling was gone.

* * *

Sometime later they reached Froghollow, where, true to its name, the frogs and bog-yelpers were singing their nightly serenade. Corbin's father Tylag and his older brothers had already gone to bed, but fortunately Aunt Suzenna was still up.

She did indeed have several fine helpings of her stew and more than a dozen corn muffins left over. She ladled each of them a fresh tumbler of chilled milk to wash the meal down. The three young men made quick work of the lot of it, leaving only crumbs on the checkered tablecloth.

"Can we camp in your yard tonight, Aunt Suzenna?" asked Jak humbly. "It's an awfully long trip back up to the common, and since we brought all our own gear we won't be any problem."

Aunt Suzenna would hear nothing of it. They were marched first into the washroom and then up the steps to the guest bedroom where they stripped off their clothes and sank into the softest feather beds that either of them could recall having touched.

"Now you boys go right to sleep, you hear?" Aunt Suzenna told them. "I know you've been taking care of yourselves out there on the Isle, but you're under my roof now. I don't want to hear that you kept Corbin up all night playing Jiggers and Swap-Cards. We arise early for chores in Froghollow. There's no place for lay-abouts."

They assured her that they would be up with the sun to help with the chores. She bade them goodnight and bustled out of the room, dousing the candles as she went. As soon as the door was shut, Jak groaned aloud in ecstasy. "Isn't this grand? I've forgotten what a proper down bed feels like.... Just the smell of it is heaven!"

Brand frowned a bit in the darkness. He rubbed the clean sheets and deeply inhaled the aroma of the bed. It reminded him of his mother and father. He even felt a bit homesick.

"Aren't we taking a bit too freely from our clansmen?" he felt compelled to ask his brother. "It seems like none of the family come out to Rabing Isle to visit us anymore. I remember the summer barbecues out on the verandah. Fresh melons and toasted mussels, dad served them every year."

Jak scoffed, but fell silent. Brand knew that their increasing isolation from the rest of the clan bothered him too. Jak had yet to take a wife, being too wrapped up in keeping Rabing Isle going to be out courting. The Isle had been family land for

26

many generations back. He wasn't about to be the one who let it wither and die.

* * *

Sometime later Brand awoke with a start. He blinked, having just been on the edge of sleep. It took him a moment to figure out why he had awoken, and then he heard it again. A flapping, fluttering sound. He rose up on one elbow, looking around the room. Pale moonlight poured into the room, as the moon was nearly full. Jak was asleep, looking younger with his face relaxed and the cares of the day forgotten.

Brand was on the verge of laying back down when he heard the sound again. He turned to the window. There, silhouetted partially by the moon, was a very large horned owl. Its huge yellow eyes were luminous orbs that radiated an eldritch light. It was staring directly at him, directly into his eyes. While he watched in surprise, it dipped its head and tore at the window sash with its powerful beak. The motion forced the bird to flap its wings to stay in place. Brand was shocked to see that it had already managed to pry up the window an inch or two from the sill.

"What kind of changeling are you?" demanded Brand, sitting up and swinging his feet out of the bedclothes.

Jak came awake with a start. He looked at Brand, and then saw the owl. "What's going on?"

Brand pointed. "It's trying to get in!" he hissed. "It's bewitched!"

Just then, there came a creaking sound from the hall. Very quietly, the brass door handle twisted and the door edged open. Jak scrambled up and fumbled beneath the bed for his crossbow, which he had stashed there when Aunt Suzenna wasn't looking. He had it out and pointed toward the door before he realized it wasn't cocked. With practiced motions, he bent the prod back and loaded a bolt into the guiding slot.

The door was open now, and an indistinct figure entered the room.

"Corbin?" breathed Brand.

Corbin's face caught the edge of the moonlight. "You're awake?"

Jak made a sound of disgust and alarm. "I nearly shot you, Corbin! Any fool knows to knock before entering!"

Corbin hushed them, easing the door shut behind him. "My father will hear, or worse my mother." He then revealed the purpose of his visit, producing a deck of stained and scarred playing cards and a jar full of polished sticks and betting beads. Tucked beneath his arm he had a loaf of bread, with a wedge of cheese in a scrap of cloth and a small jug of berrywine riding in his pockets. "It's your own stuff," he said, tapping the jug proudly. "Rabing Isle makes the best berrywine still."

Jak groaned, unloading the crossbow. "You think of nothing but your stomach."

"And of games," added Corbin with a chuckle. "By the way, why are you two awake and so flustered?"

Brand pointed to the window, but the owl had fled. They explained the incident and inspected the damage the bird's talons and beak had done. Corbin pursed his lips in concern. "An owl you say? Looks more like an eagle, by the look of these marks."

"It was strange—when it looked at me, I felt that it wasn't afraid and that it wanted to find me. There was no fear at all in that creature. Perhaps it was some kind of changeling."

It was Jak's turn to be skeptical. "For a fact, things have been odd this autumn, and the Harvest Moon is almost upon us. But I don't think that the Faerie would break the Pact with the River Haven just to get at the likes of you and me. What could be their purpose?"

"Still, this all seems quite odd to me," said Corbin. As he spoke, he methodically set up a table in between the two beds, laying out the food, wine and game pieces. He didn't even bother to ask if the others wanted to play. There was no need.

Shaken by this second unnerving apparition, Brand told Corbin about the shadowy horseman he had seen earlier on the shore. Corbin listened intently while he divided the betting beads evenly, dealt the cards, and arranged the polished sticks in the appropriate patterns. When Brand had finished, Corbin shook his head and scratched his red beard. "I know of no one like that, nor have I heard anything of such a man. But this is not to say that I doubt you, cousin," he said hurriedly, cutting off Brand's protests.

Soon, they grew tired of discussing it and turned to the games and the food. Brand was quite tired, but nothing could keep him awake like food and games. The three played Jiggers and Swap-Cards long into the night. They kept their voices low so as not to awaken Corbin's family. Corbin won most of the hands, but Brand was just as glad to have something to keep away thoughts and dreams of the shadow man at the river and the giant bird that had torn up the windowsill to get at him.

Morning came too soon and they had to fight themselves awake. Never did their beds felt better than when they tried to leave them for the cold dawn air. Shivering, they washed up and dressed in fresh clothes before tramping down the creaking spiral staircase to answer Aunt Suzenna's call to breakfast. She set a grand table that morning. Corbin's two older brothers, Sam and Barlo, were there in addition to his father, Tylag.

"Good to have you boys here this morning," said Tylag, spooning a heavy portion of mushrooms and bacon onto his plate. Brand could hardly wait to get his hands onto the serving bowl. To his joy—and Corbin's obvious chagrin—his uncle passed the bowl to the guests first. "We'll be needing help to bring across a heavy load today. The Glints have brought a mighty big offering, and they've made a deal with me to handle the crossing of the livestock."

Brand and Jak tried their best not to grimace visibly. The Glints maintained the largest flocks of sheep on the river, and were well-known to give generously for the offering. More than a hundred fat sheep and twice as many sacks of meal were likely to be involved. At the same moment, they looked at Corbin, trying to catch a trace of guilt in his eyes.

Corbin seemed preoccupied with his mug of tea. His fork too, seemed to have become worthy of study. The brothers exchanged knowing glances. Corbin had duped them into this "chore" which would likely amount to an all-day venture of sweating and straining. Brand sighed quietly, finally getting hold of the serving bowl and giving himself a heaping load of steaming mushrooms and glistening bacon. They should have known not to trust a ferryman's son who offered them free food.

"We'll be glad to help, Uncle Tylag," said Jak with all the good grace he could muster.

"Don't be worrying, boys. We'll work those corn muffins and that midnight wine into muscle instead of fat," chuckled Aunt Suzenna. Jak and Brand glanced at her sharply, and saw she was smiling. Their Uncle Tylag, too, wore a cagey grin. It was clear that their midnight festivities had not gone unnoticed.

Corbin seemed to hunker down a bit, attempting to avoid attention. It was impossible for him to truly reduce his great bulk, and the only effect was a lowering of the head and a hunching of the shoulders. He perked up when the serving bowl came close, however. Brand and Jak were working on the next one, loaded with a hash of green potatoes, radishes and spiced mutton. It was a specialty of Aunt Suzenna's. Just the aroma made Brand feel better compensated for the day to come.

* * *

Hours later they stood upon the ferry, pulling the last load across the rippling waters from the northern shore of the river to the southern tip of Stone Island where Tylag's ferry landed. Brand had discovered where Corbin's muscles had been earned. His own arms burned by now, equaled only by the burning of his hands inside the thick leather gloves that his uncle had given him. Each time he grabbed hold of the thick rope and hauled in unison with his cousins, his biceps seemed to groan aloud. This groaning, however, if it was audible, was entirely drowned out by the frightened bleating of the sheep that were roped in a cluster at the center of the ferry. The river gurgled and splashed over the timbers of the ferry, which was primarily a large platform of logs lashed together and supported with crossbeams. Gray with long exposure, the wood of the ferry was seamed and cracked and prone to giving splinters. Brand glanced back at Jak, who looked as winded as

Brand felt. Jak's blond hair was matted with sweat and stuck to his forehead in dark rat-tails.

As the day wore on it grew increasingly cold, unseasonably cold. The wind blew from the west and there was the hint of snow in it. They were approaching the cliffs of Stone Island when Brand saw the shadow man again. Atop the whale-backed ridges of the cliff stood a dark figure on a horse, his cloak a rippling black shadow. Brand's breath was ragged. His hoarse shout of alarm was carried away by the river winds. What the others did notice was that the line had slackened. Jak tapped his shoulder, shouting something that Brand never heard. Brand simply stared until the shadow man turned his horse and slid into the shadow of the pine trees that topped the cliffs.

"What's wrong with you, boy?" demanded Tylag. His uncle's voice came close and strong in his ear, and Brand made a croaking sound in reply. Tylag had once been the chief of the Riverton Constabulary, and his old training showed in times like this.

"He's gaping like a gigged bog-yelper," said Corbin's older brother Sam. He had massive arms, the biggest in the family. He walked with a dragging foot, and everyone knew he worked his arms all the harder to make up for it.

"Here now, off with you!" ordered Tylag, waving away his sons. "Back to your stations before we swamp the ferry with all you lot standing at one corner."

Brand shook himself, suddenly aware that he was sitting on the cold wet logs of the ferry, his right hand still clutching the thick rope. He noticed that his face was wet too, as river water had lapped up and splashed him. His eyes focused on his uncle, and then upon Jak and Corbin, all of whom looked worried.

"Did you see him?" Brand asked.

"Who?" demanded Tylag. He helped Brand to his feet. "See who?"

Brand looked to Jak, who looked even more concerned than before. Jak turned to look at the western shore of the river, into the Deepwood. "No, no, that way," said Brand, gesturing up at the cliffs. "Up there."

"He was on Stone Island?" demanded Jak.

31

"The shadow horseman?" asked Corbin.

Tylag was looking from one to another of the boys in confusion. "What's going on here?" he demanded gruffly. "I'm not accustomed to ignorance when aboard my own ferry!"

Brand, who was feeling better, stood up unaided and quickly explained. This time, however, he added in his feelings of numbness and cold dread. When he had finished, Corbin told the story of the great owl at the window the night before.

Tylag was left rubbing his heavy growth of beard, which was even thicker and redder than Corbin's. Sam scoffed and told them they were all scared of their own shadows, literally, but Tylag halted him with a raised hand. "No, no…this might fit," Tylag said slowly. He looked older somehow, more worried and daunted than Brand had ever seen him. Brand felt responsible and suddenly wished he had kept the whole thing to himself. His Uncle Tylag had never looked weak. Even when Brand's father, Tylag's brother, had died, he had looked stronger than he did now.

"Your Aunt Suzenna saw one of the Wee Folk just tonight," said Tylag.

"One of the Wee Folk?" gasped Brand, feeling a rush of wonder and fear all at once.

"Yes, Mama-cat chased him off. He was after her kittens in the barn," Tylag grunted and half-smiled. "She always was a good ratter. She came home with a scrap of his coattails in her claws."

"But what has that got to do with the shadow horseman?"

Tylag didn't answer for a moment; clearly he was thinking hard. "We must get news of these events to the Riverton council," he muttered at last.

They pressed him for answers on the rest of the journey, but he only shook his head at them, deep in thought. "It's been a strange autumn," was all he would say. Tylag had been the head of the Rabing Clan since Brand's father had died, being the second oldest child of Gram Rabing's family. Old Gram had passed the clan leadership to her children on her seventieth birthday, and now that she was nearly ninety she rarely did more than offer a word or two of sage advice. As the head of the Rabing Clan, Tylag was a key member of the Riverton Council.

Brand pulled the ropes along with the rest of them, his strength having returned, if not his peace of mind. He could not imagine what was going on, but felt it to be something terrible. Could the Pact with the Faerie have been broken? Wasn't the great Offering that the folk of the Haven had spent so long gathering this hard season enough?

It took only a short while to get the ferry to the stony shores of the eastern point where a cart and oxen awaited. The men loaded the cart quickly, with many wary glances cast up at the ridge. Brand himself felt the lingering dread, as well as guilt for having put so many years onto his uncle's face.

Tylag seemed to understand his mood. He stumped over and threw an arm around Brand. He squeezed with this one arm, giving him a crude hug. "You're getting so tall boy, I can hardly look you in the eye!" he said, some of his normal bravado returning. Brand noted that he was indeed several inches taller than his uncle was, although not nearly as wide. "I want you and your brother to come with me to meet the clan leaders. You too, Corbin," he said over his shoulder.

The boys nodded and a few hours later—after a fine lunch where Aunt Suzenna surpassed herself once again—they all headed back to Riverton. Corbin and Jak rode behind Tator with the load of melons and berrywine casks while Brand rode on Tylag's ox-cart. Ahead of them, the oxen lowed. All around them, the sheep that Corbin's brothers were herding to the common bleated and rang the bells at their necks. Brand glanced back at Froghollow wistfully many times. He had the feeling that he was leaving something behind forever.

Chapter Four
Telyn

On the way, Tylag grilled Brand about the details of his encounters. Before they had left, he had inspected the damage done by the owl to his windowsill as well. He had waved away Jak and Brand's apologies for the damage as irrelevant. Brand answered all the questions as best he could. It seemed clear after a time that Tylag was searching for something, some kind of hint, perhaps.

"Was this man wearing clothes, would you say?" he asked, looking at Brand with a peculiar intensity.

"Yes. A cloak at least. Although it seemed to be of some kind of odd, flowing material. Not wool, I'm sure of that."

Tylag nodded. "What about headgear? Did he bear a hat or some type of helm?"

Brand shook his head.

"Would you say that the man on the cliffs just now was the same, or a different one?"

"Most likely the same," reported Brand. *Could there be many of these shadow men?* The thought was alarming. He turned on the driver's board and eyed the forests around them. Suddenly, they seemed far less friendly. "Do you know this man?"

"I should say not!" Tylag said with sudden intensity. He was loud enough to attract the attention of Jak and Corbin, who turned to look at them. Seeing Brand's uncomprehending stare, Tylag waved away his concern with his large hands. "It matters nothing, boy. What is important is that I get you to see Myrrdin straight away."

"Myrrdin!" gasped Brand. "The Clanless One?"

Tylag nodded firmly. "The same."

Brand fell silent for a time. It seemed that all his worst fears were being realized. Myrrdin was a traveling man from distant lands who aided with the Harvest Moon ceremonies each year. It was clear he was no peddler, and no one knew where his home was or if he even had one. Some wagging tongues had gone so far as to label him a wizard, although most of the clearer heads scoffed at this idea. Wizards were myths—the talk of legends like the stories about the Dragon's Eyes, the colored Jewels of power. The Faerie, however—they were very real.

If this involved Myrrdin, then it certainly involved the Faerie as well. The thought of it made Brand go cold inside. All he could think of was the old stories that his mother had told him as a child. The terrible wonders of the Faerie were without number.

They traveled the rest of the way without talking much. The usual festive mood that buoyed up the last few days before the Harvest Moon feast was absent. Even Tator seemed dispirited, his tail and ears drooping.

They clopped and swayed their way into Riverton, greeted by passersby on the road. As they entered the town, Sam and Barlo led the sheep to the stockyards. As to their own offerings, there were many compliments on Brand and Jak's generosity, and the two young men swelled with pride. They were running Rabing Isle on their own, but they weren't slackers. Their father had brought no more or less to the Harvest Moon in years past.

They wound up the hill to where the nicer houses and the largest buildings were. In the center of town, where the guildhouses and the shops huddled close to the road, there was even a section of cobblestones. Tator perked up here, as if he were proud to pull his cart through the best street in town.

It was here that they stopped before the gates of the manor house of the Drake Clan, the wealthiest and most influential clan on Stone Island. It was at their ancestral home that the clan leaders held council. Although it wasn't as spacious as the common room of the *Spotted Hog Inn*, where the town meetings were generally held, it afforded much more privacy.

"I'll go on in and announce us," said Tylag, climbing down with a grunt. The driver's board straightened in relief. Brand watched as Tylag walked through the ancient iron gates and up the path to the manor. The gates were never locked; in fact, it had been so many years since they had been shut that the hinges had frozen with rust.

Brand felt a slight rocking of the wagon. He looked around and was surprised to see Telyn sitting beside him, just biting into an apple. She grinned at his expression.

"My, but you're getting tall," she said.

"Telyn!" he breathed, unable to get out more.

"You should look behind you more often," she commented. Brand made a wry face, but it was half-hearted. She was so pretty, even with her rather stringy-looking, reddish-blonde hair and her stained, green leathers smelling of the tannery vats. The delicacy of her face and piercing gray-blue eyes came through all that. He felt his heart leap just at the sight of her. He watched a drop of apple juice run down her hand for a moment before he was able to reply.

"You're always sneaking up on me!" he said finally.

"I like to be unpredictable," she responded with a flip of her head. She smiled at him again, and it was like sunlight breaking through a gray cloud. She took another bite of her apple and then frowned, tossing it over the wall of Drake Manor.

"What are you doing?"

"It was a cull," she said with a shrug. She stretched luxuriously, pushing her fists into the air over her head. "Just as most of those melons you've dragged all the way in from the island are probably culls."

Brand's brow furrowed. "We wouldn't do that!"

"Well, I would."

"Hello, Scraper," said Corbin from the ground. He had left his cart and now stood with Jak. Both of them grinned up at Brand. Brand blushed, feeling the blood tingle all the way down to his knees.

"Hello, Corbin—Jak," Telyn answered, fluttering her hand at them. She produced another apple and a small sharp knife from her green leathers. Slicing the fruit with quick efficient strokes, she began munching on the wedges. "Do you fancy an apple?" she asked Brand, who was staring at her. She winked at him, and he blushed all over again.

Corbin and Jak withdrew to the manor gate to have a look into the courtyard. They kept a discreet eye on Brand and his visitor while they talked.

"I wish they wouldn't call you that," he said.

"What? Scraper? That's what everyone calls me," she said, unconcerned.

He looked troubled. "But it isn't a very pretty name."

She smiled. "Look, I scrape the fur off hides at my father's vats. Most of the Fob clan works in the tanneries. The name doesn't bother me. Besides, my work has taught me to be handy with a knife."

"Okay. Where did you get all the apples?" Brand asked, attempting to shift the conversation. He never seemed to know exactly what to say to Telyn. Somehow these days his thoughts were muddled and never came out right when she was around. It had been different when they had been children.

"Where do you think? From clan Thunderfoot's offering. They have the best orchards in the Haven, after all."

Brand was scandalized. "You took them from the offering?" he demanded in disbelief.

Telyn only shrugged her pretty shoulders again. "Better that I enjoy them than some dancing Faerie that would as soon spoil my milk or lead astray a lamb as look at me."

Brand doubted that the Faerie would be so aloof to her, but he didn't say as much. Instead, he changed the subject again. "I saw a candle burning in your window last night. At least, I think I did."

Telyn slid her eyes around without moving her head and transfixed him with a penetrating gaze. Brand was immediately speechless. She swallowed her bite of apple, and then straightened purposefully, taking Brand's hand in her own. "Are you the one then?" she asked.

Brand gaped at her. He wanted to tell her that yes, he was the one, no matter that he wasn't yet full grown, no matter that his beard was barely enough to bother shaving each morning, but all he could do was stare.

"Are you the one?" she repeated in a hushed voice. "I've had one of those feelings Brand, you know, like when we were kids."

Brand nodded, remembering. "You mean like when you knew Gram Rabing had fallen off the ladder and found her? And when you told me not to let my parents go on the river, that day..." He swallowed, unable to continue.

"Yes," she whispered, leaning even closer. She was in easy kissing range now, and it made it difficult for Brand to think clearly. "Yes, just like that—only different, too. I've felt that someone is coming. Maybe several people. I've felt that they need help in getting here. That's why I've been burning a candle in my window each night. I don't know who, but I know they must get here soon."

"Before the Harvest Moon," whispered Brand.

She nodded very seriously.

Brand thought about the Harvest Moon and everything it meant to the River Folk. He tried to look calm, but he really wanted to shudder. He controlled himself with difficulty, managing a small nod. He didn't want to look like a scared little boy in front of Telyn.

"I've been seeing and feeling odd things as well," he said. Then he told her about the shadow man and the owl, managing to hold her hand in his and lean close to her fair face the entire time. He only edited the truth slightly, not mentioning that he had slipped to the deck of the ferry in numb fear.

Telyn's eyes unfocused and flittered from spot to spot while he spoke. She nodded to herself frequently. Brand knew she was thinking rapidly, her quick mind coming up with a scheme. He could recall her looking like that before he had gotten into the most daring of his childhood adventures. The River only knew what she would come up with.

"All right," she said, squeezing his hand. "I know now what we must do. I'll catch up with you later." With that, she darted forward and kissed him on the cheek. Their eyes locked for a moment.

"Brand! Corbin! Jak!" came Tylag's voice, booming over the manor wall. He heard the crunch of boots on gravel. "Come to me. We have a problem."

Brand turned to look back at the gates. He swallowed, facing the prospect of entering Drake Manor for the first time since he was a small boy at his father's knee. He turned back to say farewell to Telyn, but discovered that she was gone. He looked up and down the street and thought he caught a glimpse of her slipping around a corner, but he couldn't be sure.

"Come on, Brand," said Jak. He followed Corbin into the courtyard. With a last glance over his shoulder, Brand scrambled down and passed between the rusty gates after them.

Tylag's brow was a storm of furrows and he rubbed at his scowling face with his fist. "Myrrdin is not here. He has yet to arrive."

The three younger men all exchanged concerned looks. Brand felt more ill at ease because of Tylag's manner. His actions spoke louder than words. Tylag was usually full of bluster and never daunted by anything.

"But, who will present the Offering if he is not here?" asked Brand.

Tylag shot him a grim stare. "None other can perform it properly," he said. "None have the craft."

"The Offering must be made. It is as simple as that," said Jak, shrugging. "If it comes down to it, I will make the offering for Rabing Isle myself. The Pact can't be allowed to fail."

"Yes," said Corbin, his speech slow and rational. "The Offering will be made. It is not that, but the etiquette of the ceremony will be flawed. We must recall that the ceremony is as important to the Faerie as the Offering itself."

"We are only the simple folk of the River Haven," said Jak, spreading his hands. "What can be done?"

"Perhaps we can find the Clanless One," said Brand. "Surely, there must be some way of locating him."

"Sensibly, he would be on his way here, sailing on the Berrywine perhaps, or crossing the Border Downs," Corbin said thoughtfully. Brand felt he could see the cogs working in his mind. Corbin wasn't a fast thinker, but his ideas were often more penetrating. "Where does he usually hail from at this time of year?"

Tylag, who had been staring at nothing while tugging on his beard, glanced up at his question. "What? Oh, well, it depends. Most years he comes done from the northwest, from the wilds of Snowdonia."

Brand's eyes blinked twice at the mention of Snowdonia. He could only imagine what those white-peaked mountains were like, what strange creatures might dwell there. "From Rabing Isle," he said half to himself, "you can see the crags of Snowdon itself on a clear summer's day."

Corbin looked at him. He paused for a long moment before speaking. "It would seem likely that Myrrdin would pass Rabing Isle then—if he were going to come by water."

"Yes, unless he came through the High Marshes or the Deepwood."

Tylag smacked his fists together decisively. "Right! That would be the way of it. The thing to do is post a lookout up at Rabing Isle. You must return home, Jak. We must watch the other approaches as well. Something has delayed him and it is likely that he needs help."

"What could have delayed him?" asked Jak, frowning.

Tylag made a sweeping gesture with his thick arms. "How should I know? Anything! His boat could have sprung a leak. His horse could have come up lame."

"If he's on horseback, I doubt he will swim past Rabing Isle tonight," grumbled Jak. It was plain to Brand that his brother didn't relish the idea of returning home and missing the celebrations on the Riverton Commons.

It was Tylag's turn to frown. "Boys, I am the leader of Clan Rabing, is this not so?"

All of them nodded. Jak's nod was noticeably glum.

"I will not have it said that the Offering was rejected and the Pact broken due to the inaction of Clan Rabing," he boomed at them, hooking his thumbs in his wide belt and rocking on his heels while eyeing them each in turn. "I ask again, Jak, will you return home and try to escort Myrrdin to Riverton before the Harvest Moon?"

"Of course," said Jak, straightening and dropping the frown.

Thinking of Telyn, Brand gave a tiny sigh of regret. "It will take two to handle the skiff properly, even when it is unloaded. I will come with you."

Tylag nodded approvingly. He slapped his son on the back suddenly. "Corbin will go as well. His back is as strong as the river is wide. Besides, I would not think of breaking you boys up on such a night as this."

Corbin looked startled, but said nothing.

"When should we set out, Uncle?" asked Jak.

"Straight away, nothing is more important. Get yourselves some dinner and spend the night at the *Spotted Hog*," he said, handing Corbin a silver half-crown. "You should leave first thing in the morning. I must be getting back to the council meeting."

"What about the shadow man?" asked Brand, his voice hushed. "Shouldn't we tell the council about it?"

Tylag pursed his lips and gazed back up at the manor, as if seeing the meeting hall and the clan leaders within. "They will take it better from my lips than from yours," he said finally. "Only Myrrdin will properly be able to puzzle out this mystery, so it is all the more important that you find him and tell him what you have seen. In any case, the Pact must not be broken. We are sending out others to every corner of the Haven. Men stand watch at the borders along the Deepwood and the High Marshes. Myrrdin's attendance is critical."

"There's something I don't understand, Uncle," said Brand. "How can we speed things up? I mean, if Myrrdin's coming along a different path, or if he's going by on the water, how will we aid him?"

Tylag smiled. "There's one more person I want you to take with you. And she's very good at finding people—or helping *them* find her."

Brand looked surprised. "You mean Telyn?" he asked.

Tylag nodded, bade them farewell and crunched gravel on his way back to the manor. Brand watched him go. He didn't relish the trip back to Rabing Isle under the watchful stare of the shadow man. If Telyn was coming, however....

"Look at it this way," said Corbin cheerfully. He threw his arm around the shoulders of Brand and Jak, having to reach up in Brand's case and down in Jak's. "At least my brothers will be troubled with the burden of delivering the offerings."

"I also see it as justice for this morning's surprise chores," added Jak. They all laughed at this and walked together to the *Spotted Hog*. On their way in, they met four Hoot boys who were just leaving. The sour smell of ale was strong about them. They scowled darkly at the Rabing boys. The entryway way to the common room was low-ceilinged, and they all were forced to shoulder their way past one another in close quarters.

"Merling fodder," muttered one of the Hoot boys, a skinny slouching youth with hair that stuck up at random angles. Brand knew him to be Slet, a dockworker. Another of them snorted in amusement.

Jak reacted as if stung. He grabbed Slet's tunic, halting the two groups at the entrance. "What did you say?" he demanded. Corbin put a heavy hand on Jak's shoulder, but Jak ignored him. He only stared into Slet's face, awaiting an answer.

Slet's eyes slid around to the faces of his companions. None of them met his gaze, not wanting trouble. Slet took a moment to spit onto the floor between Jak's wading boots. "Nuthin'" he said. "For now."

Jak released Slet with a visible effort of will. The two groups separated without further incident. Corbin ordered lunch with the silver half-crown, which Brand knew was much too much money for a prince's lunch in Riverton, but such was the generosity of their uncle. With the rest of the money Corbin made several other purchases before returning to the table.

Jak ate the lunch of steak and kidney pie without interest. Brand and Corbin exchanged glances. They had hoped his mood would have improved with food and time, but it hadn't. "Jak, I'm sure they didn't mean..." began Brand, but his brother cut him off.

"You don't remember rightly. You were too young, and I was younger than you are now. When the River took our parents, they said it was Merlings. It looked like everything was finished...everything was too much..." he said. He stabbed his fork into his pie and forced down another bite.

Brand thought about what it would be like if he were left to care for Rabing Isle, all of it, right now. It wasn't a pleasant thought. He turned to Corbin and grinned in surprise. Corbin already had the tavern's Jump-Pin board out and was setting the metal pegs up for a three-way match. Without a word, he made a move and pushed it to Jak, who ate two more bites before acknowledging the game. He finally moved with a sigh and pushed the board to Brand. The three ate and played in silence. As usual, Corbin won.

The following day they left the *Spotted Hog* just after dawn. They walked down to the docks in a dark mood. Although the sun was still bright, the autumn air seemed colder, the wind stealing the warmth from their bodies and stinging their eyes with their whipping hair. Corbin soon threw up his hood as he often did. When they got to the dock and made ready to board the skiff, they were surprised to find Telyn sitting in the prow, already in the act of casting off.

"You'd better hurry up and jump down," she said. "The current is pulling me out."

"Who put you in charge?" demanded Jak gruffly, jumping into the boat and snatching the lines from her hands.

Telyn stood up in the skiff as well and put her hands on her hips. "I'm not in charge, but I'm going with you."

Jak glowered at her, then shot a look at Brand who was climbing into the mid-section. Corbin followed him. Jak tossed the coiled line down and went to release the stern moorings, throwing up his hands in a gesture of disgust and surrender.

"What's with your brother?" asked Telyn with some concern.

Brand explained the events at the tavern briefly.

"Well, I'm no Silure, nor am I a Hoot," Telyn pointed out.

Brand looked at her, suddenly realizing that *she* might well have taken offense. He was quick to assure her that it was just his brother's mood.

Telyn nodded and finally smiled at him. Her smile brought a warm feeling to Brand. "How did you know that we were going back to Rabing Isle?" he asked.

"I hear things," she said, reaching up and giving his ear a playful tug. "Besides, I'm following on the track of something

43

right now, and I'm not letting go until I find out what it's about. Yesterday, I learned that you are part of all this, Brand Rabing."

Brand nodded, not really knowing what she was talking about, but finding it easy to agree. He could think of no one he would rather have aboard for the journey. The sails were of great use now that the skiff was running high and empty and the winds were up. They were borne upriver at a steady pace.

Chapter Five
Telyn's Signal

Traveling up the river, Brand had a nostalgic, almost melancholy feeling come over him. Everything seemed to be changing, becoming more exciting and more ominous by the day. The seasons were shifting, getting colder rapidly. Even while the sun was still high in the sky, the wind carried the chill of a cold night ahead. He eyed the scudding gray clouds and wondered if it might not snow tonight. It almost never snowed before the Harvest Moon, but anything seemed possible this autumn.

"Everything seems odd to me, Telyn," he said wistfully. They sat in the bow of the skiff, while Jak gripped the tiller and Corbin tended the sails. By silent agreement, his clansmen had arranged for him to be alone with her.

She didn't answer him right away. The skiff's mast creaked and the river bubbled and splashed as the wind pushed the boat against the current. Telyn dangled her fingers in the white foam that curled up the skiff's dark hull.

"Something is definitely wrong," she agreed finally. She stretched out and Brand was taken by the way her hair fluttered freely in the wind.

They spent much of the trip in quiet conversation, and by the time Rabing Isle hove into view, Brand found that he had sidled close to her and could feel her warmth. He was almost sorry to see the journey end.

"Well," said Jak, clapping him on the shoulder as they moored the skiff at their home dock in a tiny green-water cove. "At least we've seen nothing more of the shadow man."

Brand felt a surge of well-being to be home again. The light was failing and the wind was downright cold now, but everyone in the group was smiling. Rabing Isle was a beautiful place, full of good memories for all of them.

They marched up through the apple tree grove to the foot of the only hill on the island. They followed the winding gravel path through the vegetable garden, its leafy green growth fading to brown now with the onset of winter. Corbin carried two weighty rucksacks with him, Brand noticed with a smile. One was probably full of games and storybooks while the other was doubtlessly packed with extra food.

"I hope you didn't give up all the year's crop of berrywine to the Offering," he said in a leading fashion as the heavy log walls came into view between the towering berry bush hedges that surrounded the house.

"No more than the customary one part in seven," Jak assured him. He gestured toward the winery where the family press and fermentation tanks were sheltered. "If you wish to inspect our stocks personally…."

Corbin grinned. "Ah, I'm sure that your cellars are more than adequate for my needs."

Telyn poked him in the side. "I for one have my doubts!"

They all laughed and headed into the house. It was made of rough-hewn logs with mortar filling the cracks. The windows were all shuttered and the second story wore a steep roof of shingles that resembled a farmer's hat. The house was impressively large, having been built to hold several families. Four generations ago, it had housed many people, but now most of the rooms were empty and layered in cold dust.

Telyn raced forward to the stairs with a delighted cry. "It has been years since I rode this banister!" she said, gripping the big rounded post at the bottom with a grin. "Remember when I pushed you out of the big yew tree out front, Brand?"

Brand tried to look sour. "How could I forget?"

"Perhaps you should chop some fresh wood for the fire, Brand," suggested Jak in a tone that Brand knew made it an order. This didn't bother him, however. Jak was the master of the house, and in any case, he was simply glad to be home.

"As I recall, we have *two* axes," Brand said, eyeing Corbin.

Corbin grinned and followed him out into the yard. They retrieved the axes from the woodshed and set to work. Soon, the chill air was forgotten as they worked up a good sweat. Chopping wood was something of a competition for them. Corbin had the weight and strength to split a log with a single stroke, but Brand had the finesse to be able to do it more often.

"You'll never chop faster than I. You know that," Brand said, speaking in gasps between swings.

"You're as competitive as your brother, in your own way," observed Corbin. Chips flew and caught in their hair. The thunking sound of axes falling filled the yard.

"Ha! If that's not the river calling the shore brown!" snorted Brand. "I'm not the one who would rook Gram Rabing herself in a game of Swap-cards!"

After this brief exchange, they saved their breath for lifting their axes. The wood piled up high and fast at their feet. For speed, it was nearly a draw, although Brand's pile was marginally larger. When both of them had several armloads, they headed back into the house.

Inside they all fell to talking about old times, and even Jak seemed to have shed his dark mood. Corbin talked while working in the kitchen. He donned an apron that probably hadn't been worn since Brand's parents had been lost, setting to work on a meal of astounding variety and proportions. As Brand had suspected, Corbin's rucksacks contained a wealth of foodstuffs, bought at the *Spotted Hog* with the remains of Tylag's money. They had no objections as hosts, however, recalling the previous morning's "chores" and the vast amounts that Corbin could put away in a single evening.

They feasted on smoked duck, fresh onion-bread, goat cheese and boiled Merling eggs. For dessert, big crescent slices of broadleaf melon were handed around. After dinner and washing up, they gathered at the fireplace and sipped berrywine. Jak built up a big fire with twice as much wood as usual. Outside, the wind had come up and began to howl.

"There's no doubt of it, we're having our first winter storm tonight," said Jak. He put his feet up over the side of his overstuffed leather chair, in just the fashion that their father had long ago complained about. Now that he was the master of the house, though, none spoke. "Still, it's good to have friends in the house again."

Brand felt a wash of well-being. It *was* good to be home with friends when winter's first breath was blowing outside. The house had been empty for too long. He looked at Telyn and his thoughts drifted pleasantly. She was brushing her hair out and staring at the fire. Her lips curved up in a delicate smile, and he knew she was aware of his attention. A blush, heated even more deeply by the wine in his belly, crept up his neck and cheeks.

"Swap-cards, anyone?" asked Corbin, nonchalantly. Jak rolled his eyes to the ceiling then finished his wine with a gulp. His boots came down with a thud. "Okay, but this time you lose," he said. Brand seconded the motion.

Telyn played for three hands, winning two of them. Corbin's eyebrows were comically high as he watched her fingers flutter over the cards and nimbly snatch up the polished sticks and set them in the appropriate patterns with a flourish. Next to his deliberate movements, hers were like lightning. Still, she somehow seemed distracted. After the three hands, she decided to retire early.

Brand watched her go up the creaking steps with concern. The allure of the game was too much to allow for worries, however, and the night wore on quickly. The majority of the betting beads ended up on Jak's side this time.

Corbin took the loss with easy confidence. "Every dog has his day," he said.

Jak slapped his legs and began pulling his waders back on. "Well," he said, "It's high time we set out lamps for Myrrdin. If he's out there on the river tonight, he'll need them just to avoid capsizing on the shoals."

Brand made ready to go with him, but Corbin volunteered for the duty, claiming he needed the exercise. Corbin donned his waders and they helped Jak with readying six heavy hurricane lamps of tarnished brass. Each tall lamp had its wick adjusted and its oil vessel filled. Carrying three lamps each, Jak and Corbin threw open the door and stamped outside. Brand was surprised by the wind's strength—it tousled everything in the room, spraying the swap-cards like fallen leaves and making the fire gust up and sputter. He pushed the door shut after them, packed away the cards, and tended the fire.

Crouched before the crackling flames with a poker in his hand, he felt eyes on his back. He turned and Telyn was there, standing just a few feet behind him. He blinked in surprise. "How do you do that? I know this house so well, no one can move through it without me hearing their steps on the boards."

"The wind drowns out sound," she said with a slight shrug and a tiny smile. She pushed back her hair from her face. "Besides, I'm no great thumping river-boy with wading boots on."

"But I know every creak and groan those stairs make," he protested. It just didn't seem possible. But then, she had always moved differently.

She silenced him with a finger to her lips. "It doesn't matter." She extended her delicate white hand. "Come with me. I want to show you something."

Brand hesitated for a moment, then set aside the poker and took her hand. The look in her eyes told him she was serious about something. She led him up the steps to the old nursery.

"You're sleeping in here?" he asked.

She nodded. "It's the room I have the best memories of."

Then he noticed the candle in the window. It was a single taper of waxy white tallow, not like the ones they had kept in the house.

"But the shutters are closed," he pointed out. "You can't hope to signal Myrrdin with that."

"Not Myrrdin, necessarily—"

"But it doesn't matter *who* you're trying to signal," he said, still staring at the tiny flame. It bothered him, somehow. He couldn't put his finger on it, but there was something odd about it. "No one can see it through the shutters. Only the hurricane lamps can be seen from the river, and then only if they are on lampposts at the shoreline. The River knows that a candle would just blow out if you opened the shutters, anyway."

Telyn silenced him with a single finger to *his* lips this time. She gave him one of her knowing smiles. "How did you see the one in my window last night, then?" she asked.

His mouth sagged open. "Are you saying that—that your shutters were closed?"

She made no attempt to answer. Instead, she guided him out of the room with light touches of her hands. Hardly aware of it, he moved at her slightest touch, and soon found himself standing in the hall. "You should know better than to be caught in a lady's room this late at night," she scolded, closing the door.

"Wait!"

"Good night," she said sweetly.

He was left standing in the dark hall, at a loss. Later, when Jak and Corbin had returned from their work, stamping their boots and rubbing their hands, he went to bed. It was then, staring at the ceiling, that he recalled what was odd about that candle.

It had not flickered, even when in the window, where drafts and gusts always came through the shutters. The flame had been perfectly steady and still. Even in a light wind, much less a storm, it should have flickered and danced and perhaps even been blown out by the drafts. He fell asleep trying to remember if Telyn's hair had been tousled by drafts that should have affected the candle, but that just got his mind onto the subject of her face, and then it was hard to think at all. His dreams were troubled.

Chapter Six
The Battleaxe Folk

Many hours into the night there came a loud hammering at the front door. The storm was at its peak. It howled and clawed at the shuttered windows, seeking to slip in cold fingers and pry away the protective boards. Brand, who had been dreaming of owls and strange lights and Telyn's fine face, awoke with a start. Beads of cold perspiration were on his forehead and cheeks. It took him a moment to realize where he was and what had awakened him. Out in the hall he heard the boards creak beneath Jak's feet, then Corbin's heavier tread. The hammering came again: *thump, thump, thump.* He scrambled out of the bedclothes and pulled on his trousers, shivering in the cold.

Telyn, wearing a nightdress that would have set Brand's heart to pounding if it hadn't been pounding already, was the first to reach the door. She seemed in a terrible hurry, her cheeks flushed with excitement as she lay her hands on the bar that held the heavy oaken door. Although most folk on the Berrywine River rarely barred their doors, Rabing Isle was close to the northern border of the River Haven and things had not been well this autumn. Jak had decided to bar the door tonight as a precaution.

"Hold it!" Jak shouted as she made ready to throw up the bar and open the door. He extended his hand, palm outward.

Telyn paused with a visible effort of will and stepped to one side. "You set the lamps out," she said. "You wanted them to come, so why do you hesitate now?"

"'Them?'" questioned Jak. "I wanted Myrrdin to come, none other."

Telyn crossed her arms beneath her breasts, looking cold and a bit cross. "Perhaps it is Myrrdin, his beard white with frost and his feet half-frozen in their boots."

Thump, thump, thump. The door resounded with heavy blows.

Suddenly, Brand felt a bite of concern. Would Myrrdin's fist fall so heavily? It sounded as if a smithy's hammer were being wielded full force upon the door. Despite its heavy oaken timbers, it shook and rattled with each blow. What kind of man would come to Rabing Isle on such a night?

"Who hammers on my door in the deep of night?" Jak demanded loudly.

Thump, thump, thump. The hammering was the only reply.

Jak scowled, his mood turning dark. Before Brand could caution him, he had thrown up the bar and swung open the door. Corbin raised the lantern he was carrying a bit higher so that all could see into the dark night. The figure that stood outside in the raging blizzard was not what they had expected. It was not tall like Myrrdin or a shadow man, nor as short as one of the Faerie.

It was clearly one of the Battleaxe Folk. Although he stood very tall for one of his race, almost as tall as Telyn, he was built along the lines of all his folk: The head was massive with crude, overlarge features and a heavy beard of coarse, red-and-gold hair. The arms were long and thick and the legs short and thicker. His powerful barrel-like chest made up the rest of him. Brand was taken aback, for although he had seen a few wandering Battleaxe Folk trading fine goods, he had never seen one nearly as large as this. He had to weigh as much as Corbin, at least. Brand's eyes drifted uncontrollably to the heavy, doubled-bladed battleaxe that hung on a leather thong from his wide belt.

Jak crossed his arms and glared at the visitor. "Who disturbs our rest on such a night?"

"I am Modi of the Warriors," answered their visitor, haltingly, but clearly. It was obvious that he was not used to their speech.

"I am Jak of the Rabing Clan," said Jak, frowning less. "What can we do for one of the Battleaxe Folk on a night such as this?"

Modi's lips worked for a moment, his huge brows furrowed in concentration. "Gudrin—she is of the Talespinners—she sent me. She saw your light."

At this, Telyn took a half-step forward. Brand eyed her, thinking of her candle. Surely, Modi meant the light from one of the lamps set out to guide Myrrdin.

"There are more of you? Do you need shelter?" asked Jak.

Relief flooded over Modi's face. "Yes, shelter. There is only I...and the Spinner."

"Why didn't your companion come up with you?" asked Telyn, slipping herself into the narrow space between Jak's shoulder and the doorjamb. "Is she sick? Too weak to walk?"

Modi eyed her critically for a few moments before answering. He seemed to see something that made him uncertain. "Gudrin is not sick. She is...burdened. She rests in the boat."

Donning their boots, cloaks and hats, the four of them followed Modi down to the docks in the swirling blizzard. The path was pitch-blackness streaked with white. The world lost its form only a few feet away in every direction. Only the stones along the path kept them from losing their way. Brand realized that the hurricane lamps would only have been visible from a few yards out on the river. He wondered if the Battleaxe Folk had keener eyes than did the folk of the River Haven.

Despite his short legs, Modi marched quickly down the hill. The others had to hurry to keep up, except for Telyn, whose light tread barely seemed to sink into the wind-fluffed powder. Brand was surprised to see that the snow had already piled up in drifts two or three feet high in places. Modi plowed through it all as if it was nothing, giving the impression that snow was no more worthy of notice than mist on a fine morning. Likewise, the freezing wind that whipped his weathered cloak of earthen brown wildly about seemed no more to him than a light summer's breeze. The questions that they shouted at his back were snatched away by the wind, and in any case he answered them all with only broad, vague gestures of his long, thick arms.

When they reached the docks they found a small boat there, made of stiff hides sewn together in the fashion of the Battleaxe Folk. In the middle of the leather boat sat a hunched figure wrapped in cloaks. At their approach, the figure stirred, but didn't rise. Telyn skipped forward, jumping down into the boat beside the figure. Modi stumped forward in sudden concern and stood on the dock, watching Telyn and his companion closely. Brand had a sudden feeling that his eyes were less than friendly. He noted that one bulging fist now gripped the haft of his axe.

Brand rushed forward, putting a hand on Modi's huge arm. It felt as if he had grabbed onto a boulder. "There's no need for that, sir," he said. "She only wishes to help. She is a good healer."

Modi looked at him as if seeing him for the first time. His eyes were the color of tarnished steel. Then he returned his attention to the two in the boat. His hand remained where it was, as if Brand were not worthy of concern. Brand wondered if he could even slow the warrior down, should he decide to act.

Gudrin rose up and climbed out of the boat. She mounted the dock with deliberate movements that weren't those of someone frail or sick. She stood on the dock between them all. Telyn jumped up and stood at her side. The River Folk all stared at Gudrin, while she eyed each of them in turn. Modi watched the River Folk. His fist was still firmly planted on the haft of his axe, as if rooted there. Feeling a bit foolish, Brand let his hands slip down to his sides. He knew he was a strong man, very strong for his young years, and he could not but wonder how strong Modi was.

"That's enough, Warrior," said Gudrin. She made a gesture, and Modi reluctantly released his hold on his weapon. "We are clearly among friends."

Gudrin, unlike Modi, spoke their tongue flawlessly. Also unlike Modi, she was of normal size for her race, being perhaps four feet in height. The barrel-chested build, long arms and large features were all there, but her hair was dark gray shot

54

through with streaks of white. She wore a black cloak, a tunic and trousers of leather, high boots and an old wide-brimmed hat of stone-gray material. On her back she carried a heavy rucksack of riveted leather and tucked under her arm was a large package of some kind.

"Greetings, good folk of the River," she said, her voice booming in the storm. "I am Gudrin of the Talespinners."

They all nodded politely and introduced themselves. Corbin and Brand moved to help pull the boat up out of the water, so that it would not capsize during the night with the weight of the snow, but Modi waved them off with his large hands. Stumping down into the freezing water, he grabbed ahold of the boat's prow and dragged it up onto the shore single-handed. Lifting up two heavy packs, he unloaded the boat. Then without a word to anyone, he moved back to Gudrin's side, slinging one of the heavy packs over each shoulder.

With Corbin and Brand trailing behind, the party marched back up the hill to the house. Once inside, Jak stoked up the fire to a cheery blaze and Corbin worked in the kitchen to feed them something. After his guests had settled and been given steaming mugs of hot spiced tea, Jak asked them if they had caught sight of Myrrdin.

Gudrin looked up sharply at the name, her eyes narrowing and her lips pursed. She seemed to hold the package under her arm closer to her chest. Her eyes burned into Jak's, and for a moment Jak's face seemed emotionless, frozen. Then Gudrin nodded, as if to herself or someone unseen, and lowered her head. "Yes, yes, we've seen Myrrdin, but not for some time. It is he, in fact, that we've come to find."

Jak explained why they were on Rabing Isle rather than attending the festivities at Riverton.

"So Myrrdin is not in the Haven to maintain the Pact?" asked Gudrin. "That is bad news indeed. I can think of nothing that would delay him from such an important task. Yes, bad news indeed. I believe it is as the signs portend." She sighed and shook her head. She sipped her spiced tea, while Modi still eyed his mug doubtfully. "Ah, thanks for the refreshment. It has been a long journey."

"I assume you hail from the North?" asked Jak.

Gudrin nodded, doffing her hat and cloak. "We came to the light," she said.

"The light?" said Telyn, leaning forward. "How could you see a light in such a storm?"

Gudrin turned to face Telyn, who had been staring at her intently for some time. "And you, my fair lady," she said. "Where do you hail from?"

Their eyes locked for a few moments, and then Telyn dropped hers. She opened her mouth to speak, but then closed it again. Brand could not hold his tongue. "She is Telyn of the Fob clan," he told Gudrin. "She is from Riverton, on Stone Island."

Gudrin looked at him, and for a moment Brand felt the power in her eyes and knew why the others had been acting strangely. Those eyes were incredibly blue and as deep as the open sea—and as wide as the sky on a clear summer's day. There was something there, something he'd never seen before. Gudrin gave him just a flash of her eyes before returning her gaze to Telyn. Brand swallowed in relief when Gudrin's attention shifted.

She eyed Telyn a few moments longer and Telyn, for her part, bravely returned her gaze this time for several seconds before again dropping her eyes. Gudrin pursed her lips again and nodded. She tapped the package clamped under her arm. Brand had the sudden impression that it was a large book of some kind, probably wrapped up to protect it from the river and the weather.

"Children shouldn't play with flint and tinder, lest they burn more than tallow and timber," Gudrin quoted. Brand half remembered the old rhyme from his childhood, but he was at something of a loss to understand its meaning now.

Telyn, however, jumped as if struck. Her hands twined about one another. Brand realized Gudrin suspected Telyn had used magic…

And that she could be right.

Chapter Seven
The Shade

It was then, in the awkward moment of silence that followed, that Brand saw the rucksack on Gudrin's back jump, just a little. It was really more of a twitch, as if something inside had suddenly moved or shifted uneasily. He wondered vaguely if Gudrin had a rabbit in there or some other kind of captured game. Out of politeness for other people's customs, he decided not to mention it.

"I don't understand your meaning, madam, but I do know that I have offered you hospitality and you don't seem overly gracious about it," said Jak. Brand and Corbin exchanged glances. Brand knew that they were both thinking Jak was perhaps pushing too far. The Battleaxe Folk were known to be honest and just, but often gruff and surly as well.

Gudrin dropped her powerful gaze, and for a moment she looked truly old and burdened. She leaned her head forward, rubbing the back of her neck. She sighed and looked back at them, smiling. It was a very different effect this time; her eyes no longer seemed to bore into one's head. They looked friendly and tired. "I apologize. You are clearly all good folk. You must understand that we are tired and have journeyed far. All the world is not at peace like the River Haven. In fact, very little of it is. We of the Kindred have suspicious natures that should be left at the border, but it is hard to change one's nature so quickly."

"Yes, I can understand that. It's very late. I think it's time we retired," said Jak, nodding. His tone indicated that the apology was accepted. "Brand, Corbin, show our guests to their rooms when they're ready."

And so the lights were doused again, and the two strangers were given rooms in the back of the house with many apologies for the dust and old linen. As Modi mounted the steps, Brand felt sure they would give way under his weight. He now recalculated the warrior's weight to be greater than Corbin's. Considerably greater. On his way back to his own room, he passed by Telyn's room, and noted that the candle she had burned all night was now out. Telyn caught him by the arm as he went by and dragged him in, shutting the door.

"They make me nervous," she said. "Don't you feel it? Gudrin has a power, I'm sure of it. That's why she saw my beacon." Telyn was speaking very quickly. Before Brand could comment, she snatched the candle he had been carrying to light his way and took it over to the window. With it she relit the candle in the window. "Well, I'm not going to have some old talespinner scare me out of my plans with a few words."

"Telyn, are you saying you think they saw your candle?" Brand asked. "How could they have?"

She looked him in the eye. "*You* saw it last night, even though the shutters were closed," she said. A far-away look came over her face. "To one of the Kindred, especially a wise one like Gudrin, it must stand out like a brilliant point of light visible for a great distance."

"But how?" he demanded, thinking he knew the answer, but not wanting to hear it. "How is such a thing possible?"

"Because it is a magical beacon. I've had visions about how to make it—the tallow is not normal tallow, there are many ingredients—but none of that matters now. I—" she came forward and took his hands. "I've got a bit of the power in me, Brand, just a spark. I've known it for a long time: the visions, this beacon, other things…."

Fear came over Brand, a more direct and immediate fear than even the shadow man brought. He felt that he was losing Telyn. How could she ever be his when they reached marrying age if she indeed had some kind of power?

"Telyn, in the River Haven, such things aren't looked upon favorably. Magic is strictly to be kept out of the Haven—for the River's sake girl, that's what the Pact with the Faerie is all about!"

Telyn looked up at him. "I know. That's why I must meet the Faerie."

This time he reached out to her. He took her hands into his. "No, that's impossible, Telyn. I won't have you following a will-o-wisp or becoming a new trophy for the Wild Hunt."

Telyn pulled away from him with an irritated gesture. "I'm not suggesting anything so drastic. If I could just learn a few more things from them. They are so wise...."

Brand's mouth felt dry. "Wise, yes. But also fickle and as full of malice and deceit as kindness and wisdom. No one but those performing the ceremony can even watch them in safety."

"I could. I could use your help as well. We'll go around behind the Faerie mound, to the side where the forest comes close, and then—"

"But we have no wards! We would be at their mercy!" burst out Brand.

She shushed him with her delicate hand. She looked to the door and listened a moment before speaking further. Satisfied that no one had heard his outburst, she lifted her hand from his mouth. "I'm not a fool. I have wards. We will be in no danger."

Brand sighed aloud, finding it difficult to believe that he was having this conversation. See the Faerie? This was one of the greatest fears of any sensible person, not something that was planned for and sought out! Truly, this plan of hers topped them all.

"Are you with me, or do I go it alone?" she demanded. She had the cast to her face that Brand knew meant a bout of stubbornness was near at hand. She had a stubborn streak as wide as the slowest part of the river.

"I'll have to tell your mother. I'll tell everyone, I can't let you be led astray," he said resolutely.

Telyn tilted her head and gave him an amused half-smile. "You think you can stop me? You think you or anyone else in the Haven can even catch me?"

Brand paused for a moment, considering. He sighed and looked dejected. "No, probably not. You'd just disappear into the trees or something...."

"That's right," she said, walking around him in a slow circle as she spoke. "I would. And then I would face the Faerie alone."

Brand rolled his eyes, unbelieving of his misfortune. "Okay, I'll come with you."

Telyn, who was halfway around on her circle jumped up with a happy sound and kissed the back of his neck. This sent a wave of nerves tingling and singing down his back.

After that, she swore him to secrecy and he bid her goodnight. Just as he left, he looked at the candle again. She had placed his beside hers. His candle guttered and danced with the drafts, but hers burned steady and clear. This time there was no doubt of it. Telyn had worked magic.

He went to bed for a second time that night with troubling thoughts. As he fell asleep, he wondered what other things might be attracted to her beacon.

* * *

By the following morning the blizzard had stopped. The world had changed from green and brown to white and dark gray. Hoarfrost and icicles were already growing from the house's eaves. One particularly long icicle hung down in front of the doorway like a frozen dagger. It broke way and shattered when Brand went out to fill two tin pails at the covered well in the yard. Corbin followed him out to help.

"Well, what do you think of them?" asked Corbin as they wound up the rattling chain. Far down in the echoing depths of the well the bucket sloshed and clattered against the stones.

"I don't like this whole thing," Brand replied.

"Oh now, let's not be like your brother Jak," said Corbin. "They are a bit rough in their ways, but I can imagine that Gudrin has many an excellent tale to spin. I've never heard one of their stories first hand, but they're said to be the best.

Wouldn't it be quite a feather in our caps if we could present them at the feast?"

"What about Myrrdin?"

Corbin made an expansive gesture. "Perhaps Gudrin could perform the ceremony. She seems as wise as any."

Brand looked at him quizzically. "Everyone around here seems so taken with outsiders lately."

"What's wrong?" asked Corbin, squinting at him. Just then the bucket came into view and they hauled it up and filled one of the tin pails. The bucket dropped back down with a long clinking rattle of the chain and a distant, echoing splash.

Brand frowned before answering his cousin. Should he tell Corbin of Telyn's insane plans? She would be angry when she found out, but perhaps he could come up with some way to stop her. Still, he was reluctant to tell Corbin something she had told him in confidence. It was a troubling dilemma, he couldn't recall ever having held something back from Corbin before.

"I don't know," he said at last. "Nothing seems to be the way it was a few weeks ago."

They hauled up the bucket a second time, and Brand waited for Corbin's mind to digest this. He began to fear that somehow Corbin already knew everything. It sometimes seemed as if he knew things that no one else did, simply because he reasoned them through so carefully and clearly.

"It must be something about Scraper—Telyn, then," he said slowly, piecing it together. Brand oftentimes thought of Corbin's head as a miller's wheel and stone. He always ground down hard facts into a fine dust. "She was acting oddly last night...almost as if she expected someone besides Myrrdin. But not a pair of the Kindred, either."

Brand glanced at him and chewed a bit on his lower lip. He looked away, lest his eyes give away the rest of the puzzle somehow to Corbin's millstone. The bucket rose to the top a second time and they filled the second pail in silence.

"Ah, I have it!" said Corbin triumphantly. "She expected to see the Faerie at the door!"

Brand and Corbin looked at each other. Brand shook his head in defeat. "I was never good at deceit, and you are like a wolf hunting a lost lamb if there is a fact missing in the world."

Corbin's look of triumph faded quickly, as more ramifications came to him. "But how is such a thing possible? And why would anyone *want* to meet the Faerie on their doorstep during a midnight blizzard?"

Brand sighed. He explained what little he knew. He cautioned Corbin to secrecy, but knew that there was little hope that Telyn wouldn't figure out that Brand had told him of her schemes. She was almost as good as Corbin at delving into the truth, and Corbin was probably worse than Brand at hiding it.

It was when they were trudging through the new fallen snow back to the house that Corbin dropped his pail of water.

"Corbin, what are you doing, man?" Brand demanded. Then he himself stopped as he noticed that Corbin was standing stock still, looking out through the opening in the hedge where the path led down into the apple orchard. "What's wrong?"

Corbin backed way to Brand's side. He pointed into the white encrusted trees. "There," he hissed. "Beyond the fourth row. I saw something moving about."

They crouched down like hunters, Corbin pointing. To both their ears then came the sweet music of distant pipes. Corbin looked into Brand's eyes, their faces close together, the white plumes of their breath fogging the space between them. Brand knew the truth before his friend spoke.

"It was your shadow man, Brand. I'm sure of it. I feel his spell now, calling us to come and dance."

The two of them rose up and ran into the house. Behind them the two tin pails spilled their water onto the snow, melting dark patches in the smooth expanse of white.

Brand, always fleeter of foot, won the race to the door and burst through it. "Jak!" he shouted to his brother. "Get your crossbow!"

Jak, who had been sitting on his favorite chair with his feet hanging over the arms, jumped up in alarm. He spilled the tea that he had been sipping. Modi surprised everyone by producing his battleaxe, which he had placed out of sight behind his chair. He leapt up and charged to the door as if an army was on the island. Brushing Brand and Corbin aside, he pushed shut the door and barred it, putting his broad back against it. Only then did he turn to the boys.

"What did you see?" he demanded, his bass voice ringing with command. He gripped his battleaxe in both hands, at the ready.

"The shadow man," said Brand, pointing toward the orchard and the dock beyond. "Corbin saw the shadow man who has been following us for some time."

Modi's eyes narrowed. He went to the shuttered window nearest him and released the latch, peeking outside. White light illuminated his weathered face and hard eyes. "Just one man?"

"Yes, but he is very mysterious," replied Brand.

"Are you sure it is the same one?" Jak asked them.

Corbin shrugged. "I don't know. This time we heard the music of pipes."

"Perhaps we should go out and thrash him," suggested Jak, rolling up his sleeves and donning his cloak and boots.

Corbin shook his head. "He is not a normal man. It was like Brand said, I—I felt a cold dread come over me. Even to look at him was difficult. Perhaps he is one of the Faerie. One of the Dark Ones."

Modi slammed the shutters and latched them. They all jumped at the noise. "I see nothing. Faerie, you say?" he said, snorting. "What do River Folk know of Dark Ones?"

Before any could answer him, Gudrin and Telyn came into the room. "I'm sorry, but I seem to have slept late," said Gudrin. Brand was a bit amused to note that although she wore a nightshirt, she still had her package under her arm and her rucksack on her back. Gudrin looked at Modi and sighed. "I see your weapon is ready again, Modi of the Warriors. What is all the commotion about?"

Brand quickly explained about the shadow man while Jak went upstairs to get his crossbow. While Brand was describing the shadow man, Gudrin became increasingly concerned.

"And the length of the weapon you saw the first time...."

"I couldn't be *sure* it was a weapon," interrupted Brand.

"Yes, yes, but if it was, would you say it was the length of a dagger or a sword?"

Brand pondered for a moment. "In between, perhaps."

Gudrin nodded, kneading her chin. She held her package to her chest, as if it gave her comfort of some kind. Brand watched her and noticed that her rucksack gave a tiny twitch again, as it had last night, a small movement. Brand blinked and frowned. He surmised that Gudrin must have some kind of odd tick in the muscles of her back. Perhaps it only showed up when she was thinking, the way old man Tad Silure's cheek would twitch when he spoke before the Riverton council.

"We must investigate this, Modi," Gudrin said to her companion.

Modi shrugged his massive shoulders. "It is but one man."

"They describe not a man, but one of the *shirik*," said Gudrin.

At this, Modi came alive. He strode forward to Gudrin's side. They spoke briefly in their own tongue, which, to the ears of the River Folk, sounded both crude and subtle. It was a language of many hard sounds and careful inflections. Each word seemed clear and clipped; none ran into the next as words tended to do in their own tongue. Only Telyn seemed to enjoy the sound of it.

"There was one other thing," said Corbin. "We heard the sweet music of pipes after the phantom had disappeared."

Gudrin and Modi exchanged glances. "Man-sized? Bearing a long knife and playing sweet pipes? It can only be Voynod," said Modi.

Gudrin nodded, but gestured Modi to silence. "It is best not to name them so casually when one is near," she said.

Telyn had followed Jak and his crossbow to the door. In her hand she held a long thin dagger. Brand frowned at her blade.

"Wait," said Gudrin. She raised up a thick-fingered hand. "You must not confront the *shirik* now. It is weak so far from home, I'm sure, but not so weak as to fall to an honest crossbow bolt or dagger."

"I didn't want to kill the man," said Jak, a bit taken aback. "I just wanted to warn him off."

Gudrin nodded. "It is not a man. It is a *shirik*—a *shade,* as you would call it in your tongue. A powerful servant of the Enemy. This one you saw, that Modi has already unwisely named, is the Enemy's bard."

"The Enemy? Do you mean Herla?" asked Brand.

Gudrin raised her hands to her face and made shushing motions. "Shhh! Don't speak his name aloud with one of his servants near!"

All the River Folk stared at her with mouths open. Brand had heard stories of bogies such as the dreaded shades, free agents of Herla and his Wild Hunt, but the idea that there was one of them stalking about outside was just too much.

"Well, that's it," Jak said, throwing up his hands. "That's just grand."

"How do you know?" Brand asked Gudrin, ignoring his brother's outburst.

"I can feel it. Now that I know it is here, its presence is clear to me," she turned then and leveled an accusatory finger at Telyn. "I believe it was some of your doing that it is here this morning. I warned you about the beacon, but still you saw fit to burn it. There are many things, even here in the Haven, that should not be disturbed by a call from one without the wisdom to deal with them."

Telyn hung her head, but by the set of her jaw and the way she toyed with her dagger, Brand suspected she was not cowed. Gudrin looked at her and sighed. "Still," she said, "it wouldn't be fair to blame you entirely, as the thing has been following these boys of Clan Rabing for some time now, even without your aid in marking them."

"What shall we do?" asked Jak, his voice sounding weak and betraying that he was at a loss as to how to protect his home and his guests.

"We will have breakfast," said Gudrin simply. The only one who smiled at this idea was Corbin.

Posting Modi as a lookout at the front window, they ate around the fire and made plans. While eating, they all felt the presence of something outside, something that wished them ill. Occasionally, they thought to hear the soft playing of sweet pipes, but they were never sure, as it might have been only the wind whistling around the eaves of the old house. The music, if music it was, brought them no joy. There was no laughter in the house, and somehow the food tasted less appetizing, despite Corbin's excellent cooking. They plied Gudrin with questions, most of which she answered vaguely. Some she refused to answer entirely. Telyn was the most persistent questioner.

"But madam, you must tell us about Herr—ah, that is, about *the Enemy*. He is just one of the Faerie, is he not?"

"Yes, and no," said Gudrin. She swallowed another two strips of bacon, seemingly whole, before continuing. "The Enemy is one we must not speak of just now. Not if that is one of his servants outside."

She paused for a moment to gaze at the closed shutters, her eyes seeming to focus on the snowy scene outside and whatever might lurk there. A tinkling sound came to them all then, a soft half-melody, felt as much as heard. Frowning, Gudrin turned back to the group. She leaned forward and lowered her voice. The others all leaned inward to hear her words.

"The Faerie aren't like humans, Merlings, or the Kindred. They come in myriad forms, the next one looking and acting completely differently from the last. They do not have families and kinfolk quite the way that we do. A Faerie elfkin is able to sire a dryad or one of the Wee Folk, or even a goblin. What results depends on magic and the nature of the parents. Many of the Faerie seem to be unique examples of their kind, freaks that are never born twice. Some of them were once human, and are now forever cursed to live with the Faerie—not alive, but Undying.

"Among them, there are wide varieties of temperaments and tendencies. The Enemy and his servants are unique in this way. Too, many of them were once human, the sort that embraces cruelty and the absence of light. It is part of your Pact with the neutral Faerie that they keep away these Dark Ones."

Jak made a gesture of annoyance. "You mentioned Merlings in the same breath as River Folk and the Kindred. The Faerie are strange, but at least they keep their bargains. I'd

66

rather not be likened to one of the baby-stealing, muck-crusted Merlings."

Gudrin shrugged. "True, they steal your young, but do you not eat their eggs when given the chance? In fact, you inhabit the same lands and waters as the Merlings for the same reasons. They too, fear the Faerie and reside in the Haven to avoid their torments."

"You make them sound intelligent," said Jak with a snort. "I've never thought of Merlings as much more than dim-witted savages."

"A fair assessment," admitted Gudrin. "But regardless, both your peoples reside here in an uneasy truce, both thankful to be out of the reach of the Faerie."

"But I thought the Pact was only to appease the Faerie, to keep them from stealing from us and playing their awful pranks," said Brand, chewing a brown-bread muffin. He sipped a mug of coffee to wash it down. "You make it seem as if much more is at stake."

Gudrin rolled her eyes to the ceiling. "Oh, how short are the memories of humans. The Pact, which seems almost a new thing to my Kindred, appears to you River Folk as ancient history, the origins of which are only vaguely understood," she said, shaking her head. She drained her coffee mug in a gulp and wagged it at Corbin, who promptly filled it again. "The Pact is really a bargain, my good young man, struck between the Faerie and the River Folk. You see, although their needs are slight, the Faerie aren't farmers. They have always found it easier to steal what food they need than grow it themselves.

"However, the rising of the Enemy in days gone by was the real reason for the Pact. Rather than stealing from and hunting one another, your two peoples decided to cooperate. Your part of the bargain was to give one part in seven of your crops each year to feed the Faerie of *Cymru*. For their part the Faerie would perform no tricks, sour no milk, blight no crops and set no changelings in the cribs of your mothers. Also, they had the task of guarding your borders against malicious creatures of every type," Gudrin finished. She scooped up another forkful of scrambled eggs, which quickly disappeared into her face.

Brand noticed that even at the breakfast table she wore her leather sack over her shoulder and kept her package laid across her knees. He was about to ask her about it, but Telyn bubbled up with another question.

"So the Faerie should have kept out this shade?" she asked. There was an odd light in her eyes that spoke of a hunger for knowledge, rather than food. Brand noticed that she had barely touched her plate.

"Aye, they should have," said Gudrin. "It is a disturbing thing that the Enemy's bard has so much strength as to be able to get past them." Her plate was empty and she sat back, loosening her belt and readjusting her rucksack for comfort. Brand thought he saw it jiggle oddly when she moved it, as if a heavy object had shifted inside.

"Are we strong enough here, on our home isle, to face this thing and ward it off?" demanded Jak.

Gudrin considered. She picked up the package on her knees, which Brand was now certain was a book, and closed her eyes. After a moment she nodded. "Yes, I feel that we have strength enough if he is alone. The Shade is weak when alone and in the daylight. Especially when working hard to keep the Faerie from noticing him.

"But that isn't the real question," she said, placing both hands on the table and eyeing each of them in turn. Her blue gaze had that hard spark of light again that was painful to look upon. "The real question is why the Enemy has sent his bard to watch you."

Chapter Eight
King Herla's Story

Gudrin aimed a stubby finger at Telyn. "I would blame you and your beacon first, were it not for the fact that the shade was seen by Brand even before you lit the fool thing."

Telyn frowned at her nearly full plate of cold breakfast.

"It doesn't matter why," said Jak, rising and taking up his crossbow. "You say we can ward it off. Let us do so and be done with it. I'll not have such a creature wandering about my island and creating mischief if I can prevent it."

Gudrin shook her head. "No," she said, in the tone of one commanding children. She took another gulp of coffee, then turned her baleful eyes full force onto Jak. Jak stood where he was, his legs and face twitching, but not moving.

Brand felt a heat come up his neck and into his face. He stood up, rising to his full height. He was considerably taller than any of them. "Gudrin of the Talespinners," he said in a loud voice. Some quiet part of him wondered just what he was doing, but a greater part of him pushed past all doubts and worries. "This is the house of Clan Rabing, on Rabing Isle. My brother is the master of this house, and you have taken of his hearth and food. I demand that you reconsider your words."

Everyone looked at him in surprise. Telyn smiled. Modi's hand moved to the haft of his axe. Gudrin was the last to react. She stood up too and faced Brand. She clutched her package to her barrel-like chest and her rucksack shifted on her back as though it held poached game. Her eyes cut into Brand's gaze and they locked there. Brand resolutely returned the stare, refusing to look down, although it seemed one of the greatest efforts of his life. Vaguely, he wondered if having suffered through the dreadful gaze of the shade he had seen twice now had somehow strengthened him for this encounter. Through sheer determination he held on, managing not to avert his eyes.

Finally, Gudrin nodded. She dropped her eyes first. She rubbed her face, eyes downcast for several long moments. When she lifted them again, the power in them was all but gone.

"You are right. I have behaved without consideration for my host," she said, then she sighed and took her chair again. The others relaxed as well. Jak came back to life and Modi let go of his axe. Gudrin suddenly looked older and smaller. "It is just that you do not know what it is that you wish to face. It is a horror beyond description."

Brand was a bit amazed to find himself standing there, facing down Gudrin. It was not his normal role to play. He frowned and sat down slowly, shaking himself slightly, wondering what had overcome him. Then he knew: he had not been able to stand his brother looking so weak. Jak didn't deserve that.

"Tell us what you can then, and let us decide," said Jak.

Gudrin looked around at them, then stood and donned her cloak and her wide-brimmed hat. "There is no way to explain such a thing. It must be seen."

They all followed her out into the cold gray morning. Corbin led them into the orchard to the fourth row where he had spotted the shade. Jak had his crossbow loaded, Telyn carried her knife, and Corbin and Brand carried the axes they had chopped wood with the day before. When they neared the spot, Modi stopped them with a gesture and stumped forward. He crouched to examine the snow.

"That's no use, Modi," said Gudrin, stepping forward and waving the others to follow. "The shade will leave no tracks."

For once, Modi didn't heed Gudrin. He raised his thick-fingered hand again, signaling her to stop. Scowling, Gudrin obeyed. She grumbled something about the warrior class of the Kindred. Modi moved around the trunk of the tree with care,

70

until at last he halted with a grunt of recognition. He waved the others forward.

"As I said..." began Gudrin, then stopped. "By the dragon's breath!" she breathed. "There are prints!"

The River Folk crowded around and they could all see the tracks too. Just four horse tracks, all alone in the fresh snow, as if a horse had appeared by the apple tree and then vanished. There were no tracks leading to the tree, nor away from it. Nor was there any way that someone could have jumped a horse to that spot through the trees. The white frost on the branches was undisturbed.

Gudrin was rubbing her face. She scowled and clenched her package tightly to her chest. On her back, Brand saw her rucksack lurch not once, but twice, as though something had fallen to one side and then the other, by itself. Gudrin jerked her head in annoyance. "Quiet!" she whispered over her shoulder. Then she caught sight of Brand watching her.

Brand frowned and stepped toward Gudrin. He wanted to know what was in that rucksack once and for all.

"This is very bad," said Gudrin before he could speak. "The shade is strong enough to take bodily form, even if for just a moment or two." She shook her head.

"Doesn't that just mean we could hurt it with our weapons?" asked Jak.

"I doubt it. I'm not sure even Modi of the Warriors here could best one of them," said Gudrin, her face was a mass of deep lines. Brand thought she looked older when she worried. "It takes more than ordinary steel to injure a shade."

"What should we do?" asked Telyn. Gudrin startled a bit, turning around to notice for the first time that the girl had come up behind her to stand close.

"You are a quiet one, aren't you?" Gudrin asked. She waved her hands for everyone's attention. "Jak, we must leave this place. We must flee. I don't know why the Enemy has his shades after you, but that doesn't matter. We must run to a safer place. And after that, we must find Myrrdin. He may know why you are hunted."

Jak nodded in agreement. "I think we should head for Riverton. The Harvest Moon Feast and the Offering must be performed. There is no more time. If I can't bring them Myrrdin, then you will have to do."

Gudrin raised her hands in protest. "But I'm not fit to perform the ceremony! I haven't the craft!"

"Neither have we, nor have any of the other folk of the River Haven," argued Jak.

Gudrin clutched her package and clenched her eyes tightly, as would someone in prayer. Brand saw her rucksack shift twice more. He and Corbin exchanged quizzical glances. His cousin had seen it too.

Finally, Gudrin raised up her head, and all her years seemed to run through her in a shudder. Brand wondered just how old she truly was.

"I will do it," she said simply.

They gathered their things quickly and went to the dock in a tight, nervous group. All of them felt that they were being watched. When they reached the shore, they discovered that a third boat was there, a small rowboat. The faded insignia on the prow, painted on the weathered wood, identified the boat.

"That's Arlon Thunderfoot's rig, the hunter from Hamlet," exclaimed Brand. "What's he doing here?"

"Careful boy, it may be cursed," said Gudrin, holding back his arm. They all watched as Modi moved forward to peer into the boat. He signaled for them to approach.

Inside the boat they found only one oar. There was frozen blood on it.

"Where's Arlon?" asked Brand, already guessing the grim truth.

"He's Merling food, by the look of it," grunted Modi. He turned to Gudrin. "We must sink what we don't take."

Gudrin nodded. She turned back to the empty rowboat and the stunned River Folk that had gathered around it. "I grieve with you all." She raised up her package above her head in both hands.

"The River gives, and the River takes. In the end, the River knows us all," she said. Brand was honored she had quoted a proverb of the River Folk. It was only right, as this was a benediction over one of his people.

Gudrin then gestured to Modi, who quickly struck a hole in the bottom of the boat and pushed it out into the flood. The warrior moved to the leather boat that the two of them had come in and scuttled it as well.

"We will all take the skiff," said Gudrin. "Come."

Numbly, the four River Folk climbed aboard after Gudrin and Modi and they cast off. Even though he had not known Arlon all that well, it was difficult to accept that he was dead. Brand couldn't remember having ever heard of an actual murder before—but the Battleaxe Folk seemed so sure they'd just discovered one. Certainly, there were accidents along the river now and then, but never an *intentional* killing. Except for Merling attacks, the people of the Haven rarely died violently. He took in a deep breath and nodded to himself. It had been the Merlings, of course. He felt sure the Merlings were guilty, just as they had slain his own kin.

For several minutes they traveled in silence, letting the current sweep them away from Rabing Isle. Brand looked back at it. With the recent events and the new mantle of white snow, it didn't look friendly. It hardly looked like home at all.

For sometime Gudrin sat on the centerboards, hardly moving.

"Gudrin of the Talespinners?" said Telyn in a soft voice.

Gudrin stirred and looked up at her.

"What is it that you carry on your back?" Telyn asked in a hushed voice.

For a few moments, the river made the only sounds that any of them could hear. The water gurgled as it rushed over rocks near the shore. A bird called in the Deepwood and was answered by another back on Rabing Isle. Brand thought the call was a strange one, perhaps a type of bird that he had never heard before.

Gudrin finally spoke. "It is my burden," she told Telyn, as if this answered everything.

The River Folk were subdued on the voyage back to Riverton. The sky was gray and the water was the color of shadowed steel; even the skiff seemed less full of life and only drifted south with luffing sails and bobbing prow. Telyn now had eyes and ears only for Gudrin, urging her to tell them a tale of ancient times. Brand smiled, missing her attentions, but knowing that when her curiosity was piqued she could not be distracted. Gudrin at first seemed reluctant, but finally let herself be persuaded with Telyn pleading so persistently.

Gudrin opened her package and removed a large book. The book was bound in ancient, scaly leather and had clasps of bright brass or perhaps even gold. She clicked open the clasps and opened the book with slow reverence. Brand could see only that the pages were filled with the odd blocky script of the Kindred. Gudrin flipped through a page or two, muttering to herself. At length she looked up at them, nodding absently.

"So, you wish to know of the Dark Bard, my curious young lady? Not an unreasonable request. However, any tale of the Dark Ones must necessarily begin with the tale of..." glancing about and leaning forward, she all but whispered the name, *"Herla."*

Brand noticed Telyn's eyes, which were serious and eager. Gudrin sat back against the boat's rail and made herself comfortable. The River Folk moved about the skiff, settling themselves—without thought or urging from Jak—in places that would both balance the skiff and allow them to hear the tale over the sounds of wind and water. Modi alone rode in the bow, where he listened without appearing to.

As the tale began, Brand felt a chill wind come up the river against the current. It made the sails luff and flag. He and Corbin moved to lower them and drift with the current.

"Herla was one of the first human kings of Cymru, which is the ancient name for this land," said Gudrin.

"So he was once human?" asked Jak in surprise. Gudrin halted and glared at the interruption.

"Human indeed and a great man as well. The Teret tells of his fall. Once, many years ago, King Herla met another king who was a pigmy, no bigger than a child. This small creature, so the story goes, was mounted on a large goat. He was gaily attired in a cloak and pants made of the dappled hide of fawns. He wore no shirt however, and his chest was bare and milk-white."

"Oberon," whispered Telyn. Gudrin paused and glanced at her. Telyn blinked. "Sorry."

74

"Indeed, Oberon it was, but then he was a young lord. He was more wild and playful in that millennium than he is in this. He introduced himself to Herla as follows: 'I am lord of many kings and princes, an unnumbered and innumerable people, and have been sent, a willing envoy, by them to you.

Let us agree, therefore, that I shall attend your wedding, and that you shall attend mine a year later.'

"Sure enough, the elfkin king appeared at Herla's wedding with a huge train of followers, bringing wonderful food and drink for the feast. And a year later, just as he had promised, Herla went to attend the elfkin king's wedding, which was held in a magnificent palace in the depths of a mountain. The only entrance to the palace was by the way of a cave in a high cliff. When the time came to leave, the little king loaded Herla and his companions with gifts. Many delightful and intricate mechanical toys and finely wrought clothing and jewelry did he give the king. Lastly, he gave the king a small bloodhound to carry, strictly instructing him that on no account should any of his company dismount till the dog had leapt from the arms of its bearer.

"When Herla came out of the mountain palace and into the sunlight of his own kingdom his joy was short-lived. He asked news from a shepherd, and he learned that not one year, but many hundreds of years had passed since he had last been there, and he himself was only remembered as a king of ancient times who had vanished into a cliff and had never been seen again.

"The king, who thought he had only stayed for three days, could scarcely sit upon his horse for amazement. Some of his company, forgetting the elfkin king's orders, dismounted before the dog alighted and instantly fell to dust. Realizing why they had dissolved, the king warned the rest under pain of like death not to touch the earth till the hound had leapt."

Gudrin paused here to light her pipe. To the others, listening closely to her tale, it seemed an infinitely slow and tedious process. At last she had the bowl glowing redly and blew several gusts of blue smoke into the open air. "Alas, from that day to this, the hound has never leapt."

"Never?" asked Brand in surprise.

"Never," repeated Gudrin. "And so through all the long centuries, the king and his mad coursers have wandered on horseback ever since, never alighting, never touching the earth, nor bed, nor even feeling the warmth of a campfire. And—although the curse has held them ageless for centuries, they still need to fill their bellies."

"But what kind of men could stay on horseback for centuries, even if ageless?" asked Jak incredulously.

Gudrin shook her head. "They were men no longer, but cursed, undying creatures. They were ageless, but they weren't changeless. They became darker of spirit and came to prefer the night over the day. As hunters they were soon unequaled. Instead of his crown, Herla came to wear the great antlered stag's head that is now familiar to us."

"But the worst change was due to the curse. For soon, the huntsmen learned why the bloodhound was so named. At first, it would eat nothing, though they offered it every kind of meat that they could kill from the backs of their cursed steeds. The small hound thinned and sickened, and Herla despaired. He cursed Oberon, and wanted nothing more than to avenge himself upon the trickster. Many times, he pondered alighting upon the earth and ending his torment, but stubbornly he refused. Only the hope of vengeance kept him going.

"So it was very important to him that the hound didn't die. He ordered his coursers to bring him every variety of food imaginable, and it was quite by accident that they first learned the dog would lap at the blood of a stag, served to it in a wooden bowl.

"The hound would drink the blood, but it did not return to health. They fed it stag's blood, but still it sickened, although its decline was much slowed. After a time, Herla came to know the truth in his heart.

"'Find the shepherd with whom we first spoke,' he ordered his coursers. 'Find him and slay him. Bring back his body into the forest that we might empty his blood into this wooden bowl.' Grimly, his coursers did as they were told. When served this bowl the hound relished it and soon grew strong again.

"In this way Herla and his followers learned to feed the hound, and in time it robbed them of the last of their humanity.

For men can't take and drink the lives of other men in a perpetual hunt without changing. They became cursed horrors of the night. Worse than the Faerie themselves—worse than those who had created them.

"Oberon came to regret his trick and his curse. Many times have the paths of Herla and Oberon crossed, and always it has been a grim meeting."

"And now these horrors have taken an interest in us?" asked Brand in dismay. "Why? Why is the Dark Bard here?"

"That I do not know," replied Gudrin.

"So the bard is one of Herla's coursers, Talespinner?" asked Corbin thoughtfully. "And if any of the Wild Hunt step down from their mounts, they will fall to dust? Perhaps all we need to do then is coax them to alight."

"Ah, a fair assessment, Corbin. But few have managed to get any of the Wild Hunt to leave the backs of their horses. The bard in particular is tenacious. He too was cursed by the Faerie to live in death, to walk the Earth undying. He too, was once mortal, and lives on through the strength of his vengeful will. He is unusual in that he can be apart from Herla and his hound and still exist."

"Are there other agents like him?" asked Corbin.

"Aye, several, but it would not be good to speak more of them now."

With a ritual of movements, Gudrin quietly closed her book, fastening the clasp and testing it. She then rewrapped the book in the waxed package and slid it comfortably under her arm.

The River Folk were quiet, each thinking his or her own thoughts for a time. Telyn was the first to speak. "Herla and his coursers are nightmares. But the Faerie, they seem at once wonderful and terrible."

"They are," said Gudrin, speaking as one would from experience. "They are both joyful and sad, young and ancient. It is beyond mortals to truly understand them."

"It would seem," Corbin said, "that our judgment of their actions should be based upon whether or not they benefit us."

"This is one way to view them," Gudrin admitted with a shrug.

77

"What about the Dark Bard? How did Herla meet him and enlist his aid?" asked Telyn.

"I want to know more of the Merlings," Jak interrupted, sounding disturbed. "How do they live? Where did they come from?"

"What I want to know is the nature of these shades that were once human and seem to have taken an interest in us River Folk. You must tell us more about them," said Brand.

Gudrin held up her hand. "Those are all other stories, which I will tell you some other time. Now we grow close to Stone Island, if I'm not mistaken."

To the surprise of the River Folk, she was right. They rounded a bend in the great Berrywine River and the granite walls of Stone Island hove into view. Soon they busied themselves with the approach to the harbor.

This time, with the feast of the Harvest Moon this very night, there was no space at the public docks. They were forced to beach the skiff, dragging it ashore and tying it to a gnarled old pine tree so that it wouldn't drift away. All of them came splashing ashore, carrying their packs and the weapons they had brought with them. Brand felt rather silly carrying his woodaxe. He exchanged glances with Corbin and could tell that he felt the same.

"Perhaps we should leave these in the boat," suggested Brand, lifting the axe to Jak. Before his brother could reply, however, Modi stepped close to Brand and laid one of his broad hands on Brand's arm.

"Keep it with you," Modi said.

Brand looked at the warrior's huge face. He could find no mockery there, nor any humor of any kind. All he could do was nod.

They all toiled up the lane to Riverton under the watchful eyes of those Hoots and Silures that were not away working. For the most part, they were elderly men rocking in their chairs and sucking on cheap clay pipes and old women, beating half-heartedly at filthy rugs. Their stares were more than unfriendly—they were shocked and downright distrustful. Brand could all but hear their thoughts: *Now those Rabing boys are consorting with Fobs and Outsiders! Even Battleaxe Folk,*

78

no less! They should change their names from Rabing to Rabble! Huh!

Chapter Nine
Old Man Thilfox

It was a long walk uphill, but soon they came to the main cobbled street of Riverton. They halted at the Spotted Hog where they had had lunch just the day before. It seemed like a week had passed since then to Brand.

"We must find Uncle Tylag and Constable Hirck and tell him about the boat and Arlon's disappearance," said Jak.

"Yes," agreed Brand, "Uncle Tylag will know what to do."

After a short discussion, they decided that Jak, Modi and Gudrin would report to the constable, while Brand and Corbin would find Tylag. As Brand had no doubt she would, Telyn wished to accompany the talespinner. They all agreed to meet up at the common, where most of the town would be in any case.

"Don't forget about our business, Brand," Telyn hissed to him as the two groups parted. She looked Corbin up and down critically. "You can come along as well, since I can see that you've wheedled the story out of Brand."

Brand and Corbin exchanged grins as they went into the Spotted Hog, deciding to check there first. Inside, one thing led to another, and Corbin was soon ordering a large quantity of food for lunch. Brand huffed, but didn't refuse the plate of smoked fish and fresh bread placed before him.

"She knew immediately," Corbin said when he'd finished stuffing his lunch away.

"Of course," replied Brand. "I never doubted that she would."

"I think I know what you see in that girl."

"And what would that be?"

"The fact that she can see right through you. It's enough to intrigue any thinking man."

Brand kept his opinions about Telyn to himself and finished his plate quickly. He noted that a fire was going now in the stone hearth at the back wall of the common room. Winter was upon them early this year. He knew from years of experience that Innkeeper Blunner would keep the flames going all day, every day, until spring.

"Well," said Corbin after he'd finished a mug of warm mead. "I think it's clear that my father isn't here."

Brand agreed, grinning, and the two of them settled their accounts and stepped out into the street again. The snow had melted off by now, and the sun was even shining weakly. It was good to walk on cobblestones instead of slush and mud.

All of Riverton was bustling in anticipation of tonight's feast. A Mari Lwyd parade came up behind them, bells jangling and criers bawling for all to beware. Remembering when it had been their year to carry the Mari Lwyd, they stepped out of the way into the entryway of Yudo the Tinsmith's shop and watched the procession.

First came the criers, girls all, wearing white dresses with wings made of sticks and gauze. Then came the smaller boys, hopping and leaping with agility, each wearing a top hat and a waistcoat of bright green, yellow or crimson and swinging their canes at the crowds with mock ferocity. Next came the huntsmen themselves, boys and girls nearly as old as Brand and Corbin. First came the biggest of the boys, bearing the Mari Lwyd itself, the ancient symbol of Herla, which consisted of a horse's skull draped with white cloth and decorated with rosettes and colored ribbons. The eyes were of bottle-glass and the antlers were those of a stag killed long ago in the Deepwood. Behind this boy came the other coursers, riding mock horses of white or black.

Brand watched the procession go by, and for the first time felt some of the old excitement of the Harvest Moon feast run

81

through him. "The children think it's all a game, but there they are, imitating Herla at the head of the Wild Hunt. But perhaps I shouldn't mention that name aloud...."

"I remember our year," said Corbin in a thoughtful voice. "You bore the Mari Lwyd because of your great height, and I was one of your coursers."

"To think that tonight we may catch sight of what we were playing at just a few years ago," said Brand. "The whole idea is mad. We must try to stop Telyn. I have no interest in being chased down by Herla and skinned to make new boots and cloaks for his coursers."

Corbin looked doubtful. "I don't want to meet up with this Enemy either, but Telyn is not easily dissuaded from anything."

Brand made a gesture of exasperation. "She wants to do something crazy, possibly risking all our lives or even more. We are well within our rights to stop her. She doesn't know what she is toying with. After listening to Gudrin today and seeing Arlon's boat and those bizarre footprints on the isle, I'm beginning to realize how important all of this is."

"It's far more than a child's game," agreed Corbin.

The two of them followed the procession to the gates of Drake Manor. The high stone walls were scaled by green tongues of ivy. The boys passed between the rusted gates and crunched up the gravel walkway to the steps. As they approached the manor itself, both of them slowed somewhat. It was difficult to overcome their childhood fear and reverence of the place. It was here that the Drake Clan had built their homestead to house their many relations. Riverton had been built up around this one corner of the estate, which made up a goodly portion of Stone Island. The Drake lands stretched all the way to the western cliffs along the far shore of the island. To the north, the estate bordered the town common upon which the festival would be held and upon which the Offering would be made tonight. The manor house itself was an impressive thing, four stories high and rambling, with dozens of apartments big enough for whole families to live in. In fact, more than twenty families of the Drake Clan still lived in the manor.

Brand hadn't faced the Riverton Council since he was a child. He hesitated at the foot of the steps, then plunged ahead, swinging the knocker and sending an echoing clatter through the halls on the other side. After a lengthy wait Brand made ready to lift the knocker again, but the door swung open even as he reached out his hand. He snatched it back hastily.

The man who answered the door was an elderly fellow with bushy white eyebrows and a squint. He took one look at them and waved them away. "You've come for courting early, eh? Anyone you boys would be looking for has already left for the common," he said. He made as if to shut the door, but then leaned out to have one more word. "And watch that you don't make free with the young ladies of the Drake Clan tonight, gentlemen."

"Sir, excuse me," said Brand, stepping forward. "We are looking for Tylag of Clan Rabing, sir."

"Eh, what's this?" asked the man. "Tylag?"

"Yes, sir. He sent us to look for Myrrdin."

"Myrrdin?" asked the man in surprise. His eyes slid back and forth between the two boys and then narrowed suddenly. "Is this a joke? We don't take well to jokes here. I'll have you whipped off the estate!"

"No, sir," said Brand, taking a step back in surprise. "We aren't joking."

The man squinted at Brand closely. "You're Jan's boy. Jan Rabing's boy. Only Jan could have had a son so tall."

"You knew my father?"

"Of course," he snapped. Then he eyed Corbin. "And this great lout must be Corbin Rabing. Well, well."

"Is Tylag here, sir?" asked Corbin.

The man made an impatient gesture. "Of course," he said. He turned and walked away quickly. A crooked finger over his shoulder was the only hint they had that they were to follow. They stepped into the entry hall and shut the door behind them. The hall was everything that Brand had remembered, but perhaps with an extra layer of dust on it. The mosaic floor was a spiral pattern of black and white that gave one the impression of falling into a whirlpool if you stared at it too long. The grand staircase that swept down into the hall from the second story was of carven stone and heavy oak beams. It was up these steps that the old man currently disappeared.

Hustling after him, the boys took the steps two at a time. In the sudden presence of wealth, they were now acutely aware of their simple clothes and muddy boots. Brand began to self-consciously stuff his shirt into his pants.

They reached the top of the steps and for a moment thought they had lost their guide. "There!" said Corbin, pointing to a door that was just swinging shut at the end of the nearest hallway. Brand marched for the door down a hall of dark-stained wood. Embroidered tapestries of various heroic acts performed by Drake Clan leaders lined the walls of the dark hall. Brand grabbed hold of the door handle and twisted. They walked into the room beyond.

They blinked in brilliance. The entire back wall of this room—and much of the ceiling was made up of stained glass. Brand stood in wonder, recalling the colored lights of the council chamber from when he was a boy. The floor was carpeted with several huge silver wolf pelts taken from the Deepwood. An oval table of great size sat in the middle of the room with twenty-one chairs arranged around it, one for each of the clan leaders.

There were only five people in the room now: the man who had answered the door, Tylag, Gram Rabing, old man Tad Silure and Irva Hoot. Brand could tell that they weren't getting along.

"Sorry about the delay, gentlemen," said the man who had let them in. "These louts of yours, Tylag, seem to have returned early—and without Myrrdin."

"Well, it was a long shot, Thilfox," sighed Tylag.

"Thilfox?" asked Brand, stepping forward. "You're Thilfox Drake?"

The old man made an impatient gesture. "Of course, boy."

"I apologize, sir. I didn't..." Brand began, but the others were all talking, ignoring them. They were trying to decide who should perform the ceremony of the Offering. Old man Tad Silure and Gram Rabing seemed particularly bitter, while Irva Hoot looked bored.

Brand stepped forward, but Corbin took his arm. "Perhaps we should just go."

"No, we must tell them about the Kindred and about Arlon."

"Eh? What was that?" demanded Thilfox suddenly. He rose up and approached them. "Did you say something about the Kindred? What would you boys know of such the Battleaxe Folk?"

Brand was a bit taken aback. Thilfox seemed at times deaf and at other times possessed of the keenest hearing. "I—I would like to tell you that we have brought with us Gudrin of the Talespinners and Modi of the Warriors. Gudrin has much craft and lore, and I believe she may be well qualified to perform the Offering."

"Oh you do, do you, boy?" asked old man Tad Silure, rising to his feet. He was a balding man of both exceptional age and vitality. He had a habit of smiling and sneering at the same time, which revealed his long yellow teeth. "Who are you to make the council's decisions for them? Like everyone in your clan, you think you own the River itself."

"Why don't we all control ourselves and hear what they have to say, Tad," suggested Tylag, checking his own anger with an obvious effort.

"Yes, boy, make your report," said Irva Hoot. She adjusted her clay pipe so that it poked from the opposite side of her mouth and peered at them dubiously.

Brand explained at length what had happened to them for the last couple of days, including their encounters with the shade, the Battleaxe Folk, and Arlon's boat. He left out any mention of Telyn's odd candle, or her plans for this evening. When he was finished, Thilfox eyed him oddly.

"Arlon, you say?" Thilfox asked. "Did you find the boat on the shores of the Deepwood?"

"No sir. We found it on Rabing Isle."

"Could it have been cast adrift so it floated your way?"

Brand considered it. "Possibly."

Thilfox told him then that Arlon had been reported missing in the Deepwood, and the fact that his boat had traveled to

Rabing Isle was quite strange. Brand agreed. An uncomfortable pause followed.

"That's all you wish to say, Brand?" asked Thilfox.

Brand looked down. "That's all, sir."

"Then we will discuss this shade at greater length later," said Thilfox, turning away from the Brand. "Right now, all that matters is that the Pact is maintained."

The clan leaders began to debate the issue heatedly. Only Gram Rabing stepped over to the boys and asked them a few questions about Jak and how they were faring out on the Isle alone. She tipped her head back toward the others. "They will come up for air shortly. In the meantime, why don't you boys go find these friends of yours?"

"Why are they fighting so fiercely, Gram?" asked Brand.

"None of them want to perform the ceremony, but neither are any of them willing to entrust another. That's why Myrrdin was so helpful. He was always a neutral party. Now, why don't you boys move along? There isn't a lot of time left before the event. Be back by twilight. By then they will be desperate to get anyone to do it."

They turned to go, and found Thilfox holding the door open for them. As he let them out, he gave the boys a rare thin-lipped smile. "You did well to bring back the Talespinner. If she is as you say, it might just save the Pact. Now don't dawdle! Flirt with the girls only sparingly!"

Shaking their heads, Brand and Corbin trotted down the gravel path to the street and turned toward the town common.

The snow had almost all melted away, except for occasional white mounds beneath trees and sheltered by boulders. On the common the celebration was in full swing beneath the great domed tents and out on the playing fields. Children laughed and capered in circles, making faerie rings of their own in the icy grass. Young girls, wearing multi-hued dresses and mock wings of gauze chased one another in the wooded area. Vendors hawked sweetmeats and rainbow-sticks, which bore ribbons of every color that would flutter in the wind or when a child ran with it held aloft. Wheelbarrows loaded with cider and gingerbeer moved through the crowds, making frequent sales.

"Too bad we are on such an urgent mission," said Corbin regretfully.

Brand agreed. The two of them searched through the crowds. Brand wondered if the mood of the people would have changed if they knew that it still had not been decided who was going to make this year's Offering.

After they had searched for several minutes, Brand felt a tap on his back. He whirled to find Telyn smiling up at him. "You never do look back, do you?" she asked.

"Telyn! It's good that you found us. Gudrin needs to go to the council right away."

Telyn led them to the second great dome tent, where the livestock for the Offering were kept. There they found Jak, Gudrin, and Modi. Modi had already downed several mugs of ale and wasn't pleased to have to leave the festival. Gudrin quieted his complaints with a gesture.

Sometime later they all arrived back at the door of Drake Manor. This time Modi did the knocking. The door was flung open almost immediately. Thilfox ushered them in and up to the council chambers.

Irva Hoot and old man Tad Silure were the most reluctant to accept Gudrin as a genuine authority. They seemed to think that the Rabing Clan had brought her in to upstage them somehow. Tylag quickly grew exasperated.

"Here, here," said Gudrin finally, holding up her hand. Her voice was such that it carried to the limits of the chamber and brought quiet with the power of its volume. "I will tell you a bit of what I know of your Pact. Recall that for the Kindred, only a handful of generations have passed since the Pact was made. Our memories are therefore fresher."

With the same careful ritual that she had performed this morning, Gudrin unwrapped her leather-bound book. The clan leaders craned their necks to see what was written on the page, although Brand doubted that any of them could read the odd, blocky script of the Kindred. "To tell the story of the Pact, it is first necessary to know that it was Myrrdin who forged it."

Thilfox made an impatient gesture. "We know this, spinner. Pray continue."

87

Gudrin gave him a baleful stare and Thilfox recoiled visibly. Gudrin then turned her attention to her book, thumbing through the pages and muttering. Finally, she closed it and let it rest in her lap.

She began to speak and while her lips moved, so did her eyes. She caught each of theirs in turn and locked stares for a moment. Even though he was ready for it, Brand sucked in his breath when he met Gudrin's watery blue eyes. They all fell silent and listened to the Talespinner as if mesmerized.

Chapter Ten
Myrrdin's Tale

When Myrrdin was yet young, he lived with the Faerie. As many have claimed, he indeed has much Faerie blood in his veins. Some say that his mother was a human princess exchanged for a changeling at birth, others that his father was an elf of almost human stature. All this aside, there is no doubt that Myrrdin is a being of rare talents.

In his early life, he was raised by the Faerie themselves. He lived in their wondrous lands, which, as all know, can be found by mortals only at twilight or midnight, and only at the foot of a rainbow or widdershins nine turns 'round an enchanted fairy mound. In this place, Myrrdin grew wise and tricksy, and though he was not ageless, age took a great while to catch him.

It was on his hundredth birthday or so that manhood finally began to take him. He began to know the females among the Faerie then, in their mryiad forms. He was quite popular among them, as his true youth and semi-mortal life were refreshing and innocent to the ancient ones. He knew enough to avoid those that would kill with their embraces. He had grown wise in their tutelage. The lovely green-complected mermaids of the sea and the elusive dryads of the forests were his favorites.

It was on a day like many others that Oberon came to find him. Myrrdin had been chasing a fleet-footed dryad with exquisite brown eyes like burning knotholes through a forest of hazel trees. Oberon appeared to be only a boy of twelve summers or so, but Myrrdin knew him to be much older. He was, in fact, a lord among the Fair Folk and Myrrdin's benefactor.

"What service can I perform for you, my lord?" Myrrdin asked respectfully. With some regret, he gave over chasing the dryad. He stood nonchalantly as always when facing one of the powerful ones. His muscles sang like the taut wires of his fiddle, but he hid his tension by leaning against a tree trunk. His eyes he let fall to the ground, that he would not meet Oberon's sparkling, terrible gaze.

"It is time, I think, to expand your knowledge of men, my adopted son," Oberon said, "I wish you to follow me."

Myrrdin did as he was told and though he was long of limb and fleet of foot, he was soon winded and panting as he chased Oberon through the endless forests. After a time they came to a wall of black rock that had no seam or opening, but Oberon made one with the touch of his hand. They stepped through and Myrrdin, for the first time in his memory, found himself in the world of men and the Kindred. He stood, in fact, in an open field of grasses. It was in a place not far from Stone Island, where an ancient human lord's barrow had formed a fairy mound. The time was twilight, when the sun touches the sea and turns the sky red. This last was a shock to Myrrdin, for in the lands of the Faerie, it is ever brightest day or blackest night, with no in-between.

"How is this possible, my lord?" he asked. "The sun bleeds red like a dying creature."

"There are many things of wonder here," answered Oberon, who led him further toward a nearby farm. There, working in the fields, they found two maidens wearing woolen skirts and hats of woven straw. Such was the softness of their approach that they were very near the maidens before they were noticed. One took fright, dropping her hoe and running home, but her sister stood frozen, having met Oberon's gaze.

Then, in the way of the Faerie, Oberon enticed her to dance with him. Myrrdin too, he begged to dance. Which Myrrdin did, but with some reluctance, as he had never danced before with a mortal. She was one who was not to be feared, but rather was at his mercy. They both danced with the maiden, Oberon playing pipes and Myrrdin playing his fiddle, and in time

Oberon did lead them back to the fairy mound. There, in the last dying gleams of light, they made sweet music and danced upon the mound and around it in a circle with many others of the Faerie, who had come forth to join in. Winged sprites, flaming bright, danced alongside those with hooves and those with the faces of white-skinned children and even the pointed-eared goblins.

When these last came near the girl, Myrrdin saw fit to intercede, placing his dancing form between the twisted flesh of goblin and fair face of the girl. He knew all too well that evil actions delighted these weakest of the Dark Ones and he did not trust them. As he was part mortal and therefore not tireless, he began to weary as the dance went on and on in the darkness with the same wild intensity with which it had begun. Even as he felt the first pangs of fatigue, it was clear that the girl was exhausted. Still, she danced on. She knew nothing but the wild thrall of the dance, and her body twisted and twirled with the frenzied energy of one overcome.

Eventually, she fell to the earth, and then Oberon, who had been touching her lightly, smiled down at her. At last, Myrrdin could take no more. He dropped his fiddle and dared to reach out a long arm, pushing back his lord.

Oberon turned his gaze upon him, and this time Myrrdin met it, although the effort was painful to him. "Are you Faerie, or mortal, manling?" demanded Oberon, enraged at being touched.

"I am both, and neither," said Myrrdin. "To see the Faerie as a mortal is a thing apart from seeing a mortal from the eyes of the Faerie. It is not in me to prey upon weakness and innocence."

"It is I then who have taken in a changeling and treated it as my born son!" cried Oberon. His arms he raised up, holding aloft the Blue Jewel known as Lavatis. He wielded Lavatis, calling to the rainbow for the power to strike down his adopted son.

Such was his greatness that even in the absence of light and rain the rainbow did march from across the seas and lands to do his bidding.

Myrrdin took these moments to grab up the fallen maiden and run with her toward the farmhouse. Before he reached the door, a savage rainstorm brewed up and lightning chased the rains and came crashing to the earth. At the door the farmer who was the girl's father came to Myrrdin's hammering. But instead of joy, he was met only with despair, for the girl was already dead. Her heart had exploded within her chest like that of a horse ridden to death by a drunken lord.

Myrrdin looked down at the maiden's dark wet ropes of hair and bloodless white limbs without comprehension. He knew less of death than the maiden had known of the Faerie. He and the farmer regarded one another.

Myrrdin, soaked and cradling a dead girl, learned much of what it was to be mortal that night. He gave over the farmer's daughter with what grace he could, and then ran into the storm and into a new world that he little understood.

His childhood and upbringing at the hands of the Faerie were at an abrupt end. Never again would he call Oberon his sire, and never again would any of the Faerie call him kin.

* * *

At this point, Thilfox loudly cleared his throat. Gudrin swept her gaze over to him, but Thilfox kept his eyes focused on his pipe as he said, "Your tale adds detail and color to what legends we've heard whispered before, but now I would like to move on, as time is pressing—"

"It's not time that will press you all this eve!" roared back Gudrin, face blazing. She held out her ancient book and clapped her hand upon it. "Ever are the biggest fools among us the most impatient to get on with things!"

"A fool, am I?" huffed Thilfox, rising to his feet. "I'll not be—"

Gudrin threw up her arms, imploring both him and the heavens. "I spoke tactlessly. Please, seat yourself and allow me to finish my tale. I promise you will not regret it."

With ill grace, Thilfox flopped back into his chair. Scowling at the spinner, he made a broad gesture, indicating that she should continue.

"Myrrdin," began Gudrin anew, "after he had left the lands of the Faerie, didn't immediately join the River Folk, although he resembled them more than any of the other races of Cymru. He wandered for many years instead, and came to join the Kindred, befriending many of our lords who dwelt beneath the mountains and upon them. There are many tales to be told of these times—but not this eve.

"Those years were an unfortunate time for humans, as their numbers had been greatly reduced by wars among themselves and with the Faerie—and even, though I am loath to say it, with the Kindred."

Here, Modi gave a low growl in the back of his throat. All eyes swung to him, and inevitably to his axe. Brand knew that it was from these times that the Kindred had come to be known to the River Folk as the Battleaxe Folk.

Gudrin ignored the interruption and continued with her tale.

* * *

The great kings of the past fell, one by one, and in time there were no more true kingdoms of humanity. Feeling beholden to humans, Myrrdin took it upon himself to walk among them and learn what could be done. He learned that they were both delightful and wicked, innocent and cunning, silly and wise. He came to love humans for their short lives and varied temperaments. Living among the elder races he had found less spice to life. But with humans, each few years brought another fresh generation, eager to learn of the world, to conquer it and to be conquered *by* it.

But even though the humans had ended their conflict with Kindred, the Faerie continued to plague them. The same sort of idle wickedness that Myrrdin had first witnessed with Oberon still occurred, and worse things had begun as well.

It was rumored that one of the Dark Ones had gained a Jewel. Herla had found one of the Jewels of power, although none knew the color and name of the Jewel. Clearly, it was known that he wielded it with evil intent. Leading the Wild Hunt upon a mad course, he ravaged the remaining human lands with impunity. They hunted humans like animals, taking their skins and skulls as trophies and making adornments from them.

It was in this situation that Myrrdin rediscovered the humans of Cymru. It took him but a short time to realize that if no one acted, there would possibly be no humans left alive in this part of the world. He took it upon himself to mount a campaign against the Enemy. Marshaling a small army of men and Kindred, he marched through the Low Marshes, over the Border Downs and into the Black Mountains, where the Wild Hunt was often seen.

But ever Herla and his coursers evaded him. They would march after their quarry through forests and over mountains and into deep ravines, only to see them rise up into the sky and vanish. For years they chased the Wild Hunt, until the human and Kindred army—hungry and desperate, riddled with foul curses from the Faerie—was set upon and decimated in the quiet depths of the Deepwood.

Myrrdin and a handful of others escaped. After many trials, they came to the shores of the Berrywine—which was then known as the Great Malvam—and crossed the flood to stagger onto the rocky beaches of Stone Island.

A widow of one of Myrrdin's soldiers took him in and nursed him back to health. When he had his strength back and was ready to leave, he took note of the babe that lay in its cradle near the warm fire.

"Is this your child, Tabitha?" he asked the widow.

"Why yes," she told him. "He is last of my sons yet to live. He is always hungry and never satisfied. He has never left the cradle all these years, never yet spoken a word or taken a step. Hope is all I have for him."

Myrrdin eyed the fat infant in its cradle, and it did regard him with a flat stare of dislike. "No normal child stays to its crib for more than a decade," he said, tugging at his beard, which had grown overlong in the mountains and the forests. Despite the widow's worried protests, he gathered a fresh egg

94

and blew out the contents, filling the shell with malt and hops. It was the first step of exorcism, of course, and watching him do it, the widow's tears flowed freely. Once the egg was ready, he began to brew over the fire.

At this a laugh bubbled up from the cradle. "I am old, old, as old as the night and the moon," said the changeling, "but never has anyone brewed me a draught of beer in an egg before!" Then it gave a terrible scream, for Myrrdin had taken after it with his walking stick. Around and around the cottage it ran, as fleet-footed as any spring hare, that which had never left its cradle for so many long years!

Myrrdin chased it out into the yard, and finally down into the river itself. There it vanished, and Myrrdin cast about, hoping that the widow's son would appear, as is sometimes the case with changelings when they are discovered.

But there was only the lapping water and the sound of the wind in the pines. The widow's true son never returned. She sat upon the rock where the changeling had vanished and cried aloud with grief. Feeling for her, Myrrdin vowed that the Dark Ones among the Faerie would not continue with their wicked amusements.

For long months, as spring shifted into summer, he wandered the land, deep in thought. One night, he found a farmhouse where a woman had set out milk for a cat. He thought to hear the cat, growling and spitting in the yard. He watched from the road and saw one of the Wee Folk, all dressed in waistcoat and top hat, as was their way, vying with the cat for its milk.

A dark rage filled Myrrdin at even so slight an offense, and he moved to charge and drive off the intruder. Only at the last moment did he check himself, deciding to watch the Wee one instead. After a goodly bit of stick waving and hopping about, the tiny Faerie drove off the cat and ate his fill of the sweet milk. When finally he had scampered away, wiping his tiny mouth and beard, Myrrdin watched the spot where he had vanished for a long time.

The next night, he told the farmer to turn out the lights again and had them set out two bowls of milk. The Wee one returned, as he had hoped it would. On the third night two of them appeared, one in crimson and one in green. They fought over the milk for a time, until finally deciding to share it. After that, Myrrdin set out more goods. More Wee ones appeared, and each night he set out even more food. He asked the whole village to help, and they did so, because they were indebted to him for his help in the past. Fresh bread, melons, sweet yellow corn, roast fowl and salted venison heaped upon platters in the moonlight.

On the tenth night, he moved the offering out into the yard, instead of upon the porch. On the twentieth, he placed it in the forest outside, each night moving it further away, into the woods and toward the clearing where the nearest faerie mound was to be found.

As the nights went on, autumn grew stronger, the leaves fell and the air held a hint of the snows to come. Each night he made the offering larger, using his powers and the efforts of the last of his faithful soldiers to aid him. Many of the Battleaxe Folk were among his soldiers. Each night the offering attracted more of the Faerie, including ones of greater power and wisdom. Soon the air shone with the fiery light of sprites and the pale glow of the elves.

On the twenty-ninth night, he placed the offering upon the faerie mound itself, and that night Oberon himself came. From concealment Myrrdin and his soldiers watched the phantom feast. Each of the men and the Kindred, save Myrrdin who was immune, had plugged their ears with beeswax so that they couldn't hear the luring pipes of the Faerie and be enticed to join the dancing ring. Still, it took great efforts of will for them all to keep from coming out into the glade, such was the allure and beauty of the Faerie, even without their sweet music. Heavy smells of spices and wines filled their heads. Shimmering images of fantastic beauty assaulted their eyes. To their great credit, none of them broke.

On the thirtieth night, the feast was repeated. Oberon came again, and all his retinue were on hand. But the food was not. Instead, it was placed at the edge of the forest where Myrrdin and his company waited. When the Faerie approached, the mortals stepped forward and placed themselves before the food.

"What trick is this?" laughed Oberon, bounding forward and halting before Myrrdin with his hands on his hips. He cocked his head and recognized Myrrdin in an instant. "Why do you trouble me again, my changeling?"

"We have fed your people for many nights now," said Myrrdin, his voice carrying not just to Oberon, but to the others, who were eyeing the food with hunger. "We have been free with our gifts, but now we ask a boon."

Oberon shouted with laughter and danced away, playing his pipes. "Bring the food to the mound that we all may feast!" he said, speaking to Myrrdin's soldiers. None moved, as they could not hear him nor his magical music. Oberon soon stopped playing and appeared annoyed. He then ushered forth the dryads and the nymphs, hoping to lure them with the bright, unearthly beauties. Myrrdin's company were all veterans of such things, but still they were hard put. They averted their eyes or squeezed them shut. Some chewed at their tongues or stabbed their own hands with their daggers until they bled freely upon the grass of the glade. They moaned aloud and fell to their knees, but none stepped forward.

Again Oberon displayed annoyance. "You hold rein over your mortals well, changeling. It is to your credit. However, it's not our custom to pay for our needs," he told Myrrdin. "We will take that which we require."

Oberon ordered forward a wave of goblins and elves with their tiny magic bows. Myrrdin and his company fell back to the woods, without fighting.

With a cry of delight, Oberon was the first to up-end a cask of wine and drink from it. In an instant, he cast the cask aside and screamed in rage. "Vinegar!" he cried. All around him, there were similar cries of dismay among the elves and the other Wee Folk as they bit into rotten fruit and tasted of spoiled milk and maggot-filled meats.

Into this scene, Myrrdin stepped forward once again.

"I should have hunted you down and struck you dead the first time you ran from me!" raged Oberon. He held aloft Lavatis and the Jewel released a brilliant blue radiance which none could look into. "I will summon the rainbow and destroy you all!"

"Then you will have no more feasts, my lord," pointed out Myrrdin.

"Then so be it!" cried Oberon.

Myrrdin sighed, he had hoped it would not come to this. "Then I have no choice but to check you with Vaul," he said, producing the Green Jewel of power and holding it aloft. It exuded its own bath of green light, which conflicted with Lavatis and together the Jewels cast an eldritch brilliance the blue-green color of the sea. Myrrdin's company and Oberon's retinue both retreated in dismay, shielding their faces from the awful twin glares of raw power.

For once, Oberon was truly at a loss. "How?" he demanded.

Myrrdin shrugged. "In the Deepwood, I was driven into the underworld by Herla. Many of my comrades perished, but we did rediscover this lost power," he said bravely. Inside he was nowhere near so calm, as he had only begun to understand the workings of the Jewel. It was all he could do to command Vaul to cast a brilliant glow. He had hoped to keep the Jewel secret from those of power for some years so that he might master it fully.

Oberon had lost his rage, and now had turned thoughtful. The rainbow he had summoned now marched up behind him to stand upon great shimmering legs. It was a terrible sight for mortal eyes, and some perished quietly in the forest that night from sheer fright. "I am certain that I have a better mastery of Lavatis than you do of Vaul. Perhaps it is best that I destroy you now and so become master of two colors.'"

Myrrdin shrugged again. "It is all one to me. Many times tonight I have surprised you. One more time will be enough, should you require it. But...."

"Of what do you think to speak?"

"It does seem to me a big risk to take over a simple matter of food. We will provide for you and yours, but we ask a boon."

"Speak!" commanded Oberon. "What do you ask?"

"Each year, at the end of harvest, we will give you one part in seven of our goods, which is enough to feed you all. We will make this Offering on the night of the Harvest Moon, which is tomorrow night. In return, you will swear not to allow your people to harm us, lure us from our homes, place changelings in our cradles, or execute curses against us. In essence, your people will not be allowed to walk these lands, and they shall be recognized as the lands of humanity."

There were a few twitterings and catcalls among the Faerie at this. Oberon silenced them with a wave of the hand. "What else?"

"I further propose a Pact between us, against the Enemy and his Dark Ones, which is to say, those among your kind that have elected to become his minions. You must keep them from harming us, and we will do what we can to keep them from harming you."

At this point, many of the Faerie voiced their contempt of the humans and the Kindred. They called out shrill insults toward the humans, and some tried to slip away into the trees and circle around behind the mortals. Oberon deliberated for but a moment.

"I accept," he said, as Myrrdin had gambled he would, for Oberon himself was almost as afraid of Herla as was Myrrdin. The added power of Vaul would do much to hold his nemesis at bay. The Faerie were shocked, and quieted suddenly. Bright eyes suddenly slitted and became dark as many of them vanished into the trees to show their disapproval.

Despite their misgivings, the Fair Folk honored Oberon's word, ceasing their cruel tricks. The rainbow strode away toward a distant storm cloud without releasing its wrath. On the thirty-first night, a great Offering was gathered. From that year to this, for many centuries, when the moon waxes gibbous and heavy with orange light and hangs low and full in the sky, the Offering is made. In this way has the Pact and the peace been maintained.

Chapter Eleven
The Shining Lady

There had been a gasp or two when Gudrin had mentioned Stone Island, the very land on which they stood, but everyone had managed to keep from interrupting her story until she was finished.

"The town common! You were talking about our faerie mound!" broke in Tylag, his eyes gleaming.

Gudrin didn't take offense this time, as she could tell that her audience was well in hand. She merely glanced up and nodded, a smile playing on her lips. She took a long draught of beer from a mug that was offered her and sat back to rest. With the now familiar ritual, she closed her book, wrapped it, and tucked it under her arm.

After thinking about Gudrin's story, there was little debate left in the council members. It was speedily decided that the Talespinner should stand in for Myrrdin. As twilight was only a few hours away, they adjourned and everyone headed for the town common.

The Harvest Moon Festival was in full swing now, with many folk from Riverton, Hamlet, North End, Swampton, and even distant Frogmorton, feasting and reveling. There were contests of strength and speed, foot races and tree felling. The berrywine casks flowed freely and many of the people wore masks with floating ribbons and gauze in the guise of the Faerie. Usually stolid and unwavering in their conduct, men and women danced with partners that they would not recall in the morning. Children formed their own faerie rings around tall poles, winding ribbons of every hue into shimmering rainbows.

As twilight fell, bonfires were lit upon the common. Yellow firelight illuminated the dome tents and cast wild shadows of the dancing revelers upon them. Brand watched the shadowy forms on the tent walls and once thought to see the capering form of a true goblin. He turned to examine the dancers, but all were human.

Above everything, the moon waxed full and washed the common with its dusky orange light. As it was every year, something of the Wilds slipped through into the River Haven. Things that were held at bay during the rest of the year awakened under the Harvest Moon. The term of the old Pact had ended and the new Pact had yet to be renewed, and in that brief span of time, the people were lost to the effects of the Fair Folk and the full moon.

Brand looked upon the festival differently this year, finding a kind of terror in it to think of a world where every night was lost such as this one was. What would the world be like without the Pact? Everything good and solid in his life now seemed to him as a treasure suspended above flame by a tiny fragile thread. Should the thread ever break, all he had ever known would be lost.

Gudrin climbed the hill at the end of the common to the grove of trees that hid the faerie mound. Only Modi accompanied her, against the wishes and warnings of the clan leaders. Modi had promised not to enter the glade, but only to stand in the trees and observe. The council warned him that only the Talespinner should be present, and that any other entering the clearing did so in peril of his life and soul. Modi only grunted in acknowledgment before stumping after Gudrin, who had already begun the trek. Gudrin walked as one burdened, and appeared to everyone to be older than she had at any other time. She kept her wide-brimmed hat pulled low over her brow, bore her odd rucksack over her hunched shoulders, and kept her book clamped beneath her arm.

"It's time, boys," hissed Telyn in their ears. Brand and Corbin turned to find her face poked between the two of them. "Here are your wards," she said, handing each a circle of river stone with a hole worn in the center and a thong of leather run through it. They took them and hung them about their necks. "I found them in stream beds, worn through naturally. Drilled holes wouldn't work."

"Where's yours?" asked Brand.

"This lucky ash leaf is even more potent, but more fragile," Telyn said as she fluttered her charm at him. The lucky ash leaf bore two terminal leaflets instead of one. She met his eyes and he frowned at her, reaching to take her arm. This was all the warning she needed. With a laugh, she evaded him and ran away into the darkness behind one of the domed tents.

"By the River," swore Brand, "she'll not escape us so easily this time!" He and Corbin ran after the fleet-footed girl, cloaks flying and heavy boots crunching the slushy earth.

"Hey!" shouted Jak behind them. "Where are you off to?"

Brand and Corbin made no attempt at replying, knowing that they would need all their attention to keep Telyn in sight. She led them on a merry chase, darting between vendors' carts and under tables spread with fine foods. Corbin, rather than following her every step, chose to drop back a bit and cut the corners of her winding, twisting path. He even managed to snatch up a leg of roast fowl on the way past a table that boasted an excellent feast. Brand, lost to the chase, ran on his long legs with great loping strides.

There were many cries of distress at their passing. "Hey you louts!"

"Stop running!"

"The Rabing boys are after that Fob girl! I wonder what she's stolen now!"

"You've crushed my foot!"

"Off with you then!"

Soon, a pattern emerged from Telyn's mad course: each twist, every turn, took them closer to the wooded area at the base of the hill that backed the common. Brand, worried that she would vanish in the murk below the trees, put on an extra burst of speed. Corbin, huffing and blowing, groaned and then followed suit.

Telyn glanced back at them, and for a moment Brand was gratified to see her teasing face take on a cast of concern. They were clearly gaining on her. She stopped laughing and gave herself to running directly toward the woods.

She did actually reach the trees before Brand caught up. She danced behind a tree and Brand fell against the other side, eyeing her around the trunk, and breathing hard.

"Brand Rabing, don't you touch me," she gasped between gulps of air.

"Give over this folly, Telyn! I'm not about to have you taken to serve some ungrateful elfkin as a foot maid!" said Brand, reaching for her. She shrieked and ran laughing into the forest. Knowing he was about to lose her, Brand threw himself at her, and managed to catch hold of her foot. They both fell in a tangled heap, leaves flying.

They sat up and regarded each other for a second. Brand thought she was the most lovely thing in the world, seen only in the light of the bloated Harvest Moon, with twigs and leaves in her hair and streaks of dirt on her face. He bent forward to kiss her.

"Hullo there!" shouted Corbin, huffing into the trees and cupping his hands to call to them. He tossed aside a clean bone from the fowl he had devoured on the way. Brand and Telyn straightened suddenly, feeling foolish. Brand helped her to her feet. He kept one hand on her arm, even after she was standing.

"Oh, there you are," said Corbin, putting his hands on his knees to relax and breathe more freely. "Oh, I can't believe you caught her, Brand. I would sooner chase one of the Wee Folk into the High Marshes!"

"Yes, she will see nothing of the Faerie tonight," said Brand.

"Oh, but how wrong you are," breathed Telyn. The boys turned to her with questioning looks, but she was looking away, into the forest. They followed her gaze.

There before them, deep in the forest, moved a stealthy shape. In the darkness, they would not have been able to see it, but it gave off a pale blue-white radiance. It went from tree to tree in a crouch, ignoring them and heading for the top of the hill. Brand estimated the creature to be perhaps half his height. An elfkin? A manling or a goblin? He couldn't tell.

Reflexively, his hand went to the ward hung around his neck. Relief flooded through him to find that it was still there.

"One of the Fair Folk," whispered Telyn. Her voice was that of one seeing the divine. While they watched in stunned silence, the creature turned to look at them. Its eyes slitted and its ears laid down as would a cat's, then it opened its mouth to reveal thin delicate fangs that glistened with unearthly light. It turned from them and moved deeper into the forest.

"A goblin," whispered Brand, half to himself. "I had never thought such a creature would be so entrancing." He turned to look down at Telyn, but she was no longer at his side. He looked around wildly, then noted that the disappearing goblin had a fluttering shadow following it that did not glimmer in the darkness.

"Damn her silent feet! We must go after her, Corbin," Brand said, beginning to run.

"I rue the day I became your cousin," lamented Corbin, trotting after him.

They caught up with Telyn at the edge of the clearing in which the faerie mound stood. The goblin was nowhere in sight, but what Brand saw in the clearing quickly made him forget everything.

A hundred of the Faerie or more thronged the clearing. Winged figures fluttered about in a circle, dancing about the ancient barrow as though walking on air. Many more earth-bound shapes cavorted and leaped in the grass. There were tall ones, almost as big as a man, and tiny ones, no larger than sparrows. All of them, even those most alien of aspect, held an unearthly beauty that took the breath from the mortals. All were sleek of limb and easy of movement, their impossibly smooth muscles rippling beneath their pale white skins. From each of them, a pale blue-white nimbus glowed. From the entire assemblage a powerful combined radiance shone, so that the clearing was lit up as if by the light of a dozen full moons. Brand knew that they reflected the moonlight, which was the source of the radiance. On nights such as this one, when the moon was round and full, the Fair Folk became the Shining Folk.

Oh, and the music, the sweet music! It filled Brand's head with glories untold! The heady scents of honey and hot spices and wild flowers assaulted him as well, overwhelming his senses. Caught and paralyzed like a rodent beneath the stooping falcon, he could do nothing but stare.

The Faerie floated and danced, feasting upon the Offering, which covered the mound and much of the clearing. One of them took notice of the River Folk and flittered close. Brand stared at the tiny form, a perfectly-shaped nude female with hair of gossamer and wings of fragile crystalline light. So exquisite was her beauty that he took a step forward, all but entering the clearing. She smiled at him, and came closer. She could not have been more than a foot in height, but he could little resist her beauty all the same. He felt a restraint, and looked down to see that Telyn had his arm and was trying to keep him from walking forward.

"Hold your ward close!" she hissed to him. He did as she told him slowly, like one moving in a dream. The tiny female Faerie halted her advance and backed away. She flittered back to join the others, giving him a final regretful shake of her tiny head.

Now that he had his ward in his hand, Brand found that he could think somewhat more clearly. A bare sliver of concern impinged upon his mind as part of him realized how close he was to his doom. He blinked in confusion.

A booming voice rolled across the clearing and the crass rude tones of it ripped a hole in Brand's heart. The entrancing power of the Faerie left him, and he felt a terrible wrong had been done. That a sad, sad mistake had been made. He missed the power of their spell with all his being.

The voice belonged to Gudrin, who now stumped into the open. She spoke to the Fair Folk as though they were worthy of no special reverence, as though they weren't exalted beyond all mortal pretenses. Brand felt she was a crude thing, insulting, an animal with the presumption to speak to its betters. It took some moments before he was able to comprehend the words.

Reading from her book, Gudrin spoke at length in a ritualistic fashion, presenting the Offering to the assembled Faerie. The Fair Folk all but ignored her, seemingly intent on little other than devouring all they could of the feast. When the Talespinner asked who among them would accept the Offering on their part and renew the Pact, there came from the Faerie only scattered tittering laughter.

Gudrin closed the book with a thump audible across the clearing. She took a step forward, brushing aside a Wee one that had gotten too near her heavy boots. She raised her arms on high and held her book aloft. "I demand that your lord come forth to meet me!" she cried. "I speak on the behalf of all the River Folk!"

Suddenly, a figure of astounding beauty appeared before her, as if stepping through a door in the empty air. She was tall and lithe, dressed all in white, with long hair of spun gold and eyes of silver. Her unearthly beauty struck through to Brand and Corbin, so that both of them gasped and went weak at the knees. No human woman could ever possess such beauty, for she was perfect. Brand felt a rush of blood run through him. He was suddenly full of heat and passion as he had never felt before. His mind burned. Corbin took a half step forward, and then fell to his knees groaning and holding his ward to his eyes.

"The Shining Lady!" gasped Telyn in terror. "Brand, Corbin, avert your eyes! She is one of the shades in league with the Enemy!"

The boys tried to turn their faces, but only Corbin succeeded, keeping his ward to his face in trembling hands. Brand couldn't tear his eyes away from the most beautiful female creature that had ever lived.

Even Gudrin was affected. She staggered forward, and then halted, swaying slightly. Still, her hands were outstretched above her. The golden clasp of her book glinted in the moonlight.

"Look upon mine beauty," the Lady said to Gudrin, "Accursed, ugly creature, constructed of oil and filth, is it not thy heart's desire to share in my perfection?" The glimmering figure drifted down the mound ever so slowly.

"Lady," said Gudrin, her words coming with difficulty. "Lady, why are you here? Why do you torment us?"

"Brand, something is wrong!" Telyn hissed in his ear. "Brand, we must get away from here!"

106

"A kiss, only one kiss," mumbled Brand.

She shook him, and Brand was distantly aware of her, but his mind was focused upon the Shining Lady. He took a full step forward and now stood at the edge of the clearing. Sweat poured from him, his head had filled with sweet music and the powerful smells of lilac and mint. In desperation, Telyn tugged at him, but against his tense muscles, she could do nothing. Corbin remained on his knees, clutching his ward and shivering.

The Shining Lady took notice of Brand then, and did turn upon him. She drifted closer, swaying a bit. Her hands wove themselves together in mock embraces, her lips moved softly. Brand knew what she wanted. It was only a kiss she wanted, just one single kiss. Her radiant skin shone through her white gown, revealing all but her feet, which were said to be the talons of a bird of prey.

He took another halting step toward her.

Chapter Twelve
Goblins

Telyn moved between Brand and the Lady and talked insistently to him, but he didn't hear her words. He saw only the Lady.

Telyn blocked his vision with her hands and body. For a spare second, he managed to glance down into her face. Telyn was beautiful to him as well, an earthly beauty.

"Telyn," he said.

Then, somehow the spell had broken. He stumbled backward and turned his eyes from the Shining Lady.

Gudrin swayed no longer. Gathering herself, she held her book before her as the River Folk held their wards. "I banish you! Offer us nothing! Your embrace will result in no beauty for me, but only ugly death. To touch you is to know death, agony and ecstasy, triumph and terrible defeat. By the Teret, the book of the Kindred, I banish you!"

Brand glanced back, and was sorry that he did. The Shining Lady paused and a sadness came over her that was hard for him to bear. With a final, regretful, heart-wrenching tilt of her head, she glided back and away. Her golden hair floated about her lovely face, but there was no breeze. She paused, and then looked over to Brand. She smiled then and raised her hand in a gesture of farewell. Brand might have run to her, but she winked out, sliding away into nothingness.

Gudrin dropped her arms. Her head lolled against her chest and her shoulders slouched forward as if she had undergone a great exertion.

But her trials were not at an end, as another shadowy figure on horseback walked his dark steed forward. The elfkin and the Wee ones fled from him, crying out their fear in their small voices. His horse had lavender eyes and a long mane and tail of white which shone against its sleek coat of black. It snorted and tossed its head, as if wanting to be away and galloping. "It is you who are banished, talespinner," said the shadow man, his voice at once melodic and sinister.

"The shadow man," said Brand vaguely, coming partly to his senses. He was still captivated by the Shining Lady. Corbin regained his feet, but leaned on a tree trunk for support.

"We must leave!" insisted Telyn, trying to rouse them. "Things are not as they should be!"

"Ah, Voynod the Bard," said Gudrin, nodding to the shadow man in recognition. "I have been tracking your whereabouts of late. You and your master have done much to circumvent the Pact. Oberon will no doubt chastise you for your adventurousness."

Voynod chuckled, a sound like the music made by water in a rocky stream. "The Pact is broken. It will not be renewed. Go back to your mountain burrow, talespinner. These muck-dwellers are not your people. You need not die for them."

With those words, Voynod turned his horse's head and retreated, and the forest swallowed him whole. The goblins, sprites, elfkin, and Wee ones that remained continued to eat and drink, feasting as would stray dogs that have starved for many days in the wild. The sounds of their gulpings and slurpings filled the clearing. Brand saw them with a new clarity now. He saw more and more goblins it seemed, and in fact, among them were others that did not shine. They were like goblins, but larger, more man-like. These hairy, fanged creatures were bestial in their manner, and openly took the remains of the ravaged Offering from the smaller Faerie. One of the Wee ones, holding fast to an apple it had claimed, was scooped up and tossed across the clearing. It caught itself and ran with great hops into the forest, clutching the apple with its coattails fluttering behind.

Gudrin cried aloud several times for Oberon to come forth—for *any* lord of the Faerie to accept her Offering and renew the Pact. None answered her save the snickers and catcalls of those that were gorging themselves upon the goods that the River Folk had worked so long and hard to gather.

The three River Folk, having regained enough of their composure to retreat from the clearing, set out for the common. Their mood was one of deep shock and dismay. The idea that the Pact was broken was unthinkable.

"What will happen to us all?" asked Corbin aloud. "Will we all find changelings in our cradles? Will the Shining Lady croon promises of lust and beauty outside our windows at night and drink our lives?"

"Did we have anything to do with this?" asked Brand, voicing his greatest fear.

"No," said Telyn firmly. "The signs have been evident for months. The Faerie are no longer keeping the Pact with any devotion, that is clear to see. Many things have crossed the borders, and we have been stalked by such as Voynod himself across the breadth of the Haven."

"Could they perhaps have waylaid Myrrdin? Perhaps this is all part of a plot that has been long building," said Brand.

"And what were those things that ate with the Fair Folk? Were they beasts or men?" asked Corbin.

"At least I can answer that," said Telyn. "I believe they were rhinogs."

The boys looked at her in horror. "Half-breeds?" said Corbin, aghast. "The offspring of goblins and human women? Such are strictly against the Pact."

Telyn could only nod. Brand numbly realized that if rhinogs were being bred, that could only mean that war was at hand. The brutes were good for nothing else.

Corbin pointed off at a glimmering shape half as tall as a man that stole forth to leer at them before disappearing again into the trees. "Isn't that fellow the goblin we followed up here?" The others agreed, and they all walked with greater care. The shadowy forest seemed to be hiding something.

"Hello?" came a call from down the hill. Brand thought it was Jak's voice.

"Hello?" Brand answered back.

"Hello, hello, hello?" mocked strange voices from all around. The three of them halted in sudden apprehension. The dark woods seemed to close around them, hemming them in. The trees were no longer friendly. Peering into the gloom, they picked out half-seen shapes that flittered and glowed. Somewhere to their left, the metallic edge of a weapon gleamed.

"Brand, Corbin?" came Jak's voice again, more distantly this time, from somewhere downhill in the blackness.

"Brand, Corbin? Corbin, Brand? Hello?" mocked strange voices. The trio halted again and wheeled, trying to locate those that stalked them. The boys wished that they had not left their woodaxes at Drake Manor. Telyn's long thin knife appeared in her hand.

"The goblins hunt us," hissed Telyn.

"Hunt us."

"I think Jak is downhill somewhere," Brand whispered to the others.

"Hunt—"

"Jak—downhill."

"Hunt us—"

Stealthy shapes moved closer. They could feel them now, a closing ring. Here a bush rustled, there a fallen leaf cracked. Instinctively, they put their backs together and circled, hands and eyes wide. Brand and Corbin groped at the ground for a rock, a branch—anything.

Heavier footsteps crashed through the brush toward them. A single thought ran through Brand's mind, turning it to ice: *Rhinog.*

He felt a rock and heaved it up in both hands, ready to smash down, ready to kill.

"Brand?"

"Jak!" shouted Brand, coming forward in relief. "Look out, they're all around us!"

The goblins attacked. Small bows hummed. Glimmering shapes charged forward, leering. Jak cried out and fell, then stumbled back to his feet clutching at his leg.

"Run for it!" roared Brand. He rushed their tormentors, heaving his rock at them. Corbin and Telyn charged with him, yelling. On the way he lifted up his limping brother and they all ran blindly into the darkness. Behind them feet pattered on dry leaves as the goblins gave chase.

In the darkness, Brand lost Corbin and Telyn, who ran on ahead. It was not their fault, he realized. In the darkness they had not understood that Jak was injured. Blindly he and his brother stumbled forward, Jak limping, Brand holding his arm across his shoulders and half dragging him. After a time they came to a place where the land seemed to bottom out. There was no clear way to go that was downhill. Brand realized that they were lost and he all but despaired. He listened for a moment, but heard nothing of Telyn or Corbin or the goblins. He could hear only their labored breathing and the night sounds of the forest. Crickets chirped and a chill wind rattled the finger-like winter branches.

"Come on, Jak. We've got to get back to the common," he whispered. Jak made no reply. Brand helped him up and started forward. Jak was limp now, he was only dragging him. He stopped, realizing that his brother must have passed out. With hands fumbling in the darkness, he felt his brother's body, searching for wounds. He found one arrow in his leg, another in his breast. The wounds were sticky with blood he couldn't see. Should he pull out the arrows? No, he thought, not when he could not see to staunch the blood.

He took a moment to gather his thoughts. Blind panic would probably lead to both their deaths, he told himself. He had to think. Where were the goblins? In which direction lay the common?

Of the goblins there was no sign. He hoped that this did not mean that they had gone after Corbin and Telyn instead of him. He reasoned that if he just kept on in any direction, within a mile or so he should come out of the trees. He was on the corner of an island, after all, much of which was inhabited. This section was perhaps the most wild, due to a natural tendency of folk not to live too close to the faerie mound, which was the only place that the Fair Folk could appear on Stone Island that he knew of. The forest was not endless though, and he had to come out somewhere along the line.

So Brand picked a direction, heaved up his brother, feeling very glad that he had outgrown him, and set out. The going was hard. There were thickets of berry bush to be crashed through or circumvented. Everywhere the trees blotted out all but a rare gleam of moonlight. Soon his legs were wooden and his arms as heavy as lead. Jak grew heavier and wheezing coughing fits wracked his body. Brand walked on as if in a dream, wondering if Jak would be dead in his arms when he won through the forest, as the farm girl had been in Myrrdin's arms so long ago.

He wept for a time in fear for his brother's life and for all the Haven, but kept going all the while. Blinking and stumbling as if in a waking dream, he became aware that he was not alone. Someone was pacing him, off to one side. He pressed forward, not knowing what else to do. He cast about as he went, but could find no suitable weapon. He bitterly recalled Modi's words when he had sought to relieve himself of his woodaxe. *Keep it with you,* the warrior had said. Better words had never been spoken.

The thing pacing him was stealthy. Whoever or *whatever* it was, it made almost no sound. Fortunately, it seemed content to simply walk through the forest, shadowing him, no more than a stone's throw away. Every now and then he caught sight of a glimmer or heard a tiny sound from this shadow. Brand worried and fretted, but tried not to show it. Was it a goblin captain? Was it Voynod, toying with him? Or worse yet, the Enemy himself?

Finally, he could stand it no longer. "Speak, shadow!" he commanded angrily.

"Hush! Sing not aloud for the Dark Ones. They hunt thee still," came the reply. It was a soft, odd sound. Words such as the winds might speak, if they had a voice.

"Are you friend or foe?" whispered Brand, refusing to be commanded to silence by another of the haughty Faerie.

"I am thy friend, and thy foe, both and none."

113

Brand was in no mood for riddles. "Then you must serve my enemies. Begone!"

"I serve none but myself," came the reply.

"Then why trouble me?"

"We hath both lost something precious. Thou hast lost thy way through the woods, and I have lost something of perhaps even greater value. We hath this in common, among many other things. My future is intertwined with thee. Thou art a potential ally and foeman, both together."

They walked on a while, Brand pausing every so often to see if Jak still lived. Each time he heard his brother take another gasping breath, he felt both relief and pain. He wondered if the forest would ever end. He estimated he had been slogging through the trees for an hour or more. The only possibility was that he had taken the longest possible route, missing the cliffs and all roads, walking across the wild back end of the Drake estate. Another idea struck him: could he be walking in circles? Perhaps that was this creature's foul game.

"I will be stalked by you no further," he said, halting. "Either come forth and try to kill me if you dare, or leave me to my suffering."

The other stopped for a minute as well and both fell silent. Brand had begun to wonder if his shadow had fled, when it spoke again. "I have decided. I will neither kill you nor leave you to die. I will point the way."

Suddenly, the figure revealed itself to Brand, and he took an involuntary step backward. The Faerie appeared as a boy of perhaps twelve, but with pointed ears and eyes that held wisdom and great age in them. He was as white-skinned as boiled milk. Despite the bitter cold, he wore only a pair of soft leather pants. Even his feet were bare.

"Look there!" said Oberon, for Brand knew in his heart that it must be the Faerie lord. He pointed over Brand's shoulder and into the depths of the trees.

Brand turned, and thought to see a tiny glimmering light, like that of a single candle in the distance. He felt relief flood over him. The candle meant home and hearth, a house and other human beings. Perhaps Jak would live through the night.

He looked back, but his shadow had fled. With only a moment's pause, Brand stumbled forward, toward the light. He knew he could be walking to his death, lured into a trap by trickery, but he had run out of options. The forest could have gone on for miles, and he doubted he could bear his brother through the whole of the frozen night, even should Jak live so long.

Chapter Thirteen
Elf-Shot

Half dreaming, Brand made his way toward the beacon. Although at first it seemed that it must be very near, he trudged on and on without end. Only very slowly did he approach it, as if it were at the end of a long, long tunnel through the night and trees. Jak grew heavier with each step. Now he no longer checked to see if his brother lived, for even if he had died, he would not drop the body, but the knowledge would dispirit him. As it was, only dogged determination saw him through the hours, putting one foot before the other, then repeating the process. Nothing else mattered to him. His head soon dipped to his chest, coming up only after every score of slow steps to see if the light yet burned ahead. Each time it was still there and it would seem a trifle brighter, giving him heart. After he had traveled this way for what seemed the entire night, he came into a stretch of bog. The muck slipped and slished beneath his tired feet, and it was all he could do to struggle onward. He groaned aloud, but was barely aware of it. The light did indeed seem brighter now, and its promise kept him going.

The moon waned and began to set, making the darkness of the forest total. Up ahead in the dimness, he thought he heard something coming. He halted, swaying, and listened. The clopping sound of a horse came to him. He let Jak sag down to the wet ground. Could it be help? More likely, he thought bitterly, it was some other of the Dark Ones, perhaps Herla himself, leading his coursers forward to finish the hunt. If it was the Wild Hunt, he sorrowed that he would give them little sport, for he was utterly spent.

The horse came closer and a lantern shone in the night. Brand now wondered if it was the lantern of Old Hob, the eldest and worst of the goblin lords. Was this the light that he had spent the night trying to reach?

The horseman wandered near and passed, not seeing him where he stood motionless in the dark. He seemed to be looking for something, and there was a familiar shape to him beneath his cloaks. Brand straightened, but before he could hail the horseman, the other had cupped his hands to his lips and shouted, "Brand!"

Brand tried to speak but couldn't. Only a dry croak issued from his throat. He swallowed, coughed, then tried again. "Corbin!" he rasped.

The rider halted in surprise, then turned and saw him. The rider came closer and Brand saw that it was indeed Corbin, straddling the shaggy brown carthorse, Tator.

"Brand! We thought that the goblins had taken you back to their land forever!" Corbin shouted, dismounting and coming to meet his cousin. He halted when he saw Jak's crumpled form. "Is that Jak?"

Brand only nodded, too weak to speak. Corbin wasted no more words. He lifted Jak as gently as he could and placed him in the saddle, where he was forced to hold him in place. Together, they set off.

"How did you come here?" Corbin asked him. "I've only just set out, and I didn't think to find you for miles. We all thought that you were lost in the wilds of the Drake estate."

"I have followed a light all night. Am I not on the Drake estate? Where are we? Is there shelter near? I fear for my brother's life."

"Shelter indeed, cousin. Look!" said Corbin. Brand looked up and halted. Before them stood the rambling house of Tylag and Suzenna Rabing. Somehow, he had won through to Froghollow, and never had a sight been more welcome to him.

"There, there is the beacon!" said Brand, pointing to an upstairs window. But even as he spoke, he realized that the window was shuttered, and that no light issued forth—nor could any have possibly done so.

"Scraper's candle," said Corbin as he helped Brand along with a guiding hand. Tator moved with delicate steps, almost as if he were aware of his injured rider. "She lit it again tonight, for you and Jak. Perhaps she is a fledgling sorceress after all."

Brand was too weary to answer. Now that they had made it to shelter, his strength left him. Corbin shouted and brought all the household out to meet them. Brand was vaguely aware of a swarm of concerned faces and questions, to all of which he only blinked in confusion.

Gudrin appeared and took charge of Jak. "Aye, he lives yet, but only just. We must remove the arrows and hope fortune is with him tonight."

Aunt Suzenna cried aloud at the sight of the black-feathered arrows that had pierced Jak. "If you have the craft to heal him," she told Gudrin. "I will be your aide."

Gudrin nodded and prepared for the surgery. She shouted orders for all the lanterns, oil lamps, and mirrors in the house to be gathered into the kitchen. They arranged the lights and the mirrors to concentrate the light upon the table. Finally, when all was ready, she and Tylag bore Jak away to the kitchen table while Corbin saw to the horses.

"I imagine you have quite a tale to tell, boy," said Modi, who had come and taken Brand's elbow. It took Brand a moment to realize that the warrior was leading him toward a couch, not into the kitchen where Jak lay dying. He protested, but Modi's grip was like that of a boulder shaped into a hand. "You need rest, boy. You listen to me—this time."

Brand met the warrior's eyes, and they were stern, but not unkind. He let himself be led to the couch where he collapsed.

* * *

Well after daybreak, he slowly became aware of someone bathing his forehead with a cool damp cloth. His eyes fluttered open to find Telyn bent over him, her face pinched in worry. He thought he had never seen a lovelier sight, not even the

Shining Lady could move him the way this tanner's daughter could. "Telyn, does Jak live?"

"Of course," she answered, her face brightening. "He is feverish, but should recover. Gudrin is a miraculous healer. There are so many crafts I could learn from such as she."

"The shafts have been removed then?" he asked.

Her face clouded. "Yes, but—"

He gripped her arm. "But what?"

She pressed him down again, and he let her do it, for in truth he felt as weak as a kitten. "You must rest, Brand. You are not well either. You strove mightily with the Faerie last night, and such things take a grim toll from mortals, to say nothing of dragging your brother through miles of forest."

"Ah, yes," said Brand, remembering the long night. "I saw your beacon Telyn. It was my only hope when all else was lost. It was your sorcery that saved us."

Her hands plucked idly at the damp cloth she held. "No, it was all my fault that you got into this in the first place. Jak is almost dead because I wouldn't listen to reason. It's fine for me to endanger my own skin, but I can't forgive myself for nearly killing us all with my rashness."

Brand sat up, although it was a mighty effort. He took her hand and squeezed it. "I'll not have that! I was the one the shade began tracking in the first place. I could just as easily say that the breaking of the Pact was on my head!"

"What utter foolishness," said Telyn, but he could hear the gratitude in her voice.

"Now, tell me the whole truth about Jak."

She cast him a concerned glance, then looked back to the cloth in her hands, which was now wound into a knot. "The shafts came out easily, Brand, but the heads did not."

"What do you mean?" asked Brand, feeling cold inside.

"I mean that the arrow points are still in him, somewhere...Brand?"

But she was talking to his back, for he had already started for the kitchen. There, in the brightly lit room in which he had supped so well, Jak lay. His flesh was bloodless and white, but his breathing appeared regular. Brand gripped the doorjamb for support. Gudrin held something pinched in a pair of tongs which she held aloft to the light. It was a tiny flint arrowhead. She rubbed her chin then dropped it into a pewter pitcher. The water in the pitcher bubbled and hissed briefly, then fell silent.

"That's one," grunted the Talespinner. She eyed Brand sharply, but didn't order him from the room.

"Is that from his chest?" asked Brand.

Gudrin nodded. "The other has gone deeper still. I only just decided he was mended enough to go for them, and it was critical that I did so now."

"Why?"

Gudrin gestured to the pitcher. Brand stepped forward and peered into it. There was no sign of the arrowhead. "What happened to it?"

"The arrowheads are enchanted. There is no question about it: your brother was elf-shot."

"Elf-shot?" Brand echoed. Stunned, he looked at his brother's leg wound. "There is still one of them in him?"

"Yes, worming its way to his vitals. Were you attacked by the elfkin?"

"No, goblins only. At least, we saw no elfkin."

"Strange," said Gudrin. She shook her head and prepared to dig into Jak's flesh to remove the other arrowhead. She stepped to the sideboard for a moment, where her book lay open, and read a page or two before returning to her work. Brand noted that her rucksack was stowed carefully beside her book. "That's what the others said. But it is for certain that these arrows are elf-work. Goblins have not the craft. Either these arrows were stolen or there are elves in league with our Enemy, which is fell news indeed."

Gudrin began her digging and cutting then, bidding Brand to hold his brother still. Even in his unconscious state, Jak moaned and writhed in pain.

"Make sure he doesn't reopen his chest wound!" ordered Gudrin. The work was bloody and it was all Brand could do to keep from retching. Modi and Tylag were finally called in to help, while Aunt Suzenna did what she could to make her elder nephew comfortable. Brand wondered if he could ever enjoy a meal at this table again.

Forcing himself to watch, he looked into the splayed flesh of his brother's thigh. There was a black shape, buried down near the bone. Gudrin reached for it, but it wriggled and half vanished into red bloody flesh again.

"The River save us!" breathed Brand.

Finally, Gudrin got a grip upon it, and lifted it up. "There's the cursed little thing."

Aunt Suzenna, who was the best and fastest with needle and thread, set to sealing the wound. Jak's agonized moans subsided. Gudrin and Brand stepped aside and examined the arrowhead.

Gudrin reached out and touched the river stone around Brand's neck. "A River ward, after the fashion of your folk. Hmmpf. Well-made, too. Your work?" she asked Telyn, who nodded. "You have an eye for the craft. If it was not for these wards, or if the goblins had used normal weapons, you would have all been killed. Notice, the arrows struck only Jak, who wore no such ward."

At this point she yelled aloud and swore in the tongue of the Kindred. She dropped the tongs she had been holding aloft and clutched at the hand that had held them.

"What's wrong?" asked Brand, but Telyn had already snatched up the tongs and grabbed Gudrin's hand. The palm was pooling with blood. Only a stub of the arrowhead was still visible as it burrowed into the talespinner's flesh.

"It got away from me! I'm a fool! An old fool! Can you get it, girl?"

Telyn made no answer, but instead thrust the tongs into the open wound. Red blood spilled and splattered the floorboards. Gudrin grit her teeth and hissed through them, but did not pull away. Brand suddenly became aware of Modi, who was standing very close, watching everyone intensely. His knuckles stood out white upon the haft of his axe.

"Got it!" shouted Telyn, pulling the tongs free. With two quick strides she took the arrowhead to the pitcher and dropped it in. The water bubbled and hissed and soon the cursed thing was no more.

Gudrin swore again, wrapping her hand. "I should have done that in the first place. Thank you, girl."

121

Chapter Fourteen
Warriors All

"How can we stand against weapons such as these?" demanded Brand aloud.

"Your wards protected you, as I said," Gudrin told him. While she talked she set a prepared poultice of healing herbs on Jak's wounds. "And we may not be completely without our own special armaments. What puzzles me is why they would use such weapons on young harmless folk such as yourselves. It is a mystery coupled with Voynod's stalking of you. It is clear that the Enemy regards you as some kind of threat. I must have a smoke and a think upon it," she said. She donned her hat, slung her rucksack, clasped her book, and slid it back under her arm.

After checking on his brother, who was now less deathly pale, Brand followed Gudrin out onto the porch. Corbin came after him and pressed a sandwich and a mug of milk into his hands, for which he was grateful. All three of them sat on low-slung porch chairs. Gudrin smoked a delicately carved pipe, the bowl of which was shaped like a bear's head. Blue smoke rose from the bear's gaping jaws.

Outside, the day was a fine one, but there was a chill wind up, and winter could not be far off. Brand enjoyed the feel of the sunshine and waited while Gudrin had her think. Then, however, he recalled his meeting with Oberon. He found it strange that he had forgotten about it until this moment. Even now, he wondered somewhat if it could have all been a waking dream. He told Gudrin about it, filling in every detail he could recall.

Gudrin leaned forward, puffing on her pipe. She asked several details of Oberon's appearance, and then at last leaned back, satisfied. "It was Oberon, that's for certain. It's a wonder you can recall him so well, however. Perhaps your ward is working better than even it should."

"Why should I forget seeing him?"

"That is one of the powers of Lord Oberon: he can make folk forget seeing him, speaking with him. It is useful in his manipulation of events," she said, then fell silent for a time, puffing on her pipe. "But why is even Oberon so convinced of your importance?"

"I find it hard to believe that it's just me. Perhaps we are confusing something. I'm only a river-boy from a small isle on the Berrywine. I know nothing more than how to travel water, chop wood and gather berries."

Gudrin swept away his arguments with a wave of her bandaged hand. "Nonsense. All of you River Haven folk sell yourselves short. The blood of many champions runs in your veins. You must recall that you are the survivors, the descendants of the best of your race. Originally, you were warriors all, and a quarrelsome lot, if the stories are to be believed."

"River Folk? Warriors all? That is hard to swallow."

"Believe it. It is written in the Teret," said Gudrin, striking her book soundly. She took her pipe from her mouth and tapped out the smoldering ashes, then refilled it with fresh stock.

Soon Modi came outside. He stood on the porch near them for a moment, the boards sagging beneath his weight, before moving out into the yard.

"He guards you closely," said Brand.

Gudrin shrugged. "He is of the Warriors. His father is a great clanmaster among the Kindred. All of his clan are warriors."

"If they are as big as he is, I can see why," mused Brand. He watched as Modi set up a row of pumpkins on the fenceposts near the road. He readied his axe and began to

124

exercise with it, chopping the pumpkins like the heads of enemies. Each of them fell neatly in half, then in quarters. His swings were precise and powerful. "He cuts only pumpkins, but still I am impressed."

"Modi's clan is an old one. Many of his folk were those that survived Myrrdin's campaign and faced the Faerie when the Pact was forged. It is sad that he should be here to witness its breaking."

"What are we to do, Gudrin?"

Gudrin compressed her lips, sucking on her pipe for a time before answering. A cherry-red glow brightened in the bear's mouth. "I must march in search of Myrrdin," she said with a sigh. "Only he might know how to reforge the Pact, or perhaps some other way to save the Haven. Besides, my business is with him in any case."

"So you will leave us soon?"

"Yes, as soon as I am sure that your brother will live. Most likely, we will leave at dawn tomorrow. It seems that Myrrdin is delayed elsewhere, although I can think of little save death that would keep him from renewing the Pact. I fear the worst, but still I must find him. I only wish I weren't so weary of travel."

Gudrin's rucksack was at her side. This and her Teret, the book of the Kindred, were never far from her hand. Brand eyed the rucksack and wondered what was the nature of the burden within that it could slow someone as tenacious as Gudrin. He watched it, wondering if it would move, but it did not.

"My burden sleeps," said Gudrin. Brand gave a guilty start. Gudrin turned to look at him with a twinkle in her water-blue eyes. "You interest me, boy. You alone of your clan can meet my eyes now without flinching. That is a rare thing, and I'm not simply boasting. The Talespinners of the Kindred have a power in their eyes, and I'm the leader of my clan."

"It would seem that clans work differently with the Battleaxe Folk," said Brand.

"Indeed. Let me explain. Among the Kindred, craftsmanship is valued above blood lineage. Each clan has a craft, or a set of crafts, to which its clansmen are born. Therefore, our clan names are representations of our craft, rather than our lineage—although they are generally one and the same."

"But what if one is born a natural warrior into the clan of Talespinners?"

"This is rare, but upon such occasions, a clanmaster or the King can grant a kinsman release from his clan. He is then free to join another, if they will have him."

"Then as a clanmaster and a clanmaster's son, you and Modi are akin to lords. Why do you trouble yourself to travel alone like this? What could be your mission in the peaceful River Haven?"

"It doesn't seem all that peaceful to me," Gudrin chuckled. "But we travel alone because a large group would only attract more notice. We wished to go unrecognized. That, of course, was undone by last night. As to the rest, well, we are searching for someone, and we need Myrrdin to find them," she said with finality.

"What should we do to prepare for tonight?" asked Brand. "It seems like the Faerie might put in another appearance now that the Pact is broken."

Gudrin shrugged.

"There is little to be done. I would suggest that you gather all the animals into the barn and ready up a large pile of firewood."

Firewood. Brand groaned inside. He didn't want to show it, but he was very spent from the previous night still. Splitting wood right now sounded like punishment.

"Let Corbin do it, boy," said Gudrin, reading his thoughts.

Brand nodded, but stood up. "I'll help a bit." Brand did feel much better than the half-dead state he had arrived in last night, but he groaned aloud when he took up the axe. Corbin told him to just take it easy, and the two of them soon made chips fly.

After perhaps a hundred strokes from Corbin and ten or so from Brand, they were both sweating. Modi came up to them to watch.

"What are you doing?"

Corbin glanced at Brand with a twinkle in his eye, but Brand gave his cousin an imperceptible shake of his head. He didn't think it a good idea to jest with the warrior, which he

126

could tell from long experience was what Corbin had in mind. Corbin scowled a bit, and simply continued chopping. Brand turned to Modi, his hands resting on his axe. "We are splitting firewood."

Modi nodded, as if this were a weighty statement. He examined Corbin's strokes for a few moments. Corbin ignored him. Brand was a bit taken aback by Corbin's manner, as it was not normal for him.

"Corbin has a better build for the axe," said Modi at last. "But you Brand, despite your fatigue, are more skilled with it."

Corbin halted, his sides heaving slightly. Sweat stood out on his brow despite the cold. "Perhaps you would like to demonstrate for us."

Modi eyed him for a moment, then nodded. Corbin handed over his woodaxe and backed away. Brand glanced over toward the porch, where he saw that Gudrin still sat and puffed her pipe, watching them.

With deliberate movements, Modi selected a large piece of oak. "There are two difficult points," he said, touching two knotholes with the heavy axe, which he held in one hand and moved about as if it were a delicate wand. With two smooth motions, he clove away the knotholes with a minimum of wasted wood. Then with four more powerful blows, he divided the wood into even pieces.

Brand was impressed. Corbin, however, seemed a bit out of sorts. He pointed to a heavy stump that lay on its side like a rotted tooth. "Can you cleave that in two with a single blow?" he demanded. Brand shot him a quizzical glance.

Modi took the question in with all seriousness. He eyed the stump and then the woodaxe in his hand. "Not with this," he said finally. "The head is too small, and the haft would break."

"Thank you, Modi," Brand said politely, turning back to the job at hand. He wondered if Modi was serious. Could the warrior have done it? There was no question that the haft of the little wood axe would break with the force of such a blow. But if the weapon were larger and more sturdy....

Could Modi really be that strong?

Modi walked to the front yard, where he began to practice with his battleaxe again. More pumpkin heads were halved and quartered. When he was out of hearing, Brand asked Corbin what had gotten into him.

"I'm sorry, but Modi has started to grate on me. He is so arrogant, so obviously disdainful of us. There is something about him that I don't completely trust."

"I'm shocked to hear this from one who's self-control is legendary," said Brand. He explained to Corbin who Modi and Gudrin were among the Kindred. Corbin's eyes grew wide to hear that Gudrin was the clanmaster of the Talespinners.

When the two of them had split enough wood to last for several days and had hauled it into the shed that adjoined the kitchen, they stopped to watch Modi's exercises. After a time they asked him to give them a lesson in using their woodaxes for war. Modi was happy to oblige and for the first time to their knowledge he seemed about to smile. Modi taught them how to close with an enemy, how to hook his weapon with their own, where to strike for a kill. By the end of it, they both felt that they had learned something. The trio exercised and sweated for two hours until lunch was announced. All the while Gudrin watched them quietly from the porch.

Jak had been carried aloft to rest in the spare bedroom. Brand found that he *could* eat on the kitchen table that had only hours before seen desperate surgery. Brand and Corbin ate like famished men, as did Tylag and Corbin's brothers, who had returned from the ferry at the base of the cliff to eat.

Tylag was full of ill tidings. "We've been busy all morning. It seems that everyone is leaving the island. The word is that the Rabing Clan broke the Pact and have brought a curse upon all the River Folk."

"That's ridiculous!" shouted Telyn. "Who says such things?"

Tylag spooned up a load of steaming mussels. "The Hoots and the Silures are at the bottom of it, I expect. But all the folk are scared, and at such a time they will say things they may come to regret. But there is no doubt that the Faerie are no longer protecting our borders from the Dark Ones among them. All of us should move with caution. No one of this clan should be alone after dark."

128

After the others had promised to follow his advice in this matter he made another announcement. "Tonight Suzenna and I go to a closed council meeting at Drake Manor. There is talk of a muster."

Everyone looked up at that. "Are things as bad as all that?" asked Corbin's oldest brother Barlo. "Surely, the rift with the Faerie can be repaired."

"That's as may be, but we must prepare for the worst," said Tylag. "No one knows what twilight may bring."

"But a muster?" burst out Barlo. "What's wrong with the Riverton Constabulary? They have always served us well enough. Let them mount a watch with archers upon the fairy mound and feather the little devils when they come!"

Aunt Suzenna stood up, and everyone turned to her, all thinking of what a muster could mean—and that she had three sons and no daughters. She looked at them sternly. "If there is to be a muster, all my sons shall go, or Clan Rabing will truly be disgraced."

Barlo could not meet her eyes. He said no more of the Riverton Constabulary. Talk shifted to the unusually cold weather and preparations that they should make to defend the household. Tylag announced he would lock the doors tonight, both front and rear. The boys discussed building an outer fence to circle the homestead during the following weeks. Telyn talked of gathering wards for the lot of them.

Brand noticed that Modi and Gudrin said little. At one point, however, he believed that he saw them exchange glances. He thought to see regret and perhaps a touch of sadness in their eyes. This disturbed him and he left the table early, his head full of thoughts of the coming nights and what they might hold. He didn't think that Tylag and the others had a realistic idea of what they were facing.

The afternoon passed swiftly. Twilight came all too soon for Brand's taste. Each day grew shorter with the approach of winter, he knew, but tonight darkness seemed to fall with great suddenness, as if a cloak had been cast over the eyes of the land. Tylag and Suzenna had long since gone to Drake Manor for the council meeting, taking Barlo with them. Sam was out using his thick arms to split wood and dragging his lame foot about as they tended the livestock, while Corbin and Brand played Jiggers and Swap-Cards in the parlor. All three of them were content, however, as Sam liked nothing more than to work his body, while the younger boys liked nothing more than competing with their minds. Upstairs, Gudrin and Telyn tended Jak in the spare bedroom, while Modi haunted the upstairs hallway. By the groaning of the floorboards overhead, it was easy for Brand to track his pacing.

"Modi seems anxious to be away," said Corbin in a low voice. "I wonder how much they know about what will happen here in the River Haven."

"I don't know," sighed Brand. He was in a reflective mood. All around him were sights and sounds that were among his favorite in the world. He had played in this parlor as a child. He and Corbin had often bounced themselves upon the couches until they were discovered by Aunt Suzenna and chased from the house. Along the walls was a shelf containing a row of perhaps thirty books, each of which that he had read at least twice. A painting of his mother and father, one of only three that still existed, hung from the wall behind Corbin's head. He felt his eye drawn to his mother's image. Tall and sleek she was, with flaxen hair and a mouth that ever curved into a smile. Jak more resembled her, while he more resembled his father. Holding to the tiller of their boat in the painting, his father was dark-haired with a heavy mustache. His eyes were stern and he smiled little.

"Do you really want to play?" asked Corbin softly.

Brand dealt the cards without interest. "Perhaps we should post a lookout," he suggested. "The night is black and the moon has yet to rise."

Corbin shrugged. "Tylag locked the door and Sam is out in the barn. Surely, he will serve as a good lookout until he gets back."

Brand agreed, and played out his hand. When he had lost three hands in a row he conceded the night to Corbin. Thinking of Modi and his lessons today with the woodaxe, he went to the woodshed that adjoined the kitchen and fetched one. Returning to the parlor, he sat with a cloth and whetstone and worked the edge of the blade.

"Don't let my mother catch you with that in her parlor," was all Corbin said as he packed away the cards, the betting beads, and the jigger-sticks.

"I just wanted to work out the nicks that we put into the blade this morning—" Brand broke off when they heard a shout from outside.

"That's Sam," said Corbin.

"Sounds like he's in trouble. Let's go!"

The two of them ran outside, Brand still carrying the woodaxe. The big doors were hanging open, and the sheep were crying in their pens nearby. The barn was dark; there was no outward sign of Sam or his lantern. After the one, brief shout, they heard nothing more from Sam. Corbin stood in the entrance and called for his brother.

"I'll light a lantern," said Brand. He handed the woodaxe to Corbin and took down a lantern from its peg.

Corbin walked away into the darkness, shouting for Sam. Brand burnt his fingers getting the lantern to sputter into life. Sucking on them, he stepped after Corbin in the lantern's flickering circle of yellow light.

"Get out of here!" shouted Corbin suddenly, swinging the axe with great force. An old wooden stool exploded beneath the blow. Brand saw something bound away and clamber up the haystack. He got a better look at the thing when it crested the mountain of hay and stood at its peak, looking down at them. Brand marveled at the lightness of the creature. It did not sink into the hay at all.

There could be no doubt that it was one of the Wee Folk. The manling was male and stood about two feet tall. He had a thin face with sharp features: the nose was like a blade and the chin tapered to a point. The overlarge mouth was stretched into a perpetual grin. Brand examined the tiny clothing in wonder. Tight-fitting hose covered thin legs and the feet wore pointed boots. The boots and his russet-brown waistcoat seemed to be made of doeskin. All the clothing seemed woven with impossibly fine workmanship, each stitch smaller than any human tailor could produce. The manling leered at them and rested his overlarge hands on his bent knees.

131

"Where's my brother!" shouted Corbin, threatening the creature with the axe.

"He's in several places!" said the manling in his piping voice. This reply seemed to greatly amuse him. He wrapped his thin long arms about himself and shook with laughter.

Corbin moved to swing at the manling, but Brand reached out to stop him.

"At least he's talking to us," Brand told his cousin. He turned back to the manling. "I've spoken with your lord, Oberon. He has helped me, so you must do the same."

At this the manling's eyes narrowed. His eyeballs were glass-like beads the color of flint. His grin took on the aspect of an evil leer. "Oberon has been deposed, so his words have no weight."

"You serve a new lord then?"

The manling shook his head. "The new lord is even less to my liking."

"Are you still loyal to Oberon then?"

The manling looked about the barn, as if seeing things invisible to the two men. Which perhaps he did, reflected Brand.

He appeared to come to a decision. He bent forward conspiratorially. "I speak for Oberon. He would bid thee to run from this place, man-child."

"Why? Where should I go?" asked Brand, stepping forward and lifting his lantern higher.

The manling squinted into the yellow light. "Join the Kindred, help them find Myrrdin and learn what must be done. The Wanderer will explain matters."

Brand nodded. "Thanks for the advice. Can I call the Wee Folk friends?"

The manling's face grew sorrowful then, he shook his tiny head and tsked at them. "Ever it is so with thy folk," he sighed. His face grew long and mournful. A hint of his true age showed in his cheeks then, which grew new wrinkles, and his bright, black eyes, which dimmed. "Ever thou wouldst mistake the slightest aid for friendship. True friendship is something which must be earned and which is never given. So big thy kind grows, yet thou hast the minds of children."

Still making tsking sounds, he bent down and began brushing away the straw at his feet. Brand watched in confusion as he cleared away the yellow straw from what appeared to be a patch of dark fur. The manling glanced at them, and tsked further at their incomprehension. With a sudden sweeping movement and a puff of breath blown through his thin fingers he revealed what was hidden in the haystack.

It was Sam's head.

Chapter Fifteen
Dando

Sam's head had been severed at the neck. The eyes were open and staring, the mouth sagged. The manling was standing atop the head, the dark fur that flipped and curled over his pointed shoes was Sam's hair.

Shock froze the two men. The manling watched them with keen interest. Brand felt disconnected from the real world at that moment. It couldn't be that Sam was dead, but his cousin's severed head was undeniable proof. He looked at the manling, and wondered what alien thoughts were in that tiny creature's mind. He seemed very curious at their response, as if he were studying them. Perhaps, for the manling, human grief was a mystery.

Corbin was the first to come to life. Without a word, he stepped forward and made a sweeping cut with his woodaxe at the manling. The manling, ready for such a response, bounded straight up into the air and did a complete spin as he came down, landing again on his gruesome perch. Corbin swung again, and this time the manling performed another impossible leap, bounding up into the hayloft overhead. Brand came to life as the manling flew over their heads and he snatched up a pitchfork. Grimly, not speaking, the two of them clambered up the shaky, steep steps to the loft. Corbin reached the top first and he made a soft sighing sound and fell to his knees. Brand rushed to him, wondering if he had been stricken. He followed his cousin's gaze and found himself staring at the rest of Sam.

The headless body, looking oddly incomplete, lay at the edge of the loft. Clearly, the head had been lopped off and had tumbled to fall on the haystack.

"Look, he took one with him!" said Brand grimly. He pointed to Sam's thick-fingered hands. In the grip of his dead hands was the dark, furred neck of what could only have been a rhinog. The rhinog was dead, its neck broken.

"Sam must have surprised it in the barn," said Brand aloud.

They became aware of a scrabbling sound. The manling was trying to pry back a loose board in the wall and escape. Corbin rose swiftly and advanced in a crouch. He held his axe at the ready. There was a low growling sound emanating from his throat.

The manling looked up in alarm. "I didn't do it!" he squeaked. "It was the goblins and their rhinog offspring! They follow the Dark Bard! He is in the bogs even now! We must flee him!"

Corbin continued his advance and the creature fled with great flying bounds, like those of a hare when a fox's teeth are right behind it. He darted beneath a pile of wooden crates. Corbin demolished them with heavy blows of the axe.

Shrieking, the Wee One bounded about, circling the loft. Corbin slashed about with the axe in wild abandon. Brand made a calculated thrust with his pitchfork and managed to catch the creature's deerskin boot, pinning it to the rough wood of the loft.

Corbin roared in triumph. The manling shrieked in terror and struggled to free himself.

"Wait, Corbin!" shouted Brand. "Don't kill him! We need answers!"

For a moment Brand feared he had not gotten through to his cousin, who was no longer acting like the boy he had grown up with. His wrath was something terrible to behold. Brand felt that he understood that uncontrollable fury. It was the same feeling that had gotten him through the previous night and allowed him to save Jak. He understood that Corbin was beyond reason, and may well kill the manling in his grief, though he had not committed the crime.

The axe descended, and the manling cried in fear. The blade thunked into the old planks of the loft, making the timbers shudder. Corbin had spared the creature.

"Do not play with our grief, manling," Corbin told the quivering creature. He jabbed a finger into the manling's side.

A dark look crossed the manling's sharp features, and Brand thought that he hungered to play a trick on them, perhaps thinking to singe Corbin's finger or turn the offending nail black and rotten. But he didn't dare.

"Now we shall have some quick answers," said Brand, squatting and setting down the lantern.

"Ever it is with River Folk," said the manling. "Always blaming the messenger for bad tidings."

"Tell us your name," demanded Brand.

The creature paused and looked as if he were about to fabricate a name. Brand moved the lantern very close to him, so that the heat of the fire inside could easily be felt. The manling shrank away in discomfort.

"I am Dando."

"Where are the rhinogs that did this?" demanded Corbin.

"Outside, in the forest, in the bog, wherever their masters lead them."

"They are led by goblins?"

"Of course. Rhinogs will only follow their sires."

"How many of them are there?"

Dando shrugged his small shoulders. "Three goblins have brought their broods. They each have ten or so offspring with them."

Brand frowned. "The goblins have so many human women to breed such numbers of rhinogs? Don't the rhinogs have families of their own?"

Dando looked at him as if he were a fool. "Rhinogs are mules, boy. As to the prolific qualities of goblins, they are legendary. It is not uncommon for a birthmother to gestate six spratling rhinogs at a time."

"What a hellish life those poor women must lead," said Brand.

"We must do something for Sam," said Corbin.

Brand turned to him. "We will, cousin, but first we need to know what we face." To Dando he said, "Since the people of the River Haven have long been off limits I suppose that most of the women have been taken from the wagons of the Wandering Folk."

Dando nodded. Brand noted that now that the manling was forced to answer, he was speaking quite openly. He seemed to be enjoying the interrogation, as would the town gossip. What strange creatures were the Faerie.

"Why do they plague us, manling?" asked Brand.

"Ah, good question!" said Dando. His eyes shone with the reflected glow of the moon. His broad smile revealed many white teeth. "Why indeed? I'll tell thee this: they hunt for something lost, and care not one whit for thee nor any others of the River Folk."

"Enough of this!" growled Corbin. "We must get back to the house."

"Hold, cousin," urged Brand. To Dando he said: "So, what is their next move? If there are thirty or forty of them, why doesn't Voynod just lead them against us and burn us out right now?"

Dando laughed, some of the swagger returning to his manner now that it was clear that they were not going to kill him out of hand. "That is not the way of the goblins. They are raiders by nature. They value their offspring and would rather isolate and kill thee one at a time without endangering themselves."

"So we would be the next easy prey, as we are out here on our own," said Brand. He glanced at Corbin, but his cousin was no longer listening. The shock of his brother's death had glazed over his eyes.

There came a sound from outside then. It was a splashing, slapping sound, such as large, flat feet would make in the bog. Then came a human cry, a high-pitched one, like that of a child or a young woman in trouble.

Corbin and Brand rose, taking up the lantern and the woodaxe again. Brand looked down at the manling, who was furiously tugging at his pinned foot.

"Before you go, Dando, tell us what we hear outside."

137

"It's a goblin trick, fool man-child! Hast thou not heard their mocking voices before?" he hissed. "Now free me!"

Brand eased up the pitchfork, and Dando sprang free. He bounded to the edge of the loft, and then glanced back over his shoulder. "Remember, if thy fate is to survive the night, find Myrrdin!" he cried, then sprang out into space. Brand watched him sprint down the far side of the haystack and out the door.

He paused at the doorway and there was a blinding flash of blue light. Where the manling had stood a large barn owl now hopped into the air and took flight. On silent wings it vanished into the night.

"The owl..." said Corbin. "Was that the bird you saw at your window two nights ago? Has that changeling been haunting our barn for weeks?"

"Forget it," said Brand. "We have to run for the house!"

"What about Sam?"

Brand squeezed his shoulder. "We will have to do what we can for him in the morning."

Corbin nodded grimly and followed Brand down out of the loft. They left the lantern in the loft so that it might appear that they were still there. Signaling each other with gestures, Corbin took Brand to a small side door that led into a toolshed. Moving carefully, they opened the creaking door an inch or so to peer outside. When their eyes had adjusted to the starlight, they could see that dark shapes crept about the foundations of the house. Now and then one of the creatures would raise itself to a window and take a quick, furtive look inside.

The rhinogs were much larger than goblins, but smaller than the average man. It was difficult to see just what they looked like as they seemed to carry shrouds of darkness with them, or perhaps it was only that they excelled at crouching in the deepest pools of shadow available. From their general forms Brand made out that they had long arms, overlarge hands and crooked legs that seemed permanently bent backward at the knees, not unlike the hind legs of crouching wolves. Their eyes were two glittering rubies of evil swimming in the darkness enclosed within their drawn hoods.

There were more movements, at the front and rear of the barn. Clearly, the enemy lay in ambush, waiting for them to come out into the yard. Brand squeezed Corbin's shoulder, they exchanged glances and set themselves. They would have to make a run for the house. Brand's legs tensed as he readied himself to sprint across the yard.

Together they launched themselves at the front door of the house, hoping no one had locked it since they left. They knocked an old rain barrel aside as they tore out of the barn. In the still night the sound of it clattering to the ground seemed deafening. An odd hooting sound of rage went up behind them. Brand could sense rather than hear their pursuers. Dark, hunched shapes that sulked beneath trees and huddled against the house rose up and turned toward them.

Brand focused on reaching the door of the house before they could halt him. A dark shape scuttled close and reared up before them. He caught sight of glittering red eyes. Corbin swung the woodaxe wildly, there was an awful thunking sound and a squeal rent the cold air. As they scrambled past the rhinog, a clawed hand caught at Brand's boot. He kicked at the thing and jerked away. Talons scraped and dug into leather, there was another snarling sound, but then he was free.

Brand reached the porch and the door first and all but fell into the house, with Corbin right behind him. They slammed the door in the leering faces of hunched shapes that mounted the porch steps behind them.

"Modi!" shouted Brand, his chest heaving. For a moment no answer came, and a new fear gripped Brand. Had the enemy taken the house already? Had he risked everything only to enter a new trap? Visions of Telyn and Jaks' headless corpses came unbidden to his mind.

Heavy footfalls came down the stairs then, causing Brand to heave a sigh of relief. Only Modi had such heavy boots.

"Enemy?" questioned Modi as he emerged from the darkened hall.

Brand nodded. "Rhinogs. They chased us from the barn."

Modi looked to Corbin and frowned. "Is he injured?"

Brand followed his gaze and saw Corbin's ashen face, drawn tight with lines of grief. He shook his head. "It's his brother—Sam. The rhinogs killed him."

Modi nodded. He moved to look out a window, and that's when the door seemed to heave against their backs. Brand and Corbin were still leaning against it, and on the far side the rhinogs had gathered, whispering and hissing. It wasn't as if the door had been shoved, but rather as if it had suddenly come alive and taken in a great swelling breath.

"They work a cantrip!" shouted Modi. "Away from the door!"

Brand and Corbin staggered away from the door and it burst open behind them. The hinges came loose from the doorjamb and the lock shattered into metal shards. Beyond were the smoky, dark shapes of three rhinogs. Long serrated knives gleamed in their clawed hands. Red eyes gleamed beneath their cowls.

Modi strode forward with his battleaxe raised. "Return to your dens! I am Modi of the Warriors, and many of you will I slay before this house falls!"

A puff of smoky darkness seemed to obscure the three shapes, and Brand knew sorcery was at hand. He steeled himself for their charge, but instead of attacking, the three shapes seemed to fade from sight. After a moment the magical darkness faded and the porch beyond was empty.

"Have they given up?" asked Corbin.

Modi shook his head, scratching his beard. "It is not their way to fight openly. They have no stomach for it. They are assassins and footpads by nature. Their goblin sires will pull back and devise some new cunning trick."

Telyn and Gudrin came down then to join them and everything had to be explained. Modi lifted the battered door back into place and used spikes from the woodshed to hold it in place again. Brand armed himself with another woodaxe and helped the others rearrange the furniture into a barricade.

Suddenly, Telyn raised a hand to stop their talk. Brand's mouth opened to ask her what she meant, but then he heard it too. A crackling noise, coming from the back of the house. Moments later smoke poured out of the hall.

"They've fired the house!" hissed Telyn, voicing everyone's thought.

Upstairs, Jak cried out hoarsely and there was a thumping on the floorboards overhead. Brand felt sick, his brother was trying to get out of bed and had fallen. He rushed into the smoky hall.

"Brand!" Telyn cried after him. The smoke-filled hall was a cavern of hanging gray tendrils. His eyes burned immediately and his lungs rebelled with a choked cough. He ducked low, moving in a crouch and it was better, the air cleaner. He passed the kitchen and saw the lurid glare coming from the woodshed. They had fired it, and smoke was pouring into the house. Yellow tongues of flame licked up at the cabinets above the woodshed door. A rack of towels near the sink caught and flared brightly.

Then he was on the stairs and the smoke was worse. He could hear his brother upstairs, coughing and dragging himself across the floor. At least they hadn't crept in the upstairs windows and killed him yet, he told himself.

He found his brother mostly by feel on the floor of the upstairs hall. The lamps had gone out somehow. He set down his woodaxe and groped in the dark. He got a hold of Jak under his arms and heaved him up. A groan of pain escaped his brother's lips.

"Brand?" Jak whispered. "They're up here, Brand."

Brand caught a fluttering movement in the front bedroom.

"I'm getting you out, Jak," whispered Brand. He reached for a lamp, thinking to relight it. To his surprise he burnt his fingers on it. Looking closely, he saw that it was still lit, but that it gave only the barest glimmer of smoky, gray light. A lump of ice grew in his stomach as he realized he faced magic. The choking smoke had fogged his mind, but in a flash he realized that they had lured him up here by making Jak cry out. They had succeeded in drawing him apart from the others to slaughter him in this inky smoke.

Brand began to drag his brother to the stairs, when he thought he heard a stealthy sound behind him. He looked back and saw the assassin. Visible only as a patch of deeper darkness in the hallway, the rhinog glided with an oddly inhuman, scuttling gait toward his exposed back, a long silvery knife poised low for a killing thrust. There was no time to reach his woodaxe, so Brand did the only thing he could think of, he grabbed up the hall lamp from its bracket on the wall and hurled it at the creature.

The lamp exploded into yellow flame, the glass oil-vessel shattering and soaking his attacker. A horrible keening erupted from the rhinog and it sunk down, engulfed in flames. To Brand's eyes it seemed to melt like a candle tossed into a roaring fire.

He dragged Jak past the burning creature, which soon fell silent and stopped thrashing. At the top of the stairs he got Jak to his feet and drew one of his brother's arms around his shoulders. Struggling and coughing, trying not to stumble, he headed down the stairs.

At the bottom of the stairs he looked back. A second, smaller shape now stooped over the smoldering remains of the rhinog. It was the lithe form of a goblin, and Brand knew in his heart he faced the dark creature's sire. He and the goblin met one another's gaze for a moment, and never had Brand felt from another such vile hatred.

Then the smoke obscured the scene and he was out in the front room again, where the others had repelled a sneak-attack through the windows. Aunt Suzenna's prized shutters, which she had painted with rosettes and curling vines of her own design, now hung down, battered and scorched. Smoking black drops of what served the creatures for blood splattered the shutters and the sill.

"Brand!" cried Telyn, hugging him. She took up Jak's other arm. "Is he all right?"

Gudrin stepped forward and examined Jak briefly. "He's breathed too much smoke, but he should make it. If any of us do, that is."

"They've taken the upstairs," Brand told them when he could speak. All of them were crouched in the front room, where the smoke wasn't too overpowering yet.

"They're firing the house to drive us out into the dark," said Gudrin.

Chapter Sixteen
Berserker

"It is best that we try to break through immediately," Gudrin said, "rather than waiting until they expect us and we are entirely blinded by smoke."

"The manling we met in the barn said there were three goblins with their broods here, plus Voynod himself," said Brand. "Can we hope to win through such a force?"

Gudrin looked out the window for a long moment. Her face took on a cast of great age and weight. "There is a way," she said, her voice almost a whisper.

"You should leave me behind," Jak told Brand. "I'll only slow you all down. Don't die on my account. Someone must tend the isle."

"Forget it," said Brand.

"You could put me in the cellar, where I might live through the fire," suggested Jak. He grimaced with pain at every step. Brand didn't even bother to reply to his brother, thinking that the cellar would never survive the fire that was coming. He felt a pang of sadness for Aunt Suzenna, wondering where she was and hoping she was okay. If the rhinogs didn't kill her outright, he thought that the sight of her beautiful home burnt to the ground would.

At the front door barricade, they held a hurried council.

"Modi, you are of the warriors, what do you suggest?" asked Gudrin.

"We must break through them," said Modi. For the first time since they had met him, the River Folk saw him in his true element. He talked more quickly and acted with greater decisiveness. There was a light in his eyes that had not been there before. Brand thought that he perhaps was only fully alive in the heat of battle. "They are attacking at the front of the house to lead us to attempt an escape at the back, where they doubtless lie in ambush. Therefore, we will exit here, at the front door. Straight into their ranks we will charge.

"But," he said, turning to Gudrin and locking eyes with her. "We need help. I see no alternative but to wield the axe."

Gudrin nodded in agreement. "I will wield it. You must be my second, Modi of the Warriors."

Modi's eyebrows shot up. "But *I* should wield the axe. You are not of the Warriors."

"It matters not, for I'm still of the Kindred."

"But you have lived for so many seasons," protested Modi, but he halted at a sign from Gudrin.

"I will hear no more of it. I bear the burden, so I will wield it," she said. While they spoke, the room had filled with a pall of black smoke and heat from fires in the back of the house washed their faces. Moving with care, Gudrin held up her rucksack, and for the first time opened it. A golden light shone forth from the rucksack, lighting up Gudrin's face. Something seemed to shift, to move inside the golden light. Reflected specks of gold glinted in her eyes. The River Folk backed away in fright.

"What sorcery is this?" demanded Jak.

"High Magic!" cried Telyn, her eyes bright and her mouth curved in a broad smile.

Gudrin made no answer. She slipped her book into the rucksack and it vanished into the golden light. "For now," she said solemnly, "I relinquish the wisdom of the Teret and take up the fury of Ambros the Golden. Throw back the barricades!"

Modi and the others hastened to obey her. Resetting the rucksack upon her back, Gudrin reached over her shoulder. Into her hand jumped the handle of a bone-white axe with twin, curved blades of great size. As she drew the weapon from its

144

concealment a great change overcame her. Her aspect shifted from that of a talespinner to that of a warrior, lusting for battle. Her eyes shone with a light terrible to see, and her lips parted into a snarl of fury greater than any rhinog had ever produced. The bone-white axe she lifted high, and in its center was a great yellow Jewel. All there knew without being told that it was the Golden Eye of Ambros, one of the Jewels of Power. A mixture of fear and wonder filled Brand to know he witnessed magic of legendary power.

With an inhuman bellow, Gudrin charged into the shocked faces of the enemy. Behind her came Modi, his battleaxe also lifted high. The others followed, feeling a rage overtake them as well.

Gudrin thrust up her bone-white axe so that the enemy might see the Eye of Ambros, shouting, "Know, foul ones, that you face the wrath of the Golden Dragon! The Lord of Wind and Sunlight is upon you!"

The rhinogs fell back. A band of three stood in the yard, but melted back into the trees at their approach. With a shocking burst of speed, Gudrin charged to where they had vanished. As she reached the treeline, not three but five rhinogs appeared from the brush and tree trunks. They glided forward, springing an ambush. Brand released a cry of anguish as Gudrin, who had somehow outrun even Modi, faced the ambush alone. Stealthy dark shapes came at her from all directions in hunched postures. Their weapons, eyes and gnashed teeth gleamed in the brilliant golden light of the Jewel in the axe. Brand ran faster, sure he was about to witness the talespinner's death.

The axe flashed twice. Each time the white axe rose and fell the Eye of Ambros flashed, illuminating the night for a moment like a stroke of lightning. Two smoking carcasses fell and the rest of the band broke. The rhinogs ran toward their goblin sires, who now glimmered near the barn.

Gudrin made not for the road, but rather for the goblin sires that were gathering their broods to them for a hasty retreat. Modi and the River Folk could do nothing but follow her. The goblin sires gathered their rhinogs into three ragged lines and led them off into the trees. To Brand's surprise, Gudrin still gave chase, running as Brand had never seen one of the

145

Kindred run before. She caught up with one of the spry goblins when it ran into a thicket and had to turn. Its offspring showed no loyalty and fled in all directions in a panic. The goblin flew at Gudrin, all fangs and long-fingered hands stretched out like claws, but she lopped off its head. Gudrin then ran after another goblin. Deeper in the trees she went.

"We must stop her!" cried Brand, running after Gudrin. "She can't get them all! They'll kill her!"

"The *Berserkergang* has her in its grip," said Modi. "It is best that you let her give chase."

Brand paid no heed, worried that the enemy would fall upon her alone in the forest and shoot her down or take her from behind. He had to run like the wind, but finally he caught up with Gudrin and laid a hand on her shoulder, spinning her around.

Gudrin wheeled with the axe upraised. Brand wondered to see that despite the slaying it had done, the axe had not a single stain upon it. The Golden Eye of Ambros flashed in the blade, lighting up the dark forest as though it were day. The golden flecks still lived in Gudrin's water-blue eyes and Brand thought to see a hint of madness there.

"We've won Gudrin! Control yourself, Talespinner!"

The axe blade flashed, and Brand thought he had forfeited his life, but it struck instead a great oak, biting deeply into the trunk. The entire being of the tree shivered, the finger-like winter branches rattling far above them.

Brand looked down to see Gudrin on her knees, her face in her hands. The axe was buried in the mighty oak's trunk so deeply that only the handle protruded. Amber light gleamed out of the crescent-shaped cut like the mouth of a jack-O'-lantern.

"How will we ever get the axe free?" asked Brand in wonderment.

Modi appeared at his side. "I will remove it," he said, taking a step toward the tree.

At this, Gudrin came alive again. "No, Modi! Don't touch the axe!"

Modi's hand stopped, but it didn't retreat. Brand watched Modi's face and his huge hand, frozen in the middle of reaching for the axe. He knew there was a great struggle there.

146

Clearly, he wanted the axe for his own. In the end Modi retreated. Gudrin stood weakly and took her book from her rucksack.

"Lay your hands on the handle, Brand," she said.

Brand stepped forward, blinking. How was he supposed to pull the blade out of a foot of hardwood? What would the axe do to him?

"No!" said Modi.

"Silence!" shouted Gudrin with what seemed to be the last of her strength. "You will obey me and you will honor the words of your father."

Modi backed off and turned away. His shoulders hunched and his head hung low as, he glowered at the ground fiercely. No one came near him.

"Brand?" Gudrin called.

Brand stepped up. He glanced at Modi once, then at the others. Everyone watched him.

"Remove the axe and place it back in my pack," she commanded.

Brand nodded and laid his hand upon the handle.

He felt the power of it course through him. It was as if he held the reins of a massive horse that shivered at his touch. He was reminded of the presence he'd felt when he had confronted the Shining Lady and Oberon.

"Bruka!" Gudrin cried in the language of the Kindred.

In response, the axe worked itself out of the hard flesh of the tree. Brand tugged at it, but it was the axe that did the work. He felt as though he drove a powerful animal, merely guiding it.

It came free in his hand and he felt a greater surge of well-being of...*power*. The axe made him feel stronger. So strong that its heavy curved blades were as light at a wand in his hand. Slowly, a wide grin opened his lips and spread over his face.

Gudrin opened her rucksack and offered it to Brand.

Brand froze, just as he had seen Modi do in reaction. He stared at the axe, and the Amber Jewel in the blade shimmered back at him, as if in acknowledgment , or perhaps as a form of greeting.

Gudrin shook her rucksack suggestively.

147

Brand knew what she wanted. But the thought was unthinkable. He couldn't put down the axe, he couldn't let go of this power. She was asking too much. She wanted a thief to give back the master's purse. She wanted a prisoner to slam the dungeon door closed. She wanted a starving beggar to give up a leg of roasted ham.

He thought of the Shining Lady and of Corbin's dead brother Sam and of Telyn. Beautiful Telyn.

He stuffed the axe into the open maw of the rucksack. The mesmerizing Jewel vanished into darkness again.

Everyone relaxed.

"It is done," said Gudrin.

She sagged down to one knee, and then collapsed.

Epilogue

The battle was over, but they all knew that the war was just beginning. Suddenly tired and calm, Brand and the others picked themselves up and did what they could to staunch the flames. But Froghollow would be a ruin by morning, none of them doubted that.

In the flickering light of the burning house Brand had loved so much, Gudrin came to him and spoke with unusual gentleness. "You are a strong one. Strong of spirit as well as of limb. Few can willingly release Ambros once they have taken it up, and fewer still can do so without getting blood on its curved blades."

Brand nodded. He knew it was true, he had held Ambros and knew the power of it.

"The enemy has been driven off for now. But life will not be easy for the River Folk from this day forward."

"We will have to make weapons and prepare for war," he said grimly.

"Perhaps," said Gudrin. "What is certain is that your people and mine have a great problem, Brand," said Gudrin. "I'm asking for your help in solving it."

Brand looked at her seriously. Her face was old and craggy and worn. Females of the Kindred are rarely attractive, but Gudrin was perhaps even less so than the average. But still, he saw in her a certain beauty, a certain inner strength. She had done everything she could for him and his people by taking Myrrdin's place.

"I'm grateful for all you've done," Brand said. "I'll help you in any way I can."

She nodded. "I knew that you would."

Book II: SKY MAGIC

Translated from the *Teret,* the compendium of Kindred wisdom:

On the topic of Wee Folk: Do not discount them!

Wee Folk are common members of the Fae, and come in many varieties. Most have faces and bodies that resemble tiny, thin humans. Often confused with elves, goblins, and wisps, they are a unique race. All Wee Folk are smaller than any elf, as elves are generally the size of small adult humans. They are smaller than goblins as well, who can be distinguished by their evil, toothy faces, cat-like eyes and ears, as well as their normal height of approximately three feet. Wee Folk can't be classified as wisps, either. They possess much more intellect, and are larger than wisps. Most significantly, despite their ability to make huge leaps, they completely lack wings. Another clear differential trait is the preference of the Wee Folk to wear clothing like humans. They are not, however, exactly like small humans in appearance. When examining one of their type, a human will often describe them as doll-like. Their faces resemble a caricature of a real human face, their features often pulled and exaggerated, with noses like waxy candles, hair like straw, or eyes like glass marbles.

Wee Folk do possess some natural craft with magic. For the most part, their magic is weak, but it's always helpful in their favorite pastime: trickery. Many have the ability to shape-shift, but it is limited in its specificity. Most Wee Folk capable of shifting can only change into one thing, usually an animal or other type of small, mundane person. In the vast majority of cases, the shape-shifters can only change into something that is approximately the same size and weight as their original form. The humans refer to such creatures (and to other Faerie capable of similar tricks) as *changelings.*

Those able to change into human shapes are the most feared of the changelings. Often, the Wee Folk can establish an easy life by simply changing into the shape of a baby or small child, thus reaping the benefits of a caring human mother indefinitely. Since—in order to succeed—such a scheme requires the kidnapping of the mother's real infant, it is considered by the humans to be one of the most vile tricks of the many performed regularly by the Faerie. The child in question is just as likely to be cared for and raised among the Faerie as they are abandoned to die in some wild place far from home and family. Such is the naturally fickle and unpredictable nature of the Faerie.

Although the humans fear them, our people do not. From the point of view of the Kindred, the Wee Folk are generally dismissed as trivial annoyances. For starters, being creatures that favor windy, wild places, the Wee Folk rarely venture deep down into our stone fortresses. We of the Kindred are largely resistant to their tricks and we fall prey to their magicks far less often than do the hapless humans they love to plague.

However, their kind does pose a potential threat in the mind of this author. Unlike the other varieties of the Faerie, they have the ability to thrive and travel in our world, even in broad daylight. They are not restricted to Faerie mounds, nor do they only haunt specific locales like the ghosts that drift about in any ancient ruin. They come and go as they please and aren't tethered to their own domain. Equally disturbing, they are common and numerous.

As a people they are chaotic and totally lacking in organization. According to all accounts, they tend to be solitary individualists, each creature bent only upon achieving its own desires. In their current anarchic state they pose no threat. However, should this strange race ever form a union of some kind, a collective as large as a nation—should they ever appoint their own king—it is the studied opinion of this author that they would become a new and powerful force in our world as well as theirs. An organized army of magical, tricksy Wee Folk is something no other race would ever want to face.

—Jerd of the Talespinners, written circa the Third Era of the Earthlight

Chapter One
The Giant

One of the last beings in Cymru to hear that the Pact had been broken was the Deepwood Giant, Twrog. A flittering wisp told him, whispering tinkling words into his huge, flap-like ears. He took a few clumsy swipes at her at first, as if she were some kind of annoying gnat. But after some of her words sank into his thick brain, he gave pause to his hopeless attempts to catch her and listened instead.

"Whut?" he asked with thick lips and teeth as big as walnuts. He wasn't good at speech, which normally didn't matter, as he rarely had anyone to talk to.

The wisps were natural messengers. They loved gossip and flew far and wide with any tidbit of news to tell every creature who would listen. Today, they had important news indeed to spread. The Pact between the River Folk and the Faerie had been broken. The borders of human lands were no longer protected by the word of Lord Oberon.

While it was true that Twrog was one of the last to hear about the fateful night that had ended the centuries-long truce between the humans and the Faerie, he was one of the first to take action. Being a giant rather than one of the Faerie, he didn't share their cautious nature. The Faerie had incredibly long lifespans, and centuries of experience had taught them to be suspicious of any change in the order of things. One of the keys to a long life, as any oldster will tell you, is to approach life with a fair dose of caution. When they first heard of the broken Pact, they suspected a trick of some kind.

Tricks were, in fact, one of the things the Faerie always expected from others. They lived by trickery, and swore by it. Among themselves, they bragged of every fool they had taken, of every surprise they had sprung. As beings so accustomed to duplicity, they were the very first to suspect its use by others. And so, although they knew that the Pact had been broken, they mistrusted such a huge change.

For many long years they had been punished by their lord for any transgression into human lands, particularly the lands along the Berrywine River. On the banks of the great river lived the humans known as the River Folk. These were the same accursed humans who had managed to forge the Pact in the first place and had meticulously kept their end of the bargain for more than two centuries. The very events which led to the forging of this Pact were considered by the Faerie to be base trickery. And so when they were told the Pact had ended, many of the Shining Folk mistrusted the news. What new trick did the River Folk have in mind for them? Had they spent the long years of peace preparing some foul surprise? Were they so very confident in their defenses, so contemptuous of the Faerie, they had allowed the treaty to drop? What awaited the first of the Shining Folk who ventured to accost a human maiden, no doubt working a field alone at dusk just to bait a hapless shade into making a horrible mistake?

None of these thoughts occurred to Twrog, however. In the first place, thoughts of such complexity rarely bothered him. Secondly, he was a giant, and his race was a people apart from the Faerie—trickery was not his strongpoint. He had, however, been bound by the Pact. Part of that agreement stated that the Faerie would hold back creatures such as himself, keeping him from violating the borders of the rich lands of the River Folk. He had been forced to be content with trudging through the Deepwood, satisfying himself with the stringy meat and tough bones of the occasional huntsmen who ventured too deeply into the forests tracking a lung-shot stag.

Today, Twrog stood at the very border of the Deepwood. For long years he had traveled to this spot on the edge of the

155

protected lands of the River Folk. Even the ground here was well-worn, the leaves having been pushed away by his heavy tread. The exposed dirt had been churned into a patch of dust.

From this vantage point, under a rowan tree on a hillock, he could see the pig farm that had been the object of his daily scrutiny for so long. But it wasn't the sights of the farm, so much as the smells of it, that drove his heavy jaws to drip and salivate.

He had not tasted a true, corn-fed, farm-raised pig but for once in his life, when he had caught a human with a knapsack that bulged with a salted ham hock. The human had been tasteless and uninteresting, like all his kind. But the ham hock had changed Twrog's world. How unlike the flavor of his usual fare that ham had tasted!

Salting a meat and smoking it, these were things beyond Twrog's capacities. He did often cook his meats, of course. He would spit a good catch and toast it, usually unskinned, so that the fur burnt with the flesh. The flavor was always gamey and half raw, but never salted or smoked. When he did manage to spear a wild boar, he always hoped it would taste like the ham hock, but alas, it never did. Something the River Folk did to those pigs made them delicious. Perhaps it was in the preparation, but he suspected it was the pigs themselves that were different. They were nearly hairless and tame, clearly a different variety of animal compared to the wild ones.

So it was, in broad daylight, that he stepped out from the rowan tree. A single sweeping stride took him over the border he had never dared pass before. Shouldering a stout oak club, the thickness and weight of which was greater than the fattest man in the Haven, he walked on toward the pig farm.

He reached a fence of split rails, about five feet in height, and stepped over it rather than just kicking his way through. It was best to make less noise than to summon the farmer, who might have a bow handy. Twrog didn't really fear a few arrows. He didn't look forward to their bite, but like a bear raiding a beehive, he accepted that a few stings were to be expected and were simply part of the business. Reasoning that the best course was a direct one—and hardly being capable of

156

reasoning anything more complex—Twrog marched up to the pigpen, which was crowded with very surprised pigs.

They snorted at him and turned up their tiny eyes in a frozen moment of disbelief. Never in their short lives had any of them even scented one of his kind, much less been approached by a giant. He seemed to them to be similar to a man, but muskier, with the odor of blood and the wilds on him. Like the occasional huntsmen that came to visit, they classified him as human, but distrusted him immediately. They trotted away to the far end of their pens and stood there, watching his approach.

It was not until he swung his club and bashed one of them to the ground that they set up a horrible din of squealing.

Chasing them around in the pens, club upraised, Twrog managed to dash three more of them in rapid succession. His last swing, unfortunately, had caught the corner of the roof of their shelter and brought it crashing down. He paused to blink down at the squealing, circling pigs and the smashed roof. Someone would come to investigate this, he was certain.

Compared to catching wild game, this was easy. He could have killed them all. But there was hardly any point to that. Four pigs were already as much as he could easily carry. He stuffed two in his game sack, gripped the third and tucked the fourth under his arm—his free hand still holding the oaken club. It was a good club, and had always brought him luck. Today's kills were further evidence of just how lucky that club was for him.

Twrog marched back toward the Deepwood with a feeling of triumph. His mouth could still recall the flavor of ham hocks, and tonight he promised himself he would cook these pigs properly and enjoy them to the fullest.

He heard shouts behind him and hunched his shoulders, expecting the sting of an arrow. He tried to move faster, but he couldn't run while carrying so much meat.

The first arrow sailed safely by. The second sunk into the rump of the dead pig tucked under his arm. The third, however, struck home. He knew it was a crossbow bolt, as those often sunk more deeply into the thick flesh of his back than an arrow could have when propelled by a huntsman's bow. He winced

157

and dropped the game sack. He briefly considered abandoning it—he could move much faster to the tree line—but the very thought made him angry.

These River Folk had eaten like kings for as long as he could remember, refusing to share with the likes of poor Twrog. Now, even as he was setting things right, they had the gall to shoot at him!

He turned around with a low roar. Three shocked River Folk faced him, all armed with bows. Despite their apparent fear, they were in the act of working their weapons, reloading them to cause him further undeserved harm.

"Shoot Twrog NO MORE!" he roared at them. They all froze, their faces showing slack-jawed surprise. None of them had ever met a giant, much less heard one speak.

Then Twrog threw his lucky club. He launched it high, so that it flew end-over-end. The humans, who consisted of the farmer, his eldest son, and his eldest daughter, paused for a moment in astonishment. When that moment had passed, they dropped their bows and scattered, but it was too late: the huge rotating club was already falling toward them. The club seemed to hang in the sky, causing flashes of black shadow and brilliant sunlight to fall upon the River Folk.

It struck the ground with tremendous force, throwing up a geyser of black earth mixed with clumps of grass. The three humans were sprayed with dirt, but none were yet crushed.

But the club was not done.

It bounced, still flying end-over-end. When it came down a second time, it caught the farmer himself and crushed him down.

Twrog made a great honking sound, a heavy laugh that would forever after haunt the grieving dreams of the farmer's children. As the giant carried his four pigs into the Deepwood and vanished in the gloom under the trees, he hoped that losing his lucky club had been worth it.

Chapter Two
The Changeling

Among all the Faerie, the Wee Folk were perhaps the most curious and impetuous. Despite the Pact, they had never stopped playing occasional tricks upon humanity. Because of this, they were well-remembered by the River Folk, whereas many of the other less common, less adventurous creatures had been all but forgotten. Banshees, for example, had become mythical in the minds of the people of the Haven. But the Wee Folk were very real. No one had forgotten them.

That same curiosity—that same willingness to take a risk—drove many Wee Folk to cross the river to Stone Island and search for victims the moment the Pact was reportedly at an end. Such was their eagerness that some of them had already arrived on the island and had been skulking about, marking likely targets for days before the ceremony itself.

This was nothing new. Each year, there were always rumors among their kind that this would be the last time the humans would escape the Wee Folks' tricks. The winged wisps told tinkling tales of the humans' lack of faithfulness. Each year it was said that surely the River Folk would not put up another feast. That *this* year, the Faerie would be released from nonsensical Pacts and times would be good again. That *this* year, every porch would have a welcoming clay pot of ale set out, and every infant would be placed in a crib near an open window, easy for the plucking. But alas, despite the rumors, these happy times had never materialized.

This harvest, however, was different.

Piskin was one of the braver, more dedicated of the Wee Folk. He was one who had made the early trip to Stone Island, hoping. The year itself *felt* different to Piskin. The air was colder and tinged with the spice of magic. And he had seen so very many years. In fact, he was old enough to well-remember the days before the Pact had been forged. He had enjoyed life much more fully then. All of the humans had been at his disposal. Every night, their farms had been like picnic tables and their young like slow, fat fish in a quiet stream.

Piskin was a changeling. He had only a few magical tricks up his sleeve, but the best one, the only one that really mattered, was the power to shift into the shape of a human infant. Back in the olden times, this single power had made life very sweet indeed. He had never missed a full meal, never gone a week without a delicate, soft-fingered bath, nor had a night ever passed without snuggling against the cushion of a young mother's breast.

He longed to return to those happy times. For many, many harvest nights he had watched with teeth-grinding fury as that fool incarnate Oberon had allowed the humans to buy him off with a pathetic pile of earthly goods. What benefit was a single fat feast each year, whilst all the food and comfort of a lifetime lay right there for the taking in any rich woman's crib? Each year he came to the Haven and hoped…and after the Pact was renewed he snarled in disappointment.

But not this year. This year, the vile Pact had been broken, and peace was at an end.

He wasted no time. He did not even wait until the cover of darkness to move. All he could think was that the fool Oberon would relent. That somehow Myrrdin, that cursed wizard, would manage to trick their fool of a lord yet again. Piskin planned to be in a cradle long before nightfall. Even if the Pact lay broken for only a single day, he planned to be back in the arms of a pretty maid.

He had his new young mother all picked out. Lanet Drake was her name. She dwelt in Riverton, the only true town the River Folk had on their island stronghold. Her house was the biggest and finest structure in town, Drake Manor. Freshly married, Piskin's maid-to-be had long red hair, a perfectly upturned mouth, and a new baby that was barely a season old. Her voice was melodic, her breasts were ample and her squalling brat got the best of everything. Equally important, the father was often away up the river working as a foreman of herdsmen. It was always best, Piskin knew, that the husband was away at first. Sometimes, the fathers became wise to him, but rarely the mothers. And, even if she did begin to suspect the truth, a maid who's first born was a changeling would protect him instinctively.

He bounded over the absurdly low wall that surrounded Drake Manor and bounced from tree to tree in excitement. It had been so long! He tried to stay low, but so great was his joy that he almost sprang out in front of a guardsman. This last surprised him. He had been all over the manor during the preceding weeks and had never seen an attentive guard on duty. The walls themselves were a joke, of course. They had no wards on them and he doubted they would have kept a three-limbed rhinog out.

But there he was, a guardsman, eyeing the trees with suspicion. He had a bow in his hands and although he probably couldn't have hit a cow with it, Piskin eyed the thing with worry. A single arrow could take the life of a Wee One, like a man pole-axed. The humans seemed to have an idea of what was in store for them. Luckily, they were clearly ill-prepared for the likes of him.

Circling the guardsman and staying under cover, Piskin made his stealthy way to a certain third floor window. There, from inside, he could hear the sweet humming of his new maid. He dared not peek inside and gaze at her. There would be plenty of time for that sort of thing later. She would feed the brat by four, he knew, and with any luck he would have completed the switch by then.

There were only two tricky parts to the work of a changeling. The first, of course, was getting the mother to leave the child alone long enough to steal it. Some mothers seemed to hover over their children night and day, which could be quite frustrating. The second part was even harder. He would have to make off with the infant, dispose of it somewhere where it would never be found, and then return to the crib to take its place. His plan in this regard was simple. He would spirit away the child to the nearest cliff overlooking the Berrywine River. A loop of leather around one chubby foot and a hefty stone attached to the leather cord would do the deed. That was all that he needed. They would never find the child.

Naturally, all of these steps had to be completed quickly and quietly before the mother grew wise. Some changelings worked with an accomplice for this very reason. One would carry off the child, while the second would spring into its bed and shift into the guise of the infant on the instant.

Piskin preferred to work alone. Others of his kind would at best get in the way, or at worst, disrupt the operation. He thought about waiting for nightfall, but his greatest fear was that another of his kind would come along with exactly his plans in mind and beat him to this fresh-faced maid. He had to move fast, before every Wee One in the Haven came for what he already thought of as *his* infant.

And so it was that when another tiny throat cleared itself nearby, Piskin bared his teeth in way of greeting.

The intruder stood only a few paces away, at the corner of the very ledge Piskin stood on. The other had come around the corner of the building, just as calmly and nonchalantly as you please.

The invader wore a derby hat. He tipped it to Piskin in the manner of one greeting a fellow.

"Sirrah, this window is taken," hissed Piskin, his lips curling away and his nose crinkling.

The other walked a few steps closer, seemingly unsurprised by Piskin's mood.

"Dando's the name," he said, offering up a long-fingered hand.

Piskin stared at the hand and fumed. "You'll not have her," he growled. "I've marked her, and she will be mine. No one touches that brat but me."

Dando eyed him with upraised eyebrows. "No need to be rude about it."

"Piss....*off*," Piskin told him, pronouncing each word with exaggerated slowness and clarity.

"You are a thick one, aren't you?" Dando said, tapping his candlestick nose.

Piskin stepped forward menacingly. If his rival wanted a fight, he would have one.

Dando put up a stopping hand in his face and tsked at him. "Foolishness. One sound from me, one bound in that window, and she'll be wise to us. You'll never get past her after that."

Piskin breathed hard and fumed. "What will make you go away?"

"I want to help," said Dando. "We will do this together. But after, I must have the child."

Piskin blinked at him. "You want the child? To what purpose, Sirrah?"

Dando shrugged. "What does it matter to you? I have my own reasons."

Piskin considered, but at length he gave in. There was no easy way for him to remove Dando from the equation. Worse, if he waited around any longer, more of his kind might show up. He would have to trust that Dando wasn't a fool, and would escape cleanly with the infant.

And so it was done as Dando had suggested. When the maid went for a moment to brush her long red locks, the switch was made. Dando carried the infant off and away into the forest, under the very nose of the pathetic guardsman, and in his new third-floor home Piskin shifted into the form of the baby he had replaced. He pulled the warm swaddling over himself. Happily, he settled in and waited for his four o'clock feeding.

When Lanet Drake returned to the crib to check on her baby for the thousandth time of the day, she cocked her head. She did not frown, but rather looked perplexed. She had not thought that an infant could smile so widely at such a young age.

But her baby boy was indeed grinning at her. Grinning hugely.

163

Chapter Three
Blighted

Mari Bowen was seventeen today. This was a fact that everyone in the Bowen household was keenly aware of, because she hadn't stopped talking about her birthday all morning. Mother had tired of it, promising her sausages, butter, and marmaladed pumpkin bread for supper if she would only stop going on about it.

Mari pouted. What she really wanted was a new calico dress she'd seen in a shop down in Riverton. By bringing up her birthday approximately every two minutes, and the dress perhaps once every eight, she'd hoped to somehow convince her family to buy it for her. Instead, she was sternly ordered out of the house to find an ash leaf with two terminal leaflets. Rather like four-leaf clovers, such ash leaves were rare, but possible to find given a keen eye and enough time. They were considered lucky, but in addition to that they were powerful wards against the Faerie. Mari's mother worried that her family had no good protection against the little beasties. Mari thought it was a lot of fuss about nothing. So what if a little manling came to steal their pies from the windows, or to drink the cat's milk? She wouldn't mind seeing one, if the truth were to be told.

And so it was that she found herself at the edge of the Haven Woods, where her family farm ended. There was a large stand of ash trees there, so it seemed as good a place as any to start looking. She wanted to find the ward quickly and get back to the house. If such a ward were truly lucky, perhaps it would help her get her new dress.

She worked her way along the edge of the trees, examining the leaves that still hung on and rattled on the trees first, watching as they fell to the earth. Then, pulling back her tresses, she bent to eye each one on the ground. She carefully toed them apart and looked at them critically. She stepped delicately, not wanting to finally find her ward and realize she had crushed it with her foot all at the same time.

An hour passed, perhaps more, and she began to grow frustrated. Her smile had faded and turned into a furrowed frown. Her hands were still in her hair as she examined the fallen leaves, but now they were tightly balled fists. *This was a fool's errand*, she thought. Slowly, as the second hour was wasted away, she came to believe her mother had sent her here to spend her birthday alone on a hilltop. All to save a few pennies. They could have simply bought one of Old Tad's wards down at the Riverton docks. It was ever so with parents: they appreciated their coins more than their offspring! Toeing leaves with increasing disdain, she had taken to kicking them up into fluttering puffs.

It was after one such kick that she thought to hear something. She looked up from her search, blinking. Was that the sound of distant pipes? Had some of the boys from the festival come out to play upon the commons again? She thought of the well-dressed Drake boys with their fine cloaks. She also thought of the strapping, if simply dressed, Rabing boys. Both of these mental images met with her approval. She smiled, listening to the music, which slowly grew in intensity and volume.

She looked around at the trees that surrounded her, and realized she had stepped inside the grove of ash trees at some point in her search. Her father's field was only a dozen yards away. A fine spring crop of grain stood ready for harvest outside in the sunlight. Each stalk waved in the breeze. All together, the stalks resembled a thousand cat tails, moving in unison.

She frowned and blinked, eyeing them. *Could it be?* She thought that the grain moved with the music she was hearing.

She watched for a moment to be certain, and soon she was. Could the music just be the sound of the wind? Had some clever soul built a pipe that played as the very wind itself blew through it?

Intrigued, she took two steps toward her family's field of grain. Then she heard a voice begin to sing behind her.

It was a fine voice, a voice that was pure and clear and which uplifted slowly, more beautifully than any birdsong. The words of the song were unknown to her, but the voice was more lovely than any human throat she had ever heard, or that any human in history could have produced. Entranced, she turned around slowly.

A smiling boy stood under the ash trees. His skin was pale, and it seemed to glow, just a trifle. He was about her height, and somehow looked both her elder and her junior at the same time. He had a black shock of unruly hair on his head. Around his shoulders a cloak fluttered, having caught the same breeze that waved the grain and made the music. She could see his teeth inside his smile, and each of them was white, square, and perfect.

The sight of him awoke something in her. She felt a rush of heat from her midsection that spread out like an explosion to her limbs and finally her head. She took a deep breath, partly closing her eyes. A heady scent of flowers overwhelmed her. Such freshness! Such fine scents! As a farm girl, she rarely had known fragrances that were kind to the nose. Her hand came up and touched her own throat.

She forced her eyes to open again. She feared that the boy in the cloak would have vanished, but he had not. Some part of her knew what he was. It was clearly an elf. She had been told all the tales of such beings. But it was a very different thing, listening at the knee of oldsters telling warning tales versus being right there in an elf's glorious, intoxicating presence.

She need not have worried about the elf vanishing. In fact, he was closer now. He never took a step forward while she watched, preferring to move when her eyes were shut.

"Who are you?" she managed to gasp.

He smiled more broadly. "I'm an old friend of the family," he said.

166

She frowned, very slightly. Really, it was only a twitch of her brow. She closed her eyes to concentrate, knowing that when she opened them he would be closer still. "Tell me your name, elf," she said. She recalled, vaguely now, that knowing the true name of one of the Fair Folk gave you a certain power over them.

The elf chuckled. She opened her eyes again and discovered that he was not only closer, but was off to her left now. He had circled her. She turned to face him again.

"I will tell you my true name," said the elf, gazing into her eyes, "but first, you must do something for me. You must dance with me while I play my pipes. It has been so long since I've danced with a true maiden."

"Dance?" she asked, feeling almost sleepy.

"Yes, girl...dance with me," he said in a husky whisper, and then he began to play his pipes.

The music was unlike any she had ever known. Far more powerful than the musical winds she'd heard before, the music erased thoughts from her mind. The very sound of it overwhelmed her senses. She was powerless, swept up in it. She began to move, in random steps and jerks at first, but soon, as the musical tempo increased, she found herself twirling and performing leaps she'd never seen another human manage.

The elf chuckled and praised her. He played and he played and he danced with her, matching her wild movements easily. As they danced, the light grew more dim, and her breath grew heavier. She caught sight of her family grain fields, and they were distant now as she and the elf had danced further into the woods.

Then he touched her, as they danced. Just a tiny contact to her wrist, or her flying foot as she kicked, or a grasping caress of her hair as it flew freely. Each contact sent a jolt of desire sweeping through Mari. Never in her life had she felt such sensations, and each time he touched her, she danced harder.

She knew, in some small part of her mind, that she was lost. This was how it happened, she knew. But she had never understood until now how a person could let themselves become bewitched. Always she had told her siblings that the person in the story was a fool, a weakling, one that could never be like *her*.

And so it was, as she danced, that they came under a huge ash tree. A thousand leaves carpeted the ground beneath it, and a thousand more hung to flutter overhead from its twisted branches.

She spun, then spun again, caught up in the dance. She was tired now, more tired than perhaps she'd ever been in her life, but she continued dancing. Nothing else was possible.

Then, by chance or design, she saw it. A single leaf hung apart from all the others on that greatest father of old ash trees. The leaf hung from the last twig on the longest, lowest branch of all.

It was a leaf with two points.

Thinking not of the elf at all, but of her mother—and her birthday—she reached out from her wild gyrations and snatched the leaf from the twig. It hung on for a desperate moment, making the twig dip as she tugged. If the leaf tore, it would be of no use, but that didn't matter to Mari in her dream-like state of mind. She only wanted it to complete her quest. With it, that calico dress down in Riverton might yet be hers. That thought was still so strong in her mind that it won through the enchantment, and allowed her to take this single, snatching action.

The leaf came free, and the music died in her ears. She fell to her knees, holding the leaf in her hands.

The elf stood before her. Even *his* sides heaved slightly. He was far from winded, but she was strong for a simple River girl, having danced for longer than most.

He reached out gently and touched her chin with his delicate hand. "Are you finished so soon, my dear? Are you ready for me now?"

She looked up at him, barely comprehending his words. She struggled not to pass out upon the moldering bed of leaves. Taking huge, gulping breaths, she slowly met his eyes, and then lifted the leafy ward up to him.

He took in a great breath when he saw it. He did not exactly hiss. Rather, it was the opposite of that sort of sound—it was the sucking *in* of air, rather than the heavy expelling of it.

168

"Where did you manage...?" he asked in exasperation.

"I want to know your name," she said, still gulping in air as might a man who had been freshly drowned and reawakened. "We have danced. Now tell me your true name as was our bargain."

The elf reached with his hands to take up two bunches of his black hair. He pulled at it, and after his hands came away, his hair stayed up in two drooping spikes.

And so it was that the elf told her his true name. The girl shuddered to hear it, for although it wasn't a name she had heard before, such as Oberon, it was still a powerful name. Their bargain complete, the girl regained her feet and walked back to her mother's house, where marmaladed pumpkin bread awaited her for her birthday supper.

Behind her, standing at the edge of the grove of trees, the elf watched her go. In an act of sheer spite, he lifted a single long finger and let its tip grow black and oily. With that finger, he reached out and touched the crop of grain.

Every stalk in the field darkened, curled, and grew noisome.

Chapter Four
False Wards

Old man Tad Silure was the head of the least reputable clan in all the River Haven. His clan had no proud homestead. Rather than impressive structures, his folk were known for ramshackle cabins that perched along the riverfront on rickety stilts. They fished by hanging nets down into the flood of the Berrywine, as there was no easier way to put food on their table. Most of their time was spent, however, smoking pipeweed in cheap clay pipes and sipping corn whiskey from rarely corked jugs.

Old Tad had another business on the side: he sold wards against the Faerie. It was easy work, but it only provided him enough coin to purchase a new jug of whiskey every week or so. The one exception to this was the time directly preceding the festival and the annual renewal of the Pact. During that one week, he often outsold the rest of the year put together. Every superstitious farmer, hand-wringing new bride, and general idiot worrier came to him then—concerned the Pact had seen its last gasp—and bought a trinket for protection. He considered them all fools, of course. Dammed fools. But they had coin, and he always managed to smile his snaggled teeth at them when they laid it into his fish-smelling palm.

Business was brisk on the night the Pact ended. In fact, he found he was running low on wards even before the disaster out at the Faerie mound. When he heard the news, he trebled his prices immediately. Wards flew from his shelf, and he multiplied the price by ten. His customers snarled at him then, rather than thanking him, but that didn't bother Old Tad. What did bother him was that he ran out of stock very fast and cursed himself.

He noted the desperation in the eyes of each additional fool that came to his dirty booth, only to be turned away empty-handed. He had sold out much too cheaply. He could have demanded much more. He thought of buying back some of his stock and redistributing it to the most wealthy in town, perhaps even demanding titles to land.

It was too late tonight of course, as everyone was busy barricading their doors in the midnight hour. No one would venture forth until morning, scared as they were of the Faerie. What an opportunity he'd missed! Certainly, he had the cash now to keep his jug full for two winters at least, but that could have been just the beginning. He saw this as a once-in-a-lifetime chance. If he managed to get these folks what they wanted so badly, naturally at a steep price, he could change the status of the Silure clan itself. He could build a clanhouse if he wanted, on prime property. And all those snots who had looked down their long noses at his family could come begging then.

He fumed and smoked as the town shuttered down for the night.

Then an idea struck him. He smashed his fist into his palm. He stood up on his creaking porch and grinned.

He tipped Slet, his worthless grandson, out of his hammock with a rude toss. Slet scrambled up, ready to fight until he saw it was crazy Old Tad.

"The town had better be on fire," Slet growled.

"None of that tone now," said Old Tad. He might have slapped the boy on a different day, but not this night. He needed him. "I've got two silvers for you."

Slet's expression froze. He eyed the coins disbelievingly as Old Tad slid them under his nose. "What for?" he asked warily.

"I want you to go down to the river shore, this very minute. Take the wheelbarrow and gather me a load of flat stones, about the size of good wards."

Slet's eyes flicked to Old Tad's, then to the coins that stared back at him like two flashing eyes.

172

"Can it wait 'til morning? I've got a headache."

Old Tad snatched back his hand and the coins with it. "Oh sure, it can wait. But the coins will be gone by then."

Slet blinked. "Okay then. I'll do it right now.

"That's a good lad."

"But stones like that won't do no good. They've got to be natural worn with a hole for the...."

Slam! Old Tad struck him a hard one, right behind the ear. It wasn't the first time Slet had felt such a blow—life in his clan had delivered many such hard knocks—but he wasn't expecting it and as far as he was concerned, he didn't deserve it.

He got to his feet. "Look, old man—"

But Old Tad cu him off. He stopped the boy's complaints the best and fastest way possible, by sliding out the hand again, this time with five coins on it. Slet's voice halted.

"Two now. Three when you finish. And no questions. No word of this to anyone, not ever. Deal?"

Slet rubbed at his head. He nodded, taking the two coins Old Tad gave him. He said not a word.

"There's a good lad. Be quick now, or maybe I'll decide to dock your final payment."

It took Slet nearly an hour to return, and by that time Old Tad was pacing the creaking boards of his shack with growing impatience. He had already prepared all his tools and counted out every leather cord he had. But there was only so much he could do without having the actual stones in his hands.

When Slet finally rolled up with the load, he sighed in relief, forgetting about his plans to slap him and dock his pay for slowness. Instead, he paid the boy and ordered him out of the place for the night.

Slet didn't argue. The boy put the coins at the bottom of his only pocket that *for certain* had no holes in it, and left.

By morning, Old Tad had drilled and manufactured dozens of new wards. He had, in point of fact, never found a real one. He had never even bothered looking. It was simply too much work. A well-made forgery brought just as much money for a fraction of the effort. When he was found wandering down on the river shoreline, people had always assumed Old Tad was searching for more wards, but in truth he was probably drunk and staggering.

He drilled each hole carefully, as he had done in secret for years. He brushed away the dust from each hole, and made them look worn. Creating them previously had been something of an art form for him. He had long studied the way a naturally worn stone looked and had taught himself to simulate the appearance with a tapping hammer, a file, whetstone, and steel brush.

He knew, of course, the wards would do nothing to stop the Faerie. But they would, he was certain, line his pockets with silver in the morning.

Whistling as he worked, Old Tad labored longer and harder than any time he could remember in his life. He argued with himself cheerfully about what price he would set. Ten silvers? Twenty? He settled on the princely sum of thirty silvers each. After the first dozen wards, he ran out of leather cords. He figured he would drop the price on those by a coin and people could just darned well make their own cords.

When dawn finally broke, he took a deep breath and smiled tiredly. People were already tapping at his shutters.

He spent the day selling his wards at grossly inflated prices. The Pact had been broken, and that might just have been the best thing that had ever happened to him.

Chapter Five
Sam's Funeral

Brand was tired and saddened the morning after the Pact had been broken. In the morning light the remains of Froghollow looked even more dismal than it had after the fire had been put out the night before. Wisps of blue smoke spiraled into the trees and drifted there. The only building of significance that had survived the battle with the rhinogs was the barn, but there was no comfort or shelter to be found there.

The floor of the barn was a thatch of straw mixed with Sam's dried blood.

They were trying to decide how to break the news to their elders when Uncle Tylag, Aunt Suzenna, and Barlo had returned to the house. Corbin had to explain to his tearful parents that during the night their home had been attacked and set ablaze. Before the flames had grown too high, they had gone back into the house and saved what they could, but with the coming of daylight, it looked like a pitiful pile of belongings. Even the painting of Brand's parents had been burnt.

Worst of all, of course, was Sam's death. In the bright, revealing light of morning, Uncle Tylag and Aunt Suzenna began the process of burying their son. The kitchen table, made of stout oaken beams, was badly scorched, but had survived the fire relatively intact. The house had partially collapsed around it. Tylag and the grim-faced Rabing boys cleared a path through the rubble to drag the table free. Setting it in the yard

175

beside the well, they stretched Sam's beheaded body upon it. They set his head in its rightful place, using wads of cloth on either side so that it wouldn't roll off into the dirt.

At first, the men had kept Aunt Suzenna from her son, but she protested strongly. "I'm no shrinking towngirl. I must be allowed to fix my boy properly," she said.

With Telyn's help, she did all the things her mother had taught her. With great care, she bathed the skin and the hair, hid the severed neck with a scarf from her own throat and set coins on each eyelid. To turn away Merlings and worse things, she had Barlo dig up a whole clove of garlic in the ruins of the root cellar. This she placed in her son's dead mouth, which she tied shut with a strip of leather.

Telyn wrapped a river stone ward in the palm of his hand, tying the thong to the dead, white hand. "Lest the Faerie find you," she whispered to the corpse.

For a shroud, they used Sam's woolen cloak, which was just long enough with the hood sewn shut and the hem cinched tight around his ankles. In the afternoon, they began the procession as properly as they could. As they carried Sam down to the cliffs, Brand's face was slick and wet with tears. From behind and around him, he heard a dry sobbing, but he didn't look to see which of his relatives it was.

Gudrin and Modi, silent during the rituals, followed the procession at a discreet distance. Unlike some of the other clans, the Rabing clan traditionally held very private funerals. Outsiders were rarely allowed. The Battleaxe Folk understood this and respected it.

As was also their tradition, each of the clan members present spoke a few words, recalling Sam in life. When it was Brand's turn, he didn't hesitate, but told them all of catching the largest dragonflies he had ever seen with Sam, who knew so well the marshy haunts of such creatures. He described the flittering wings of the blue-greens, the largest—and Sam's favorites. As boys, his cousin had taught him to coax the insects to light upon his finger if he remained very still and held it just so.

Aunt Suzenna's turn came last, as was custom, since she had birthed the boy. Unexpectedly, she turned to the two

Battleaxe Folk. "I would ask that our guests be allowed to speak. With your blessing, of course, Tylag."

Uncle Tylag, blinking back a tear, nodded.

Modi looked about uncomfortably. "I apologize, but I have not the craft, my lady."

She nodded in understanding. She looked expectantly at Gudrin, who stepped forward.

"I will speak from my own experience, as is your custom," she said, for once not consulting her book. "Although I did not know your boy, I am no stranger to grief. I was born and raised in the place known as the Earthlight, a great complex of caverns that exist beneath the blue-white peaks of Snowdon itself. There is no sunlight there. Instead, the lurid red glow of the lava flows illuminate the primary caverns. The Great Eastern Cavern was my home. Each day it is illuminated and warmed by light reflected up from the red depths of the mountain. For thirteen hours each day, the huge metalworks that work to shutter and unshutter the light from the rivers of fire stand fully open. It takes an hour each day to open and close the great vents, thus providing the Kindred an hour long dawn and dusk. The great vents were in the slow act of closing during the time which I'm thinking of.

"Thus it was in the evening dusk of the Earthlight, at the furthest edge of the Eastern Cavern, that I learned of my brother's death. I lived then where the lava-fires were only a crimson flickering in the distance on my Uncle Hakon's mushroom farm. We subsisted there on the frontier, far from the town of Darrowton, on the edge of the eternal dark that bred the eyeless monsters of the underworld. I was raised on that farm, my Uncle's farm, as my parents had perished soon after my birth.

"My older brother Eirik had been my only surviving sibling. He had been killed on the distant surface, which at that time I had never seen." Here she paused, and all could see that she grieved still.

Brand noted that she didn't mention how her brother had died, and wondered if it could have been at the hands of the Faerie, or perhaps the hands of men. Could Gudrin recall the

177

centuries-gone wars between men and the Kindred? How old could Gudrin truly be?

She continued. "My clan members and I trudged in silence, through the mushroom thickets and the rolling jambles of stonefalls from the distant roof of the cavern, to the temple in Darrowton. That evening the service went the long and slow way of such temple services. Each of the golden bells was rung in turn by the initiates. Twelve silver hammers were laid upon their anvils and heated to the point of incandescence by the robed and cowled priest-smiths. I was impressed by the appearance of twelve hammers. From my Uncle's depreciative comments about the expedition that my older brother had gone on, I would have thought Eirik would have rated no more than seven, or perhaps nine hammers, at the most.

"Once the last horn had blown and the last dirge had been played, the empty urn that represented Eirik's lost remains was hoisted up the rocky hillside toward the lava-pits. I and my Uncle carried one side of the pavilion, my Aunt Syla and my eldest cousin lugged the other. Sweating due to the intense heat of the lurid lava chamber ahead, we bore our burden silently. We stopped before a vent that spewed up heated gasses from the depths of the Earth, allowing these hot winds to instantly dry and sear our sweat-beaded brows. Uncle Hakon mumbled a memorized passage from the Teret, and together we all heaved the urn into position, sending it sliding down into the fiery heart of the Earthlight.

"I lingered, despite the intense heat, to watch the urn be consumed in a plume of yellow fire. There was such power there, I could feel it. Then I followed the others back down to the temple. Soon after, tired and sullen, I and my relatives trudged back to the stone farmhouse. We carried lanterns, as the Earthlight vents were now just three glimmering red lines in the distance—and even the eyes of the Kindred need some light to see by."

Here Gudrin paused to hold her hands, palms outward, toward those assembled. "I speak these words to tell you how close the Kindred are to the River Folk. Here, you are about to cast beloved Sam's remains from a cliff into the great flood of the Berrywine, much as I did cast my own brother's remains into the Earthlight. We of the Kindred see the Earth and its depths as our origins and our final resting place, just as the River Folk feel that they belong to the watery depths."

Aunt Suzenna finally spoke then, as it was clear that Gudrin had finished. "Thank you, Gudrin. We agree that the Kindred and the River Folk are closely related peoples. Both of us, may I add, perform this type of service to keep the Faerie from performing mischief with our dead. A month ago, I would not have taken our death rituals as anything but empty gestures. Now I know such rituals are ancient wisdom."

As everyone had finished, Suzenna looked to Tylag, and both nodded with tears in their eyes. It was time to send their son into the water for his final journey. The body, weighted now with stones, was cast into the green-white flood of the Berrywine.

As Gudrin had gazed into the Earthlight countless years earlier, Brand and Corbin lingered on the cliffs. They heard the thunder of the rapids and felt the cold gusts that blew up from the distant river.

Chapter Six
Dando's Trick

As they were the last to leave the cliffs, Brand and Corbin were the only ones to hear the baby's cry. At first, Brand wondered if the family cat had followed them out on the procession. After a moment, though, he recognized the sounds of an infant and his eyes searched the woods. He saw nothing.

"Do you hear it too?" asked Corbin, standing at his side.

Brand's eyes darkened with a new thought. "If this is some new trick of the Faerie, I for one do not plan to cooperate."

Corbin's face twisted. Brand saw an even darker emotion—that of murderous intent—on his cousin's face. After all, it had been the Faerie who had just caused him to send his brother into the floods.

Moving with quite intensity, the two paced apart and moved into the trees in the direction of the sounds. If it was one of the Faerie having a bit of fun, they were talented. They came to a thick towering pine that rustled in the breeze from the cliffs. Each young man circling around the tree in a crouch, they came upon that which they least expected to find—exactly what they heard.

It was an infant, kicking and crying weakly in the dust at the bottom of the tree. The child had few clothes on. They stared down upon it, and felt pity in their hearts.

"Where did you come from?" asked Brand, kneeling beside the child. It looked at him curiously.

180

Corbin did not kneel. Instead, he eyed the woods around them suspiciously.

Brand took off his cloak and wrapped the child in it. Could someone have abandoned it here, hoping that their family would take care of it?

"Maybe you ought not touch it, Brand," said Corbin.

"Why not?"

"Have you thought this through? The Pact is freshly broken. Never before have we found a babe in these woods, but after a very strange night, we find our first today."

Brand looked at him in growing concern. He jumped to his feet. "By the River!" he shouted. "If this is a changeling, I'm shocked by how convincing they can be!"

Corbin snorted. It was his turn to kneel and study the child...if that's what it was.

"They could hardly be successful at their business if they weren't highly convincing," he pointed out reasonably. He leaned forward and spoke to the thing wrapped up in Brand's cloak. "If you are a changeling, know this, foul creature. You will regret this trick for a long while!"

He took up a stick and moved as if to prod the child.

"That will be quite enough!" said Telyn, appearing that instant and surprising Brand and Corbin. She slapped Corbin's wrist and frowned at him. Then she studied the baby closely.

"He looks human enough to me," she said.

"Where did you come from?" Brand asked her.

"Where did you get lost in the woods?" she asked. "That's what I asked myself when I realized that you hadn't followed us for an extended time. I came looking, and it was a good thing. Here I walk up and find Corbin about to poke an infant with a sharp stick."

"We're not sure—" started Corbin.

"Yes, yes, I know, you think it's a changeling. Only, this isn't how they usually operate, is it?"

The child, while they talked about it, took a great interest in Corbin's stick and gripped it, chewing hungrily on the offending point.

"Think about it, Telyn," said Brand, "is it not the perfect plan? Aunt Suzenna has just suffered the loss of her son. How

181

better to gain her trust than to appear here now, in her moment of weakness, as a replacement child?"

At this, a tiny chuckle was heard by all of them. The three looked up, into the branches of the great pine.

Dando stood upon a thick branch over their heads. He leaned nonchalantly against the pine's trunk with one hand. He looked down at their gaping faces…and tsked at them.

"My, I had not thought River Folk were so suspicious. Poking babies with sticks after a single bad night, is it? But I must say, that scheme you laid out boy—capitalizing on a woman's grief—that's genius! I must pass that one on."

They all glared at him. Telyn slipped her bow off her back.

"Have a care, girl!" Dando said, putting a stopping hand out to her. "You all should be thanking me."

"For what, manling?" asked Corbin. "For burning down my house and slaying my brother?"

Dando gave his head a vigorous shake. "I had little to do with either. But this babe, that was indeed my doing."

"So, you admit to stealing a child? Did we thwart your vile plans by coming out to this remote spot?" asked Telyn, nocking an arrow in her bow.

"Hold, hold! Allow a hero to explain himself!"

"A hero!" said Corbin. He snorted, scandalized.

"More a hero than you, babe-prodding lout!"

Brand put up his hands to stop his friends before things got out of control. "Dando, please explain yourself without baiting us further, or things might not go well for you."

Briefly, Dando explained that he had come upon one of his own kind stealing a babe for their own purposes, and who had planned to cast the child into the river at this very spot, with one tiny foot weighted. Telyn gasped in outrage at this, while the boys glowered.

"So you helped out a changeling," said Brand.

"*No*. I *saved* a child from the Berrywine," he said. "Perhaps I misunderstood your kind, but I was under the impression you protect your own young."

"Of course we do," hissed Telyn. Corbin had the child in his arms now and the two of them were trying to quiet it.

Corbin offered it a bit of cheese from his pockets, but the baby only squeezed that to mush and cried harder.

"Why did you return the child to us?" Corbin asked.

"Recall what I once told you, man-child. Friendship must be earned, not given."

"So," said Corbin, ticking off points on his fingers as he spoke, "you steal a child and return it, insult us all profusely, and expect us to be grateful? Are we such moon-calves? Why don't you light my boots on fire and then offer to extinguish the flames? Surely, that would make us close confidants!"

"You do me a disservice, fat one."

"Fat one!" exclaimed Corbin in annoyance.

"Shush," interrupted Brand. "Let him speak,"

"Yes," said Dando huffily. "I want you to know, I have taken no offense at your rude remarks. I, of course, did not steal the infant. I rescued it from where it had been abandoned in the woods."

"I see. And who did steal it then?"

"Why, the changeling who lies even now nestled in its mother's loving arms, of course."

"So, you deny that *you* are a changeling?"

Dando shrugged. "I deny that I can take the form of a human, infant or otherwise. There is another of my kind, a less civilized fellow, who has usurped this child's cradle."

Now that they knew it was a true babe, they began carrying it back toward Froghollow to look for something to feed it. Dando followed them, though prudently staying safely up in the trees.

"No gratitude? None at all?" the Wee One demanded.

"Dando, we are warily grateful," explained Corbin. "But you must understand we don't know your motives yet. Why did you return the child? If it was to gain our trust, then perhaps you simply stole it with this scheme in mind."

"That would indeed be diabolical, but I can prove my good faith."

He went on to explain who the babe was, where he had gotten it, and exactly what they would find in the crib eating the child's lunch.

"Okay, we will investigate," Brand told him. "I can see you are trying hard to earn our friendship. Might I ask why?"

"Because, you and I have great futures ahead of us."

"You and I?" Brand smiled. He found it hard to think that any two creatures had less in common.

"Yes, just so," said Dando seriously. "Right now, neither of us appears to be important to anyone. We are just going through our daily routines in life. We are not notables. But, some know the truth. Like those that burned you out of house and home."

Brand frowned and blinked. He really didn't know what to make of what the manling was saying, but he couldn't deny that someone out there thought he was important—even if those thoughts were malicious.

"And so," Dando continued, beginning to strut back and forth upon a high branch as he spoke, reminding Brand of a proud rooster at dawn, "I think that two individuals like us—two who are rising stars, so to speak—such folk might be in a position to help each other. Such folk may well find common cause."

"Okay," asked Brand, "so why are we so important?"

Dando beamed at them all with a very broad smile. "I believe that will become evident in time." With that, he tipped his hat and bid them farewell. He bounded off into the woods. Just as he was about to vanish from sight, he caused a brilliant blue flash that lit up the forest. Then he was gone.

They walked back to Froghollow. Corbin muttered distrustfully of magical midgets and eyed every branch on every tree as they went. Arriving at the smoking remains of the farm, Aunt Suzenna did indeed make a fuss over the baby. Still, they soon began packing up what they could in the cart, having decided to head to Riverton to return the child and find lodging. There was little left for them at Froghollow, as they couldn't reasonably hope to begin rebuilding until spring.

While the others prepared to leave, Brand wandered off into the forest to rest against the great oak tree that had been cut open by Ambros the Golden the night before. He plucked at the fallen leaves there, deep in thought. He found disturbing truth in Dando's words. It seemed clear to him now that the

Dark Ones wanted to slay him. Why else would they have come here in numbers? Nowhere else in the Haven had they attacked in such force, although his uncle had told them of rumors in town of changelings and fairy rings that had led away young folk. It did seem to him that he had indeed somehow brought a great curse to his clan and to all the River Haven. What had Oberon said? That he was both a great potential ally and enemy at the same time. He couldn't understand how this could be, but that mattered little. If the Dark Ones believed it, then they would keep coming until he was dead—or worse.

Gudrin came out among the trees with him and sat upon an old weathered stump. She took out her bearhead pipe and puffed on it. "Your thoughts are troubled, boy."

Brand nodded. "I think I must leave Stone Island. I can't understand it, but somehow my presence is threatening all the River Haven."

"And why do you think this?"

"The dark bard followed me first. Oberon and Dando both hinted that Herla has some evil purpose for pursuing me. The attack last night was too much. That was far more than sour milk and the like. Tylag says that no attacks of such ferocity have occurred anywhere else on the island yet. What if the Wild Hunt had arrived? Would we all have perished, impaled on their boarspears?"

"Where will you go?"

"I don't know," said Brand, but even as he said it, he was struck with a thought. "No, I *do* know. I will accompany you to find Myrrdin and beg him to help reinstate the Pact. That is, if you and Modi will have me."

Gudrin took a moment to tap out her pipe and refill it. She relit it and took a puff. Blue smoke wound up like a transparent snake into the sky. "We'd be honored to have you, but what of your family and friends?"

"I will go alone," said Brand determinedly. "It was me that Voynod came after each time he appeared. Oberon has indirectly confirmed this. I'm the source of the trouble, while my friends are blameless. I wouldn't want to lead them into danger—that is the whole reason I'm leaving."

185

Gudrin nodded sagely. "Don't you think you should ask them about that, though?"

Brand frowned, then heard a twig snap behind him. He turned and saw that Corbin was perhaps a score of yards away, listening and trying to sneak closer. He was about to yell at him for eavesdropping when he felt a tap at his shoulder; Telyn was there. She had been hiding behind the oak's trunk.

"How long have you been there?" he asked in exasperation.

She laughed. In spite of his displeasure, he had to grin a bit at her. It was good to see her laugh.

"If Corbin hadn't come crashing nearer, you might have written your will right here and caused me to burst out laughing."

Brand made a half-hearted grab for her, but she danced away.

Brand looked to Gudrin, and her eyes were shining with amusement. "I feel like a fool," he said, sitting back down. "But I must do it, I must leave the island. And I won't be going back to Rabing Isle, either."

"Then you will take us along," said Corbin, having taken the moment Brand was talking with Telyn to come forward and join them. "We are all in this together, Brand. It was *my* brother who was killed."

"But *I* am the source of the trouble. Why follow the source? Why not stay home and be safe with your families?" argued Brand. "Telyn, you could answer the muster. Corbin, your family needs you to help rebuild Froghollow. If you follow me, you are placing in danger two of the people that I most want to protect by leaving!"

"I believe it's true that the dark ones last night were out to destroy clan Rabing, and have come primarily for Brand," said Gudrin, and all their eyes swung to her. "But this will not be the case for long. The Pact is broken, and the old dark times of the past have returned. It will not take long for the ancient ones to recall their ancient ways. Changelings will again appear in cradles. Crops and livestock will again be hexed, the fairy rings will abduct the young and the trusting. Worse things, too—such as the Shining Lady and the Wild Hunt—will come."

"But why me?" asked Brand in exasperation.

"I'm not sure on this point. I do know that Myrrdin has always thought very highly of your clan. I know too, that among his captains of old, some of his greatest champions were known by the name Rabing."

"You mean our ancestors were important?" asked Corbin.

"Of course," said Gudrin. "Did you not all hear my tale? You are all descendants of Myrrdin's original army. Clearly, the Enemy recalls the name Rabing from those days."

"So my clan is being pursued for something heroic done by our forbearers? Something which we can't even remember?"

Gudrin nodded. "Recall that for Herla, each year is as a day, until the bloodhound alights and frees him of his curse. The point is that Brand's leaving will not return the River Haven to peace. The only thing that will bring peace will be the recovery of the Pact. Or the forging of a new one. Leaving may, however, distract the Dark Ones that are charged with hunting him.."

"So we should all go, to help you find Myrrdin," said Corbin. "Too bad Jak is injured. We could use his hand on the skiff's tiller."

"Someone must manage Rabing Isle," said Brand. He stood and faced them all. For the first time he noticed that Modi was there too, off among the trees, listening to their talk. It seemed that everyone was in on this. "Okay, I know when I'm beaten. If I were to try to go alone, you would find some way to stow away or follow in another boat—I know you too well. But I say this! We must all have Tylag's blessing, for he is the leader of clan Rabing and he may have need of us."

They all agreed to this and went to consult with Tylag. Brand's uncle was distraught by the loss of his son and his home, but he listened to them seriously. Barlo snorted once in disbelief as they told their tale, but his father silenced him with a scowl.

"So you have decided to leave in search of Myrrdin. I see that I have lost a son, and now must risk another." Their hopes seemed dashed, when Tylag asked "Where will you go?"

At this, they were at a loss. Gudrin stepped forward. "I think we will follow the river north into the Deepwood and on toward Snowdon. Last I heard. he was in that region."

"It seems an opportune moment to say that we, the Riverton Council, finally received word from Myrrdin last night," said Tylag. "News of my son's death had driven the thought from my head until now."

"Myrrdin lives?" said Brand. "This is good news indeed."

"Where is he?" demanded Gudrin.

"A messenger came from the village of North End. Myrrdin wandered out of the High Marshes two nights ago, on the eve of the Harvest Moon, in fact. He had been waylaid, lost his horse, and was on foot. He had not eaten or slept in weeks, but still attempted to gain passage to Riverton. He did intend to reach Stone Island and perform the ceremony, but he was too late. The village hetman convinced him that he would not arrive until the day after the ceremony. Once he realized the truth, the messenger says he collapsed in their arms and had to be borne away to rest."

"Is he injured?" asked Brand.

Tylag shook his head. "We don't know."

"We must go and consult with him," said Gudrin. "We must leave before dark tonight."

"I give my blessing to your journey. The River Haven would be better served by learning all there is to be learned from Myrrdin than by a few extra bowmen in the militia," said Tylag. "May the River guide your boat."

Brand had one more person to consult: Jak. He went to the wagon, where Jak had been stretched out in the shade. He was still far too injured to help them.

"Hello, Jak," said Brand, feeling like a runaway, a deserter. Jak needed him to keep up Rabing Isle, now more than ever.

Jak's eyes opened. "Hello, brother. I feel useless, today of all days."

Brand knew no easy way, so he simply blurted out his words. "I'm leaving with the Battleaxe Folk to find Myrrdin."

Jak nodded. "Go then. I only wish I were well enough to go with you."

"But the Isle, Jak—what will you do?" Brand asked.

"It doesn't matter. You must try to heal the rift, to mend the Pact. There is no more worthy quest."

Thus it was decided, and they worked the rest of the day to make their preparations. It seemed to Brand that all the world was soot and ashes and twists of blue smoke. He felt sad and guilty to be leaving his clansmen in such a time of dire need, but in his heart he knew he could better serve them on this mission. In the afternoon they set out on the road to Riverton. There were many hugs, handshakes, and tears. Not an eye was dry, with the exception of Modi's, who only appeared anxious to get moving.

Chapter Seven
Twrog's Tree

After losing his club, Twrog was despondent. At the moment, it had seemed like a fine idea to throw it. He did not regret killing the farmer, nor the stinging arrows the River Folk had left in his hide—but he came to regret the loss of his lucky club.

As always when he felt poorly, his thoughts turned to a special, secret spot in the Deepwood only he knew about. This spot was open to the sky, yet surrounded by overgrown thickets of thorny plants. Not even deer liked to enter the region for fear of being pierced by the stabbing needles that every twisted vine seemed to produce. It was a private place for Twrog, a spot where he could gather his thoughts and think at his own pace. Almost on instinct, he set out for the secret glade. He had not been there in many seasons.

As Twrog strode through the woods, he thought he heard the subtle sounds of pursuit. He glanced back over his shoulder. Something or someone did indeed follow him. Probably, the smell of pig's blood had attracted a scavenge, as he still carried three of the pigs he had stolen from the farmer's pens. He increased his pace through the trees, no longer ambling, but now striding with purpose. His pursuer kept up with him.

Twrog was not frightened. Rather, he was cunning. He wanted to know the nature of the thing that dared shadow him.

By speeding up and discovering the pursuit continued, he knew the other was at the very least persistent.

After night had fallen, Twrog found a spot strewn with stones and a fallen tree. He halted his march and decided to cook one of the pigs. The odor of seared pig often drove animals mad. With luck, if it was a bear or a dire wolf, the creature would attack and that would be the end of it.

He labored for minutes with flint and tinder, finally managing to spark a cookfire. This being a large pig, he required a spit of hardwood. He chopped loose a branch of beech with a knife the size of a short sword and whittled the point until it was as sharp as a lance. Poking the pig through end-to-end, he hung it over the fire and turned it now and then. He built the fire up higher, then went to gather more wood. Frequently, he flicked his eyes back to the sizzling pig. The smoke and fine smells filled the forest with aromatic clouds. The unguarded pig still remained upon its spit however, unmolested.

Twrog returned to his camp with an armload of wood and stoked the fire into a fine blaze. He nodded and muttered to himself. Whatever his stalker was—it was a patient creature. Most likely, it was not a beast. Few could have suffered this long in the presence of fresh meat without having revealed themselves.

After an hour or so of cooking, Twrog ripped loose a meaty haunch. Juices flowed from the rest of the beast into the fire. The fat made the flames sizzle, flare and pop. He opened his mouth, but paused, not eating just yet. Instead, he turned his head this way and that, and held the haunch high overhead.

"I call to thee," he said carefully. "I give thee leave to share my fire, whatever ye may be."

Nothing happened. He set about eating the haunch noisily. He did not know if his invitation had been heard and understood, but he listened closely while not seeming to. At last, as he finished the first haunch and reached for the second, a stealthy rustling met his ears.

Twrog shifted his flapping ears toward the trees behind him. He glanced back to see what it was that approached. There was a faint glimmer. Could it be one of the Fae? he wondered. He knew a short moment of concern. If he had invited an elf or one of the shining Dead….

But no. The shine of it, reflecting the unseen moonlight that bathed the leaves overhead, proved it was one of the Fae. Seeing the rest of the creature made Twrog snort in amusement. There was nothing to fear from this one. It was no great lord that had stalked him. The creature that emerged was small, with cat-like features and smooth, green skin. It was a lone goblin.

Twrog shook his head bemusedly. He had never sat at camp with a goblin. Had he known…but he had not, and the invitation had been issued and accepted. There was nothing for it. By the rules of honor which almost all creatures in Cymru adhered to, he was bound to tolerate its presence.

The goblin slunk forward, ears twitching. It nosed the air and flicked its eyes everywhere, suspecting duplicity. Twrog continued eating and chuckled to himself. He could not believe his foolishness at having invited a goblin to dine with him.

"Name?" asked Twrog.

The goblin hesitated. No doubt, it considered a dozen lies. "Frakir," it said at last. The eyes flickered uncomfortably.

"Twrog," Twrog said.

When the other came at last to rest on the opposite side of the fire, the giant handed a foreleg to his guest.

"Here," Twrog said. When Frakir did not reach for it quickly enough, Twrog grunted and shook it at him. Hot grease splattered his hand and the goblin's face. Finally, the frightened, scowling goblin took the meat and sniffed it suspiciously, as if he believed it might be laden with poison.

Twrog snorted again. "Meat good! Not even have salt on it, fool goblin!"

"I have your word it is good?" asked Frakir in a sibilant voice.

"You speak to Twrog? Good. Boring guest is one that can't make speech with me."

The goblin's eyes narrowed. "The meat is good?" he asked again.

"Yeah, yeah!" roared Twrog in sudden irritation. "No more ask that! I will eat it myself, if you don't!"

Frakir's ears folded down, and he took the offered foreleg in both hands and ripped into it with the sharp, rippled teeth of his kind. They were teeth clearly made to eat meat and nothing else.

For a time, the two beings ate hot pig meat. Finally, however, after the second haunch, Twrog threw the bone down into the fire. Sparks loomed, coals and ash blew up as if thrown. The goblin hopped to its feet and crouched warily.

"Not the same!" shouted the giant.

Frakir cocked his head wonderingly.

Twrog pointed to the half-eaten carcass that was now white with showers of ash. "Taste! Not the same taste! Is not fair. The River Folk tricked Twrog."

The goblin's tongue snaked out and whipped back into his mouth. He eyed the rest of the pig.

Twrog made a wild, sweeping gesture with both hands. "Eat more! Is garbage!" he roared. Then he stood up and walked away. Internally, he raged. The taste was good, but it was *not* the taste of a ham hock. Somehow, the humans had misled him. They were tricky, and they hid their best meats. They kept them from Twrog. He would make them pay for their cruel deceptions.

The giant left the goblin, the pig and the fire behind and made his way into the forest. He was tired, it was late, and he really should find a spot to sleep in. But he did not. He wanted to see the tree in the glade more than ever. He had gotten his lucky club there. It had grown upon the hugest oak he'd ever found. There, in the center of that strange glade, the lone tree was a huge oak and the club had been ripped free by Twrog after an hour's work, sweating and heaving to pry it loose.

The journey took nearly until dawn. He was tired and grumpy by the time he reached the spot, but also exultant. He knew the place well, and always when he came here it filled him with memories of his youth. He'd played here by himself among these same silent trees two centuries ago. In particular, he'd played upon the great oak.

At last he found it. The thicket surrounding it was, if anything, more profuse and tangled than he remembered. He circled around twice before finding the secret entrance: a tunnel in the greenery which allowed entry without a thousand spiny stings. He slipped through and after suffering no more than a dozen pokes and scratches, he reached the center of the glade.

Inside the ring of thickets was an open area where a great tree grew. A massive oak loomed high overhead, the dark, dead branches clawing at the sky. So large was the oak that it dwarfed even Twrog. The tree itself had been broken, the top half having long ago been torn away. Like a broken black tower, the trunk stood alone in the glade. The giant rested his back comfortably against it and settled amongst the black, snake-like roots.

His earliest memories were of this place. He had been born here, as far as he could determine. For the giant, this secret retreat was home.

He dozed until dawn, when one eye snapped awake. His ears twitched. Could it be? Did he hear a rustling nearby? He turned his head a fraction and stared into the thickets. A stealthy shape moved there. It was hard to tell one goblin from the next, but Twrog felt sure it was Frakir. Each step he took was performed with exaggerated care. Like a tiny, stalking predator, the goblin circled the glade at the edge of the thicket.

Twrog let his head roll back. He appeared to be dozing, or uncaring. Every minute or so, though, he let an eye open to a slit to check on the goblin's progress.

When the goblin had made a half-circuit around the glade, and was thus as far from the entrance as it was possible to be, Twrog jumped up and trotted to block the only exit. He looked back around, eyes wide, lips flaring.

But the glade was empty. Could the creature have escaped him? He peered in the growing sunlight.

"Come forth, Frakir," he boomed.

Nothing occurred for a full minute. A second minute passed, and then Twrog thought to see movement. There, behind the trunk of the huge oak, a single ear and a single matching slitted eye peeped around to look at him.

"Come out," the giant said.

"I call upon your honor," said the goblin. "I am your guest."

Twrog snorted. "You a spy!"

"You have offered me sanctuary."

"Fire and pig. Nothing more."

"Do not dishonor yourself in this fashion, Twrog," the goblin said, tsking and tutting. "I grieve for your kind. I hope none of them ever learn of this travesty."

Twrog's eyes narrowed. He did not know what a travesty was, but he was sure he didn't like the goblin's tone. "No my dishonor. *You* dishonor."

Frakir revealed his full head now, but kept his body behind the tree trunk. "How so? You offered me friendship, Twrog. You brought me here to this strange spot. How can I be blamed for—"

"QUIET!" roared Twrog. Such was the power and volume of his shout that a nearby flock of ravens took flight, squawking their way up into the sky. "Twrog called to fire. Not here. This *my* place."

Frakir had retreated fully behind the oak when the giant boomed. His voice came from the other side of the tree as he spoke now. "I apologize, dear Twrog. I was wrong to come here. I misunderstood the nature of your invitation. I hope you will accept my apologies."

Twrog nodded slowly after thinking it over. "Yes," he said. He stepped away from the exit.

Frakir peeped out again. Seeing Twrog no longer blocked his way, he came out from behind the tree and stepped forward. He walked confidently toward the hole in the vines where the thorns were thinnest. Twrog watched him and waited.

When the goblin came near and tried to pass by, flipping the giant an easy salute, Twrog's big hand flashed out with surprising speed, catching Frakir was, who squawked in surprise.

"What is the meaning of this?" the goblin demanded.

"It means you die," said Twrog calmly.

"Old Hob will hear of this! You will be named a goblin enemy for all time!"

"No," said Twrog, shaking his great head. "You came to spy on Twrog. Old Hob must never hear of this place. That is why you die."

Twrog felt Frakir's stringy body struggle and writhe in his hand. The creature bit him. Bright blood flowed as those triangular sharks' teeth made a rippled pattern in the giant's leathery palm.

"Rawrg!" roared Twrog, but he did not let go. Instead, he squeezed. The goblin's ribs snapped, but he did not stop struggling. He did not stop biting, either. In the end, Twrog pulled Frakir's head from his body. It popped loose and took part of the spine with it. The strings, cords, and gushing blood warmed the giant's wounded hand.

Twrog threw the head into the thicket, where it bounced and rolled a hundred paces or more. He threw the tiny green body after the head, then went to look for something to clean himself with.

Chapter Eight
Exorcism

For Brand, the trip to Riverton was strange. People met them on the road, but shouted no greeting. Most of them hurried by, with many fearful glances. When Riverton was in sight, they met the elderly Fiona Thunderfoot, out from Hamlet. Most of the Thunderfoot clan had made their home in the Haven Wood on the east bank, but a goodly portion of them had settled in Hamlet on the west bank, her poor, missing son Arlon among them. Fiona had doubtless come to see the festival. She wore the dark cloak of mourning, her face hooded. She wore a mourning ring—a hoop of gold that expanded at the shoulders where there was a hinged bezel with the designs of her clan in black enamel. The hoop was inscribed: *In memory of beloved Arlon.* The bezel would contain, they knew, a picture of her son. Arlon had been presumed dead. Tylag, who had come with the party to see them off at the docks, attempted to express his sympathies, but she would have none of him, turning away and then giving them all a venomous glare over her shoulder. She stood at the side of the road as they passed, her back to them, her body trembling as she wept in grief.

"Isn't that poor Arlon's mother?" asked Telyn as they passed out of her hearing. "It seems that she blames us for her son's disappearance."

"She is distraught over her loss," said Tylag.

"Everyone seems to be blaming us for everything," observed Corbin in a grim voice.

"It will pass," said Tylag, although Brand thought he heard worry in his voice.

In Riverton they drove down the cobbled main street and passed by Drake Manor. Brand was stunned to see that the hinges of the old iron gate had been oiled and worked so that they now were closed and locked. This was the first time in any of their memories that such a thing had been done. Further, two guards had been posted, wearing the powder blue cloaks of the Riverton Constabulary. They came to attention as Tylag stopped in front of the gates, and he acknowledged this with a nod.

Tylag, Brand, and Telyn took the baby up to Drake Manor—Telyn insisting on carrying the baby herself. She pointedly stated that she didn't trust Brand to carry the boy, and wanted Corbin nowhere near him. She still seemed ruffled about the stick-prodding, even though the men took pains to point out that they had never *actually* poked the child.

Tylag knocked once, and reached to knock again, but found the door had popped open. Thilfox Drake poked out his head with eyebrows riding high. He ran his eyes over Brand and Telyn, standing together with a baby in the girl's arms. His eyebrows, although Brand might have sworn it was not possible, raised even higher. He cleared his throat and looked at Tylag.

"My good sir," he said. "I've heard the news. Let me offer my condolences to you and Suzenna."

"Yes, we sent our son Sam out into the flood this afternoon."

"A terrible thing. And the news about Froghollow is almost as horrible. I'm wondering if you would be needing lodging?"

"Ah," said Tylag, "we planned to stay at the Inn for a bit, or with our cousins out south of the commons. We can't really rebuild until the winter has passed."

Thilfox shook his head, claiming he would hear nothing of it. "Nonsense—you'll stay with us. Half of this place is empty, you know," he said, waving at the rambling manor. Four stories of it stretched behind him, enough room for twenty families.

"That's very generous of you," said Tylag, although he was having some difficulty accepting charity, even though he needed it. Brand knew the offer must sting his pride.

"Again, nonsense," Thilfox said. "We've got work to do, desperate work for the defense of the River Haven. Nightly meetings on the topic, that's what I'm planning. We'll not be sitting about sipping sherry and smoking pipeweed all winter, I'm afraid."

Tylag nodded. "I suppose we need a headquarters, and your place is the obvious choice since we lack a keep."

"A keep," said Thilfox wistfully. "I never thought I'd see the day when we wished we had one. Come inside, there's a chill wind blowing upriver."

They followed him into one of the private parlors on the second floor. A cherrywood fire burned merrily on the hearth, and Brand felt the welcome warmth of it sinking into his bones immediately.

Thilfox bent toward them after he'd slid the door shut and spoke in a hushed voice. "I see that you have another problem at hand," he said, flicking his eyes to Brand, Telyn, and the baby. He smiled a flickering, knowing smile.

Tylag frowned. "Um, yes and no. We do have a delicate matter to discuss."

"Indeed!" laughed Thilfox.

Tylag looked annoyed, and Brand realized that he might well get insulted and angry at any moment...although he wasn't sure why. Then it dawned him: Thilfox was suggesting the child was an illegitimate surprise to the Rabing family! He didn't want his uncle to throw a fit and get himself kicked out of the manor with winter about to set in, so he jumped into the conversation.

"Uncle," said Brand, "don't you think you should check on Aunt Suzenna? She probably should be told the welcome news."

"What news?" barked Tylag. Thilfox frowned at him, not quite understanding his mood.

"About your plans to stay here at the manor for the winter. She's probably at the Inn with Corbin arranging long-term lodging now."

Tylag's mouth opened, then snapped shut. "Good thinking, Brand," he said. He summoned up what graciousness he had left and thanked Thilfox. He leaned close to Brand, saying, "You can give him the good news yourself then."

Brand nodded and Tylag let himself out.

"Is the good news what I assume it to be?" asked Thilfox, looking bemused. He pointed with his chin to the child in Telyn's arms.

"Um, in a manner of speaking, yes, but it's not what you might imagine," said Telyn.

Thilfox threw up his hands. "Nonsense, girl. I've had a number of children myself, you know! I'm no stranger to the process. And there is no need for any shamed faces here. Not in my house, and especially not on this year. What we need now are more young, strong mouths to feed."

They tried to break in, but he wasn't listening. Telyn had turned bright red, and Brand felt his own face heat up as well. He stole a glance at Telyn and hoped she wouldn't blow up at Thilfox— after all, he meant well.

"Now, let me think," said Thilfox, rubbing his chin in thought. "You two will of course be needing your own apartments. It will have to be the fourth floor, I'm afraid."

"Clanmaster Drake," said Brand, trying to interrupt.

"Now, you two *are* married, right?" he asked, and he knew the answer from their surprised, embarrassed faces. "I see. Not even a moonlight ceremony out on the mound? Well, that won't do. I'll perform the ceremony myself tonight. We must at least keep that level of decorum, don't you think?"

"Clanmaster Drake, please listen," demanded Telyn. She held the child out to him. "This child isn't ours. It's *yours*. It's your grandson."

Thilfox's face registered shock. He blinked at the child, then squinted. "I do believe you're right. That's Lanet's boy. However—"

200

"He was stolen," explained Brand, thinking it best to leave Dando out of it for now. "We found him in the woods. There's a changeling in his place."

Sick understanding and revulsion came over Thilfox's face. "I see it all now. I've been the fool. The delicate situation was *our* situation."

"Lanet must be told," Telyn said firmly.

"Of course. We can't let that thing spin enchantments for one more second. I really hadn't thought they would come so quickly. I should have more wards out."

As they followed him up the stairs, they saw Thilfox Drake strap a dagger onto his belt and loosen it in its sheath. Brand and Telyn exchanged worried glances.

By the time Thilfox arrived outside Lanet's apartment, he looked resolute. He was scowling. They could hear Lanet inside, singing softly to what she no doubt believed was her beloved baby.

"How do we handle this?" Telyn wondered aloud in the hallway.

Thilfox glowered and shrugged. "She'll be so heart-broken. She'll be under the thing's spell. But what must be done shall be done."

He rapped smartly on the door. After a moment, Lanet answered. They were all relieved to see she didn't carry the changeling in her arms.

"Lanet, could you come out into the hallway for a moment?" asked Thilfox calmly.

"What is it? I don't like to leave—"

"Of course not, we'll only be a moment."

Brand glanced into the apartment. Near the window, he saw what must be the cradle. As the door swung shut, he thought to see a tiny face, looking at them with one eye overtop the blankets.

"Telyn, if you please," said Thilfox, gesturing.

Telyn held out the child for his mother to see.

"Who...?" asked Lanet, pausing with her hands up before her. "What is that?"

"I want you to look at this child closely. Who is it, my dear?"

201

"Father," she said, almost as if in a dream. "It's a baby."

"*Whose* baby?"

She peered at the child, coming close. She blinked and after a moment her face broke into a smile. "Why, he's my baby."

"That's right," said Thilfox. He nodded to Telyn, who handed the baby over to its mother.

"He's hungry," said Telyn. "let's take him downstairs for a moment."

She led Lanet down the stairs with her child. She walked slowly still, as if she had just awakened.

Thilfox turned to Brand, and his face was grim. "Quickly now, let's do what must be done before she gets wise."

They entered the apartment and let the door click shut behind them. Brand eyed Thilfox worriedly. Would he really be able to thrust that dagger into something that so resembled his own beloved grandson? He hoped that he would never be faced with such a task.

Thilfox slid the window shut, then stood over the crib with his hands on hips. He frowned down into the crib.

The baby inside was the twin of the other. Brand shook his head. The only difference he could detect was the eyes. Their nature was too knowing, too wise for an infant. But the changeling did put on a great show, kicking its feet and cooing at the old man.

"You'll not find our folk so easy to fool as all that, manling," said Thilfox in a quiet, threatening voice.

The changeling eyed him and the dagger which had now appeared in his hand. In an instant, it's manner changed drastically. It sucked in a great gout of air and bellowed with wild cries and screams. Outside on the landing, they heard running footsteps. Lanet was at the door. She rattled the knob, but of course Thilfox had locked it.

"Please father, don't hurt him."

"Go downstairs, daughter," he said in a commanding voice.

Brand heard Telyn talking to Lanet, but she wouldn't be consoled. She pounded on the door again.

"You must be skilled, to so convince my daughter so quickly," said Thilfox.

"Sir," said Brand at his shoulder. "Should we prep an egg? Don't we need to perform an exorcism?"

Thilfox smiled grimly and shook his head. He slapped his dagger into his palm. "There is no need. We have the child back."

At this news, the changeling waited no longer. It sprang out of the cradle and raced around the room. Thilfox slashed the air behind the creature, still in the guise of his grandson, as it flew about the place in great leaps and hops.

Brand made a grab for it, but it ducked and slipped under him. In a moment, it had found the second window, which they had not thought to secure. It flew out into the courtyard. They leaned out after it, and watched it bound by the befuddled guardsman. He'd never seen a naked baby, especially not one performing ten foot leaps, and it cleared the outer wall and disappeared into the forest.

"We lost it," said Brand, "I'm sorry about that, sir."

"You have nothing to be sorry about. I dithered, rather than striking at once. I suppose I just wanted to be sure. I am in your debt, Brand Rabing."

Brand nodded, not knowing what else to say.

At the door, Lanet finally made her way in. She held her real child, but still felt the hurt of losing the other. Tears ran down her face.

"You were bewitched, my daughter," said Thilfox gently, "but we've chased the faker out. We must be more careful."

"But I had wards," said Lanet. Telyn inspected her wards. There was indeed a flat river rock on a fresh thong in the child's cradle. She looked at it closely.

"This hole," she said, "it's been drilled. Where did you get it?"

"I don't know...my husband bought it for me before he went away."

Telyn and Brand exchanged glances. Both knew there was only one man who sold wards in Riverton.

Chapter Nine
The Riot

They spent a relatively peaceful night at Drake Manor. The beds were warm and the sheets clean. There seemed to be no end to the fresh food. In the morning, however, they heard that many bad events had occurred over the evening across the Haven.

A giant had killed a farmer, young people had been led astray, changelings were discovered. Every mother in the Haven eyed her own infant with suspicion and sick worry.

Before midday, Tylag struck out with Brand and his companions to the docks. They would set off from the harbor to search for Myrddin immediately. There were no surprises on the trip to the docks until they passed into the winding section of road where the rickety houses of the Hoots and the Silures were perched. There they met a great party of folk dressed in the simple dirty garments of dockworkers and miners. They had gathered around Old Tad Silure's shack, and they were in an ugly mood.

As they rolled their cart down the road past Old Tad's place, the oldster himself pointed them out to the crowd. "There they are! They provided me with the wards! Seek your refunds from them!"

The crowd surged forward to surround them.

"What do you want?" demanded Brand, speaking in a commanding voice as he thought his brother Jak might have.

One among them was Slet, the skinny unkempt dock worker that had gotten into an argument with Jak back at the *Spotted Hog* a few days ago. Brand could tell that it was partly due to his humiliation on that day that he headed up this mob now. "We are arresting you! That Fob girl is a cheat and a witch!" he said, pointing to Telyn.

Brand took a step toward him. He controlled himself with great difficulty.

"You others are guilty of witchery, too," Slet said. "By your foul craft you have ended the Pact, which is treason against the River Haven." He looked a bit nervous, but there was rage in his voice and his courage was bolstered by the support of the mob around him. There were snarls and catcalls from the crowd.

Tylag, who had been walking behind the others, leading Tator with their supplies, stepped forward. "Where is your writ? I am of the council, and no one has come to me with such a request."

Tad Silure stepped further out of the shadows of his dilapidated old shack. "I have scribed such a writ!" he cried loudly. "They are in league with the Faerie, I tell you!"

"You forget that I was once Chief of the Constabulary. It takes three signatures from the council even for the writ to be legal. Who has signed it besides the Hoots and the Silures?"

"Bah!" roared Old Tad. "You are no longer a Constable, Tylag. Take them, boys!" In response to his command, many of the younger men surged forward. They slowed however, as Tylag's clear, calm voice rose above the clamor.

"Without the third signature even this arrest is illegal, and all of you are guilty, not us. Besides, where are the Riverton Constabulary among you to perform the arrest?" demanded Tylag.

"The writ is legal, Rabing. There will be no weaseling out of this," shouted Old Tad. "What's more, Rabing Isle will be forfeited as payment for damages, after these witches are cast into prison! Forward! Take them lads!"

The front of the crowd surged hesitantly, and Brand tensed for a fight. They were only rabble from the shacks along the docks, made up mostly of Silures and Hoots, but there were a lot of them. Then Modi raised his battleaxe and gave them pause. Gudrin waded forward, holding aloft her Teret, her book of the Kindred.

"I am Gudrin of the Talespinners. Among the Kindred, the Talespinners hold the books of law. It rests with us to judge the guilt or innocence of our kinsfolk. I have sat in judgment over many of my folk. I can say from centuries of experience that you people want nothing of justice. What you want is a scapegoat." She gazed out upon the mob. Somehow, she seemed taller than a man then, and she burned the minds of those that met her eyes.

"You are of the Battleaxe Folk!" shouted Old Tad, shaking with rage. "Your words bear no weight here, story-teller!"

Gudrin affixed him with her gaze, and Old Tad all but swallowed his tongue. "You are the guilty one here!" accused Gudrin, leveling her finger upon Old Tad. "Speak if you dare to deny that you have misled these fine honest folk with your dark-loving words of fear. Speak if you did not drill these false wards yourself!" Gudrin demanded. While she spoke, she held his gaze, burning into Old Tad's head. Old Tad's eyes appeared to be starting from his head and his lips worked, but no sound issued forth. Gudrin too, fell silent, while she and Old Tad strove against one another's wills.

Tylag took this moment to speak further. "I am loath to say it, but Old Tad seeks only his own personal gain in this, good folk. He divides us against ourselves, and in the very face of the true enemy, which are the Dark Ones among the Faerie. Last night my home at Froghollow was razed and burnt to the ground. My eldest and strongest son Sam was killed. What horrors will this night bring to your homes while we stand here deciding who is to blame? On behalf of the Clan Council, I ask you all to pull together, set aside your recriminations, and answer the muster of the River Haven. Only united can we hope to stand against those that will come against us in the night. Behold! Twilight is almost upon us! Tonight the War Beacons will be lit, for the first time in a century! Have you all readied your wards? Are your homes bolted and stocked with weapons and supplies? Go now, and see to your families!"

There was a stirring at the back of the crowd, and even before Tylag had finished it was clear that many had quietly deserted Old Tad. They fell back, muttering among themselves, some arguing that it was indeed almost twilight, others claiming that they were being bluffed and that trickery was afoot. Old Tad, who had been unable to speak, regained his voice and screamed that he had been enchanted, that Gudrin was a witch and a Faerie to boot.

Things might still have gone poorly, had not a knot of folk, including a squadron of the Riverton Constabulary, appeared in the road. They were marching down from Riverton, and were being led by several of the Fobs, Telyn's relatives.

Tylag lay his hand on Brand and Corbin's shoulders and spoke with urgency. "Go now, my lads, while you have the chance. Farewell and good luck to you," he said, squeezing them with almost painful force. Brand thought to see his uncle's eyes mist over with tears, but he didn't weep. Then they had broken through the evaporating mob and were headed to the docks. Modi, Gudrin, and Telyn walked with them, their steps hurried.

Quietly, they boarded their skiff. They swiftly unloaded their packs from Tator and turned him loose. "Go home, that's a good boy!" said Corbin, slapping his rump. The horse trotted upslope a ways, then turned as if to see them off, tossing his head.

And so, with few words spoken between them, the four young River Folk and the two Kindred slipped into the waters of the harbor and out into the open river, turning north. The winds were up and their sails billowed full, catching the early evening breeze. To the west the sun was setting, and its dying light turned the waters to jet-black, shot through with dancing threads of silver and gold. The western sky was orange and lavender, while in the east it turned to blue then finally black as night stole forth.

Thus they left Stone Island to the unknown fate of nightfall, and their hearts were heavy.

* * *

That night they made it to the big fork in the river, one leg of which led up to Rabing Isle, the other of which led to North End. They swung northeast and headed for North End. Brand stared long and hard to the northwest where his home lay just a few miles off.

"It's time we found a place to camp," said Gudrin after a time.

"Yes, it's dangerous to sail the river at night, even for those of us who know it so well," agreed Brand. "But where can we stop and camp that would be sheltered from the Faerie?"

Telyn spoke first. "Skydrop Falls! They are quite near— we will be hearing them soon. They are surrounded by the Haven Woods, where there are no fairy mounds."

"Still, I would not like to sleep exposed beneath the stars if we can help it. If a pack of rhinogs came upon us we would be lost," said Corbin.

"We can sleep under the falls," said Telyn. "Remember, when we were kids, we would go on hiking trips through the Haven Woods? There is a big cave behind the falls. We can camp there, where the Faerie may hesitate to enter."

The idea met with approval, and Corbin, who sat at the tiller, set course for the falls. In time the roar filled their ears. When they could feel the water moving faster and cold mist touched their faces, they poled swiftly for the shore. Brand leapt to the land and made the skiff fast with heavy ropes. Then they all climbed out and walked beneath the dark canopy of the Haven Wood.

Burning lanterns and walking carefully, the group slipped behind the falls and entered a wide, flat cave. The walls were wet with mist, but the sandy bottom was dry enough for comfort. They lit a small fire and Corbin cooked a fine dinner of leeks and toasted shellfish with a dessert of dried peaches prepared during the summer.

"I'll say this," Modi chuckled, slipping a notch on his belt. "You River Folk certainly know how to feed yourselves."

"At least Corbin does," added Brand, to which they all laughed and saluted Corbin's excellent cooking and preparation.

Corbin accepted the compliments with a smile and a nod. His mouth was too full of dried peaches to allow anything else.

Modi took the first watch, so the rest bedded down and the night passed swiftly with only one interruption. Brand awoke to find Modi standing at the cave entrance, looking out into the night. He came and stood at the warrior's side. Noticing him, Modi pointed out the cave mouth into the woods. There, beneath the dark canopy of the trees, tiny lights circled and darted.

"The Faerie..." breathed Brand. "Here in the Haven Wood!"

Modi nodded, gesturing for him to be silent. Brand watched them for a time, then headed back to his bed. They appeared to be of the harmless sort, he thought, and soon enough it would be his turn at watch. It was when he was coming back to bed that he saw the little man stealing their food.

He grabbed up a stick from the woodpile and charged after the manling, who turned and fled with great bounds that carried him over the sleeping figures of Telyn and Gudrin. The Wee One wore a waistcoat of bright blue and carried an armful of dried peaches from their supplies. One or two of them fell upon the sleeping figures.

Brand gave chase, but it was hopeless, as the Wee Folk were far too swift for a man to catch on foot. With a final act of frustration mixed with amusement, he hurled the stick after the creature, which thumbed its nose at him as it disappeared into a hole that doubtlessly led to the surface. Shaking his head, Brand returned to his bed and after a time slept again.

* * *

In the morning they found that their boat had been ransacked. The sails were gone as were the poles. The plugs at the bottom of the vessel had been pulled and it had half-sunk, scudding along the bottom in the current.

"Merlings!" cried Brand. "First the Fae, and now the Merlings plague us as well!"

"It would only make sense," Gudrin told him. "For the creatures you call 'Merlings' have never been happy with your dominance of the River Haven. They see it as their home, and now that the Faerie plague you, they will crawl forth from their dens and stake their claims upon your lands as well."

"But we are familiar with Merlings," complained Corbin. "Why have they always beleaguered us even when the Pact was in force?"

"Because the Pact only provides protection against the Faerie and various monsters they consort with," explained Gudrin. "The Merlings are a simple, mortal race, and not bound to Oberon."

Brand sourly inspected the damage. Only the thick ropes, which had apparently defied the attempts of the web-handed Merlings to untie them, had kept the skiff from drifting over the falls as they slept.

"Damned nuisance!" complained Brand as they hauled in the damaged boat and began to bail it out. It took hours to repair it and cut new poles. It was half way to noon by the time they set out, all poling hard to keep from being sucked over the roaring falls. Brand looked out upon the beautiful Haven Wood, so friendly during his childhood. Now what was to become of it?

The group worked the poles and sweated. It would take them another day or two yet to reach North End without sails. Brand hoped that Myrrdin had some answers. He wished to return his home to the way it had been.

Chapter Ten
Myrrdin

North End was a small village bordered by Old Hob's Marsh to the west and the Faerie Wood to the east. Further north were the Dead Kingdoms, a vast region once thickly inhabited by humans. The Dead Kingdoms were outside the protected boundaries of the River Haven. Now none lived there but ghosts, ghouls and darker things. Even the Faerie and the Wandering Folk avoided the area as it was as full of ancient evils as ancient glories.

North End was primarily a fishing settlement, and a fleet of sailing sloops loaded with fine-woven nets thronged the docks. The tallest building in the town was an Inn called the *Blue Lantern*, which stood three stories high. Thrusting up from the sole muddy street, it was built of orange bricks that were weathered and pock-marked. Swinging and creaking in the ever-present wind, the *Blue Lantern's* namesake glowed above the entrance and guided travelers into its common room.

Brand and the others came up from the docks and followed the blue glow. They entered and were quickly ushered to a table by the rotund innkeeper, Pompolo. He, like most of the folk in North End, was of the Sonner clan. Pompolo had only one hand, the other having been lost long ago in a boating accident that had ended his career as a fisherman and brought him into a new career: inn-keeping. Always good-natured, he claimed that the hook the physician had attached to his severed wrist worked better than his old hand, as he could gather the handles of more empty ale tankards with it.

"Pompolo, my good man! Never has a sight been more welcome to my eyes than your round face," said Brand as he took his place.

"Ah! Master Brand and Master Corbin! Excellent to see you lads. It has been months since you came to taste my beer," said Pompolo, placing great frothing mugs of his home brew in front of them without even asking. His eyes passed over Telyn and the two Battleaxe Folk, and his smile faded, then came back on, full force. "But you must tell me, where is your brother Jak? And what's this news I hear that something has gone amiss with the Pact?"

Brand and the others exchanged glances. Finally, he cleared his throat and briefly explained the events of the past nights, leaving out the details of the fighting at Froghollow and the suspicions of many that the Rabing and Fob clans had caused it all. That news would come to North End soon enough.

"Oh, such grim tidings! Whatever will we do with the Wee Folk running amok in our village? My beer will sour and the fish will slip our nets as if oiled," cried Pompolo, slapping his hand to his forehead.

Brand took a good slug of the beer, not bothering to wait for the foam to subside. It was excellent. His new mustache of white bubbles made the others smile. "It will take more than an army of the Wee Folk to sour this beer, Pompolo," he declared.

Pompolo dipped his head to the complement, beaming. He waved to one of his two barmaids, the one called Serena, Brand thought. She came to take their orders for food. As she did, Gudrin said "We are searching for Myrrdin, whom we heard might be lodging here. Where could we find him?"

Pompolo took on a look of great thought. "He is indeed somewhere in North End, although I can't say that I could pinpoint his whereabouts just now. I've been so busy, what with all the traffic to the Harvest Moon festival and all."

"So he is up and about, fully recovered?" Pompolo nodded. "This is good news," said Gudrin. "If you see him, be sure that you tell him we wish to have words with him."

Pompolo assured her that he would.

212

Brand drank more of the beer. It was strong brew, and on his empty stomach the warm feeling of it was already spreading through him pleasantly. "I should introduce my friends," he said, waving to Telyn and the two Kindred. "First, this lady is Telyn Fob, of Riverton—"

"Everyone calls me Scraper," she announced, interrupting.

"And this is Gudrin of the Talespinners and her companion, Modi of the Warriors. They are friends of the River Folk and already have used their strong hands and quick minds in defense of the River Haven."

Pompolo took all this in with a sweep of his eyes. Brand watched him, knowing that he was sharper than most people credited. He was, in fact, the Hetman of North End, although he didn't put on airs. There were many questions in his gaze, but the first one he asked was: "The defense of the River Haven? You sound as though we were at war, lad."

"You are," said Modi, draining his mug with a gulp and wiping his mouth and bristling beard with the back of his hand.

Pompolo flicked his eyes at him, then shifted his attentions to Gudrin. "Well, madam, did I hear correctly that you are a Talespinner?"

Gudrin nodded, smiling.

"Excellent! The reputation of the Talespinners of the Battleaxe Folk reaches far and wide. It is said that the Faerie themselves will put aside their mischief to listen to one of your stories!" Pompolo swept up Modi's empty tankard with his hook and replaced it with a fresh one even as he spoke. "Should you feel moved to tell the folk here one of your tales, your food and lodging will be free for the night."

Gudrin stroked her hair. "If we have the time, and if the mood is right, I will do so," she said after a moment's contemplation.

"As you say milady, as you say!" gushed Pompolo. He excused himself then and rushed to a knot of fisherman as they entered the common room.

Corbin chuckled and leaned close to Brand's ear. "I have the feeling Gudrin might have told a tale even if not asked," he whispered.

213

Brand smiled and nodded back. "Right you are, Corbin, the beer is excellent."

The food came soon after, and they set to devouring a load of fried trout and river cod. Tubers from Old Hob's Marsh were on hand as well, and they didn't taste quite as bland as usual to the hungry travelers. At one point, Brand took a moment to notice the others in the common room. They were mostly fishermen, with a few foresters and flap-footed marshmen among them. The fin-like marsh shoes of the marshmen were stacked along the wall at the entrance. One old granddaddy of a marshman sat in the corner by the fire, warming the chill from his bones.

Then the conversation at the table caught his attention. The others were discussing where Myrrdin might be and how he could be reached. Modi spoke little, but seemed the most distrustful of Myrrdin's motives for not showing up, suggesting that he knew the Pact would not be remade. "A battle not fought is a battle not lost for one such as Myrrdin, but we all lose just the same," he grunted.

Brand looked out the window and thought about the unpleasant changes that were overtaking the River Haven. Outside the inn dusk stole over the land. The people of North End vanished with the dying light, closing up shops and locking their doors. A few harried-looking souls trotted down the muddy street, hoods pulled low, trying to get home quickly. Brand frowned and shook his head—it was wrong that people should so fear twilight.

"Where is Myrrdin?" demanded a voice loudly. Brand turned from the dimming scene outside to see it was the granddaddy marshman at the fire who spoke. "Not only has he missed the Harvest Moon, but he has yet to appear and make his excuses!" There was muttered agreement around the common room. The old man held aloft the stick he had been poking the fire with and waved it in the air.

"Where is he? Does he stalk the fair maidens of North End, playing upon their honest new fears of darkness and the Shining Folk? Or perhaps he has even fled as far as Hamlet by now, shirking his duties to the Haven and now pretends to be some other wandering personage!"

All eyes in the common room were now upon the old marshman, who stood with stooped back and hooded face. He made sweeping gestures with his walking stick, causing those near him to duck their heads and raise their hands to shield themselves. Brand glanced at Gudrin and Modi, who looked annoyed.

"You don't know what you're talking about," Gudrin said to the man. "Myrrdin would not abandon these folk."

The marshman wheeled on them, very spry on his feet for one so aged and bent. His long white beard flew about his head as he advanced on their table. Taking everyone by surprise, he swung his stick and struck the table a resounding blow. The stick came down between the two Kindred, the loud crack of it making everyone jump. There was a flash of fire and a wisp of smoke rose up from the table, which was blackened where the stick had landed. Orange sparks leapt about the table. One fell in Brand's mug of beer and sizzled there. Brand blinked in wonderment and could only imagine that the tip of the stick had been burned to coals by the fire.

Modi was not amused. With a roar of challenge, he stood, his chair springing away from his legs. His hand flew to the haft of his battleaxe, which was now revealed to all as he swept back his cloak. The double-curved blades gleamed redly in the firelight, echoing the killing light in his eyes.

Gudrin gestured for him to be seated, but for once he ignored the Talespinner. Modi and the marshman faced one another.

With a fluid motion, the oldster seemed to grow before them. His back straightened and his shoulders rose. Finally, he threw back his hood. The craggy, weathered face beneath had white brows and flowing white hair. The face was like that of a hawk, complete with a hooked nose and dark, shining eyes.

"Myrrdin!" shouted Gudrin, coming to her feet and stepping toward the man, who was indeed missing wizard. A clamor arose from the common room around them as people exclaimed in surprise.

"The Clanless One," breathed Telyn, looking as she had when first seeing the Faerie.

215

Only Modi seemed unmoved by the revelation. He continued to eye Myrrdin angrily. "You don't take my duties seriously enough, Wanderer."

Myrrdin returned his gaze. Amusement danced in his eyes. "Why, Modi of the Warriors, you seem less than happy to see me."

Modi shrugged, his huge shoulders rising and falling. "I spotted you at the fire when we first entered."

Myrrdin cocked his head, eyeing Modi for a moment. He nodded. "I do believe you did. Hhmm...interesting," he said, sounding less than pleased. "And so your goading remarks make more sense."

Gudrin could contain herself no longer. She pushed forward and clasped Myrrdin's hand in both of her own. She ushered him to a spot beside hers at the table and called for more beer. Pompolo himself hurried over with fresh mugs for all.

Modi, clearly disapproving of Myrrdin's antics, waited until all the others were seated before he eased his bulk into a chair. His face was grim and he maintained a stony silence. Brand noted to himself that Modi didn't have much of a sense of humor.

The group exchanged greetings and introductions for a time, and all the River Folk were surprised when Myrrdin recognized each of them. With ease he named each of their parents and close clansmen. He even seemed to have foreknowledge of their personalities, which Brand found most fascinating.

Myrrdin turned his gaze to Brand last, and Brand felt something of the sensation that he felt when he met Gudrin's eyes. There was power in them, perhaps even more so than was the case with the Talespinner, but it was a gentler power. He stood up to it unflinchingly, and thought to see Myrrdin give a tiny nod of approval.

"Nothing about this party surprises me, save one thing," said Myrrdin. "Where is your brother Jak?"

Brand told him, then began to describe the events of the last few days, telling Myrrdin far more than they had told Pompolo. He found that without even considering it, he was speaking of things that he had edited previously. Corbin stretched a leg under the table and crushed his foot briefly with his huge boot, but after only a momentary glance of confusion at his cousin, Brand went on speaking rapidly. When he got to the attack by the rhinogs at Froghollow, Myrrdin stopped him with an upraised hand.

Brand stopped and blinked. He noted with embarrassment that he had the attention of everyone in the common room. Shocked looks, hidden gestures, and buzzing conversation swept the room. He had been speaking of fighting with the Faerie firsthand, an idea both foreign and terrifying to simple people such as those of North End. It wasn't this that bothered him the most, however, for they were sure to learn the dark truth in the next few days anyway. What annoyed him was his lack of control. He blamed it on the beer partly, but that did little to make him feel better. He chided himself not to fall under Myrrdin's more subtle influences so easily again. He was no child, not any longer.

"Perhaps this is something best discussed in private," suggested Myrrdin, and the others all agreed, many with relief.

After a bit of lighter talk, they moved to the large sleeping room that Pompolo had provided for them. The North End folk watched them go with a mixture of suspicion, relief, and disappointment. After checking the doors and windows, and making sure no one was eavesdropping, Myrrdin bade Brand to finish his tale. Brand did so, and when he stopped Myrrdin heaved a great sigh. Again he looked old and worn, but soon he brightened and sprang to his feet with new vitality.

"Things are bad. Worse than I or any of us had imagined," he said, but looking bright of eye all the same. "But I believe here in this chamber there are answers for many of our problems, should we all listen and think."

Brand smiled, liking Myrrdin for his optimism, at the same time wondering just how old Myrrdin was, marveling at the way he seemed both old and young at the same time. "Could you tell us your tale now, Myrrdin?" Brand asked.

Myrrdin rose up to his full height, which was greater than any there save Brand himself. He grinned at the River Folk and the Kindred alike. "Finally, the question comes."

Then he settled into a chair, kicking up a footstool to place under his feet with a precise movement. He sighed, suddenly appearing old all over again. Brand shook his head bemusedly.

"It is a sad tale. The grim tidings from the north attracted me, as no doubt these good folk have told you about," he said, gesturing to Gudrin and Modi.

"We have heard of some dark whispers from the north," said Corbin, speaking slowly and clearly. "But not from Gudrin and Modi."

"What!" shouted Myrrdin, and Brand half expected him to leap to his feet again. This time he only straightened bolt upright and faced the Battleaxe Folk. "You haven't told them of the wars in Snowdonia!"

"There was no need to frighten them further," said Modi. "They've been trembling like rabbits just at the hints and the casual contact with the enemy they've had."

Telyn scowled. "I believe we fought the rhinogs rather well for rabbits."

Modi glowered at her for a moment, then nodded, grudgingly. "Your courage was true, I admit. But you don't yet comprehend what you face."

"And what would that be?" asked Corbin.

"Numberless great black ships come across the sea each day from the land of Eire. They bear goblins and their broods of rhinogs from the dark castles on that nearby island. Led by their goblin sires, rhinogs spawned in Eire war with the Kindred. We've fought them in the Black Mountains and even upon the very heights of Snowdon itself," said Gudrin, meeting no one's eyes. "The surface is for the most part under their control now. Only the great caverns are still ruled by the Kindred. Most of our strength lies below ground, but still the situation is not good."

"But your strongholds beneath the mountains are legendary," said Telyn. "Surely, they will not fall."

"The mountain fortresses are vast and self-sustaining. They are all but impregnable, it's true," said Gudrin. "But they are divided and unable to come to the aid of one another. If all of Herla's forces gather to destroy one of the fortresses, the others can do nothing to stop them. One by one, the great halls will fall."

"Nothing is fated," growled Modi. "The Kindred may all perish in one hall, but they shall inflict such great losses that the enemy army shall be broken!"

Myrrdin nodded, but continued looking grim. "We have no way of knowing how things will progress, but we do know that the enemy are great in number and their ranks swell daily. If they can gather enough strength, the Kindred will indeed be rooted out and slain, one fortress at a time."

The River Folk looked from one to another, stunned. All of them had the same thought: if the enemy was so great as to overcome the Kindred, what chance did the peaceful River Haven Folk have? With the Pact broken, they were at the mercy of the Faerie and the rhinogs.

"And so now you can imagine my reasons for delay," said Myrrdin. "I managed to slip by the enemy host and into Snowdon, only to find the Kindred garrison even weaker than I had feared." He looked at the Talespinner. "Although your craft at making tools for war are great, Gudrin, I fear your people aren't prolific enough to replace the soldiers you lose in battle. Ten rhinogs may fall to each of the Kindred, but this may not be enough.

"In any case, when I left to come to the River Haven—over a month ago—I was greatly slowed by the presence of the enemy army. I dared not come down the Berrywine, because it was being watched by archers. I was forced to turn east, into the Deepwood, and then I crossed the river and went south through the Dead Kingdoms to reach this marsh.

"Still, I might have made the meeting had not that damnable storm come so early and turned Old Hob's Marsh to frozen slush."

"I don't know what you could have done," said Gudrin. "Oberon was not there, and clearly you weren't expected to be either. The ceremony was a farce, a chance for the Faerie to stuff themselves one last time at the expense of the River Folk."

"Perhaps you are right," said Myrrdin, heaving a sigh. "But perhaps I could have done something."

"I doubt it. I was asked to stand in your stead," said Gudrin, "although this wasn't my real purpose in coming here. It made no difference"

"I understand," said Myrrdin. "Thank you."

Brand, though, thought of something the Talespinner had just said. "So what exactly *are* you here for, Gudrin?" he asked.

Gudrin and Modi moved uneasily at that, exchanging glances. Gudrin finally answered. "I suppose there are no more secrets to hold back now. We came for two purposes. We had wished to add the Kindred to the Pact, making it a three-way alliance for mutual protection. I am greatly saddened to see that there is no more Pact for us to join."

"All is not lost, Gudrin," said Myrrdin. "A new Pact may yet be forged."

All eyes swung to him. "A *new* Pact? Can't we just reinstate the old one?" asked Corbin in concern. He voiced the thoughts of all the River Folk, who had always assumed that somehow the Pact would be remade and things would go on as before. Anything else was too painful to bear thinking about.

Myrrdin shook his head. "Everything is different now. The old Pact is broken. A new one, if it is to be forged, will be entirely distinct from the first. The Faerie are fickle and capricious. Rarely do they perform predictably."

"What I fail to understand is Oberon's lack of interest in maintaining the Pact," said Gudrin. "He must fear Herla nearly as much as the rest of us. No one is hated by the all the Wild Hunt more than Oberon, who stole their very lives from them."

"That *is* a puzzle," said Myrrdin. "And I believe now, after hearing Brand's tale, that I may have an answer."

Myrrdin paused here, knowing that he had their full attention. He took the time to weigh his walking stick and rub its ashen tip before speaking. Brand noted in surprise that his stick—which he had thought had been burnt in the inn's fire earlier—was only coated by a thin layer of ash. After a bit of rubbing, it was all brightly polished wood once again.

"I believe that Oberon has lost Lavatis," said Myrrdin in a low whisper.

"The Blue Jewel?" gasped Telyn.

"Of course," said Gudrin. "That would explain his ending of the Pact. He has not the strength to maintain it."

"But then who has it? The Jewel, I mean?" demanded Brand, half-expecting Myrrdin to produce it from the depths of his shaggy beard.

Myrrdin turned to him. "Good question! That is indeed the question, and the riddle that must be answered to forge a new Pact."

"Could Herla have it?" asked Brand.

"Let us pray not," said Gudrin, "for if he does, all is already lost."

"Only if his grip on it is firm," added Myrrdin. "For even if he possessed it, he must attune himself to the Jewel in order to wield it."

"Let me understand this," said Corbin, the slow logic of his mind clearly engaged. "Oberon has lost his greatest source of power, Lavatis. Thus, he can no longer hold Herla at bay, who seems to wield a great power of his own. But if we can recover the Jewel, we can bargain its return for a new and more favorable Pact with the Faerie."

"Well summarized as usual, Corbin," said Telyn, not without kindness. "My mind is already leaping to new concepts, however. We must find the Blue Jewel first, and win it, in any way we can. The thought of stealing such a prize makes me glad for every apple I ever palmed from a farmer's cart at market."

Brand shifted in his chair and looked embarrassed for her, but no one else seemed to notice. Something occurred to him. "But you said, Gudrin, that you came to the River Haven for two reasons."

"Aye. We also came on the behalf of King Thrane of the Kindred to find a new bearer for the Jewel Ambros. Besides parlaying our way into the Pact, we are to return with a new Champion who could wield the axe and slay the armies that besiege the Earthlight."

"But why not select a Champion among the Kindred?" asked Corbin.

"Humans have ever made the best Champions, and the best of humanity is known to be here in the River Haven," said

Gudrin. Modi's eyes rolled up to the ceiling as she spoke. "I had hoped that with Myrrdin's counsel, one could be found."

"It seems to me that my counsel is hardly needed," said Myrrdin.

"What do you mean?" asked Gudrin.

"Why Gudrin, your judgment is legendary! Can you not see? Your Champion is in this very room!"

At this, they all became deathly silent. Modi took a half step forward, and his eyes were alight. His hands made grasping motions in the air. "What do you mean?" he demanded.

"The River Folk!" cried Myrrdin, as though they all had to be blind. "What better selection could one ask for? Two of the Clan Rabing, one of the Clan Fob. You know your histories as well as I. Knights once rode to battle beneath the banners of their ancestors. Already they have met the enemy and done well. You have only the final decision to make."

"Bah! What utter nonsense!" Modi said. He made a sweeping gesture of disgust and turned to stump away to the door. He crossed his arms and leaned his weight against the door, which brought a groan of protest from the old wood.

"Modi is of the opinion that since the axe bearing the Jewel Ambros has long been held by the Kindred, it should be wielded by one of the Kindred," explained Gudrin. "This is a compelling argument, but history shows its dangers."

Myrrdin nodded sagely. "Your King is wise. The freshness of spirit needed to contain the fury of the weapon is hard to find among the elder races. I imagine that even for you, great among the wise of your folk, Ambros is a heavy burden."

Gudrin looked pained. "Yes. Ever the Jewel weighs upon me. It wants nothing more than to slay, and senses danger and evil where none exist. Only by sheer force of will have I stayed my hands from murder until now."

Brand thought of the night in the woods when Gudrin had turned upon him, clear murderous intent in her look. He shuddered to think that it had been the Jewel that had looked out through Gudrin's eyes and desired his death.

"Do you then agree with my assessment?" asked Myrrdin, indicating the three River Folk with a wave of his hand.

Gudrin rubbed her cheek for a time, holding her Teret clamped to her body. She eyed each of them in turn. Brand felt the intensity of her gaze, and it was painful. "Yes."

Modi made an exasperated sound, but said nothing.

"Which is it, then?" asked Myrrdin quietly.

All eyes were now on the three River Folk, who sat dumbfounded. Corbin opened his mouth, but no words issued forth.

Telyn was the first to find her voice. "I don't wish to wield the axe. If it were a knife or a bow," she said quietly, "perhaps it would be different."

"Women have been Champions in the past, Telyn," said Myrrdin gently.

She shook her head. Then all eyes turned to Corbin and Brand. Brand felt his heart race in his chest. His throat was suddenly dry and taut. It was difficult to swallow.

Finally, Modi could contain himself no longer. "These are but weak children!" he burst out. "Surely Gudrin, you can't be serious. Neither of them has yet seen twenty summers! By the white peaks of Snowdon, kinswoman, I beg you to reconsider."

Gudrin now stood angrily. She faced Modi and held her Teret aloft. She slapped it soundly. "I sit as judge among the Kindred! You have sworn to escort me on this mission, ordered by our king. Perform your duties as sworn, or it is *you* I shall next pass judgment upon."

The two stared at one another, and the battle of wills was such that Brand began to feel oddly unwell. It twisted at his gut and made his stomach, still full of good food and beer, roil inside him. Finally, Modi dipped his head and stepped back.

"My duty is clear," he mumbled.

Gudrin took a step forward, once again face to face with the warrior. "It is my decision to give the choice to you, as the wiser judge of warriors. Which one of these two boys shall be our Champion?"

Modi blinked in surprise. His hand went to his chin, and he turned to view the River Folk anew. His eye traveled from one to the other of them. "Corbin has more the natural build for the axe, but Brand is more skilled," he said, echoing his words from days ago. "What is more important, Corbin is more

223

thoughtful, while Brand exhibits more qualities of leadership. It is clear that between them, I would make Brand the Champion and Corbin his Second."

Gudrin nodded. "I agree," she said. "If Brand accepts, of course."

Brand opened his mouth, then closed it. "I suppose..." he trailed off. He paused, wondering what new course his life was about to take. He felt his brother Jak there, telling him he was no Champion, only a farmer, steeped in muck up to his waist and with rainwater for blood. Then he glanced at Telyn, who brightened visibly. She was flushed with excitement, clearly overjoyed that he might be given this honor. It came to him that she would be infatuated with a man who wielded such an unknown power.

"I accept," he heard himself say.

"All is settled then!" said Myrrdin, springing again to his feet. He stood among them with his hands on his hips, beaming. He made a sudden movement, and Brand felt a pressure against his chest. He looked down and saw that Myrrdin's walking stick was pressing against him there. He swallowed, wondering if Myrrdin were indeed a wizard.

"You," said Myrrdin, poking the stick harder against him. Brand pushed it away. Myrrdin smiled. "You are to be the bearer of Ambros the Golden. I think it is best to tell you that the axe isn't always willing to accept a new bearer. If it finds you lacking, it will rid itself of you, probably in an act of terrific mayhem."

Brand felt his face whiten. He distantly recalled the normal days of his life. Only a week ago he had worried about the heat of the sun upon the berrywine casks. The quiet sounds of the river had been all that came to him in his sleep. Now he was to be tested by one of the Jewels of Power.

"The axe will want to test you," said Gudrin. "I think it is best that we counsel you for a time, allowing you to decide to accept the axe and allowing it to decide to accept you—"

"Yes," agreed Myrrdin, interrupting. "There must be a period of attunement before you take up the axe."

Gudrin looked annoyed with the interruption. "Yes— attunement. In time you shall bear the axe as I do. After a time, you will learn its tricks and build a resistance to its power. Only then should you pit your will against Ambros and attempt to wield it."

"This is much the same as with all the Jewels—there is a period of attunement, followed by a struggle of wills," interjected Myrrdin again. "Rightfully, Brand needs years of training before taking up the axe. It is unfortunate that we may not have so long."

"So," said Brand carefully, "you are saying that I might learn to wield the axe, but not be able to control it."

"Exactly. So for now, Gudrin shall continue to bear the axe until you are ready," replied Myrrdin solemnly. Then, with another rapid change of expression and demeanor, he whirled to face the others. "With that settled, there is a question for us to now ponder: Where might we hunt for Oberon's lost Jewel?"

"Can't *you* tell us?" asked Corbin. He had a knowing look that was familiar to Brand. Brand wondered what he had figured out.

Myrrdin tilted his head, a smile playing about his lips. "Perhaps," he admitted.

"Let me see," said Corbin, taking on his expression of deep thought. "We know Oberon would not give up his greatest treasure willingly. And he is too wise to lose so great a prize in a wager. Therefore, it must have been stolen from him."

Myrrdin was nodding in approval. He returned to his chair quietly and closed his eyes, as if asleep.

"It would take a great thief for such a crime," Corbin continued, "and there are no greater thieves than the Faerie. Many among them are known for their thieving ways, but probably the goblins and the Wee Folk are the most accomplished."

Brand smiled now, watching Myrrdin's eyebrows raise a twitch over his closed eyes. It was fun to see others when they were first faced with Corbin's methodical wits.

"However, a goblin would attract too much attention if he were to come close to Oberon. I would think that the likely culprit would have been one of the Wee Folk," finished Corbin.

Slowly, Myrrdin's eyes turned to slits, then opened widely. "Are you quite finished, sir?"

225

"For now," said Corbin thoughtfully. He began to munch upon a marsh tuber from the sack he had brought up from the dining room.

"Astounding!" shouted Myrrdin. He shot up out of his chair and bounded into the center of the room. Modi, who had been in the midst of yawning, lurched and blinked. He shook his head in annoyance.

"Simply astounding," Myrrdin said, smiling. "What an excellently logical mind you have, my good Corbin. I concur with your conclusions. The Jewel had to have been stolen, for if Herla had taken it by force, Oberon would have to be dead. And you're correct: he would never dare wager it. Thievery would then be the most likely answer, and the Wee Folk the most likely culprits, as you point out. Now, what other treasures will your mind grind out for us, good Corbin?"

Corbin pondered. Two of the marsh tubers disappeared, followed by most of a third. "I would say that Herla doesn't have Lavatis in his hands yet. It would seem more likely that the thief still has it."

"And why is this?" demanded Myrrdin. As he spoke, he went to the room's only large window and threw up the sash. A gust of cold air blew into the room. The fire guttered, but no one protested, as the room had been getting a bit too warm.

Corbin shrugged. "Would not Herla have already swept us all from his path if he bore two Jewels?"

Myrrdin shrugged in return. "Possibly, although history tells us that attuning oneself to two Jewels is somewhat like adopting two jealous wives...the results aren't always as one would envision."

"Presuming it has been stolen, and presuming that the Wee Folk have it," continued Corbin unconcernedly, "then we must find them and take it back."

"A tall order indeed," muttered Gudrin.

"Absurd," said Modi. "I, for one, don't wish to tramp through swamps and forests grabbing for manlings."

"Could you be so good as to close the window now, Myrrdin?" asked Telyn, pulling her cloak around her shoulders.

"Certainly, my dear," replied Myrrdin, but he made no move toward the window.

226

"There is something that I might add about the Wee Folk," Myrrdin said loudly, speaking with his head directed upward now, as if he addressed the ceiling. He strutted back and forth before them, seemingly oblivious to the cold draft that was stealing the warmth from the room. The River Folk began to glance toward the window. Brand considered moving to close it, and he even began to get up.

Myrrdin paused before him and Brand sat back down. "I have a great secret to impart to all of you concerning the Wee Folk! A secret that many of the Shining Ones themselves don't know!"

"Well, impart it!" Modi said gruffly.

In response, Myrrdin strode to the window with two quick, bird-like strides. He turned toward them and whispered, "They aren't just the best thieves, but accomplished spies as well!"

"What?" grunted Modi.

But Myrrdin never answered. With a movement like that of a stork darting its beak down to snap up a marsh frog, he stooped and thrust his arm out the window. There was a squawk and a scrabbling sound. The long arm returned and in its grasp was the struggling form of one of the Wee Folk.

"A spy!" shouted Modi, grabbing up his battleaxe. "I'll make quick work of him."

Gudrin and Myrrdin both raised their hands. "Hold warrior!" said Gudrin.

"Indeed, hold!" Myrrdin said.

The manling, clearly terrified, increased its struggles as Modi approached. After closing the window, Myrrdin placed the Wee Folk on the center table and quickly looped a gray cord around its waist, pinning its arms. He held carefully to the end of the cord. After several mad attempts to bound away, it ceased its struggles and stood as if relaxed upon the tabletop.

The manling was dressed in the garb of a marshman, only in miniature. Its feet bore overlarge, flapping shoes, a tunic of sewn, colorless skins covered its body and a leather rain hat topped its head. Its glass-like doll's eyes regarded them.

It almost seemed curious.

Chapter Eleven
The Will-O-Wisp

Outside the *Blue Lantern* the town of North End was quiet, as if in uneasy anticipation. The moon had crept up over the town to hang in the night sky, and now shone into the window. The shine of it was in their captive's eyes and reflected from the manling's skin.

Telyn clapped her hands with excitement. "I've never seen one of them up close!"

Corbin glowered at the manling uncharacteristically. Brand knew he was thinking of Dando and his brother. He doubted Corbin would ever be amused by their tricks again.

The manling, saying nothing, studied each of them with intense curiosity. Somewhere beyond the open window a startled bird squawked angrily. Brand wondered if another of the Wee Folk even now worked to steal the bird's clutch of eggs.

"Well, what are we going to do with him?" asked Gudrin aloud.

"Let's interrogate him," said Corbin darkly, and Brand new he wasn't just talking about asking the Wee One questions.

"How do we know he knows anything useful?" asked Telyn.

"Let's go to sleep with one less spy in the River Haven to worry about," grunted Modi.

"Well, whatever we do, I don't suppose we can let him go," said Brand. He was already trying to come up with something

228

to imprison the thing. An old crate in one corner of the room that served the inn as an end-table caught his eye.

"Of course we're going to let him go," said Myrrdin. The others looked at him askance, except for the manling, who was now studying Telyn with the quiet intensity of a cat studying a songbird. Its head tilted to one side whenever she moved or spoke.

"First, however, I must make a fetish," continued Myrrdin. While the others looked on, he produced a leather pouch and filled it with a variety of ingredients. Many different withered herbs and colored powders were placed inside. Next, he took the pouch with him to one corner of the chamber and there, turned away from the others, performed some kind of ritual. There was a flash of pale green radiance. Brand was surprised by it, and for a moment wondered if he had imagined it.

Telyn gasped and looked entranced. "The Eye of Vaul," she whispered to Brand. "He has caused it to blink."

"A witch he is! Sorcery, he works! Kill thee all, he will!" screeched the manling suddenly. They all turned to it and saw that it had untied the first knot and was working on the second and third. There was a sudden desperation in its manner that belied its earlier lack of concern. "Devil! Tomkin will be no bond-servant to a half-man hedge-wizard!"

Corbin reached out and grabbed the thing around its midsection. In a flash, the manling bit him, seeming to open the whole of its head to sink in a row of sharp white teeth. Instantly, Corbin withdrew the hand. Blood welled up and dripped to the floor of the chamber.

Modi stepped forward with a gruff sound of decision.

"Hold!" said Myrrdin, coming forward with the packet he had been laboring over. The creature's struggles increased. Myrrdin stood over it, glowering down at the tiny spy. "I have captured you and made you captive, fairly and doubtless," he chanted to it, as if reading from a book of laws. "If you wish your freedom, you must grant me a boon, or your life is forfeit."

Glaring, the manling stilled. It replied in a similar, lawful tone. "Tomkin disagrees. There was no thing fair in my capture. No man could move with such speed and stealth. Thou art no man, but a foreign creature that walks in the lands of men. I call thee a cheat."

"It is all the same to me," shrugged Myrrdin. "A cheat such as myself has no difficulty in committing another crime—that of base murder."

The manling growled in its throat, the sound a small animal makes when its food is threatened. "I wish my freedom, and will grant thee thy boon, witch. But I demand a smaller boon in return, as is my right."

"Name it."

"I cannot, until I've heard of thy—no doubt grossly unjust—demands."

Myrrdin shrugged again. He held aloft the pouch he had prepared. "You, Tomkin of the Wee Folk, must swear to wear this pouch, night and day, dusk and dawn, for a year and a day. Ever you must hide it, and in no way shall you communicate its existence to your fellows or your masters."

The creature gave another cat's growl of unease. "Surely you jest! Two pieces of faerie gold would be too great a boon for such-like as thee, cheating witch!"

Myrrdin raised his walking-stick meaningfully. "Freedom or death? Choose now!"

"'Tis a geas, plain as the moon in a marsh pool at midnight!"

Myrrdin sighed. "I have no more time to waste upon you." He nodded significantly to Modi, who grimly took his axe from his belt.

"But what of my boon?" demanded the manling.

"Let us hear it," said Myrrdin impatiently.

A crafty look came over the creature's doll-like face. Its eyes slid to Corbin's hand, which was being worked on by Gudrin and Telyn now. The white strip of cloth they used for a bandage was stained the bright red of blood.

"I've tasted of River Folk tonight, and I always know best what I taste. Tonight I wish to taste of thee, cheating witch, so I may know what it is that flows in thy veins that makes thee as quick as an adder."

Modi snorted. Telyn and Brand looked concerned. Corbin rubbed at his bandage. A muscle in his cheek jumped.

230

As quickly as a snake, Myrrdin bared his left arm and thrust it out toward the tiny creature. For the first time since its capture, it smiled.

"The wound will be unclean," admonished Gudrin.

Myrrdin locked gazes with the manling as it sidled forward, beginning to grin now. "Get on with your boon, servant," the wizard said.

Again, the whole top of the thing's head seemed to come unhinged and it snapped its pointed white teeth into the bare flesh of the offered forearm. Myrrdin grimaced, as did everyone else, save Modi and Corbin, who simply glared.

After the spilt blood was cleaned from the floor and the table—and after Gudrin had staunched the flow from Myrrdin's veins—Tomkin was still rubbing his face and licking his palms. Brand now looked at the creature with disgust. "He's not like Dando. He's more animal, more feral."

"Yes," agreed Myrrdin, gritting his teeth as Gudrin's strong hands tied off the red-soaked bandages. "He is one of the more barbaric types that inhabit swamps and barrens rather than clean forests and farmlands."

At this, Tomkin chuckled. "If that's not a strange insult from a half-breed cheat! I know thee now by the blood in thy veins, witch! I know thou hast as much kin with Tomkin as these prattling River Folk!"

"Silence now, my servant," demanded Myrrdin. "It is time for you to don your new keepsake." He produced the pouch and handed it to the manling. Tomkin snapped his sharp teeth at Myrrdin's fingers once, just to make him jump. Myrrdin did jump, and his brows furrowed darkly. "You are indeed tainted by the darkest of your ilk," he said.

With ill grace, Tomkin donned the pouch. Beady eyes glared at Myrrdin.

"Now, my servant, you shall rejoin your clan and report back to me any news of that which Oberon has lost. Even if you hear nothing, you shall report back to us every week hence for the next year and a day," said Myrrdin. He turned to Corbin, who held the creature's cord. "Free him."

"But you have not asked him about what he already knows," protested Corbin.

Tomkin waited no longer, but seized the rope and began chewing through it. The others made as if to stop the manling, but Myrrdin restrained them. "Let him go. I can only ask him to do things afresh. Old knowledge he is free to twist and lie about."

Reluctantly, they watched Tomkin free himself and bound to the window sill and threw the window open. He crouched there for the moment, framed by the darkness outside. He turned and touched his thumb to his nose. Then with a great bound, he disappeared into the night.

"Can we trust him?" asked Brand.

Modi snorted.

"He is one of the Wee Folk, and a wild one at that. We can trust his greed, his malicious nature, and his instinct for self-preservation," said Gudrin.

"And," added Myrrdin, "we can trust his sworn word to a point—and the effects of my poultice."

Modi grunted and stumped to the window. He looked out into the cold night. "He's gone. Either he'll lose the pouch and his memory, or his clansmen will drown him in the marsh for treachery."

"Possibly," admitted Myrrdin with a shrug. "Time will tell. A week, to be exact."

"But, what do we do in the meantime?"

"I suggest we seek out the Merlings and see what they know," said Myrrdin.

The River Folk were stunned. "What? Are you mad?" demanded Brand. He quickly recovered. "I'm sorry, but no one in the River Haven ever seeks out a Merling...unless it is for revenge."

"Which, of course, does little to endear them to our plight," agreed Myrrdin.

Even Telyn was aghast. "The Faerie are one thing," she said. "At least we can make deals with them. But the Merlings are nothing other than evil, baby-stealing animals."

"No!" said Myrrdin. "As I've said before, they aren't unintelligent. Just primitive. They have no lost love of the River Folk, it's true. But the Pact has benefited them as much

232

as the humans in the Haven, and I think they would do almost anything to get it restored...even parlay with us."

Not long after that, the party readied themselves for bed. Sleep came slowly to Brand, and once it did finally take him, his mind was filled with dreams of ice-white teeth, snapping jaws, and webbed hands.

* * *

Tomkin bounded out the window with his heart soaring. He still drew breath! The River Folk had been fools not to slay him. His first flying leap carried him from the second story windowsill of the *Blue Lantern* all the way to the thatched roof of a marshman's hut, which was across a narrow alley. Being light and small, he didn't crash through the roof, but rather crunched into it. The landing made a sound not unlike that a tomcat might make after a similar leap. Tomkin heard the marsh people below, stirring in their beds. He did not wait for them to come out and see what had been thrown atop their roof. He bounded again, this time to their chimney, which still smoked faintly. Trotting over the crumbling mud-brick chimney, he gave a single wheezing cough and launched himself to the next roof, which covered a stable. The horses within nickered and shuffled, sensing Tomkin's nature. Domesticated animals feared his kind even more than the cowardly River Folk. Still happy with his escape, Tomkin leapt again to yet another roof. This time, a baby awoke at the sound and began squalling.

Traveling across the town of North End roof-to-roof, he began to enjoy the experience. It had been too long since he'd played games with the River Folk. Perhaps that should change…

His broad mouth spread wider and curved up at the corners. He *would* play games with them! What was the wording of the foul witch's enchantment? He must rejoin his clan and report back. Well, he needed something to report, then! He would give the River Folk events to ponder! They would not be so quick to enslave one of his kind when he was done!

Leaping from the roof of a fletcher to a wet, green field beyond, he raced out of the town toward the marsh he called home. He ran as fast as he could, knowing he had little time to waste. It was already near midnight and dawn was barely five hours off.

Finding Wee Folk in a swamp is a difficult task for any creature, but Tomkin knew his people well. He did not race about calling for them—that would only cause them to hide or possibly attack him. By his people's calendar, which revolved around moon phases and varieties of trees, this was the month of *Ngetal*, the month of the reed. Very fortunate indeed, he realized now. His kind would gather where the reeds were thickest, and of course, where else would that be other than a marsh?

Tomkin knew the difficulty in finding a group of his kind would not be in finding a large area of reeds. Being a marsh, they were plentiful. The trouble was in finding the *right* reeds. He thought he knew the place, however. There was a spot northwest of North End where the reeds were thick on an island of birch. The Wee Folk liked birch in particular, although Tomkin didn't share their taste for them.

Heading for the island, Tomkin reflected that he had not been in contact with his own kind for many years now. The River Folk had called him crude and barbaric. Perhaps they were right, he reflected. Maybe it was time to rejoin his people tonight and share in their nightly festivals.

Tomkin heard the music first. Fiddles and pipes. At a distance, one could mistake the sweet sounds for the sighing of the wind, but as he grew closer, he knew the truth. The sounds of the Fae frightened and enchanted humans, but to Tomkin they were natural and homey.

He saw the lights next. They floated over the murky pools of bog-water and cast up reflections of magenta, azure, and reddish-gold. They were wisps, he knew. The flittering creatures never could resist a good party, and if nothing else they provided some welcome illumination.

Tomkin reached the edge of the island and hesitated. The group that piped and fiddled in the midst of the three clustered birches were not known to him. They might not like his intrusion. Myrrdin had ordered him to find his clansmen and report on their activities, but the joke was on him, as Tomkin had no clan to call his own! At the time, Tomkin had thought this was a fine jest and that he would return each week to report nothing, exactly as the week before, because there was no clan to report upon. But the geas was too strong for that. Whatever guiding spirit held his reins, he was not allowed to ignore his commitments. The term *clan* was widened in meaning to include all Wee Folk, and thus he'd been forced to seek them out. The situation was most unfair, but there it was.

He took another few steps forward onto the island, and paused again. The fiddling and piping continued. He could see their shadows now, flickering as they leapt in circles amidst the birches.

Suddenly, he heard a rustling behind him. Another telltale splash, a tiny sound from pools to his left, finished the scenario. Tomkin turned and leapt high, but he was too late.

Two of his own kind leapt up to meet him. Like a group of mad hares, they met in midair and commenced a vicious fight. The other two wore top hats and tails—they were town-types, unlike him. The type of Wee Folk that liked to ape humanity. Unfortunately for Tomkin, in addition to their clothing, the others carried stout cudgels of gnarled hardwood. They swung them with urgency.

One cudgel crashed into Tomkin's scalp, while the other popped him on the back. Tomkin was knocked from the air and splashed down into a bubbling pool, but he was not out of the fight. The other two laughed and saluted one another.

"He's down, Dando!" shouted one.

"Let us crack him again!" returned the one known as Dando.

They lifted their staves, but Tomkin launched up from the mud and into their faces. He had in his hands a glittering knife. His shockingly large mouth opened, and his teeth caught one of the cudgels before it could be brought down upon him. The bitten wood snapped and the staff fell in two halves.

Tomkin put the knife under Dando's chin.

Dando dropped his cudgel immediately and looked shocked. "It was only a bit of fun, brother!" he said.

Tomkin growled in response. For a cold few seconds, they regarded one another. Two ruffians of the soft life faced a feral, clanless Wee One of the marshes. Tomkin could see they were suddenly fearful. He enjoyed the taste of their fear, and decided he would taste their blood as well. Let them savor this moment—

No! said a voice in Tomkin's mind. He knew instantly it was the spirit enforcing the geas. It felt to him as if it squeezed his mind. He gave a twisting, snarling howl of frustration. He wanted to cut these two, but he could not. The two Wee Folk looked on warily, not knowing what form of madman they'd had the misfortune to meet. The pipes and fiddles came to a halt and several others stepped forward and gathered around and see what was amiss.

"He's a wild one, step lightly!" said one of the pipers.

"It will take all of us to bring him to justice after poor Dando's brought down!"

Dando sputtered at this talk. "Nonsense!" he cried, trying desperately to sound confident. "It's only a long-lost cousin, attracted by the music to share our feast and festival. Make him welcome, everyone!"

None of the others moved. Tomkin's face continued to writhe as he fought his own muscles for control of his body. His tiny knife, however, remained under Dando's chin as if glued there.

"Be you a mad thing?" asked Dando in a hushed voice. His eyes were huge and gleaming. "A mindless assassin?"

Finally, Tomkin mastered himself enough to speak coherently. He shook his head. He stared at Dando quizzically. "Who art thee, miserable fop, to be believing thou warrants an assassin?"

Dando shook his head a fraction, but as the movement made the blade at his neck saw against his skin, he froze again. "No one, sirrah."

"How can this party be?" asked Tomkin with growing suspicion. He could not recall such a large gathering of his people in the marsh. Not ever.

"What is your meaning, brother?"

"So many of our kind. In my marsh. Why does this occur?"

"It is a party," called another Wee One who worn a lavender hat as tall as half-pint mug. "We dance in Dando's honor!"

Tomkin eyed the fancy creature called Dando with slitted eyes. He did not look important in Tomkin's eyes. Could this gathering truly be to honor such a scoundrel? He'd never had a party thrown for him by anyone. He eyed the crowd that had gathered around and didn't like any of them. They were of a different breed entirely. They thought him a wild lout—while he considered them conceited and foolish.

"This swamp is my home," Tomkin growled. "I've come to my island and discovered ruffians. I've been attacked, and did nothing but defend myself."

Several of the Wee Folk sputtered protests. They said he could not claim this land, as it was clearly sacred ground for all the Folk. Dando waved a silencing hand at them desperately, all the while keeping his gaze locked upon Tomkin.

"I apologize profusely!" Dando said. He spoke quickly in an ingratiating tone. "I am abject in my error! We are all sorrowful, and would be boundlessly in your debt fine sir—if you would only allow us use of *your* lands!"

Tomkin found his groveling disgusting, but he listened. The other Wee Folk huffed and snorted.

"'Boundlessly in my debt?'" asked Tomkin, tilting his head in a manner that was suddenly predatory.

Dando licked his lips. His eyes flashed to his comrades, who looked sour.

"Well, I can only speak for myself. But what is it you came for? Companionship?"

Tomkin stared at him for several long seconds. His hand, which held the knife, wanted to cut them all. But he could not, due to the pouch that hung like a slave's collar around his neck. He hissed vexedly.

"Companionship," he said at last. "Yes. I will partake of that."

Dando dared a fluttering smile. "Will you join us in festival then, this lovely eve?"

"No," Tomkin said. "Instead, *thee* shall join *me*. We will work our charms upon the town nearby. The River Folk have

237

offended me personally. I have declared an imbalance, and it must be settled."

"Tonight?" asked Dando. "We have not done a raid on a town for so very long. Perhaps another—" Dando broke off with a squeak, as Tomkin's knife pressed closer. A thin pink line appeared upon his skinny throat.

"Yes!" said Dando instantly. "Tonight would be excellent! I promise and do hereby swear: I will aid thee to make this night a special memory for the River Folk."

Tomkin nodded finally and gave them all a final, snarling curl of his lips. He meant it as a smile, but such expressions were not natural to him. He removed the blade from Dando's throat and the throng relaxed.

The pipes and the fiddles immediately began to play again. The colored wisps rose up and circled, brightening their glow in tune with the lighter mood. Everyone cheered and sang— except for Tomkin, who stood grumpily on the outer shore of the island.

Dando threw his arm around Tomkin and gave him a conspiratorial wink. "You had me going there for a moment, brother! You know, I could use a fellow like you at my side."

"Remove thy skinny fingers, or I'll have that hand off," Tomkin replied.

Dando's hand vanished, but his smile broadened. "Sorry! Just trying to be friendly, you understand?"

"No," Tomkin answered, staring with slitted eyes. "We shall go now."

"Where?"

"To North End."

"Oh yes, that," said Dando, looking annoyed. He sighed. "It will take most of the night, will it not?"

"Until dawn, I should think," Tomkin said.

Dando looked toward the party wistfully. There were Wee Folk maids there, and Dando obviously loathed leaving them. Suddenly, he brightened.

"Everyone! Everyone, may I have your attention please?"

Tomkin looked after Dando in irritation. What kind of delay would this weasel attempt now?

"I have a boon for you all," Dando said, throwing his voice suddenly downward into a low, conspiratorial tone. "We shall raid this town near us. We shall do as we have not done in two centuries! The Pact has fallen, and we need no longer cavort amongst lonely trees on swampy isles! Let's do as our elders did before us, as those who are aged may still remember. Let us *play*—with the River Folk serving as our toys!"

The Wee Folk considered his words with glassy eyes and waxy skins shining in the night. Suddenly, with a whoop, they began to bound into the air and shouted together: "Yes! Yes! Yes, we shall *play*!"

Within minutes, a troop of Wee Folk were bounding toward North End. They giggled, flipped, and twisted in mid-air as they went. When they reached the sleeping village, they quieted and went about their tricks and mischief as stealthily and quickly as they could.

Chapter Twelve
The Marsh

Brand and his comrades awoke to a gloomy marsh morning. The sun was a red disk that could not burn through the mist rising from the swamp that surrounded North End. After groaning and climbing out of bed shortly after dawn, the group all ate a dull breakfast of watercress and fish that tasted of grit. When they complained about the poor fare, they learned there had been a rash of small tricks and hexes performed during the night. Cows had gone dry and whole wracks of smoked fish had been stolen and spoiled. One woman even claimed that her child had been replaced by a changeling, but Myrrdin—after a very serious inspection of the squalling child—pronounced that it was only a mild case of rickets. He prescribed a remedy of acidic fruits and by ten o'clock the companions were ready to depart.

"It is well known that the Merlings have a hidden stronghold in Old Hob's Marsh outside North End," Myrrdin said. "It is there that I propose to parlay with them."

The others, rather unenthusiastically, had agreed to accompany him. Brand was silently thankful that Jak had not come with them, as he doubted that his brother would have readily agreed to doing anything with Merlings that didn't involve killing them.

They purchased marshshoes for the journey, but decided to head into the backwaters of the marsh by poling up the slow waterways on their skiff rather than going in by foot. Myrrdin cut and fashioned a parlay staff of hickory, with three long ribbons attached—two green and one white. This universal symbol of diplomatic intentions was fixed to the prow of the skiff, where the three ribbons wafted in the slow, dank breezes of the marsh. Brand wondered whether the Merlings were sophisticated enough to even recognize the parlay staff. Modi commented that the thing would only encourage attack by stating the group's probable lack of weapons.

After sailing upstream on the Berrywine into the entrance of a wide slow tributary, the skiff soon lost its wind and had to be poled. Gray-green reeds and lilies clustered around the boat, clinging to the prow and to their poles. Heavy frogs made odd, croaking cries and plopped in the water as they approached.

Brand and Corbin manned the poles in the prow and were soon sweating profusely despite the cool mists. In the stern, Gudrin and Myrrdin debated the relative natures of the Wee Folk, comparing one variety to another. Brand decided it was a good moment to talk to his cousin about recent events. "I can tell that you hate all the Wee Folk, now," he said.

Corbin glanced at him, his face grim. He made no reply.

"Dando didn't kill Sam."

"No, Dando didn't kill Sam," said Corbin. "But he did mock my brother in death. He toyed with his corpse. He played an evil prank."

Brand nodded. For all Corbin's usually easy-going nature, he wasn't one to forgive a real hurt. "I'm sure that if the little monster had danced upon Jak's head, I would feel the same. But I do hope that your spirit and nature aren't changed forever by this. I would miss the old jolly Corbin."

They poled on in silence for a time, and it seemed to Brand that the marsh was becoming increasingly still and cold. He shivered as the cool mists of the swamp stole into his cloak and chilled the sweat on his skin.

"It's just that—" broke in Corbin, suddenly. "—it's just that everything seems so wrong now." He heaved a great sigh. "I don't know. My home was burned and my brother killed. It's difficult to accept that the stories of olden times have come to be reality again. It seems unfair, somehow, that a week ago the world was perfect."

241

"Ah, but it wasn't," said Brand. "Recall the Dark Rider and the strange winter full of rainbows and all the rumors from the borders of the Haven. Myrrdin was late, everything felt wrong. All the evidence was there, but we refused to see it. We knew what was coming, we could *feel* it."

Corbin nodded. "Yes, I admit that I saw and felt strange things. Then, of course, they seemed minor and inconsequential. I only wonder what we could have done differently."

"Nothing," Brand said flatly. He could see the ugly head of self-recrimination rearing up, and he wanted to kill it right away before Corbin found a way to blame himself for Sam's death.

"Nothing?"

"Nothing. Because we can't go back and change it. Things were as they were then, and therefore they had to happen the way that they did. All we can do is learn from it and thus alter the future."

"Hmm," said Corbin. "I thought I was the thinker in this group..."

Brand laughed aloud, an alien sound in the silent cold mists, but he was glad to do it. Corbin had not made a joke of any kind for days.

Corbin glanced back at Myrrdin and Gudrin. Brand followed his gaze and they both eyed Gudrin's backpack with curiosity. "So, you are to bear one of the Color Jewels," whispered Corbin. "You'll have more magic on you than most of the Faerie!"

"Jealous?" asked Brand with a smile, not wanting his cousin's improved mood to falter.

"Me? Ha!" said Corbin. Then he lowered his voice to a bare whisper that Brand could hardly catch. "*I'm* not the jealous one."

Brand glanced back toward Modi, who was busy sharpening his weapon with a whetstone and cloth. Brand nodded, as if to himself, but he knew that Corbin caught the gesture. They had known one another too long—and been involved in so many youthful secrets—that their communication went far beyond words. Often when hunting or working the River or hiding something from Corbin's parents, they could move together with just a nod, working as a team with a single purpose in mind.

Brand wondered at their connection. He had always been more in tune with Corbin than anyone, even more than Jak, his own brother. Perhaps the fact that Jak was older and had far greater responsibilities made the difference.

Brand was jolted out of his reveries when the skiff bumped into something. He stumbled forward, but was too much of a boatsman to be thrown overboard, even when surprised.

"What is it?"

"Some kind of rope," muttered Corbin.

"Rope?" shouted Myrrdin from the stern. He sprang up and ran lightly forward. Leaning between the two heavier river-boys, he thrust his staff down into the muck and heaved up. With an expression of disgust, Brand reached into the green slimy water and helped him. Soon a rope, encrusted with gray-green growths, rose above the waters. It dripped and steamed and felt like a giant worm.

"Not just a rope!" said Myrrdin, pointing out the twisted lines of cord that hung down from the rope at even intervals. "It is a net!"

Brand released the thing and it slapped back down in the stinking waters. "We can go over it. But why is it here?"

Myrrdin shrugged. "It's a barrier, I have no doubt."

"Not much of a barrier against a flat-bottomed craft," remarked Corbin.

Myrrdin waved his staff in the air. The river-boys ducked a spray of muddy splatter. "No, no! Not to stop boats. Since when do Merlings use boats?"

"You mean the net is to stop Merlings?" asked Brand. He cast his eyes about the marsh with greater concern.

"Certainly. The tribes aren't all friendly to one another, you know. It's a good thing for you River Folk that they aren't, too. They'd give you much more trouble if they were organized into a single kingdom."

"Do you think they know that we're here?" asked Brand.

"Of course! They've known since the moment we turned into their part of the marsh, I suspect. I'm certain they have their eyes on us right now."

In response, Brand and Corbin both hunkered down in the skiff. They gripped their poles like weapons.

"Why have they not attacked?" demanded Modi. Brand looked over his shoulder to see the hulking Kindred sitting at the center of the skiff, his battleaxe across his thick knees. He scanned the shifting mists around them for signs of any threat.

Again, Myrrdin shrugged. "Perhaps they are curious, or they respect the parlay symbol," he said. "Or perhaps they simply aren't ready yet."

As no bulging pair of submerged eyes showed themselves, Brand and Corbin soon relaxed and worked the skiff over the barrier. They proceeded deeper into the marsh with more caution. Brand spoke less and shivered more. Often he wished he had Jak with his crossbow at his side. After a long day of work and tension, the sunlight began to falter. They found a relatively dry, sandy island, and decided to camp for the night.

* * *

Tomkin had enjoyed the experience of working with his fellows on a common goal. He had rarely known companionship of any kind. After a night of pranks and snickers, he felt something had changed within his heart. They had played every trick they'd known, and many they'd only heard about, upon the hapless marshmen while they slept in their moist beds. By dawn there was hardly an edible substance in the entire village the Wee Folk had not sampled and then spoiled. They had considered firing the town, but decided against it. Sorrow and grief were not as amusing as surprise and helpless rage. They wanted to impress the River Folk, to plague and harass them—not kill them. Where would be fun in that? Who would rebuild and be waiting to be tricked again the next time the Folk wanted a party?

Tomkin watched as the throng of them left the village just as dawn pinked the skies, as was the way of their people.

Everyone went their separate ways, with nothing left behind other than a wavering reed in the marshland to attest to their passing.

The wild manling was left wondering about Dando and the others. The Folk had feted Dando, and seemed to hold him in the highest regard. How was it that Dando seemed to warrant a vaunted spot among his kind, while Tomkin was unworthy of their spittle?

After rubbing his chin thoughtfully, standing all the while on a farmer's barn roof, he heard a voice shout up at him. He gazed down into the yard to see the white-haired farmer walking up from the house with two pails. No doubt, he planned to do some milking. Tomkin grinned at him.

"Hey there, get off my roof, you!" shouted the farmer.

Tomkin bowed, an unfamiliar affectation he'd learned from his Folk the night before. He did it with exaggerated movements, making the gesture mocking and insincere. "Be my guest, sirrah!" he shouted down from the roof. "Milk them well, with my blessing!"

So saying, Tomkin scuttled off the roof and raced out into the reeds. He paused to listen, however, for the farmer's shouts of dismay. They were not long in coming. Along with his brothers, Tomkin had spent the better part of an hour working the cows until they were full of nothing but thick cream near to butter.

When the farmer's outrage met his ears, Tomkin hooted. He'd rarely felt so good. He charged off into the reeds and disappeared from North End.

He wandered for the rest of the day through his swamplands. As much fun as he had the night before, he felt oddly deflated. He did not seek shelter and sleep, although he was tired. He did not take pleasure in the foodstuffs he found. Birds' eggs, toasted lizards, and the like seemed coarse fare after the delicacies he'd enjoyed with Dando's group. His comrades had carried no less than three jugs of Fae wine with them. He had tried them all: the pomegranate, the persimmon, and the gooseberry. In his opinion, the gooseberry had been the finest.

In time, he found himself returning to the isle where he'd found his Folk the night before. The place looked far less enchanting in the cold light of day. The pools were mud holes. The wisps had vanished and the three birches looked sickly, with twisted branches and half-peeled trunks.

Tomkin walked half-way around the island before he realized there were eyes upon him. He froze and cast his gaze this way and that. Could one of his Folk have returned? Might there be another party this eve? The breaking of the Pact might cause a revival of sorts, he dared hope. Perhaps his people would return to the lands of the Haven in droves, anxious to make up for lost time.

The towering figure his eyes finally landed upon was a horseman—and most definitely *not* one of his brothers. At first, Tomkin thought he might be gazing upon a man. But the absolute stillness of the stranger soon set that thought to rest. No man could sit upon a horse so motionlessly. No horse, for that matter, could stand like a statue for so long without so much as a sidestep or a whickering snort.

Tomkin did not flee, however. It was not his way to run immediately in the face of the unknown. He knew such instincts had served his people well for countless centuries, but it simply was not in his character. For one of the Wee Folk, he was remarkably brave.

After another minute, Tomkin began to wonder if he faced a statue or a scarecrow. Could his own wild Folk have left this manikin here, as a final jest to frighten him? Then, as he continued his scrutiny, he thought to hear soft music. He saw too, that the figure's eyes did move. They were not natural eyes, though. Rather, they were tiny dancing flames in the sockets. He knew then what it was he faced, and he would have rather faced the greatest knight of the River Folk—if they even had knights nowadays.

"So," Tomkin said, addressing the thing that sat upon its horse with infinite patience. "What does one of the Dead do in my marsh?"

"It is not your marsh, brash creature," answered the dead-thing.

"Thou art of the Wild Hunt, I take it?"

"Observant, but it is you who shall be answering the questions this day."

"What is it thou seeks?"

"I seek one of the Fae, one of the River Folk, and one that is both together."

Tomkin licked his lips. He seriously hoped he was not the person listed as *one of the Fae* which this creature claimed to seek. "I saw such a trio not an hour's march north of this very spot!" he said with a mocking laugh.

The other was silent. It still did not move. Tomkin wondered if he had offended it.

"Well," Tomkin said after an uncomfortable silence had passed, "I've got many appointments to keep this day. I bid thee farewell, and wish thee luck in thy quest."

The music stopped. There was a rasping sound. Tomkin saw a long length of fine steel reflecting in the sun as it was drawn.

Tomkin turned and ran.

Hooves thundered behind him. So close! The dead-thing which had sat so still was incredibly fast. He should never have sought to yank its beard in the first place. A thousand self-recriminations ran through his head, even as his legs pumped and his feet made wild-flying leaps over flowered clumps of stichwort, muddy pools, and occasional boulders. Quail burst out of hiding as he sailed over an insect-eating patch of sundew plants, then he darted under the stilted roots of a pond-ash tree.

He listened intently as the hooves thundered by and splashed away. Could he have lost the dead-thing? He dared not peep out. For all his bravado, Tomkin knew he was no bigger than a surly child to this horseman. Even the thought of sticking his blade into its desiccated flesh—or worse yet, biting into it—made him ill.

The silence went on, but the natural sounds of the bog did not return. The insects did not chirrup. The birds did not cry for mates nor warn one another away from their territory. The marsh was abnormally quiescent.

After another full minute, Tomkin poked his long nose out from under the tree roots. Immediately, a length of blade—silver-white and made of fine steel—appeared at his chest. The

247

long blade led up to a hand encased in a crumbling glove. Tomkin retreated from the tip of the sword, but the tip followed him.

"All right," he said, crossing his arms and walking out into the open. The sword tip marked him closely. "I would know thy name."

"Voynod."

Tomkin blinked. What could the Dark Bard want of him? "What is it thou desires, dead man?"

"As I've said," replied Voynod, "I seek three beings: one of the Fae, one of the River Folk, and one that is both together."

Tomkin eyed the dead-thing with vast distrust. Could this creature be thinking of Myrrdin and his friends? What did they have that would so interest the Wild Hunt? He could give them up, of course. It was well within his rights. They were clearly of interest: a half-breed traveling with a group of River Folk. Not exactly as the Huntsman described, but close enough. But Tomkin did not like this creature's manner. And he certainly did not like to be bullied by anyone. Although he had no love of Myrrdin, he would sooner trust the sneaky wizard than a pack of dead-things. He decided to avoid giving information. This was a natural attitude for him and took no special effort.

"Do they travel together?" Tomkin asked.

"Possibly."

"I have not seen such a trio. On this I swear."

The sword tip pressed closer to his chest. Tomkin stood firmly, angrily. The dead-thing suggested by its probing it did not believe him. Tomkin took this as an insult. He had seen no such party, and his word was his bond.

At last, after a tiny spot of blood showed on Tomkin's tunic, the sword was withdrawn.

"Interesting," Voynod said, studying Tomkin. "I have more questions."

"And I have prices," Tomkin said quickly.

"Why did you come here? What brought you to this place?"

Tomkin hesitated. It was a mistake, and he knew it, but he wanted to tell this creature about his gathering Folk even less than he wanted to tell it about Brand and his crew.

"What do you hide from me?" asked the Bard, leaning down from his creaking saddle.

"It is the month of the *Ngetal*—the month of the reed. At times, my people gather here during such evenings."

Voynod inclined his head and withdrew his person, sitting high upon his saddle again. "I found evidence of a celebration. Tiny, broken mugs and the like. You have spoken truth to me."

Tomkin shrugged. "Of course I have."

"Would your Folk be gathering here again tonight?"

Tomkin eyed him and shook his head. "I doubt it. It is not our way to be predictable."

Voynod murmured in agreement. He reached to his belt and tossed down a flashing, gold disk. Tomkin caught it and frowned at the object. He saw it was an old coin. Minted a millennium ago, the Faerie gold showed the head of a long dead king on its face.

"There is more gold to be had if you should help me," Voynod said.

"What would I do with this?" asked Tomkin. He did not like the weight of the coin. It would slow him. If he buried it, as his people often did, he would have to worry about its location and safety.

"Buy whatever pleases one of your kind," said Voynod, sounding surprised. "Buy yourself a top hat, at the very least. You resemble a beggar."

Tomkin hurled the coin back up at Voynod, who caught it effortlessly. "I have no need for thy trinkets! I don't like being in the employ or debt of another—and I *hate* top hats."

"Interesting," Voynod said again. He turned his horse without another word then and glided off across the swamp.

Tomkin watched him leave. His horse galloped, but did not quite touch the earth with its hooves. *That* was how the Bard had managed to double-back and approach in silence. Tomkin nodded and wondered about the coin. Should he have kept it? Perhaps he had no use for it, but another of his kind—perhaps one of the ladies of his Folk—might have.

He shrugged. What was done was done. He headed on his way, choosing to journey in the opposite direction Voynod had taken. He wanted nothing more to do with the dead-thing.

As he trotted through his marsh, he noted the natural sounds of of the swamp returned. Birds sang and whistled. Insects buzzed. Badgers and voles scrabbled in the underbrush. He was glad to hear it all, as it meant to him the dead-thing was far away.

He wondered about Voynod's quest. It seemed clear the Bard sought Dando, Myrrdin, and the River Folk. Tomkin thought it might be worth finding Dando first. He should at least give his brethren warning—if he did, he might be invited to future gatherings and pranks.

Also, he could not help but wonder: what was so interesting about those three?

Chapter Thirteen
The Axe

For Brand and his companions, the journey into the marsh went without incident for some days. It was slow-going, with many wrong-turns and wide boggy areas where the river seemed to disappear into marshy ground for miles. Often, they were forced to get out of the skiff and drag it behind them, slogging through endless sucking mud.

Several nights later, Brand awoke with a start. He immediately felt uneasy. Something was... *wrong*. He rose in his bedroll, which was shivery-cold in the dank night air. Leaning on one elbow, he peered about the campsite. The dying embers of the fire glowed and crackled nearby.

The fire! It was supposed to be kept going all night. Perhaps the cold had awakened him.

"Who's on watch?" he asked quietly. No one replied. The swamp was silent, save for the scrabbling crickets and the hoarse cries of the frogs. His breathing increased as he felt for the wood axe that had been at his side. It was gone.

His first thought was to shout for the others, but he dared not, as he wasn't sure what was happening. If they were under attack, perhaps it was better if the Merlings did not yet know he was awake. Trying to be silent, he slipped out of his bedroll and pulled on his river boots. With an odd twinge of homesickness, he noted that they were still new and stiff. Days ago he had not wanted to soil them, now such thoughts seemed trivial. He reached over to shake Corbin awake, and his mind froze over. Corbin was missing. There was nothing on his bedroll but a cold patch of slimy mud.

"Corbin? Gudrin? Telyn?" he hissed into the blackness around him. The mists swallowed the sound of his voice.

He rose into a crouch, realizing now that he might be alone. Over the sounds of his breathing and his pounding heart, he made out the slapping of flat feet on mud. A stealthy gurgling sound came from the opposite direction.

"Merlings!" shouted Brand. He broke and ran for the boat. Something on the dark ground moved and tripped him. He went down sprawling. His hands reached out and found it wasn't a Merling, nor one of his companions. It was a leather knapsack. He grabbed at it reflexively, and ran with it in his hands. Something inside it shifted, and he almost dropped it in surprise. It felt as if a small, trapped animal were inside, struggling to get out. That was when he remembered the axe; it must be Gudrin's knapsack. He thought that it might be of use, so he kept his grip on it and moved in the direction that he hoped the boat might be found.

At the shoreline, he found no boat, but he could see the dim outline of it, a few feet from shore. His first thought was that it had been cut adrift. Whatever the reason, he charged out into the marsh after it. Behind him, flat feet splashed and something hissed in excitement. The hairs on the back of his neck rose up as he feared that he might be cut down from behind.

He slogged forward, wading after the skiff. Unseen things clutched at his feet and the mud threatened to suck his boots away. As panic threatened to set in, he thought of something.

The axe!

It seemed heavier in the sack now, more deadly. He had an almost overwhelming urge to turn and face his pursuers and wield the axe. In his mind he could see their bulging eyes popping with terror, their strange skins and bones spilled open and their broken bodies floating in the stinking waters, righteously hewn down.

Then his train of thought was broken as his free hand reached the skiff. He hauled himself over the side. He scrambled up and was surprised to see a figure at the tiller. It was Telyn.

"Telyn!" he gasped. She made no reply, and her eyes stared fixedly ahead. He blinked back the red haze of the axe and forgot about slaughter and mayhem. Slipping twice on his muddy boots, he clambered to her side. He panted there, listening for the splashing of a Merling arm as trying to come over the side of the boat, but he heard only a distant, rhythmic rippling sound. It seemed that the creatures were content to swim after the skiff, perhaps not yet ready to board her. This made sense, as Merlings were always weaker and slower on boats and land than humans. They preferred to tackle only sleeping or unwary men in the darkness and close to water into which they could be easily dragged.

"Telyn? Where are the others?"

She didn't look at him, but only pointed over the prow of the skiff. Brand peered ahead, but could see nothing but blackness and drifting mists. He couldn't even tell which direction they were headed in. He laid his hands on her shoulders and was about to shake her, when he saw a light. It was a white ball of light, tinged with green. Shimmering through the fog, it danced and wavered in slow circles ahead of them. Just as quickly as it had appeared, it winked out again.

"Did you see?" asked Telyn in a hushed voice.

"Yes, I saw floating lights," answered Brand. "What were they? Where are the others?"

"Old Hob's green lantern," said Telyn.

"What?"

"The Will-O-Wisp, the dancing lights of the marshes."

"The Will-O-Wisp?" gasped Brand. He looked back into the darkness with his eyes wide. The light blinked on again, an indistinct ball of cold dancing fire. There was something about it, he could see now—a beauty that made one want to follow it and see the magical loveliness that it promised up close. No one in the River Haven knew what the Will-O-Wisp was, exactly, except that it was definitely related to the Faerie and often led the unwary into danger.

Brand looked back and watched it with Telyn for a moment. It winked out suddenly, and he was left wishing it would return. He shook his head and looked around him, recalling the Merlings and his missing companions. He became alarmed when he realized that the skiff had grounded, and was now far from the sandy island. Was the Will-O-Wisp bewitching him, as it appeared to be doing with Telyn? The softness of it belied the danger it represented.

"Telyn, what happened to the others? What about Corbin and Myrrdin? Did the Merlings take them?"

Telyn said nothing. She continued to stare straight ahead. She raised her arm to point into the mists. Brand followed her gesture and saw the Will-O-Wisp again, this time much closer. There was more than one of them now, perhaps six, and they were bigger and brighter than ever. White ones, yellow ones, and a single green one revolved around one another. Despite himself, Brand was entranced. They possessed a cold, silent beauty. Looking at them made sounds of music sing in his head and filled his nostrils with strong smells of spice and hot mead made from fresh honey.

He looked again to Telyn…but she was gone. She had already sprung out of the boat and was heading through the marsh toward the wisps, silent and intent.

"Telyn!" cried Brand, and went after her. Something tugged at his hand and he struggled briefly before realizing that it was the straps of Gudrin's knapsack. Somehow, the straps had entangled his hand. Almost as an afterthought, he took the knapsack with him.

A chase began. He felt the part of the lumbering ox, splashing through bogs and crashing through dense growths of reeds and fleshy swamp ferns. In turn, Telyn ran as lightly as a fox, circuiting the thickets he stumbled through, silent where he made a great racket, quick and agile where he was desperate and strong.

As quickly as they had loomed close, the wisps vanished from before them only to reappear moments later, this time off to the left and at a much greater distance. Brand realized that they were being led astray. He recalled his grandmother's old songs of warning, the songs that every river child was rocked to sleep by in their cradles, but it did him no good. If Telyn was bewitched, he would never give her up. And so he fell as neatly into the web as had Telyn herself.

As he struggled and panted to keep her in sight, he sometimes lost her and was forced to stand stock-still, waiting for the quiet sound of her footfall or the flittering of the dancing lights. When he received such a sign, it always seemed to be far off and at an angle to his current direction, so that he was left to charge blindly into the dark marshes to save his love.

My love? he thought.

Yes.

For it was then and there, splashing about in the marshes outside of North End, that he decided—nay, *admitted* to himself—that he loved Telyn. What other explanation could there be? Why else would he risk everything for this uncontainable woman? He asked himself this and much more during the chase, which went on for an unknowable time.

Finally, there came a moment when he could no longer see the lights, nor could he detect any sound nor sign of Telyn. Two minutes he waited, listening and casting about for any hint. Five minutes more passed, and he struck out in a random direction. Ten more passed and he halted. He despaired, his sobs—part grief, part fear and fatigue—escaped him as hoarse, choked cries. He had lost his beloved, just when he had decided that she *was* his beloved.

Finding himself exhausted by the rigors of marching through the endless marsh, Brand located a relatively dry spot and sat down to rest with his back to a gnarled tree. The tree's roots were twisted and exposed. Against his back they felt like the fingerbones of a dead, rotting hand.

He sat there for a time, in the blackness, hearing nothing but the nightbirds and the burbling of slow-moving waters. His head lolled, and he snapped back awake. He forced himself to shake off sleep and stand up; he could not give up on his love. But he was also at a loss.

Between his legs lay the backpack and within it slept what Gudrin called her burden. He became curious about it. He still found it hard to believe that he held one of the ancient Jewels. This one, Ambros, had been wrought long ago into a weapon by the Kindred.

Could Ambros help him? He felt sure that it could guide him, if only he were attuned to it. But he was no wizard! He had never even fashioned a charm or practiced a schoolboy hex. How could he hope to wield one of the six shards of the rainbow?

Pushing the idea and the knapsack aside, he tried to forget about it. In the morning, which could not be long in coming, he would backtrack to where he had lost Telyn and follow her trail as best he might.

Follow her trail? Through the marsh?

It was true, he admitted to himself, he had never tracked anything in a marsh before.

There is water. Water, water, everywhere. Not even a hound can track across water.

He would do it, somehow. He had to.

"But what if you can't?"

Brand gave a start. He peered around himself in the darkness, sure that he had heard a voice speak aloud. Nothing met his eyes or ears except the night sounds. Not even the Will-O-Wisp had come back to collect him. He sighed, thinking that he had been dreaming.

Old Hob's Lantern.

It had led Telyn off into the night. What dangers did she face even now?

She's in water.

He didn't even know if she was dead or alive. He might find her tomorrow, floating in the marsh, her lovely face down and her long dark hair matted and wet.

Up to her knees, and getting deeper. The Wisp is almost done with its game. Soon it will grow bored and drown her.

Brand gave another start. He found that the knapsack was in his arms now and that he had hugged it tightly to his chest. His mouth was open, his jaws were slack. A cold thread of spittle ran down his chin.

Save your beloved.

In a loving fashion, he rubbed his cheek against the rough leather of the knapsack's tightly cinched mouth.

Save her.

With sudden, urgent movements, he grabbed hold of the knapsack and worked at the knot. It unraveled easily, as if by its own accord, giving his blind, fumbling fingers no difficulty.

Hurry.

A brilliant golden glow, like the last dying light of a summer afternoon, streamed out to stain the gnarled trees. The trees seemed almost to strain away from it, contorting their twisted branches and shuddering. A single gray-brown leaf fell fluttering down to the marsh floor.

He paused there for a moment, stricken even as were the trees, by the beauty of it.

Hurry.

Brand reached into the sack and grasped the handle.

Chapter Fourteen
Old Hob's Green Lantern

Brand stood woodenly. In his hand he wielded frozen sunlight. The cold mists drew back from the blazing light of the exposed Jewel. The last tattered leaves that clung to the bony marsh trees fluttered as if pained by brilliance. Brand closed his eyes for a moment and willed the axe to tell him where his beloved faced mortal danger.

He felt nothing.

Confused, he turned about slowly, in a circle, trying to feel something, anything. All he could feel was the enemy. Enemies, many enemies. It seemed that the world teemed with them. But there was one powerful one...not too far off....

It was the Will-O-Wisp. Turning sharply on his heel, he headed off into the darkness. He felt no fatigue. He felt little— not the slippery mud beneath his tread, nor the dank cold of the night. All he felt was the cool pressure of the axe's flat, broad blades, which he rubbed against his stubbly cheek to soothe himself. The cold touch of it seemed to clear his head of sleep and uncertainty.

Behind him, forgotten in the dark, lay Gudrin's empty knapsack.

* * *

For an unknown time, he trudged through the marsh, oblivious to everything in his path. Twice, unthinkingly, he swung the axe, felling trees that barred his way rather than stepping around them. He was focused, he and the axe, upon a single objective. Little else could penetrate their collective thoughts.

His stride was long and purposeful. He passed over a great deal of ground with each step and never paused or wavered. When he finally saw the wisp—the first glimmer of green, drifting light—there was no change in his step. He didn't increase or decrease his pace, but rather continued on with deadly purpose. The axe now rode on his shoulder, the haft of it feeling good against his collarbone. He touched the blades to his cheek again and felt the surge of coolness run through his body and his mind.

He smiled then, and it was a wicked thing, not a smile of gladness. It was a thin, curving slit in his face, like a wound. Rather than happiness, it spoke of slaughter, gore, and rapine.

He finally came to a large open body of water. Above it, six dancing, blinking balls of fuzzy light drifted. All of them were white or yellow, the green one was not present. Like glowbugs in summer, the things winked on and off and flittered about with seemingly aimlessness movements. Always, however, their drifting was taking them farther out over the waters.

Telyn was there. He could see her now, wading up to her neck in the slimy pond. Around her head that the wisps danced—summoning her, guiding her, dragging her deeper still. As one of the lights danced close, almost touching her drowning face, Brand saw her hair floating free on the surface of the still pond. Her face was white and vague. She gave no sign of recognizing him, or her plight.

Brand never broke his stride. He never spoke. He simply walked out into the waters where the Faerie were toying with his love. The stinking water came to his knees, then his thighs, then flowed into his high boots in a slippery flood. Behind him his cloak floated on the surface. Reaching his love, he grasped her unceremoniously by the hair and yanked her back.

She gasped and struggled, but his grip was firm. He backed up, hauling her toward the shore. Around him, the wisps moved with greater agitation. They blinked in and out rapidly and drifted around the two humans. Their reflections glimmered and rippled on the surface of the cold water.

One came close enough to Brand for him to examine it. For a moment, he was stricken. He had seen the like of it before, he realized. It was a tiny, nude female. Her form was exquisite, perfect, beyond nature. She had wings of gossamer that flittered like those of a large dragonfly. Despite her impossibly small size, she somehow exuded lust. Brand's breath quickened and his backpedaling halted.

Standing as if frozen—chest-deep in the pond—he gazed up in wonder at the creature. She caressed her own cheeks and ran her tiny hands over her body in a smooth, languid fashion. Still held by the hair in Brand's inexorable grip, Telyn sought to free herself. He stared at the Faerie female in open-mouthed wonder, for the moment completely unaware of Telyn or anything else. Gradually, the other wisps began to come closer, circling around, revealing themselves to him. Each was female, each was perfect, but unique, like rare shining jewels exhumed from the hearts of individual mountains.

Then, quite by accident it seemed, Brand touched his cheek to the axe once again. A cold shock ran through him. It was as if he had been tossed into a snowbank while in a deep, warm sleep.

He staggered, almost losing his grip on his beloved's hair. The tiny nude nymph floated away, shaking her head with terrible sorrow. She felt him leaving her possession, and it pained her. Her pain was almost too much for him to bear. He took a step forward, still dragging Telyn.

"No," he croaked, "don't leave."

Then the axe brushed his cheek again and his face twisted into a snarl. He saw not a tiny beauty, but a wicked, cunning creature that sought to destroy him.

For the first time, he swung the axe in anger, and it flashed with the light of the sun when it struck. The tiny nymph fell into the pond with a small shriek, one of her wings shorn cleanly off. In that instant, the other nymphs winked out and vanished. The Will-O-Wisp that they had formed together ceased to be.

Telyn grabbed for the fallen creature, echoing the nymph's shriek with one of her own. Brand glared down at it, and saw that it would most likely live. He let go of Telyn's hair and reached for it, lifting the axe for a second, killing stroke.

"No, Brand!" cried Telyn. "You can't kill her!" She clutched the nymph to her breast and held it tightly. Then she saw Brand's face and the shimmering light of the axe, and her face changed to one of mortal fear.

Enemies.

Brand paused.

Evil. Slay them both.

Brand's arm rose. The Golden Eye of Ambros blinked then, filling the pond with the brilliance of day for a moment— like the strike of silent, amber lightning. Telyn, expecting death, cried out and shut her eyes. She protected the wounded nymph as a mother would a child.

Brand's arm rose higher still, but the axe did not fall. Within his mind and spirit a struggle went on. With a gasp, he released his grip upon the axe, and it splashed into the pond. It sank down into the stinking waters reluctantly; its light fading from brilliance to a glimmer, then a dull glow.

Taking hold of Telyn around her shoulders, he made for the shoreline. When they neared the water's edge, he turned back for the axe.

"Leave it!" cried Telyn.

"I can't," said Brand.

"Brand, you all but killed me!" said Telyn. "The axe is evil. It urges you to kill!"

Brand looked at her, then back toward the yellow glimmering spot that marked the waiting axe. His tongue snaked out and wet his lips. He wondered no more at Modi's longing for the axe. Perhaps the warrior had touched it once. Perhaps it had caressed his cheek, and had let him feel its cold bright power.

"...Brand!" Telyn cried. He realized she had been speaking to him, but that he had heard none of it. "The wisps, Brand!"

Brand found he had been gazing down and had waded forward to the axe, and was now much closer to it. But the Will-O-Wisp had returned—with a new member.

As Brand watched in horror, the new wisp rose up from the depths of pond. At first, it was nothing but a green glimmer, then a bright glow, until, finally, it broke the surface not a dozen paces from him.

The green wisp was not the same as the others, however. The green wisp was male, as perfectly formed as the females, and only slightly larger. He was caged in an old lantern of black, woven iron. His bright green glow was thus cut into many squares of shining light. Holding the lantern aloft was a gnarled hand of darker green. For a moment Brand watched as the lantern approached, shining its green light. Of Old Hob, for the moment, all that was visible was his upraised arm, holding aloft the lantern from the depths of the stinking waters. Slowly, the arm and the lantern drew closer. Around the male in his cage drifted the other remaining wisps, circling excitedly.

Brand quailed. He shrank back and looked toward the axe—so close. He paused. His mind froze over, his will to flee the approaching terror battling with the overwhelming desire to possess the axe once more.

"You must leave it! Don't touch it or you'll lose your sanity!" cried Telyn, sensing Brand's thoughts.

Still, Brand hesitated.

With a sound of desperation and fear, Brand heard Telyn coming up behind him. He blinked in surprise as he saw her reach down for the axe, using her cloak to wrap it in.

"It's mine!" cried Brand, grabbing it from her. Telyn staggered back from him, still clutching the nymph in her other hand.

It was then that Old Hob, eldest of all goblins, spoke to them. "Pray tell," he gargled in a watery voice, "who has stolen my youngest ward?"

Brand and Telyn turned to face him, and knew true fear. Old Hob loomed above them, one of the grimmest of the Dark Faerie that ever was mentioned by mother to child. The figure beneath the cowl and the robe was indistinct, but seemed to be made all of random lumps and twists, with no symmetry or natural repetition of form. The exposed arm was mottled and discolored, with horn-like growths and rough-textured bumps running the length of it. The face was cowled and invisible but for the dark crook of flesh that protruded from it. This flesh was, Brand surmised, a large nose or, perhaps, a narrow, pointed chin.

"Your ward? You mean the wisp?" asked Telyn, being first to regain her voice.

Brand felt little but for the urging of the axe to take it up and strike down this monstrosity that threatened him and his beloved. For the moment, he was beyond speech.

"Yes, the wisp, child," came the odd, watery reply. Hob took another half-step closer. The River Folk took a half-step back. "I require the seventh wisp. Her husband and sisters would be sad without her."

The other Faerie floated in lazy circles around them, curious and listening intently. Their reflections shimmered upon the water like a half-dozen full moons.

"You have imprisoned their male?" asked Telyn in disgust. "You keep them all in bondage this way?"

Old Hob shifted his lantern, for a moment partly illuminating the gloom beneath his dripping cowl. Brand saw a hint of inhuman eyes. They were the yellow eyes of an animal—perhaps that of a snake.

"They are my possessions, child. Return the wisp."

"They are such exquisite creatures," said Telyn, cradling the wounded wisp. "I would not feel right to hand a slave back to her master."

"Enough!" cried Hob. He stood suddenly, and the River Folk learned that he had been hunkering down in the water, and only now rose to his true height. The vast, dripping form towered above them, standing perhaps twice the height of Brand. The indistinct form beneath the robe now took on new menace, being of greater bulk than they had previously imagined. A wave of stinking water lapped over them, and they staggered back in shock.

"The wisp!" rumbled Old Hob, extending a grossly deformed arm that ended in a twisted, dripping claw.

"We must parlay first," said Brand, finding his voice.

"Parlay?" roared Old Hob. His arm swung to grasp his vast mid-section. He roared with unnatural laughter. "An insect seeks to parlay with Hob? In Hob's waters?"

263

"Yes," said Brand. He gripped the axe now, holding it through two layers of Telyn's cloak. He hoped it was enough to keep it from taking over his mind. He felt sure that if it had its way, there would be a bath of blood that would deepen this disgusting pond by a good measure.

"Ah, yes, the Eye of Ambros," rumbled Hob. "The other item that I require. It was good of thee to bring it into my domain. Now, cast it into the center of my pond and remove thy clothing, manling. It has been too long since I have devoured one of the River Folk— or sired a squirming litter of rhinogs!" This last he directed at Telyn, giving her a yellow-eyed wink.

Brand and Telyn took another two steps back in unison.

"Ah now, I don't fancy a chase!" said Old Hob. He chuckled then and the sound was menacing beyond any they had ever known. "I promise a clean kill for obedience, as is my custom."

"I will neither run, nor yield," said Brand, holding aloft the axe. He knew that he must seem firm, hoping that Old Hob, like all other goblins, would shy from an open and fair fight. "Should you take another step, by the Golden Eye of Ambros, I will hack your foul limbs from your body and stuff your grotesque head into that iron lantern you carry. Again, I ask to parlay."

Both Telyn and Old Hob seemed a trifle surprised by Brand's words. The wisps circled with more speed and several of them began to blink in and out of sight.

"A child wields the axe?" asked Old Hob in disbelief.

"I am a man."

"It is not yet attuned to thy spirit, fool," returned the eldest goblin.

"It is attuned enough. Gudrin and Myrrdin have instructed me."

"The child wields names to impress Old Hob, even as it claims to wield one of the Nine Jewels," said the monster. He held his lantern to his face and spoke to the green wisp inside. "What say thee, Ganleon?"

Inside, the wisp shrank back from his master.

Old Hob suddenly glared back at the two River Folk. "It is agreed then. First we parlay, then I shall devour the upstart and produce a fine litter by the half-breed temptress. I bade thee to speak."

"Great Hob—" began Telyn, but he swung his iron lantern at her so that she had to duck.

"Silence! I will speak only with the axe-bearer. I will hear enough of thy pitiful cries later, girl."

Brand held his axe tightly and battled for his will. Fatigue, the axe, and his natural terror fought against him. He tried to come up with something to say.

Old Hob, sensing hesitation, leaned forward meaningfully. "Hast thou no words?"

"Yes, I will speak," said Brand. "Why did your offspring attack my clan?"

"Thou hast the idiocy to threaten me with Ambros and still ask why we sought to claim it?" snorted the goblin. A gush of discharge fired from beneath his cowl. The dark slime splattered the pond's placid surface and clung there, refusing to sink. Brand wondered what other disgusting things they were wading in and felt ill.

"If we return the wisp and promise that the River Folk won't harm any goblin if they aren't harmed first, will you drop your alliance with Herla?"

"You dare speak of the Wild Huntsman so plainly, eh?" said Hob, sounding impressed. His free claw reached up into his cowl and touched his unseen face. "How is it that you speak in this matter for all the River Folk?"

"I do speak for the River Folk," bluffed Brand resolutely. He wondered if the axe gave him courage and put steel into his words, even when it wasn't touching his flesh. "My Uncle Tylag is the head of Clan Rabing. I've been selected to bear the axe as the champion of the River Folk."

"Ha!" roared Hob. "Could they not have found someone younger? A teat-suckling whelp, perhaps? What hast thou, boy, twenty summers? I wager thou hast yet to bed this fine wench!" said Hob, gesturing with his free claw toward Telyn. He leaned forward a bit, his great form looming over them. The dark protruding lump that thrust out of his cowl made snuffling sounds. Brand felt sure now that it was the monster's nose. "Yes, she has a pure smell. I'll enjoy myself all the more after my meal. Our parlance is finished! Now it's time to remove thy clothing, axe-bearer!"

"You haven't answered my query," said Brand. "Will the goblins cease to perform as Herla's army?"

"The goblins wield no Jewel," said Hob. "That changes tonight. Despite thy impudence, I will grant thee a boon of quick death, axe-bearer, for bringing me this unexpected prize—and as a fee for providing my evening entertainment."

"You evade the question, Hob," said Brand. "Don't you control your people? Does Herla rule the goblin sires and their offspring, or do you?"

Hob roared in anger. His lantern swept back, then forward like a great mace aimed at Brand's head. The wisp inside gripped the iron cage and fluttered his wings. His green light brightened, illuminating the trees along the shoreline. Standing waist-deep in the pond, there was little Brand could do but use the axe. Without thought, he raised the weapon. There was another flash of yellow light and a sound like the clashing of great swords. Brand's arms were stunned by the impact and he all but dropped the weapon. Somehow, he managed to cling to it—or perhaps it clung to him.

Brand looked up, sure to see Hob's maw stooping to devour a foolish river-boy. Instead, he saw the bottom of the lantern had been shorn free from the rest of it, and now the green wisp was free and floating away with the circling crowd of excited females.

Roaring with anguish, Hob now followed after his own Will-O-Wisp, which led him deeper into the pond. Taking this opportunity to escape, Brand and Telyn splashed their way toward the shoreline. Another roar of anguish came up from Old Hob as he discovered their escape.

"Thou hast wronged me!" roared Hob toward their retreating backs. "No goblin shall rest until thy bones simmer in my stewpot! And thee, wench! Thy rhinog offspring shall feed upon their own mother one day hence!"

266

Once they felt they were safely away into the trees, they paused to rest. Their breath came in painful sobs and their hearts and heads hammered with exertion.

Brand was the first to speak. "You could have left me, Telyn. I was mad to go back for the axe."

"Wrong on both counts, river-boy," returned Telyn in a ragged gasp. "We did Old Hob an injury, rather than making him a gift of the axe."

"I did not mean to make more enemies for the Haven."

"He will never be anything other than an enemy. As for leaving you, I couldn't leave the one who had followed me on my foolish way through all this forsaken swamp!"

She came close then, and kissed his sweaty cheek. "As you would not leave me, nor would I leave you, Brand," she whispered in his ear. She squeezed his arm. A shock of heat ran through him. Her kiss and touch were as powerful in their own way as the cold touch of the axe.

Brand looked at the axe. He thought of putting it down on the ground, but could not. The weight of it, when he wasn't touching it directly, seemed almost too much to bear. Now he understood why Gudrin had carried it tucked away in her knapsack, and why it always seemed to burden her.

"What scares me is that I know I couldn't have left it for my life, Telyn. The River help me Telyn, but I do love it so!" said Brand, his voice hushed and shamed.

Telyn put her arms around him and hugged him. As she did so, a tiny squeak came from her tunic.

"The wisp!" she cried. "I forgot about her!" She produced the wounded creature and stretched her out upon her palm so that the wisp's legs dangled over her wrist. She was only barely glimmering with a pale radiance now.

Brand felt ashamed to know that he had harmed such a beautiful creature.

"Don't be glum, Brand," said Telyn, reading his thoughts. "Even if this wisp dies, you freed her and her family from slavery."

Brand nodded. Still, it made his eyes burn to see the wisp hurt. It was like seeing the broken body of a child and a beautiful woman, all at once.

"Look!" Telyn hissed to him. He followed her gesture and saw lights glimmering in the trees behind them. "Hob follows us!"

Brand knew another thrill of panic. "Could Old Hob have recaptured his wisps so quickly?" he asked in a hushed voice.

"We don't know what powers he might have over them," replied Telyn. "The lights are approaching—we must flee."

Brand groaned and began stumbling after her. Fleet-footed, she headed into the thickest stand of trees in sight. The only light they had was the glimmering of the axe, but it was enough to see by. Soon, they had lost themselves in a forest of vegetation. Ferns grew here in wild profusion. Giant fronds came up out of the darkness and brushed their faces like giant, caressing feathers.

For a moment, the wisps were gone. "Have we lost him?" asked Brand.

"I think not," she said. "I'm sure he knows this land far better than we."

"How then can we escape this monster?"

"Perhaps if we keep fleeing until dawn, he will concede the chase. Goblins rarely venture forth in the light of day."

Brand groaned aloud. "I'm weary beyond belief, Telyn. I fear I might collapse. Perhaps we should make our stand on a spot of our own choosing before I lose all my strength."

Telyn looked at him in concern. "The sun should rise in two hours, maybe less."

Brand shook his head. He knew in his bones that he couldn't walk the swamp for two hours more. "I don't think I can make it. Besides, if he did catch up, we might be trapped in a bad spot, too fatigued to fight."

"You mean too fatigued to wield the axe," said Telyn. Her face was lined with worry. "In fact, you intend to wield it. Does it call to you, Brand? Does it want you to fight Old Hob?"

Brand blinked at her, thinking about it. "Yes, I believe that it does."

"I'm not sure that we should trust it. It seems to want nothing but bloodshed, and tends to see everyone as a potential

268

enemy. Like a man whose only tool is a hammer, it tends to see many nails."

Brand nodded. "I'm *sure* that we shouldn't trust it." Before he could go on though, Telyn was pointing over his shoulder. He saw the look of fear in her eyes and fully expected to see Old Hob looming above him as he whirled. Instead, it was the green wisp, the male. He floated over the ferns, lighting them with his soft, green glow. Telyn turned to run in the opposite direction.

"Wait!" he cried to her. "They might be herding us into another trap!"

Telyn suddenly veered to the left, having just encountered another wisp, this time a female of the familiar yellow-white shade. Brand crashed through the ferns after her. He now felt convinced that the wisps had encircled them and were herding them into Hob's waiting arms. He made a grab for Telyn's cloak, but grabbed only big, leafy fronds.

The desire to take hold of the naked haft of the axe became almost overwhelming. Slowing to a walk, he held it aloft before himself, so that the broad double-bladed head filled his vision. In the heart of the two blades shimmered the brilliant amber Jewel. In its light he saw a purity of color that had never been matched upon the earth or the heavens above.

The Golden Eye of Ambros brightened under his scrutiny. Some small, distant part of his mind wondered if the final decision to wield the axe would be his last conscious act of will.

Something loomed up to his right, a green glowing thing. He thought he saw Hob's face. His enemy was there, the enemy that must be struck down.

Cut down the fiend.

He felt a yearning to see his enemy cut and bloody and dead at his feet.

You must wield the axe.

Old Hob had threatened to make Telyn sire his foul offspring. This couldn't be allowed. Death for everyone was preferable.

You must...

"—Brand?" came a distant voice. He couldn't identify it right away, although it seemed familiar.

Wield the axe.

"Brand, they're friendly! Put down the axe!"

Telyn! He had it now. That's who it was. She was the one who must be saved. Her words, however, were lost on him.

Then, suddenly, something darted between his eyes and the Eye of Ambros, into which he had been staring most deeply. He blinked, and a flash of anger ran through him. With a growl, he moved to cut down the flittering thing.

Then he stopped. As if awakening from a dream, he found himself standing in the lush ferns, surrounded by wisps and Telyn. A tiny, beautiful female wisp had darted between his eyes and the Eye of Ambros. With a sick feeling, he looked about wildly.

"Did I kill her? I swear, I was not myself!"

"No, no, Brand," said Telyn, putting her soothing hands on his shoulders from behind. She hugged his broad back. "You harmed no one."

Brand looked up to see the wisp float closer to him again. She had risked her life to break the spell by passing between his eyes and the Jewel. He felt ashamed to have threatened such a wonderful creature.

"But what of Hob?" he asked.

"He has retreated to his pond, I hope," answered Telyn. "These wisps followed us. I believe they want the injured one returned to them."

Brand nodded. Telyn produced the tiny wisp from her pocket and instantly the male wisp swooped down and took her away, his family following him. He paused, looking back at the humans. He gestured to one of the yellow wisps, who separated herself from the others and returned to hover just inches from Brand's cheek.

Brand was entranced and his face, which had scowled death's own mask a minute earlier, now was wreathed with smiles.

"Not even the Shining Lady could possess such beauty," he said in wonder. Telyn made a sound of delight as well.

270

The wisp curtsied in mid-air, as if to acknowledge the compliment. She then pointed off into the swamp and made a series of short flights in that direction. Each time she returned to them and repeated the action.

Brand and Telyn looked at one another.

"Normally," said Telyn. "I wouldn't be the first to suggest that we follow a wisp, but this is a special circumstance."

Brand nodded. "Indeed. This is the first time that I ever thought any of the Faerie could be trusted. I guess it is with them as Dando said, 'Friendship is always earned, never given.'"

So saying, the two of them followed the wisp out of the fern forest and into the rest of Old Hob's Marsh, going they knew not where.

They followed the wisp until dawn began to lighten the sky. Ever they begged her to rest, but she urged them onward. They didn't know where she was leading them, but hoped it was to their companions, or a way out of the swamp, or just to the cabin of a marshman who could help them.

Just before dawn the wisp halted and pointed east, in the direction they had been going. They took it to mean that they should continue forward. To Telyn, she flittered close and caressed her cheek. Telyn smiled and touched the spot delicately. To their amazement the spot on her cheek and her hand where she touched it glowed for a time with the same radiance as the wisp.

When they looked up, they found she had gone. They cast about them for some sign of her, but could find nothing, not even a distant glimmer.

"She's gone back to her family," said Telyn. She still gazed down on the tiny spot, now fading, that glowed upon her fingertips.

"They are clearly creatures of the night rather than the day," agreed Brand heartily. He sat down upon a relatively dry spot and leaned back against a gnarled tangle of tree roots. To him they were as comfortable as a featherbed.

"Ah! I'd thought she would lead us to Snowdon before she was done," he sighed.

"Perhaps we should keep going," said Telyn worriedly, looking to the east. "Perhaps the others need us."

"Surely you jest, milady," mumbled Brand through thick lips. Already his eyes had closed. "I, unlike the wisps, am a creature of day. Also unlike them, and yourself, I need sleep."

"But the others, Brand."

"If they have suffered the night, they can hold another hour. I have no strength left to rescue them now, if that's what they are needing. Besides, we don't really know what the wisp was leading us to. Maybe this is just a garden spot of the swamp to her, and she wanted to show it to us!" said Brand, making a clumsy, sweeping gesture that indicated their drab surroundings. Even while gesturing, his eyes stayed shut. The brightening skies of dawn seemed painful to his weary eyes.

With a sigh, Telyn sat beside him.

Chapter Fifteen
Merlings

In the light of morning, Brand awoke, shivering. The tree roots had cruelly dug their way into his back and ribs, causing a dozen sharp aches and cramps. He eyed the marshlands around himself blearily, realizing that for perhaps the first time in his life he was truly and utterly lost.

Then he noted the only source of warmth that touched him. He looked down upon Telyn, asleep upon his shoulder, and smiled. Although the weight of her slightly discomforted him and the roots that dug into his back from behind made him want to stretch, he did not move. This was a moment to dream of. Telyn slept on his shoulder, touching him. A thrill of pride and contentment and protectiveness shot through him.

The sleep had done him a world of good. He lay back and breathed deeply of the morning air. It stank, but he didn't care. Out on his own like this, with Telyn, he felt more like a man than he ever had. It was exciting and daunting, all at the same time.

Soon, though, he could stand the pinching of his shoulder no longer. To relieve it, he rolled it slightly under her weight. To his disappointment she awakened almost instantly. She made a small sleep-sound that made him smile again, then she blinked at the world. She yawned and it seemed to him that even her yawn was attractive somehow.

"Morning," he said quietly.

"We've slept for hours!" she exclaimed, staggering up.

Brand winced at the pain in his shoulder and back, but tried not to let on. "Yes, we should get moving."

"You should have awakened me, Brand," she scolded, picking up her things. She emptied out her knapsack, which she still had after all this time, and handed it to him.

"What's this?"

"Put the axe in it."

"Right," said Brand, thinking of the axe for the first time. He felt a pang of worry, but quickly found it leaning against the tree beside him. "I'll look like Gudrin's over-grown son with this thing moving about like a full game-bag on my back."

The axe barely fit into the knapsack, and Brand worried that its razor-edged blades would cut through the leather. The handle poked out of the top so that there was no way to hide it.

"Well, people are going to know what you have," said Telyn, putting her things into various pockets of her muddy cloak and tunic. "But at least there is less chance of you getting bewitched again by accident."

"Yes. Now if I wield the axe, there will be no question that it was my choice to do so."

Telyn glanced at him sharply. She nodded. "Let us hope so."

After making a poor breakfast of the odds and ends from Telyn's tunic and a few swallows from Brand's waterskin, they set off in the direction of the rising sun. Soon, they came upon signs of Merlings: a woven mesh of reeds designed to trap and drown six-legged muckfish, a clutch of sucked-dry bird's eggs, and a totem made of a skull. The skull had braided strips of hide and was decorated with chips of colored glass. Brand recognized the totem as a crude effigy of Herla.

Brand felt a sudden urge to crush the effigy. He advanced on it, a growl emanating from his throat.

"Brand!" hissed Telyn. "Don't! We can't afford the noise or any obvious signs of our presence!"

Brand halted, shoulders hunched. He sighed. "Sorry. I don't know what I was thinking."

Telyn nodded with pursed lips. She gave the axe-handle that rode his back a long, mistrustful look. Then she continued eastward and Brand followed, feeling sheepish.

Speaking only in whispers and moving with stealth they approached what could only be a Merling village. Brand had never seen one before, but knew that the best time to venture near one was in the brightest light of day, when the Merlings were at their most sluggish.

They came close enough to see the earthen mounds before the River Folk quailed. Telyn sank down behind a gnarled tree trunk and Brand knelt by her. Brand studied the village with interest. The entire encampment was difficult to spot unless you knew what you were looking for. All surrounded by a central pond, he counted six of the long, low lodges made of muck and woven sticks. All of the lodges abutted trees and seemed like unnatural extensions of the trees' root systems. Brand knew from stories that each of the squat, cancerous mounds would have multiple secret tunnels that led into the surrounding pond.

"What do we do?" Telyn hissed.

"The wisp wouldn't have led us here without a reason. One or more of our companions have got to be here."

Grabbing him, Telyn pointed to a fluttering object near one of the great mounds. It was a staff of hickory with three ribbons fluttering from it, two green and one white. One of the green ribbons was torn and partially missing.

"Our parlay symbol. If they live, they are here," she hissed. "We must rescue them somehow."

"I agree," whispered Brand. Despite the seriousness of the situation, he found that it was pleasant to whisper into her ear. He enjoyed the opportunity for his lips to touch her skin. "But if they are nothing but bones in a stewpot," —he shuddered at the thought— "I don't wish to join them."

Nodding, Telyn rose up. "Wait here, I have an idea," she said, and headed off to the right. Brand half-reached to restrain her, but as usual her thoughts and actions were one and she was already in motion. He watched her closely from concealment until she disappeared from sight behind one of the mounds.

He sighed quietly, wondering if he would need to wield the axe again. The axe was suddenly alive in his knapsack, and almost caused him to cry out, thinking a Merling was pawing him. It had shifted its weight of its own accord, as he had seen

275

it do upon Gudrin's back. It made his skin crawl to think of it. It was unnatural and beyond his experience. And yet, although such a thing would have sent him off screaming a month ago, it now seemed only odd and discomforting. He reflected upon the breaking of the Pact and the great changes it had wrought upon his world.

His thoughts were broken by a burbling sound followed by a splash. He craned his neck around the tree trunk. Telyn was a master of stealth, but she had perhaps met her match with the Merlings. They had come upon her from behind, showing only their bulbous eyes above the surface of their placid pond. Lurching up out of the water with croaking sounds of dubious meaning, they stalked her. Telyn was in the middle of investigating one of the mounds, looking and listening for signs of captive humans. She turned to run, but found herself cut off.

Brand rose up and reached for the axe. Again it shifted its weight, as if eager to be out of the dark knapsack. He hesitated, wondering if he could control it this time. He drew in a breath to call to Telyn. Perhaps if he could distract the Merlings, she could yet escape. He watched as she reached first for her bow, then realizing they were too close, drew her knife instead. The approaching Merlings paused, hissing. It was not their way to face an armed human in daylight. They themselves clutched tridents and weighted cords from which dozens of sharp, barbed hooks dangled. They slowly began to whirl these cords over their heads. Used like a whip, they could bring a human down, tearing up an ankle or forearm in the process.

Brand ran now, but the Merlings hadn't noticed him yet, so intent were they on stalking Telyn. They advanced slowly, allowing time for reinforcements to slither up from the pond. Telyn backed to the end of the spit of land she was on and looked with desperation to the water on both sides.

Brand felt her fear. "No! Not the water! Keep to the land!" he cried out.

The Merlings whirled to look at him. Telyn took this moment to slash at one of them. It's arm oozed and it croaked in dismay. The pack of them retreated one step, then two.

More of them rose up from the pond and Brand saw he had no choice but to wield the axe once more. They were not going to give her up without a fight. With a silent prayer to the River to guide him, he reached back over his shoulder. He had no need to grope for the axe-handle, as it slapped itself into his hand.

Ecstasy coursed through him. It began in his fingertips, ran up the palm of his hand and forearm, then seemed to linger a moment in his bicep before racing hotly into his head. His head filled with the coppery scent of blood.

He ripped Ambros from the pack, not bothering with the flaps. The blades slid through the leather with ease and sang as they blazed into the gray light of the morning. Brand charged at the Merlings, his face split wide with a toothy grin. Most of them fled into the safe waters of their pond, slipping into the muck and filth that meant home and safety to them. But two sought to stand before him. The first swung its weighted cord laced with gleaming hooks. Ambros slipped forward and severed the cord first, then the neck of its wielder. The creature's head and the weighted end of the cord both flew out to splash into the murky waters of the pond. The second Merling fared no better and fell into the mud, clutching its spilled vitals.

Ambros gleamed happily as it drank their small lives. These killings did not slake its thirst, however, but only brought its desire to a furious boil. Whooping, Brand felt detached from himself. Almost by itself, the axe swept gracefully at Telyn's white neck. Brand turned the axe from slaying her with a deft twist, almost an afterthought, before he waded into the pond itself after the enemy. From his lips erupted an ancient battlesong, one he could not recall having heard before, in a tongue that was only remotely recognizable to him.

In the water, however, the slothful Merlings became quick and graceful. They fled from him with rapid flips of their limbs. One even broke the surface and flew through the air in its haste to avoid him, like a salmon leaping from the cold water of the river. Left without enemies, Brand headed for the nearest of the lodges. Standing over it, he hewed out great chunks of the thick walls. Woven sticks and muck flew everywhere. Inside, females and their offspring squirmed in the unfamiliar sunlight. Two clutches of eggs were in evidence. One of the females that brooded over them didn't flee. She hunkered over her eggs protectively, an odd growl emanating from her throat.

Brand paused for the first time. He raised the axe and it winked. The lightning-like flash of light blinded the Merlings so that they cried out, shielding their eyes. The sight of these creatures, so many maggots swarming upon meat, filled him with disgust, but still he did not strike.

The stewpot.

Brand blinked in confusion.

Look at the stewpot. It was there that they cooked your friends.

Brand looked at the crude stewpot that sat in the middle of the torn-open lodge. It was empty, but he knew that in just such stewpots, many humans had ended their lives, often boiled alive and screaming. Still, the female held her ground, protecting her young, and hissed at him. Again, Brand did not strike.

It was here that they boiled your parents. Their skin sloughed from their bubbling flesh.

Brand made an odd sound. He lifted the axe for a killing blow. Then, without warming, something struck his wrists and the axe dropped from his grasp.

Treachery—-! the word screamed in his mind as the axe fell.

"What's wrong with you, Brand?" yelled Telyn in his ear. "They're coming with catapults! They'll pepper us with bolts from the safety of the pond! We must flee!"

Brand whirled on her. "You must not touch the axe!"

Telyn looked at him for a moment, then grabbed up the axe with her cloak, careful not to touch it with her bare hands. She ran with it toward the shore, splashing through the shallowest part of the pond.

"*THIEF!*" roared Brand, chasing her. He ignored the catapults that snapped and sang around him. Murder shown in his eyes.

He chased Telyn into the forest, quickly outdistancing the Merlings on land. When he finally caught up with her, the madness had left him.

"I..." he panted, "I'm sorry—"

"It's okay," she gasped out, letting the axe drop to the wet ground. "I shouldn't have run off by myself. By the River, the thing is heavy!"

Brand nodded. "It is heavy when it does not want to go with you, but as light as straw when you slay with it." He looked at Telyn. "We could have been killed, you know."

Telyn nodded. She chewed her lip and her eyes were wide with fright.

"I killed Merlings." he said in wonder. "It was almost like killing men. It was terribly easy, Telyn. Part of me—part of me enjoyed it."

She just stared at him. Then he opened his arms, and they embraced, standing over the axe.

"I must learn to control it," he whispered into her ear.

"Yes," she said softly.

They both looked at the axe that lay at their feet. The mud of the marsh wouldn't stick to the Jewel or the blade. As the River Folk watched, the muck seemed to turn to liquid and crawl from the surface of the gleaming blades. Brand wondered if it would eventually kill his friends...or even him.

* * *

Tomkin searched for days before he caught up with Dando again. He'd taken to questioning wisps who had attended the party in the marsh. Wisps were notoriously gossipy and unreliable. They did not maliciously *lie*, but they definitely did *embellish* when pressed for details. They didn't like to disappoint their questioners, and tended to make things up, lost in the moment of excitement, *improving* a tale to the point of distortion.

After being led to foxholes in the dead of night, circles of stones at the bottom of waterfalls and lost Fae mounds in the Deepwood, he finally got a tip from a vermilion wisp.

Grumbling and suspicious, he followed her to the foot of the Black Mountains. There, he realized she was flittering straight up a rocky cliff. That was all very well when one had wings, but the climb looked long and it was barely two hours before dawn broke.

Tomkin hesitated there, staring up into the starry night after the reddish ball of color which was the wisp. She was oblivious to whether he still followed or not, so excited was she to have the attention of another of the Fae. The wisps considered themselves to be very low in status, and so accounted the Wee Folk as gentile and impressive, when to all others they were only sneer-worthy. The attitude was endearing, but consistent failures had embittered Tomkin. He sighed, staring upward after the wisp.

He considered abandoning the quest for the night, but then something caught his eye. Was that a flash up above? There it was again! A flicker of light from on high. Something way up, perhaps on the very mountaintop...on the roof of the world. The winds and feel of the night wasn't right for a storm. There was no thunder. If this were lightning, then it was silent lightning. Taking in a great breath, he began the climb. Perhaps, when he got there, he would at least witness something of interest.

The climb was worse than he had imagined. When he finally reached the summit, he found a bald expanse of rock, black as pitch in the night. There was no moon riding overhead, and starlight was all he had to guide him as he walked over the mountaintop. The wisp had departed by then— her kind never had anything resembling patience. She had probably forgotten who she had led to this lonely place the moment he was out of sight, and had buzzed away to irritate another fool.

Tomkin kicked at loose pebbles and wandered the mountaintop. Then he saw it again—up close and brilliant. It was a flash of such intense blue that it appeared white. He squawked, then called out: "Hullo?"

Silence met his call. He stepped forward cautiously. If it was some kind of elemental he met with—something invisible perhaps, which now hovered overhead—he had to be very circumspect.

Suddenly, like a jackrabbit bursting from cover when a hound comes too near, a figure bounded out of hiding and sprinted with great leaps toward the cliffs.

"Dando?" Tomkin cried after the retreating figure.

The other stopped and turned. He crouched upon a boulder and stared back at Tomkin.

"Who goes there?" Dando called back.

"'Tis I, Tomkin of the marshes."

Dando warily leaned forward. He all but sniffed the air. He did not rush forward in welcome, which disappointed Tomkin. He had hoped at the very least to be greeted as an acquaintance. Could the other have forgotten their night of fun so quickly? Tomkin wondered what it was like to have so many friends you could forget one of them.

"Tomkin?" asked Dando. "The bumpkin from the marsh, you say? What do you want?"

Tomkin hesitated. He decided not to ask about more parties and pranks with his fellows. Somehow, if that was his purpose, he felt it would make him feel small in the eyes of the other.

"I have news. *Something* seeks thee."

Dando laughed. The sound was sudden and bitter. "That I know bumpkin—better than I wish to!"

"Perhaps my efforts to find thee were a waste of time," Tomkin said, becoming annoyed. "Good night."

"No, no," said Dando, hopping closer. He was off his boulder and quickly covered half the distance between them. "Speak, please."

Tomkin huffed. "There is something—a dead-thing—that wishes to find you and two others. Its name is Voynod."

Dando gave a sudden, sharp intake of breath. "The Dark Bard. Yes, I know he seeks me. I do not seek him, however."

"Pity," said Tomkin, turning to leave. He could see clearly there would be no party to be had tonight.

"Wait!" cried Dando. "What dealings have you had with this other? Does it follow? Are you in its service...or its debt?"

"Neither."

"Then tell me your tale."

281

Tomkin looked at him coldly.

"Please?"

So Tomkin told him how he had met the Bard standing at the very spot of their party the day after they'd met. Dando seemed more and more worried as the meeting was detailed.

"They are so close behind now," he said. "I don't think they will give me the time I need."

"What?" Tomkin asked.

Dando shook his head, but stepped closer. "Tomkin? Have you ever thought of changing things?"

"Like what?"

"Like our lot in life. The role of all Wee Folk. We are the fools of the Fae, you know. Not even the River Folk consider us more than nuisances."

Tomkin shrugged. "Better than being a wisp."

"Perhaps," conceded Dando. "But I believe we are capable of much more. I have found power, Tomkin. I—I seek to wield it for the good of our Folk."

"Power?"

"Think!" Dando said, coming close now. He reached a hand out toward the heavens. His other hand, Tomkin noted, stayed tucked into his tunic. There was a bulge there Tomkin had not noticed before.

"Think of the world as a different place," Dando shouted, "a place where we are not the rabbits of Cymru! Must we forever run from anything that threatens us?"

"Fast rabbits live long lives."

"Perhaps," said Dando disdainfully. "But they are humiliating, fearful lives. Do you know why we play our tricks? Why we delight in them so?"

Tomkin considered. "Because they are so much fun?"

"But *why* are they so fun to us?"

Tomkin shrugged.

"Because, my friend of the fields, we seek revenge."

"Revenge? For what?"

"For every slight given us over the centuries! For every scrap tossed down to us! Long have we been dogs under the tables of the masters. We have been the butt of every joke since the dawn of time, and our only way to fix things up until now—the only way to balance our accounting—has been through trickery and pranks played in the night."

Tomkin considered the other's words seriously. They did ring true to him. Had he not enjoyed the pranks immensely? Had he not sought Dando far and wide, precisely to feel that sensation of comradery and power as a Folk again? He looked at Dando with new appreciation and nodded slowly. "What is better than tricks played by moonlight?"

Dando threw an arm around Tomkin, and although it made Tomkin want to squirm, he allowed it.

"*Power*, Tomkin. True power. That is what I speak of. You are not like the others. There is steel in your spine. Can I call upon you when the time comes? In my hour of need?"

"Will there still be parties and pranks?" Tomkin asked.

"Absolutely!"

"Then yes," Tomkin said slowly, uncertain as to what he promised.

"Excellent!" Dando cried, clapping him on the back.

Tomkin turned him a flat stare, which the other seemed oblivious to. Dando strutted now upon the dark rocks. His excited eyes shone with reflected starlight.

"Leave me now to my work, Tomkin," he said.

Tomkin cocked his head and appraised him closely. "Which Jewel hast thou?"

Dando looked startled. "Jewel?" he sputtered. "I'm sure I don't know what you speak of!"

"May I see it?"

"No!" Dando said, hopping backward.

"Very well," Tomkin said, nodding. "Be careful, brother. Do not let it consume thy soul." With that, he left Dando on the roof of the world and began the long descent, hopping down from rock to rock. Pebbles dislodged and trickled down with grit from the cliffs, but never did he stumble.

Dando looked after him with disquiet.

Chapter Sixteen
Tomkin Returns

Days later, Brand and Telyn were still lost in the endless swamp. It was morning and Brand awoke with a groan to another day of gray skies and bone-chilling cold. Telyn was already up, having taken the last watch. She had a smoky fire going, and worked hard to keep a stinking mass of wet wood and dried peat moss alight. Several large, gigged frogs roasted on a spit over the flame. One of the frogs spasmed when the flames seared its dead foot. The frogs made Brand think of the Merlings he had slaughtered. Vaguely, he wondered if Merlings and frogs tasted alike. He hoped he would never find out. Despite a slight feeling of disgust, he salivated at the smell of the roasting frogs. They had been on slim rations since they had lost the skiff.

When the frogs had been seared and smoked to edibility, Telyn sawed off a leg and tossed it to him. "Toasted to perfection!" she said.

"Thanks," sighed Brand. He gnawed the half-raw, half-charred meat hungrily.

"Shhhh!" hissed Telyn, gesturing for him to be quiet.

"Wha—?" began Brand.

Telyn made the shushing gesture more furiously. She was eyeing the marsh around them intently. Brand ate faster, wanting to fill his belly while he could. He too, eyed the trees with unease. He had learned to trust Telyn's senses, as they were keener than his own.

"Something stalks us," she whispered after a time.

Brand only nodded. He took a grip upon the knapsack, hoping he would not need to lift the axe again and wondering if he would kill Telyn this time if he did. Who stalked them? More Merlings? Old Hob himself? Some other darkling Faerie, intent upon the power of the axe?

Both of them heard a sound at the fire. They whirled around to find a tiny figure standing on its tiptoes, sawing away at their food. A frog leg came loose and the creature sat down and began munching contentedly on their breakfast.

"Tomkin!" cried Telyn softly.

"What are you doing here?" demanded Brand, watching in alarm as the Wee One ate one of their frogs. He felt protective of their meager supply of food.

The manling shrugged, then grinned. Too many white teeth were shown. "Hast thou already forgotten? 'Tis the week's end."

The River Folk nodded in sudden comprehension. "But what of Myrrdin? Why did you come to us instead?"

Again, the manling shrugged. He paused to swallow a great lump of frog meat before speaking. "Thy great clumping feet are the simplest to follow."

"Yes," Telyn said. "The spell wasn't specific as to who he should report back to."

Tomkin made no response, but simply ate more of the meat. Suddenly concerned that he might want more of their limited food, Brand hacked off another leg for himself and set to work on it. While he was up, he rotated the spit again so that the rest of the meat wouldn't burn while they talked.

"So, Tomkin, make your report," urged Brand.

The manling slid its eyes to meet his, taking another great bite of the frog meat as he did so. He finished the meal, licking the bone clean. Rather than discarding it into the fire as Brand had done with his first one, however, he waved it in the air instead.

"What dost thou wish to know?"

Brand frowned. The creature was not going to make this easy. "Who has Lavatis?" he asked.

"I know not."

285

"You mean you haven't seen the Jewel?"

"I have seen it wielded."

"Then who has it?"

"I know not."

Brand glared and began to make an angry retort. Telyn raised her slim hand to calm him.

"Tomkin, who had the Jewel when you *last* saw it?" she asked.

Tomkin slid his eyes first to Telyn, then to Brand. He gave Brand a smirk. "Dando."

"Dando has the Blue Jewel?" said Brand, almost shouting.

"I know not," said Tomkin, grinning now.

"What do you mean, you—" began Brand, enraged. The axe that still rested in the knapsack on his back shifted suggestively,,as if to say: *Slay the little liar.*

Again, Telyn intervened. "Brand, he means he saw Dando with it, but he can't know who has it now, as that was probably days ago."

Brand sat back down in disgust. He took another frog leg from the fire with a ripping motion, not bothering with a knife this time. Juices dribbled down into the fire, causing it to hiss and spit.

Tomkin said nothing, but now put the bone he had held into his mouth and crunched down on it. His powerful jaws flexed and the bone cracked. He sucked the marrow out loudly.

"I give up, Telyn," grumbled Brand. "You talk to him."

"Where is the Jewel now?" she asked.

"I know not."

"I mean, where was the Jewel when you last saw it?"

Tomkin made a vague gesture over his shoulder. "Out yonder, across the swamp."

Brand grunted in displeasure.

"Tomkin, where was Dando when you last saw him? Was he alone? Were there others there besides you and him?"

"Out yonder. No. No."

It was Telyn's turn to sigh. She organized her thoughts before continuing. Tomkin's black eyes reflected the dancing firelight like two tiny jewels. "Were there other Wee Folk with him, besides yourself?"

"No."

"Were there Merlings with him?"

Tomkin shuffled his feet. "No."

"Was Myrrdin or any other member of our party with him?"

Tomkin looked uncomfortable. "Yes, and no."

Brand growled like an animal. "Why are you being so difficult, manling?" he demanded.

Tomkin turned on him as if surprised. He pulled the pouch Myrrdin had forced him to wear out of his shirt and waggled it at him. "When thou art tied with a leash, child of the River, Tomkin will enjoy watching as thy red tongue joyfully licks mine hand as thy revered master."

Brand strove to remain calm. He shook his head as if to clear it. Anger came so easily to him now, perhaps it was some sorcery of the axe. "Look. Let's work together. The Wee Folk have Lavitis, is this not so?"

Tomkin shrugged. "Dando does, at any rate."

"Okay, then. And we have Ambros, correct?"

Tomkin narrowed his eyes. "What ship crosses thy mind, human?"

"Well, *we* have a Jewel, and so do *you*, and while Herla wants both...."

Tomkin grinned. Strips of frog meat showed in his sharp white teeth. "An alliance?" he gave an odd hoot of derisive laughter.

Brand held back his rising anger. "No, nothing so grand. Not an alliance, but rather a temporary, mutual agreement of sorts."

Seeing that Brand was doing well enough, Telyn took this opportunity to cut loose another frog leg and began to eat. She sat back and watched them with raised eyebrows.

"Speak thy mind plainly," said the manling. He stood up to take another frog leg.

Brand frowned at the little man who so freely took his food, but managed to say: "Help yourself."

Tomkin looked surprised that the food was now being offered. He sniffed it suspiciously. After a time he seemed more trusting and sat back down. While he ate, Brand

287

organized his thoughts. "Herla wants all the Jewels. Until recently, neither the River Folk nor the Wee Folk possessed one. Our holds over them are weak, as we aren't yet fully attuned. At least, I know this is the case with Ambros."

Tomkin said nothing now, but continued eyeing him with surprise. Brand figured that he was probably shocked that a human was so foolishly offering this information. Brand decided he had to offer *something* or the manling's information would be so difficult to extract and untrustworthy as to be close to worthless.

"What I'm suggesting is that we pool what information we can more openly, more as a trade, with the purpose of keeping our prizes to ourselves."

Tomkin snorted. "How can thy meager knowledge help Tomkin and the Wee Folk?"

Brand shrugged. "Would you say that it is better for us that you have Lavitis rather than Herla, and better for you that I wield Ambros rather than the Dead? The Wild Huntsmen will only use their power to gain dominion over all of us."

"Agreed."

"So, anything we can do to protect one another helps both sides."

Having gnawed the second frog leg down to the bone, Tomkin waggled it at him. "But there is no reason to trust the River Folk. Tomkin knows better than that."

"Let's start small. Friendship is never given, but always earned," he said, repeating Dando's words.

"It is always so," agreed Tomkin, looking at Brand with new respect.

"I suggest an exchange of information. Question for question, answer for answer. The more complete your answers are, the more mine will be as well. Agreed?"

"If my question comes first."

Brand hesitated. What would the creature ask him? What would he be betraying with his answer? Tomkin eyed him with great intensity as he debated with himself, which didn't make it any easier. Finally, he sighed. "Agreed."

Tomkin bounded to stand on the rock he had been using as a seat. He peered up at Brand like a merchant eyeing a fool

288

with a fat purse. Little seemed to delight one of the Wee Folk more than a battle of wits. "No dissembling, now!" he shouted.

Brand shook his head. Tomkin leaned forward, so much so that it seemed impossible that he did not topple to the ground…but he did not. In Brand's knapsack, which lay at his feet, the axe twitched as the manling's shadow fell over it. Brand nudged it with his foot to quiet it, as one might calm a growling dog.

Tomkin tossed the frog bone into the fire with a flourish. He rubbed his hands together and performed a series of standing hops. "What to ask? What knowledge to be gained?"

Brand waited in increasing apprehension. He looked to Telyn, but she only watched Tomkin with the same fascination, if not quite the usual delight, that she displayed when in the presence of any of the Fae.

Tomkin whirled upon Brand, jabbing the frog bone at his eyes. "How many times hast thou wielded the axe?"

Brand blinked in surprise. He had expected a question about the strength of the Riverton Constabulary, or perhaps something about Myrrdin's activities as the first question. "Ah, let me think…."

"No thinking! No fabricating! No deceptions!" screeched the manling. He bounded about from foot to foot upon the rocks now, the smoky firelight reflecting in his shiny black eyes.

"No, no. I just don't recall right away. Let's see, the first time was when I went looking for Telyn and found…ah, found her. The second time I almost wielded it against the wisps, but the spell was broken…."

"Wisps?" interjected Tomkin. "But did you wield it?"

"No…no, I wanted to, but didn't. Then there was this last time, at the Merling village…I've wielded it twice now, I guess."

"Twice!" shouted Tomkin. He was hopping about now, extremely agitated. He slashed at the air with the frog bone and Brand had to crane his neck to follow his movements about their crude campsite. "Tomkin is a fool, thou ken! Tomkin will believe cats dance on pins! Tomkin wouldn't know a lie if you yanked his furry ears, would he?"

"You don't believe me?" asked Brand in surprise. "It didn't seem such an amazing thing, after all."

"Cheat! Liar!" screeched the furious manling. "Thou hast forfeited thy question! The game is at an end!"

"But he *did* wield it twice, Tomkin," said Telyn gently.

Tomkin whirled to face her. In a single bound, he cleared the fire and stood in front of her. "Why should Tomkin believe the word of a troublesome woodwench?"

"Because it's true," she said simply and evenly, facing him without flinching.

Tomkin stared at her for a moment longer, and Brand felt an urge to defend Telyn. The axe twitched at his feet, as if to offer him a solution to his difficulties. He wondered if it truly sensed his emotions.

But Brand held his anger in check again and soon Tomkin came back around to his side of the fire. He did it in three conservative leaps, the last ending with him in a thoughtful sitting position back on the rock he had originally claimed.

"Do you believe me?" asked Brand.

"Ah, thou hast asked thy first question," said Tomkin, eyes shining again.

"No, no," said Brand. "I just wanted to know if we could continue now."

"Tomkin will believe—for now."

Brand thought for a moment. "What is the best course for us to rejoin our companions?"

Tomkin spread out his tiny hands in surprise. "First, find them. Then hail them as friends, and perhaps walk together out of this marsh."

"That's no answer!" barked Brand. "Look, if we are going to trade information, it must be done in a way that helps one another. If you want more from us, you must give me more than that. Remember, with all our party collected, the Jewel is doubtless safer from the Huntsman than it is now."

Tomkin produced a tiny bright blade and set to work carving a frog bone. "Very well, thy friends are holding court, if such a thing it can be called, with the Merling king. That is where to find them."

"But which direction? How do we find them?"

Tomkin trimmed off the ends of the frog bone to form a hollow tube. He made an off-handed gesture. "Too much for one question."

"I asked what course we should take," argued Brand stubbornly. Again he felt a red heat rising up his neck. The creature was being almost as difficult as before.

"Follow the river upstream until it is but a trickle. It lies to the east."

Brand sat back, taking a deep breath. Now all he needed was a night clear enough to see the stars and he could navigate his way back to his companions. Later, he might even be able to get out of this miserable swamp.

"Tomkin's turn," said the manling as he drilled a tiny hole into the white bone. "How many hast thou slain with the axe?"

Brand eyed him in surprise. Again, the question was not what he was expecting. The manling was busy with his flute, or whatever it was he was making, but Brand sensed his tension underneath. He really wanted to know the answer.

"I've killed two Merlings, but no men."

At his words Tomkin bared his teeth. They were as white and wet as the tiny bone he worked. "Two times. Two slain," he said aloud. He shook his head as if in disbelief, but this time he didn't call Brand a liar.

"My turn," said Brand. "Is Myrrdin a prisoner, or is he free to go from the Merling king's court?"

Tomkin grinned. "A little of both, child of man. A little of both."

"What do you mean?"

"He is not in a cage, but neither would he dare to leave right now from the king's nightly feast table."

"Is Dando with him?"

"Ah, ah, ah!" said Tomkin, shaking his head and tsking. "Mine question first."

Brand sighed, but said nothing.

"Twice thou hast wielded Ambros, and twice thou hast slain with it. Clearly, thy will is great enough not to wield it now, though the urge is plain to see in thy gross hands. Hast thou ever put it aside, once wielded, by thy own will?"

Brand had to think again. "Yes, the first time I did. The first time, the axe urged me to kill Telyn, but I managed to let it fall from my grasp. The second time, Telyn aided me again by knocking it from my grasp."

Tomkin tossed a curious look at Telyn, then slid his eyes back to Brand. "I see. Thou hast a second—as it must be."

"A second? Oh, yes, Myrrdin did speak of that," said Brand, rubbing his stubbly chin. "Since you seem to be so interested in the axe, I will ask about Lavatis. Had Dando already stolen the Jewel from Oberon when we met him in the hayloft?"

Tomkin's demeanor changed as Brand spoke. Instead of casual interest, he now seemed intent on delivering his answer. He hugged his odd, knobby knees up to his body and stared at Brand. "Stolen is a tricksy word. The Wee Folk are ever accused on account of it."

"But did he have it at that time?" repeated Brand.

"Of course."

Brand nodded and smiled at Telyn. "That's why he was there, then. He was on some kind of mission for the Wee Folk, he had the Blue Jewel, and even then he was scouting out the Amber Jewel."

"Do you think he meant to steal Ambros, too?" she asked.

Brand shrugged. "Possibly, although I'm hard put to envision such ambition. The axe is dangerous and twice the size of any weapon the Wee Folk could hope to wield. Maybe he was just spying, or trying to aid us so that Herla didn't have too easy of a time."

"Perhaps we should just ask our friend here," said Telyn, nodding to Tomkin.

"Turn and turn-about," replied Tomkin to their questioning glances. "This turn is mine, river-boy. What odd tricks has the axe performed thus far?"

"Ever back to the axe," sighed Brand. "Let's see. It has tempted me to slay my friends—make that anyone I meet, if they seem unfriendly in the slightest."

"And...?"

"And it flashes occasionally. It gives off a great flash of light that blinds everyone around but me."

Tomkin nodded slowly. "The wink of Ambros' Golden Eye," he said. He gestured for Brand to continue.

"Well, that's about it."

Tomkin's face wrinkled. "The crime of omission is as grave as any other!"

Brand shrugged, liking the creature less by the minute. He felt an urge to smash the manling, but contained himself. "It does seem to affect my emotions, if that's what you mean. Right now I feel like cutting you in two."

Telyn made a tsking sound, but Tomkin only chuckled. His next question he asked in a hushed whisper. "Does it ever *speak* to thee?"

Brand shuffled his feet and stirred the fire with a blackened stick he'd been using as a poker. "Not exactly."

"Evasion!" accused Tomkin. He bounded up from the rock and flourished the flute he had fashioned from the frog bone. The tip of it he held leveled at Brand's frowning eyes.

"Okay, yes," said Brand. "I'd hoped not to mention it, but yes, it does communicate words to me, now and then. I'm not sure how."

Tomkin nodded, calm again. He returned to his perch upon his rock and began to play his bone flute. While they listened to the odd, beautiful music, Brand and Telyn ate the rest of the toasted frog meat. The tiny notes warbled and thrilled, playing one lonely tune after another. None of them were known to the River Folk, yet each seemed somehow familiar. It was as if wind, rain, sun, and stones played the songs of their lives. Brand felt as though he had heard the music on every first fresh day of spring in this life, but always before with his heart rather than his ears.

Brand gave a start when the fire popped and sizzled while consuming a wet pocket in the peat. It had burned down low somehow, and looked like it was close to going out. Had he dozed off? He looked around in surprise. At first, he couldn't see Tomkin at all, but then he spotted him, rummaging through Telyn's gamebag. Then he thought of the axe. Had the little thief somehow made off with it? He looked down and was surprised to see that the straps of the knapsack were wrapped around his ankle. The axehandle was still there, sticking out of the cut flaps and resting on his shins like a sleeping pet. Brand couldn't recall having put it there.

At his attention, the axe twitched—just a fraction of an inch—but it was enough to set Brand's skin to crawling.

"Tomkin!" Brand shouted with great volume. He was gratified to see the manling give a startled hop. "What are you doing, man? You have another question to answer!"

Telyn, almost as startled as the manling, slipped and almost fell forward into the fire. She had been dozing with her chin on her hands. She shook her head and spotted Tomkin as well, making a sound of disgust. "That little trickster! He charmed us and now makes free with our possessions!"

Tomkin glared at them. "Tomkin had accepted thy invitation to dine," he said sternly. "If that invitation is now withdrawn, then this meeting is now done." So saying, he gathered up his flute and headed for the thickets.

"Not so fast!" shouted Brand. "You owe us a question yet!"

Tomkin made a dismissive gesture. "Not so. The first question was a gift. The game is at an end."

"So! You have all the answers you care for," said Brand slowly, putting it together as he thought Corbin might have. "Now you wish to skip out without honoring the last of the bargain. You seek to break your word."

Tomkin reacted as if stung. "Have a care, river-boy," the manling growled, showing his teeth.

"Will you answer our last question?" demanded Brand.

With poor grace, the manling returned to his perch. Glumly, he tossed the frog bone flute into the fire. To Brand's surprise, it caught and flared up into a tiny blue eye of flame that soon burned away to nothing.

"Has Dando yet dared to touch the Jewel Lavatis—to wield it?"

Tomkin studied him intently for a time, cocking his head as if listening for something. He grinned then, showing those teeth that had tasted of both Corbin's flesh and Myrrdin's. "In truth, I can't be sure. But I fear that he has. Lavatis is no less seductive than Ambros...perhaps it is even more so."

Stunned by the detail and honesty of Tomkin's reply, Brand was quiet for a moment, mulling it over. "Is the game at an end then, or do you wish to pose another question?"

Tomkin sighed. "The game is at an end."

"Before you go, however," spoke up Telyn, "I have another proposal."

Tomkin eyed her curiously. It seemed that the offer of a bargain always intrigued the Wee Folk. Brand filed that fact away for future use.

"Speak, witch," said Tomkin.

"I propose that you lead us to Myrrdin and Dando. That we travel together."

Tomkin hooted with laughter. His whole demeanor changed in an instant. He bounded about the camp, laughing derisively.

"Now hold!" Telyn shouted at the bounding form. "We have something to offer: your freedom!"

Tomkin halted his bounding and sprang to alight before her. He crouched there, wiry knees bent as if to leap away again. "Speak!"

"I propose that if we reach Myrrdin, you will be freed of your geas."

"Thou hast not the craft, witch!" screeched the manling, suddenly enraged. "Promise not that which thee cannot deliver!"

"Ah, but I think I can!" Telyn shouted back. "Brand here is the Axe-Bearer, the Champion of Ambros the Golden! You know this to be true."

Tomkin whirled to eye Brand speculatively, then whirled back to face Telyn.

"We aren't powerless. We will both swear to honor the bargain. I propose that we do all we can to break this spell, with Myrrdin's help or without. I'm sure he will honor our agreement, in any case."

Tomkin's eyes slid back and forth. His hands moved up to his chest, but didn't touch the bag that hung around his neck. It was plain that the thing pained him, that wearing it hurt his pride greatly.

"Well?" asked Brand. "Will you be a slave for the next year or a free creature of the fields?"

"Thou must try to free Tomkin first!" he said.

Brand shook his head. "That would be risky. I'd suggest we try to find Myrrdin first."

There was a long moment of silence between them as Tomkin considered the bargain. "Tomkin agrees..." he said at length, "but, since my freedom is not certain, a boon shall I claim."

Brand glared at the manling. "You will not taste of my blood as well, you wretched creature."

Tomkin chuckled. "No, the frog meat was enough. My wish is to see the axe...to gaze into the depths of Ambros."

"But why?" Brand asked suspiciously. The axe twitched at his feet, roused like a growling dog.

Tomkin saw the twitch and seemed fascinated by it. Taking slow, cautious steps, he approached the knapsack. "Tomkin has reasons."

"No," said Brand. Suddenly, he hated the vile creature more than ever and the urge to pull out the axe and strike it dead was almost overwhelming.

"Brand," said Telyn. "We need his help. It is a small thing. There is no danger."

Brand blinked several times and bared his teeth. "Yes," he growled finally. "I'll allow it."

Tomkin's face split wide with a savage grin then, and the yellow light of inhuman desire shown in his black, glass-like eyes.

Not daring to touch the haft of the axe, Brand moved with great care to ease the weapon partly from the knapsack. The axe remained quiet until the Jewel at the heart of it was revealed in the gray morning light. Then it flared into heatless incandescence. Amber light glared into their faces and lit up the swamp around them. Each of them cast giant shadows upon the encircling trees. Brand squinted and gritted his teeth, but didn't take his eyes from Tomkin. lest the creature choose this moment to attempt some deception.

Tomkin was clearly not in the mood for deception. He halted his approach and took two short, blind hops backward.

He hissed as if the light burned his skin. The leather sleeves of his tunic covered his eyes and only his white teeth showed, grimacing. "Stop the light!" he cried.

"I can't control it," said Brand. "Wait, though—it will die down in a moment."

Even as he spoke, the flaring light weakened and died down to a dull, amber glimmering. Tomkin resumed his approach. He took even greater care than before. His hands worked and rubbed at one another nervously as he came close to the axe.

Brand was almost amused by Tomkin's trepidation. "If it frightens you so, why bother with it?" he asked.

Tomkin only snarled at him and continued his terrified approach. He stood before the axe finally, or rather crouched there. The amber light of the Jewel reflected in lusty yellow glints from his eyes. A thread of saliva slipped from his sharp white teeth as he gazed into the depths of the Jewel.

Brand felt tension take hold of him. He realized now that Tomkin was a demon, an imp, a creature of darkness daring to creep forth to touch the forbidden light of day. When Tomkin's trembling hand extended a long thin finger and snaked forward slowly to touch the Jewel, Brand made an involuntary sound of disgust and rage. Tomkin seemed to hear nothing.

"No, Brand!" shouted Telyn, standing and taking a step forward. Brand looked down to see that his hand had reached down of its own accord, and now held itself poised above the haft of the axe. Right then he knew, with crystal cold clarity, that if the little devil defiled the Amber Jewel with its unwelcome touch, he would wield the axe and strike it dead for its gross presumption.

Just then the axe shifted. It was not so much of a twitch this time, but more of a lurch. Like a wounded creature trying to regain its feet, the axe heaved up its haft and left it wavering, close to Brand's waiting palm.

Whatever spell Tomkin had been under broke then, and he leapt back from the axe like a cat springing away from a striking snake. Landing a dozen feet off, he hissed and sputtered, speechless.

Brand stared down at his hand and the haft of the axe, just bare inches apart. Sweat sprouted upon his brow.

"Brand," came a soft whisper in his ear. "Kiss me instead."

Brand turned his head slightly, and there was Telyn, at his side. Her hand now gently clasped his wrist. He let his arm relax and the axe dropped back to the ground in defeat. Then he turned and he did kiss his beloved, deeply.

Tomkin's snide chuckle brought them back to themselves. "Now Tomkin sees how your second operates!" he declared, hooting with laughter. "What a novel way to distract him from the bloodthirsty spell of the axe! Impressive, it is!"

Ignoring him, Brand bent down and gently nudged the axe back into the knapsack. He unwound the straps of it from his ankle and slung it on his back. Again, it was heavy, a dead weight that pulled at his shoulders.

"Saved your life I did, Wee One," commented Telyn.

"That might be, witch," agreed Tomkin. "Let's be off, the sooner to remove this accursed millstone from my neck."

The others agreed. They gathered what gear they had and broke camp, setting off across the steaming bog. Soon they were lost in the gray morning mists.

Chapter Seventeen
The Redcap

With a curse, Brand stomped on yet another hissing snake, jumping over its writhing coils. It escaped his boot and splashed away into a bubbling pool of steamy water that showed the location of one of the numerous hot springs in the area.

"Another snake! May the River drown them all!" Brand complained.

"At least that one wasn't so large that it chased us off!" said Telyn brightly as she sloshed by him.

Eyeing her, rather than the treacherous muck, Brand stepped upon an orange, fleshy, bulb-shaped pod. It popped beneath his heavy tread. A vile gray discharge sprayed his boots. The stench was overwhelming.

"Aggh!" he cried aloud. "I crushed another of those disgusting pods!"

"Human skulls, they were once," commented Tomkin from up ahead. He stood lightly upon another of the large pods and tapped at it with his walking stick. His weight wasn't enough to break one open. "Legend says that these growths are the final remains of thy ancestors. 'Twas here they fought the Faerie upon this last of battlefields before being driven from their strongholds to the north."

"Driven?" asked Brand. "So the Dead Kingdoms to the north are conquered ground, taken by the Faerie?"

Tomkin made an airy gesture with his walking stick. Brand wished that the pod beneath Tomkin would suddenly give way and coat him with the clinging goop inside. "That's one view. But only the darkest of the Faerie dwell there now. Only Wraiths, ghosts, bogies...and worse things."

"As I understand it—" interjected Telyn, "—war and magic destroyed the land, so ravaging all life there that wheat won't grow, nor can sheep graze. People moved to the Haven and settled it as a matter of choice."

Brand grunted in reply. He was busy making sure that he stepped on nothing even more vile in these northern reaches of Old Hob's Marsh. *The Dead Kingdoms.* That would explain why the land seemed more sickened with each step they slogged forward into the Marsh. The mud was past ankle deep and felt like cold porridge. If it was all like this, no wonder his ancestors had left their homes and fled to the Haven.

"How can even the Merlings like it here?" he asked aloud. "With each step the land grows worse. Wetland it is, but everything here rots and withers."

"Few human hunters are here to break open their lodges and slay their young," commented Tomkin. He bounded ahead, crossing two or three of Brand's paces from one flotsam to the next without so much as soiling his boots.

"Fair enough," muttered Brand.

Morning shifted into afternoon, then approached evening. Taking few breaks, they began hunting for a relatively dry and wholesome place to pass the night.

"What's that?" asked Telyn, pointing off into the deepening mists of twilight. A darker shadow hulked among the skinny web-work of tree trunks.

"Looks like a building of some kind," replied Brand. "Ruins, doubtless."

"Better to spend the night in a tree," said Tomkin, looking at the ruins with distrust.

"Well said for you, but I weigh more than a skinny housecat," replied Brand. "These trees are too frail and rotten to support my weight, to say nothing of comfort."

Tomkin only shrugged and smiled with his unsettling rows of sharp white teeth. He followed them toward the ruin, but

300

now no longer led the way through the marsh. Brand forgave him his cowardice; he was no stout warrior, after all.

After inspecting it in the failing gray light, they surmised the ruin was that of a fallen tower. Raised mounds running off to the north and east indicated that walls had once been attached to it.

"These old walls once faced the river," commented Brand, patting the blackened chunks of stone that still protruded like broken teeth from the ground. It gave him a certain sense of pride, although tinged with sadness, that humans had once built such structures.

Tomkin still stood at the foot of the dry land that bordered the ruin. He fidgeted there uncomfortably.

"Come on, Tomkin," called Brand. "There seems to be nothing to fear. The knights all died centuries ago."

Tsking in irritation, Tomkin bounded up the slope. "We'd best leave here," he said. One of the ancient blocks of stone crumbled a bit beneath even his light tread. He skittered back from the falling stone nervously.

"Ha!" laughed Brand, putting his hand on his waist and grinning widely. "A human creation that makes the Faerie nervous! I like this place!" he declared.

Indeed, he did like it. It had a feel of home to it, a feel of something lost that he'd never felt the loss of until now, when he'd rediscovered it. The axe too, liked it here. He could sense its moods now, after bearing it for several days. It seemed buoyed up in his knapsack, almost floating of its own accord, rather than weighing him down like a great stone across his back.

Tomkin studied him closely for a second or two. He nodded curtly, making a decision. "It is a human place. Tomkin will not stay." So saying, he bounded back down into the marsh and toward the sounds of the river to the west.

"Wait!" called Brand. "Ho there, what of our bargain?"

"Tomkin will return on the morrow!" cried the disappearing figure. Already he was only a faint moving shadow in the mists. "If a morrow there will be for thee!"

As Tomkin vanished into the fog and his voice became faint with the muffling effects of the clinging mists, he cried the final words, "Watch for redcaps..."

Telyn appeared at Brand's shoulder and they looked together after Tomkin, who was gone. "Perhaps we should find a better place, Brand," she said in concern. "I don't know what a redcap is, but I don't want to find out."

"Nonsense," snorted Brand. "I'll not be put out of the only dry land in ten leagues by the words of a coward such as that."

"Is the axe affecting you?" she asked quietly. She looked up at him in concern and he softened.

"A bit, perhaps," he admitted. "But aren't you curious about this place? This is a lost piece of our history. It is a part of us, Telyn."

Telyn's eyes traveled the shrinking circle of space that she could see in the growing darkness. She sighed. "We'd best be getting a fire going before we lose all of our light."

"Right," he agreed, almost giddy at the prospect. He slapped his gloves together and knocked the muck from them. "Ah, but it's good to not be sliding with every step I take."

They made camp quickly inside the broken tower. The walls only rose up twenty feet or so at the highest, but inside they were relatively warm and sheltered from the winds that came up along the river. They built a fire and the light flickered upon walls that had perhaps not known such a human presence for many long centuries.

"There must be a reason why we have never heard of such a place in the Haven before," said Telyn after they had eaten such rations as they had left.

"There is," said Brand, eyeing the walls. He reached out and ran his finger around one of the great stone blocks, drawing its outline. Dry moss peeled away at his touch. "I believe we are just outside the borders of the Haven," he said quietly.

Telyn gasped. "You're right. Somehow, I don't know how, but I know that you're right."

"There's no need for fright," said Brand lightly. "Since the Pact ended, one side of the Haven's border is as safe as the other."

"Perhaps," said Telyn, sounding less than convinced. She huddled forward as if trying to gather more heat from their tiny fire.

The night passed uneventfully until Brand awoke with a start sometime after midnight. He wondered groggily what had awakened him until he felt another light rapping upon his shoulder.

He turned with the beginnings of a smile. Perhaps Telyn had changed her mind about waiting and wished for his attentions, clumsy and oafish although they might be. He groped behind him, but found that Telyn was not there.

The haft of the axe shifted again, right before his eyes, rapping him on the shoulders, once, twice. Then it lay still. With a sharp intake of breath, he came more awake, but didn't cry out. He was used to its fitful slumbering by now.

Lying there, he wondered vaguely what had disturbed it. Had a field mouse threatened the campsite? Perhaps it had sensed a low-flying owl or a croaking frog.

As he laid there, almost dozing off again, he became aware of a sound. It was a wet, lapping sound—very quiet. It was not unlike that of a pet cat drinking from a saucer of cream.

He rose to one elbow slowly, quietly, and looked about. The fire had burned low, but still cast good light. The red coals reflected heat off the tower's walls. Telyn was on the other side of the fire, asleep. Brand frowned at this. It should have been her turn at watch, unless she had fallen asleep and had never awakened him for his turn. But that was unlike her—she was not the slothful type and seemed to rarely sleep in any case.

His eyes widened as he saw the thing bent down before her. It resembled one of the Kindred, but was smaller. It definitely wasn't a goblin or a Wee Folk, being heavier-built than that. In one hand it carried what looked like a small mace. In its free hand was an object of some kind, which it was dipping down toward Telyn's arms.

With a roar Brand heaved himself erect and lunged for the creature, stepping right through the dying fire as he did so. The fire flared up as he passed through it. Sparks and smoke shot up around his boots, and he was glad all in an instant that he had not removed them to sleep more comfortably.

The thing turned and snarled at him. It was a manling of sorts, but with far less human features than Tomkin. Its face was charcoal, its eyes a sickly yellow. It raised its small mace in challenge and struck at his knees. Surprise and pain flashed through Brand; the creature was much stronger than it looked. He fell, and the thing was on him. He grappled with it, trying to keep it from his face. Growling like a feral dog, it snapped and swung his mace at him. There was no time to free the axe, so Brand dug his thumbs into the corded muscle that served the creature for a neck.

There was a deafening crash and his vision left him for a second. The creature had tried to brain him with its mace. He clung to consciousness and strove to shake off the blow. He squeezed harder, while it sought to bite his hands and tear with its claws.

Brand felt it gouge his hands. Desperate, he rolled the thing into the fire, still holding it at arms length. It made a keening sound and struggled free of his grasp. A shower of sparks and looming flame gave Brand a good look at its face. It seemed mad, animal, even demonic. Telyn's blood flecked its dark lips. Once free, it climbed the walls of the tower like a squirrel and crouched there, glowering down.

Watching it, Brand checked Telyn's wounds. He saw with great relief that she was not dead. Her chest still rose and fell. But blood spilled over her cut wrist. The creature had been dipping its cap into her blood and drinking it. Besides the blood running from her wrist, which he quickly stanched with a tourniquet, there was a sticky spot on the side of her head. It was clear that she had been knocked senseless.

Brand made ready to draw forth his axe should the creature show any signs of attacking again. He tossed its small mace into the fire and added more wood as well. The creature had also left its cap behind, the only scrap of clothing that it appeared to wear. The cap was thick and wet with Telyn's fresh blood. Brand was disgusted to think that the creature had dipped its cap into her blood to drink. Brand tossed the cap into the flames to burn with the mace. Something in the shadows above him hissed in hatred.

The rest of the night passed uncomfortably and sleeplessly. Brand watched the tower walls all night in nervous anticipation, but the redcap did not return. By dawn Telyn was conscious and Brand no longer cared for the ruins.

Chapter Eighteen
The Dark Bard

"A merry good mornin' to thee!" cried Tomkin, coming through a breach in the stone walls. The first pink light of dawn was at his back. He grinned at them.

Telyn and Brand jumped at his greeting. They still watched the tower walls with bleary-eyed suspicion. "Thanks for the warning," said Brand bitterly. "The red cap nearly killed Telyn."

"Oh, did it now?" said the manling with mock concern. "Ah, and I see thou hast learned the reason for its curious name."

Telyn tugged at her crude bandage, reworking it in the brightening light of day. She had very little fresh cloth left as they had spent so long in the marshes now and the muck seemed to penetrate everything.

After they made no reply, the manling continued on, "Tomkin's never seen a redcap up close, but there are many legends of them. Believe it or not, thy luck was good last night that thine eyes can see the morning today."

"No thanks to you!" shouted Brand. "You could have stayed on, helped us guard against the beast, but no, you could think only of yourself."

Tomkin looked honestly surprised. He hopped forward and perched upon a tumbled stone block that was big enough for a Wee Folk dance floor. "What of it? Kinfolk of mine would expect no more, so why should thee?"

306

"What good is a companion that knows of danger yet skips out with barely a warning at the first sign of trouble?" asked Brand, seeing that the creature really didn't understand and seemed curious about his reasoning. "A group, a team, works together for the benefit of all."

"Why? This is one of the things most puzzling about thy breed. Such an arrangement might work well for sheep, but what could possibly keep thinking beings from abandoning one another in the face of any real threat to the—herd?" asked Tomkin, eyes glimmering in amusement.

Brand frowned at the reference to people as thoughtless sheep, but tried to ignore it. "It is as you say, our Folk stick together. We are social and trustworthy by nature, and despise treachery as among the worst of crimes."

"Fascinating!" exclaimed Tomkin. "So the natural act of any thinking creature is considered a wrongful thing."

"In a sense, yes," admitted Brand. "For the good of the group, each individual suffers something. It is like an unspoken bargain between us all."

Tomkin nodded. "This explains somewhat why thy Folk could maintain the Pact. Ever it has seemed a mystery to the Faerie."

This time Brand was surprised. He had not considered Tomkin a thinking creature. He had seemed more animal than anything else before, but now the Wee One seemed to be intrigued by the philosophies of humans as much as any of the Faerie he had encountered. Brand was beginning to wonder if the Faerie were as curious about and mystified by humanity as humans were by them.

"Since we seem to be trading questions again, Tomkin has one," said Tomkin offhandedly.

Brand glanced at him, and then nodded.

Tomkin crept closer, crossing his stone block perch to the very limits and leaning over the edge toward them. "Did thee, by chance, wield the Eye of Ambros again last night?"

"No," replied Brand.

Tomkin studied him for a moment then retreated again, frowning. Brand wondered why he looked dissatisfied. Could it be that he had set them up, wanting Brand to be forced to wield the axe again? It seemed far-fetched, but Brand stored the thought for the future. Tomkin, if there ever was a doubt, couldn't be trusted beyond his own self-preservation.

After a meager breakfast of water-leeks from the river and safe mushrooms from the marsh, Telyn declared herself fit to travel. She still looked a bit pale in Brand's critical eye, but he supposed it was better to move on than to stay in the ruins. They broke camp and followed the mounds that were the fallen western walls of the ruins. As they marched upriver, their backs crawled with the scrutiny of unseen, baleful eyes. Brand felt sure that the redcap watched them from some dim crevice among the tumbled stone blocks.

The walls went on for a great distance, and Brand began to wonder at the size of the place. It seemed bigger than all Riverton! "I believe all the people of the Haven could reside within these walls, if this one we march along is matched in length by the others."

"'Tis true, thy breed is far less common now than in olden times," agreed Tomkin.

"We are mice rattling about in the bones of a dead giant," said Telyn.

For a time they trudged in silence, the only sounds that of their boots scuffling on mossy stone and dead leaves. But then something else drifted on the wind to their ears.

"What's that sound?" asked Telyn.

"'Tis music!" declared Tomkin, springing up with sudden energy. "It took thee long enough to pick it out!"

"Yes, I think it *is* music," said Telyn. She stopped marching and turned toward the river.

"I still hear nothing," said Brand, straining. He was not in the least surprised to learn that his ears couldn't match Telyn's. He'd known that since childhood.

Then part of the natural noises of the world around him shifted. It seemed that the wind's random sounds melted into the chatter of the water passing over rocks and the creaking of the swaying trees. Slowly the music grew until it became clear to him—a dark melody of somber beauty. It spoke of death and decay and the rebirth from the dark soil of new green shoots. Vaguely, he knew that this couldn't be the work of men or

308

Merlings. None had the craft it took to make music that was so entrancing.

Abruptly, the music stopped. All of them blinked in surprise. There before them—at the water's edge, shrouded in white mists—stood a tall figure on a horse of dappled gray. It was the dark man that Brand had seen days before on the cliffs above the river. It was Herla's lieutenant, the bard of the Wild Hunt.

"The Dark Bard," whispered Telyn aloud.

"Pleased to meet you all," replied Voynod. His voice was courtly and rang with even tones in their ears.

Brand looked around to see if others of the Wild Hunt were possibly approaching, but saw nothing. In fact, he saw nothing of Tomkin, either. Evidently, the Wee One's sense of self-preservation had taken precedence once again.

"I wish a word with you, if I might," said Voynod.

"We are on a journey, sir, and must be off," said Brand, surprising himself at his cavalier tone. He shouldered his pack and began to make his way along the fallen walls. After a moment's hesitation, Telyn followed him.

Voynod walked his horse along the shoreline of the river, pacing them. Brand wondered if he knocked the bard from his mount if he would truly turn to dust as Gudrin's story had foretold.

"I wish to discuss the axe," said the bard after an uncomfortable silence.

"Do you speak for your master?" asked Brand.

"I do."

"What message do you have from him?"

"My master wishes to know if you account yourself the Bearer of Ambros…or the *Wielder* of Ambros."

Brand hesitated only a moment before replying. "Gudrin was the Bearer of Ambros. I am the Wielder of Ambros." Upon his back, the axe seemed to shift slightly, and even lighten itself somehow. Yes, definitely—Brand felt lighter on his feet. He wondered if it was changing its own weight or perhaps giving his legs more strength. As his legs still ached from the night spent on the tower's stone floor, he suspected the former.

"You realize that you are but a boy of the Haven?"

"Yes," admitted Brand.

"You've had virtually no training at arms, nor have you had much time to attune yourself to the Jewel. Declaring yourself a Champion seems a trifle—shall we say—overreaching."

Brand shrugged. "How is it that you know so much of me?" he asked, attempting to apply the lessons he had learned from Tomkin. The trick of conversing with these beings was to gather more information than you gave.

"A sprinkle of silver, a sprinkle of fear. A few muffled screams in the night. Such information is easy to obtain."

Brand felt a chill. For the thousandth time in the last week he wondered what events now transpired back home in Riverton and across the Haven, what evil deeds had Herla and his huntsmen performed in pursuing him and his companions?

"Do you wish to discuss the formation of a new Pact?" asked Brand on impulse.

Voynod laughed. "Surely you jest. My master has worked for centuries to end the last one!"

"Yes, but a new Pact with different terms may be more to his liking," said Brand.

Brand was startled by a quiet voice that erupted seemingly at his feet.

"Now who speaks of treachery, river-boy?" muttered Tomkin, who had appeared again beside him. He moved in Brand's larger shadow, just inside the ruined walls so that Voynod couldn't see him.

"Ha! What's that?" cried Voynod from the shoreline. "Did my ears detect a squeaking? Yes, long we have thought that you have had help from our least trustworthy of allies."

"It seems you have many untrustworthy allies," said Brand, thinking of Old Hob.

"Alas! 'Tis true. So many of the Faerie are fearful of darklings, shades that were once human. They suspect that we have as much humanity in us as we do Faerie blood. And perhaps they are right."

Brand thought that he himself was more akin to the Faerie than to the cursed Dead such as the Wild Huntsmen, but he held his tongue.

The bard continued. "But to answer your question: no. My master does not wish to reforge a new Pact with the Haven at this time. What I am here to ask for is the surrender of the axe. In return, my master has offered to allow you and your companions to return to the Haven unmolested."

Brand snorted. He felt the axe shift on his back. It grew tense like a dog bristling for a fight. "What of the Haven's borders? Will they be respected as before by the Huntsmen?"

"Alas, we cannot promise that," said the bard, putting the sound of real feeling into his words. "After all, we must feed."

Brand's mind was brought hard around to thoughts of Gudrin's stories. The hound that Herla carried and forever waited to alight would drink only fresh human blood. Murdering cannibals they had all become, deepening their damnation. The thought of them running free in the Haven, hunting men and women like stags, filled him with revulsion and anger.

"Then we have nothing to discuss!" he shouted. "I would sooner slay the lot of you than let one hoof of your accursed horses stand free in the Haven!" Upon his back, the axe squirmed like a thing alive. But he didn't reach for it, not yet.

Brand stood facing Voynod. The dark bard paused now, too, standing motionless on the shoreline. Brand noted that no steaming white puffs of breath came from the horse, nor the rider. It dawned on him that neither of them were breathing at all.

The silence lasted for only a few seconds, but it seemed an eternity. Brand felt waves of hatred and evil strength, willing him to stand aside—to cower, to yield the axe—but he stood firm. The growing anger in him was becoming a rage. He bared his teeth with an animal desire to battle the bard.

"So be it," said Voynod.

The horse reared, then came down and set off in a gallop. The huntsman charged. Hooves thundered, kicking up great clots of rotting earth. The mists swirled and churned around the horse and rider, and something flashed silver as Voynod drew his sword. An unearthly cry erupted from his hidden mouth.

Brand backed two paces, to the far side of the wall. He knew nothing of how to face a horseman on foot. The only

311

logical thing seemed to be to jump aside at the last moment and swing the axe as the rider passed. Surely, the horse would have to slow as it got to the top of the mound where stone blocks jutted up like broken teeth from and old man's gums. But even of this, he could not be sure. He wouldn't have been surprised if the Huntsman had taken off into the air and flown, still galloping.

Brand saw the tiny, bounding form of Tomkin, disappearing into the mists. He could hardly blame the creature for taking flight, but still, it was disheartening to be so wantonly abandoned. Brand looked to Telyn, never having felt greater fear than this moment. The Faerie and the Merlings, they had been almost wholesome when compared to this cursed, animated corpse. Their eyes met, and he saw his fears mirrored in her eyes. She struggled with her bow, trying to ready it, but her injured wrist was making it difficult. It seemed inevitable that he would be forced to wield the axe again this day. He hoped that they all survived it.

Brand reached up for the axe, but hesitated. He could feel the haft straining to meet his gloved hand. Voynod was almost upon him, charging up the slope to the fallen walls. Making the decision that he would have to wield the weapon, come what may, Brand reached for it.

But the rider was slowing. Unexpectedly, a blue twist of glowing light ran across the horse's chest and flashed up into Voynod's face. The horse and rider together made unnatural, undulating sounds. More bolts of magical light leapt up from the very ground the horse tread upon and chased one another about the bard's body. The horse was slowed to a straining walk. Brand realized then that the castle walls must have some protective spell upon them that the bard had awakened.

"Slay him!" urged a voice at Brand's feet. "Slay the bard *now*, whilst he is preoccupied!"

Brand glanced down at Tomkin, then at the huntsman. He realized that the manling was right, there would likely be no better opportunity, but somehow the fact that the huntsman was no longer a deadly threat stayed his hand. Besides, there was Telyn, who was also urgently speaking to him.

"— don't, Brand! I don't trust this little blighter," she said, indicating Tomkin with the toe of her boot. "All he seems to want is for you to wield that axe. Perhaps that is Voynod's purpose as well."

Brand nodded, and let his hand drop a fraction. Voynod, by this time, had given up trying to overcome whatever charmed barrier the old walls held against his passing. Hissing his displeasure, he and his unbreathing horse withdrew down the slope to the shoreline again.

"Clever, river-boy," he said. "No doubt well-planned. It is to your credit that I had forgotten of Castle Rabing's ward. But my master has tricks of his own to overcome such ancient charms. They will not stop his powers. You can't hide forever in the fortresses of your dead ancestors."

With that, he galloped off into the mists, heading upriver. Soon, the sounds of the horse's hooves faded into the chatter of the river.

"Castle Rabing?" asked Brand, aghast.

Telyn spread her hands and shook her head. Both of them looked to Tomkin, who perched nearby in a stunted tree upon a twisted black branch.

"So quickly does thy breed forget thy own roots!" he cackled.

"So you knew what this place was?" demanded Brand. "Again, you have withheld valuable information."

Tomkin cocked his head and gazed at him unconcernedly. He seemed curious as to what Brand was going to do about it.

"And no, I'm not going to take up the axe and cut you in two for this, either. Although I'd rather enjoy it," said Brand.

"Castle Rabing," said Telyn, as if tasting the words. "Brand! Here, you are a lord!"

Brand looked about the place. The sun was a glowing disk in the sky now, trying to burn through the heavy layers of mist. It was having a tough time of it. He wondered if it was true, that his ancestors had owned and ruled this place. He had thought it had been only the influence of the axe that had led him to like it before, but now he wondered.

Chapter Nineteen
The March of the Rainbow

Soon after facing Voynod they reached the final tower along the riverfront. Ahead stretched an endless expanse of mist-shrouded swamp. The stench of rot was worse now than before. The trees were fewer and all looked like twisted black skeletons. Their imploring branches reached to the gray skies but found no relief there.

"This truly must be the Dead Kingdoms," said Brand, gazing down into the dismal scene.

"Indeed," said Tomkin. "'Tis not a lovely place."

"How can anything live here?" demanded Telyn of Tomkin. "Where is this Merling king? Where are you leading us, trickster?"

"Tomkin is leading the way to the Merling town!" said Tomkin indignantly. "Never are the Wee Folk believed! Ever is our word questioned!"

"Okay, which way is it, then?" asked Brand, leaning on the walls of the last fallen tower.

"Upriver! 'Tis almost to the headwaters we go!"

"But how can anything live here?" demanded Telyn again.

"The river still runs sweet and pure at its source," said the manling, his voice almost a growl. "There, the Merlings can live and there they are safe from attack. as no sane being would cross this swamp to pester them."

The humans had to concede the logic of this argument, and so with heavy hearts they agreed to follow Tomkin back down into the swamp once again. Before they had gone a hundred paces, Brand was already casting wistful glances back at Castle Rabing, which seemed an oasis by comparison. The redcap seemed less terrible with each step he took.

They marched much of the day through the endless swamp. After a time, subtle undulations began to appear in the land. Soon after they came upon low green hills cut with gullies filled with inky, scum-coated water. Their spirits rose as it seemed they might escape the accursed swamp.

As they topped a ridge, there were signs that a storm brewed ahead of them. A cold, wet wind blew in their faces and the clouds overhead moved in an unusual circular pattern. Tomkin seemed concerned over these developments. He mumbled to himself and spoke no more to them. He took to trotting over the dryer land, bounding like a hare from stone to stone. Brand and Telyn were hard put to keep up with the tireless manling. They called to him, but their words were sucked up and devoured by the growing winds. Finally, the storm clouds let go their bounty and lashed them with rain. Lightning flashed and boomed.

"Where is he going?" shouted Telyn.

"I don't know, but we can't lose him now!" Brand shouted back into the storm. "Finding the Merling stronghold is one thing—we can do that without him now—but getting our fellows back is quite another!"

"Look!" cried Telyn, pointing to the east. A great flashing grew in the east and loomed closer each moment. It was as if the lightning there had somehow been gathered up and held in a fist. As it moved closer, the lightning lashed out, twisted and rumbled, as if trying to free itself.

Brand and Telyn climbed to the top of a rise upon which Tomkin had halted. From this vantage point, the stronghold of the Merlings was finally revealed. To all sides lay higher and higher hills, where the headwaters of the river that fed the marshes began. Lying surrounded by these hills was a great wetland filled with the low mounds of the Merlings. Brand was surprised by the number of them. There were perhaps as many mounds as there were homes in Riverton. Encircling the wetland was an earthen wall, ranging from ten to perhaps

315

twenty feet in height. The top of the wall bristled with spear-like shafts to discourage anyone trying to scale them. The only break in the walls was the great gate of woven reeds that spanned the river. Brand supposed that for the aquatic creatures, the river was the only road in or out that mattered.

Tomkin ignored the town. He faced the east, where the fistful of lightning approached. He threw up his tiny hands to the skies, as if beseeching the heavens. Wind-driven rain lashed him but he stood firm, crying out words that Telyn and Brand didn't understand the meaning of. "Dando! Dando!" he cried over and over again, mixed with a torrent of what sounded like curses and lamentations.

"What's wrong? What's happening?" shouted Telyn, kneeling beside the creature in concern. He ignored her and continued to cry aloud in distress.

It was then that Brand saw the leading elements of the Wild Hunt. Just as Riverton children imitated each spring festival, the Hunt was led by a host of the Wee Folk, runners like hounds that bounded about with reckless speed before the hunters.

The first of the shadowy hunters followed, then a burst of coursers came up the very rise that they stood upon. Brand grabbed Telyn and toed Tomkin with his boot. He pointed toward the approaching host and Tomkin seemed to come back to himself. He gave a look of surprise to Brand, clearly not having expected the warning. He led the way to the far side of the rise where a tumble of rocks, trees, and thick brush served to hide them. They took cover and watched as the Wild Hunt flowed by on all sides of them toward the Merling town.

The Wild Huntsmen came silently. They wore skins that flapped and fluttered about them. Some wore helms, but most had wide, low-brimmed hats that hid their faces. They carried boarspears and swords of gleaming metal. With reckless speed, the Wild Hunt swept up to them. Brand could hear nothing of them until they were almost engulfed by the host. It was not until the coursers were but ten paces away that their sounds crashed over them like an ocean wave. There was nothing but deafening sound, the roar of what seemed a thousand hooves thundered and shook the ground so that speech was impossible.

Frozen with fear, the three of them huddled in their shelter, praying that they would live through it.

One courser paused near them on the top of the rise. Brand eyed him in wonder. Black cloaks fluttered over him and his horse. Atop his shoulders rode the head of a great stag, its antlers boasting a score of points. All his face was hidden but for the eyes, which shown a ghostly shade of lavender. There was a second, smaller, dimmer set of crimson eyes of another creature that crouched upon the back of the horse. They turned of their own accord and those evil eyes met Brand's.

Then the hunter put an odd, curved horn to his lips. Tatters of flesh from whatever great beast's skull the horn had been torn from still clung to it. The dead thing winded the horn. A long, clear note rang across the Merling town, cutting through the rumble of hooves and the drumming of the rain. Then the figure was gone, rejoining the charge down to the walls of the Merling town.

Brand knew he had laid eyes upon Herla, and that the bloodhound that had shared his horse with him for nine hundred years had laid eyes upon him. He was speechless with terror. Never had he felt such malevolence emanating from a creature.

When they could hear one another speak again, Telyn and Brand plied Tomkin with questions, the most important one being "What's happening?" Brand reached out to grab and shake the manling, but paused at the savage glower he received.

Tomkin bared his teeth at him, and then spoke. "The Wild Hunt comes, is it not clear?"

"What about the storm? Is Dando wielding Lavatis?" asked Telyn.

Tomkin grabbed up his hair in both hands and tugged wildly. "The fool!" he cried. "He has not the craft! He'll go feral and all will be lost!"

Down below, they watched as the coursers passed over the walls. They didn't even pause at the fortifications, but simply leapt into the air and sailed over the walls. In a steady flow, the horses swept over the walls as if jumping a fallen log.

317

"How can they do that?" cried Brand. "Why couldn't we hear them until they were upon us? What magic do they possess?"

"Herla wields Osang, fool!" Tomkin snarled at him. "Embedded in the Dragon's Horn! Osang is the Lavender Jewel, the Shadow Jewel, which rules sight, sound and movement. Hast thou been taught nothing of the world?"

A crash nearby brought their attention back to the bundle of lightning, which now marched down toward the Merling town. Brand gazed into the heart of the lightning, and after a moment he knew what he was seeing.

"The Rainbow!" he gasped. Telyn looked to him in shock. "He has summoned the Rainbow, just as Oberon did in Gudrin's story!"

"It marches to meet Herla," said Telyn. "It is the most terrible beauty I've ever seen."

Indeed, thought Brand, it was a beautiful thing. A shimmering giant that shown with every color, the Rainbow was the entity that dragged the reluctant lightning with it. It was the eye of the storm. It came to the walls and passed over them without breaking stride. With each footfall lightning struck, blasting to blackened husks trees, mounds, and Merlings alike.

Tomkin made a strangled sound. He sprang up and ran out into the lashing storm and down the slope toward the walls.

Brand started after him, but Telyn moved to stop him. "It's too dangerous, Brand! We can't face such powerful beings!"

"We must not lose him!" exclaimed Brand. "If Corbin and the others are with Dando, then perhaps we can slip by and help them escape in the confusion."

"You're mad, Brand! The axe is addling your wits again!" cried Telyn.

Her words were lost on his back. He heard them, and knew the truth of them, but the call of Ambros was too great. The battle of its siblings had perhaps excited and strengthened it. He was all but helpless to resist it.

As he rushed down the slope in the rain, half-falling, half-running, his eyes rarely left the towering image of the marching Rainbow. The only part of it that didn't rapidly shift colors was its eyes, which shone a steady blue. Brand knew in his heart that the pure, deep blue of its eyes exactly matched the color of the Jewel Lavatis.

He was hard put to keep up with the bounding form of Tomkin. Even Telyn couldn't have run with greater speed or agility. Tomkin bounded like a wild hare, like a hunted deer fleeing for its life. He headed not for the gates that crossed the river as if it were a road, but instead toward the spot where the Rainbow had stepped into the town. There, its foot must have brushed the wall, for the top of it had been blasted by lightning, and great chunks of steaming earth were all that remained in the breach.

Brand followed the manling, and reached the breach and plunged through it, running into a sludgy marsh of interconnected ponds. Running not as roads, but as boundaries between property lines perhaps, were relatively dry pathways a few feet across. Brand raced after Tomkin along these toward the center of the town, where the lodges were larger and multi-story and where the Rainbow stood now, laying about with its great fists.

In the center of town, the Wild Hunt met with the Rainbow. Stooping to smite the galloping horsemen, the creature blasted craters in the earth and muck of the Merling town. The largest lodge in the town was splattered with flying mud and wet, burning sticks. Clouds of white smoke and steam rose from the scene, but Brand could still make out the relatively tiny forms of the Huntsmen, slashing and stabbing at the shimmering stuff of the Rainbow's legs. Hunks of flashing intangible flesh were cut from the creature's legs. The gauzy material lay shimmering in the mud, the chasing colors of it dying slowly, dimming like a guttering lamp that drinks and burns the last of its oil.

Brand was close now, so close that one of the coursers galloped past him, and its rider could easily have struck him down from behind. But the huntsman was clearly intent on charging the Rainbow's legs. Shrieking a weird, inhuman battle cry, it thrust its boarspear into the mass of the leg. A swinging fist swooped low as the huntsman passed and swept the rider from his mount with an explosive blow. Brand watched as the rider melted, still shrieking, into the earth. The undying horse, now riderless, took a few trotting steps before it too, stumbled on brittle legs and turned into a heap of dust on the wet earth. Brand vowed silently to never doubt the truth of Gudrin's stories again, should he be so fortunate as to hear another.

Brand soon was near enough to the Rainbow to make out the tiny figure that stood beneath it. Between the vast spread of its shimmering legs, Dando stood, working his limbs even as the Rainbow itself did. It was as if the Rainbow were a great puppet and Dando its puppeteer.

Then Brand saw the Jewel in the amulet that Dando bore on his breast and which flashed rhythmically, perhaps with the beat of the Wee One's heart. As if in response to the sight of its sibling, the axe squirmed in his knapsack.

Take it.

Brand licked his lips. Abruptly, it seemed to him that the rest of the battle quieted and dimmed. Ghost-like, the huntsmen continued to circle and cut at the legs. The Rainbow twisted and stooped, swinging its great limbs at them. Brand saw all this only as a set of flickering, dream-like images. Nothing other than the throbbing light of Lavatis mattered.

Cut the Rainbow's feet from under it and take the Jewel.

Brand's hand moved up of its own accord to hover over the haft of the axe. He paused there, trembling.

"Hold it, Brand," said a voice in his ear.

Startled, he twisted around. A leering face met his eyes, and he wanted to strike it, but soon recognition set in.

"Myrrdin?" he asked. Then he felt a strong hand clasping his wrist. Twisting the other way, he was shocked again. "Corbin?"

They paused only to smile before urging him to take cover with them behind the blasted ruins of a great Merling hall. Modi was there too, and gave a rare slow smile at Brand's gaping mouth.

"How did you escape?" asked Brand.

"How did you find us?" asked Corbin in amusement.

"I followed the Rainbow," said Brand with a grin. He pointed up at the monster that all of them gazed at.

"Shhhh!" admonished Myrrdin. "If you can contain yourselves, we might yet live through this day. Watch the waters at our backs."

Even as the reunited party hunkered down, the Merlings finally made a counterattack against these invaders of their town. A jostling, croaking horde of them rose up from the waters of the nearby ponds and charged into the whirling melee. They fought bravely, but most of them were quickly cut down as if out of hand by the huntsmen. A few perished beneath the swinging limbs of the Rainbow. A few managed to thrust their weapons into the Rainbow and once three of them pulled down a huntsman with their barbed cords. Horse and rider melted together into the earth, but the Merlings knew this victory only briefly, and were soon routed from the scene. The few that splashed out into the safety of the waters dragged their flopping wounded and dead comrades with them.

"A brave assault for Merlings. It does them credit," said Myrrdin.

"Better that they all die so that we'd be free of them," grunted Modi.

"Perhaps we should find a way to retire before one side or the other wins this fight," suggested Corbin. "It seems that there is little we can do."

"I could wield the axe," said Brand. He couldn't hold back the words. The urge to charge in and face two of Ambros' siblings in open conflict was all but overwhelming.

Myrrdin looked at him with great concern. "No, no. You aren't ready yet. Have you wielded it on your journey here?"

"Yes, twice," replied Brand. He eyed the Rainbow speculatively. The axe had great cutting power. A few low sweeps could perhaps sever the monster's foot. Then finishing it would be easy.

"Twice!" exclaimed Myrrdin, shocked. "Have you slain with it?"

"Yes, two Merlings."

Myrrdin shook his head in amazement. "It is indeed a wonder that you live. You have not yet been attuned to the Jewel fully. To attempt to use it again without proper instruction will almost certainly drive the Jewel feral and leave you dead soon after."

"What do you mean?"

"When the wielder of a Jewel isn't strong enough to tame it, the Jewel takes over, going feral. It performs with mindless aggression in most cases until it destroys its master. Ambros is particularly famous for acts of savagery that eventually kill its champion. But we have no time for this talk now—we must retreat. Where is Telyn?"

Brand blinked in surprise. He had all but forgotten his beloved. This bothered him, as it showed the intense grip the Jewel had over him. "I—I left her in the hills outside the town—"

A great crash interrupted him. The Merling king's palace had fallen in upon itself and now burned with great choking clouds of steamy smoke. Flaming sticks and smoldering chunks of earth splashed over the battlefield. Dando was taken by surprise and hurled to the ground. The huntsmen took this opportunity to dash in and hack desperately at the creature's legs. One of them finally gave way at the ankle and the Rainbow dropped to one knee. It grasped about itself like a fallen man, destroying whatever it touched. A howling sound, like that of a hurricane wind whipping around stone crags, erupted from it. It seemed to go mad then, flailing with its limbs. Grabbing up Merlings and burning them with its very touch, it hurled their crushed, smoking bodies far out into the outlying ponds of the town.

Beneath the monster, Dando struggled up and moved again. A shock ran through the Rainbow. It reached down beneath itself and grabbed up Dando. Brand thought he could hear a tiny shriek of pain, but it might have been the wind. In a long sweep, the arm rose up to the gaping maw. Dando disappeared within it. Brand gave a gasp, wondering what it might be like to tumble down that cavernous, incorporeal throat.

The Rainbow shuddered again and struggled to rise. Its missing foot made it topple again. Reaching down, it grabbed its lost foot and placed it back onto the end of its leg. The torn, shimmering material of its body flowed together. Making smoothing motions, it melted the leg and foot back together again as if molding clay. In moments the foot was reattached.

"How does one kill such a thing?" asked Brand in a hushed voice.

"Elemental spirits can't really die," replied Myrrdin. "How can you kill a rain cloud? How do you destroy a gleam of sunlight? It is the same with the Rainbow."

"But what will it do now that Dando is dead? Will it carry the Jewel in its belly forever?"

"No. If Dando dies, the creature will soon lose form."

"If?" said Modi with a grunt of amusement. "How can you say 'if?' How could anything live after having been devoured by a monster?"

Myrrdin shrugged. "I've never been in the belly of the Rainbow myself, so I can't say."

"Stranger things have happened while one bears a Jewel," agreed Gudrin solemnly.

"Whether Dando is dead or not, it seems clear that the creature no longer has a master, and thus knows not what to do," added Corbin.

"Yes, it has gone feral," agreed Myrrdin, his face grim.

There was no doubt of that.

Chapter Twenty
Escape

They watched as the gigantic living rainbow rose up again to its full height. A look of uncomprehending agony remained fixed on its face. It gave off a wailing sound like that of storm winds over sea rocks then set off toward the river. Each tremendous foot swept forward as it picked up speed into an incredible run. Every footfall shook the earth and sent up explosions of sparks, water, and mud. The Wild Hunt gave chase, their mounts gliding over the waterways and ponds as if they galloped across hard earth. Herla winded Osang again and its long, clear note rang from the walls and the hills beyond. Brand was reminded of hunters chasing down one of the rare great elk that were sometimes found in the Deepwood.

"How can they do that?" exclaimed Corbin. "What keeps the Wild Hunt from sinking into the mire as any creature should do?"

"Osang does," replied Brand, bringing startled looks from Myrrdin and Gudrin. "Herla wields the Lavender Jewel, which has power over sight, sound, and movement."

"Well said," Myrrdin grinned. "You have learned a thing or two since last we talked, Champion."

Modi gave a grunt of disgust at the title and began to stump off toward the river. "We'd best be after them," he said.

Myrrdin looked after him. "Quite true, but I believe it will take special aid for us to catch them before events have come to a conclusion beyond our control."

They all looked at him. He made no further comment, but set off at a loping run toward the river. All of them followed.

Brand watched as the chase led the huntsman right into the river itself. The Rainbow crashed through the town gates and waded downriver. Only the Wee Folk seemed fleet enough of foot to catch up to the creature. They circled it and even ran ahead of it, playing at death with the great crashing feet. They urged and dared one another to dash across its path even as each tremendous step was taken.

"Tomkin!" shouted Brand, pointing.

"Where?" asked Telyn, running alongside him.

"There, playing tag with the others at the Rainbow's feet! I —" he faltered. "Telyn! Where did you come from?"

"Did you think I would let you chase Wee Folk, the Wild Hunt, and the marching Rainbow all by yourself?" she laughed.

Brand grinned. "I'm glad you didn't."

"What about Tomkin?"

"I saw him at the Rainbow's feet. At least, I thought it was him. He was the only one wearing dappled fawnskin rather than a top hat and waistcoat."

"But I see several like that," said Telyn.

Brand shook his head. "I don't know then, perhaps I was mistaken."

"Or perhaps our little companion is just as big of a traitor as we suspected at first," said Telyn with uncharacteristic cynicism.

The group panted as they reached the river's edge. Myrrdin was already there and was hard at work waving his staff over a large fallen tree that lay half in the river.

"The creature must have smashed this one down as he passed," commented Corbin.

Brand nodded. The tree looked as if it had been struck by lightning and blasted from its roots. The upper part of the tree still looked normal, but near the bottom of the trunk it was twisted, black, and smoldering. Brand marveled that just a glancing blow could deliver so much destructive force.

"Watch!" exclaimed Telyn excitedly in Brand's ear. "Myrrdin is about to work truly powerful magic! I can feel it gathering."

Brand felt it too. It was like the coming of a storm or the rising of a fresh breeze on a hot summer's day.

"Is this wise, Myrrdin?" asked Gudrin in concern. "If you reveal yourself to Herla now, might he not decide to attack us instead, judging us easier prey than the crazed Rainbow?"

Myrrdin, intent on his work, made no reply. With a look of fantastic concentration, he drew a line the length of the tree's trunk with the tip of his staff. He then skipped up to the leafy branches and with a flourish and a great thrust, plunged the staff into the trunk.

The fallen tree shuddered. Moments later, as they all watched, the line Myrrdin had cut into the trunk widened into a slash, then a gap, then a great hollow. The leaves and branches at the tree's crown curled up like fingers and wove themselves together to form a green serpentine head.

"It's a boat!" cried Telyn with delight. Not hesitating an instant, she clambered up into the hollow, which now bore benches grown over with tree bark. "Come on!" she shouted to the others. "Let's cast off and chase them!"

Myrrdin beamed at her proudly, continuing his handiwork. His staff had turned into a mast of sorts now, and he was busy working up this mast a sail of woven green leaves.

Shaking his great head, Modi put his shoulder to the stern of the odd craft and shoved. Myrrdin and Telyn swayed a bit as the boat shifted.

Brand and Corbin grinned as they joined in and put their shoulders into it. Gudrin helped as well, and in few moments the craft was afloat on the rising flood of the river. Climbing aboard the marvelous boat with the others, Brand smiled as he watched Telyn all but dance about them. The rain in her face and hair, he reflected, made her all the more beautiful when she was happy.

"Nothing delights you more than magic, does it?" he asked her when she drifted near, running her hands lightly over the rough bark of the deck and gunwales.

Still eyeing the craft, she smiled and gave her head a tiny shake. "You do," she said quietly. She lifted her head up and gave him a tiny kiss.

Brand decided that, live or die this day, he would remember her kiss to his last moments.

The sails suddenly caught the wind and tugged. Brand wondered that the breeze should be so strong and steady and going in the right direction. He supposed he should not have wondered about good sailing conditions when sitting in a ship magically formed from a fallen tree.

The Merlings, miserable in their smashed town, watched them leave without molesting them. Brand felt sorry for them, caught up as they were in a conflict which most of them probably had no knowledge of. So many of their homes were smashed and so many of their people dead. He resolved that, should he somehow have a hand in reforging a new Pact with Faerie, the Merlings should be part of it. For too long men and Merlings had hunted one another in a silent war. Too many babies had been stolen, pelts taken, and eggs smashed.

He turned then to see that Telyn was studying his face.

"You feel for them, don't you?" she asked.

Brand nodded. "I can't help but think of when I gazed down into one of their homes, about to kill a female and her young. Who was the monster at that moment?"

Telyn nodded, still looking at him.

"Any creature that protects its young and builds a town shouldn't be hunted as an animal," he said.

She gave his hand a squeeze, and it felt almost as good as the kiss had.

"Well, I don't suppose my opinion counts for much," he said. "The rest of the River Folk will take some convincing."

Telyn gave him another squeeze. "If anyone can do it, you can."

Sailing out of the ruined town, Brand felt good to be on the water again. A shifting deck under his feet and clean water all around felt like home to him. Fresh rain washed the sweat, grime and trials of the last few days from his face. Soon, however, he began to become alarmed as they picked up speed. The boat's hull was furling back water like a cast spear.

"Are we caught in rapids?" he asked Corbin.

"No, the water is swift and deep, but not so that it could possibly account for this speed," he replied. "I don't understand it, but it must be Myrrdin's doing."

They looked to Myrrdin, who stood at the prow, his arms wrapped around his staff-turned-mast and his intent gaze directed ahead.

"Myrrdin!" cried Brand over the rising winds. "What if we hit something, man! We'll go over in a thrice!"

Myrrdin shouted something back, but the wind carried it off.

Brand climbed past Modi's bulk. The warrior glared at him, unhappy as usual to be in another damnable boat. Brand reached up to grasp Myrrdin's shoulder. During the time it took to traverse the length of the craft, their speed had increased nearly two-fold. Looking to the shore, Brand suspected that they moved faster than a horse could gallop.

"Myrrdin! Have you gone mad, man!" he shouted into his ear.

Keeping his eyes on the water ahead, Myrrdin simply uncrooked a finger, the rest of which he kept tightly upon his staff, and pointed ahead.

Brand's eyes followed the finger and ahead of them he saw the towering form of the Rainbow ahead. They were gaining on it, slowly.

Brand shook his head and sat back down on the bark-covered benches that had grown so fortuitously for human backsides to sit upon. Normally at home in any craft, he felt out of his league now. He looked over the side and marveled at the pace with which the water was pushed from the tapered prow. Never had he seen a boat move half as fast, excepting perhaps a canoe that fell over a waterfall in the spring floods. He reflected that after the breaking of the Pact, magic had become commonplace around him. He wondered if it had always been abundant, but hidden, just beneath the river's surface or inches beyond the borders of the Haven.

The chase went on for some time. The Rainbow seemed tireless, as did the huntsmen. Slowly, though, they did gain. Brand wondered what they would do if they caught up with the hunters. As they drew closer to the fleeing Rainbow, the storm grew worse again. Soon the rainfall was so great that they had to bail to keep the vessel riding lightly on the water's surface.

Then, without warning, the Rainbow stumbled and fell. They were not close enough to see why, but now that it had stopped running, they caught up very quickly. In moments the circling horsemen could be seen, then the darting Wee Folk, some of whom had the audacity to take wild leaps over the fallen shimmering form. Although it had been brought down, the Rainbow still flailed about at its attackers. Brand saw one of the Wee Folk miscalculate and get caught by a sweeping hand. The tiny figure flew off into the river like a swatted insect. The huntsmen charged in, thrusting home their boarspears and hacking fearlessly with their broadswords. Brand wondered if they had ever faced a larger, more terrifying foe. He shivered to think that perhaps, sometime in their centuries-long existence, they had.

Finally, the Rainbow ceased its struggles. It lay half in the river and half on the fetid land of the swamp. Myrrdin slowed their craft as they approached the scene.

"We are too late," said Corbin behind Brand. "We can't fight all the Wild Hunt for the Jewel. They have captured Lavatis at last."

As the Rainbow died, its shimmering form, never entirely substantial to begin with, began to melt and fade. Runnels of bright color flowed away from it to form glistening puddles that slowly darkened. Brand saw Herla, his stag head towering over the others, trot his horse up to the melting creature and begin hacking at the great belly. All around him and the dissolving corpse the Wee Folk pranced and cavorted, like hunting dogs baying and worrying the fallen prey.

Reminding Brand of a snowman under a steady stream of hot water, the Rainbow melted quickly. The storm clouds overhead stopped their pelting downpour and slowed to a light drizzle.

A shout went up from the Huntsmen. Brand knew that they had found the Jewel. His heart sank. He had hoped it might be lost somehow in the river.

Herla turned then and his lavender eyes fell upon Brand and his companions. His dead horse raised a hoof and scraped the ground. Brand knew dread as he met his enemy's eyes. With a certainty beyond any he had ever known, Brand realized that the Wild Hunt would pursue him next, for his Jewel, and Myrrdin for his. Soon, he would be as dead and forlorn as the melting Rainbow.

We must fight!

Brand despaired. At any moment Herla would raise his fist aloft and claim another of the Jewels of Power. The axe upon his back twitched.

Have we no stomach for battle?

Herla was poking about for the Jewel now, having dug a hole into the shimmering guts of the creature. It was time to face him now, before he could master a second Jewel. Brand knew the truth of it. His only hope lay in the power and the sharpness of the axe that rode his back.

"Brand, look!" said Telyn.

Brand's hand reached up for the axe. Something grabbed his wrist. He twisted and snarled, expecting to see Herla's lavender eyes burning down into his. Instead he found Corbin holding to his wrist with both hands. Corbin shook his head. Brand's other hand formed into a fist.

"Brand, it's Tomkin!" said Telyn again, tugging at him. "Look, he's running away with something!"

Brand blinked in confusion. Telyn's voice somehow dug through the haze in his mind and he saw Corbin again.

"Sorry," he said to Corbin.

"No problem, cousin," said Corbin, releasing his grip. Brand realized that he needed his friends, badly.

He gazed the way Telyn was frantically indicating. One of the Wee Folk, perhaps Tomkin, perhaps not, was bounding away into the swamp, away from the rest of the hunters.

Moments later, Herla shouted something to his fellows. They circled and pointed in various directions. Some of them pointed to Brand and his party, but most pointed after Tomkin.

The entire company was relieved to see the Wild Hunt launch into pursuit again, this time charging after the manling that had deserted them.

"Could it have been Tomkin?" asked Telyn.

"More importantly, could he have stolen Lavatis?" asked Myrrdin. "I felt no shift of power. I believe Herla didn't get the Jewel."

"If he had, he would have come after us," said Brand.

Myrrdin looked at him. "Yes, I believe you are right. Let's sail to the scene."

The craft moved forward again. Soon they beached the boat alongside the last shimmering, melting fragments of the Rainbow. Telyn was the first to jump out of the boat. She immediately grabbed up a handful of the Rainbow's fading flesh.

"It feels odd," she said. Brilliant colored liquids ran over her hand and dripped down to the ground where they glowed for a moment before disappearing. "It's almost as if you have nothing in your hands. It's like a wad of smooth, fleshy cotton."

Brand ignored the glimmering remains and sought with the others for some sign of the Jewel. They found Dando's body instead. The tiny, twisted form was burnt and mangled.

Thinking him dead, Brand lifted the manling and laid him upon a dry grassy spot. He was shocked to see one eye flutter open.

"Dando lives!" he told the others, and they gathered around.

Dando managed a crooked smile. "Not for long, I fear," he coughed. "Tell me of the Jewel."

"It's gone," Brand told him.

The last of his strength seemed to ebb from Dando at the news. He closed his eyes and Brand suspected he would never open them again.

"Pity," he rasped. "It was such a lovely thing. I had dreams of treating with you, Brand. Like my folk, your people have lived for so long as nothing, as slaves and fools for greater folk."

"Perhaps your dreams will yet come true, Dando," said Brand. "This struggle is not yet over."

Dando smiled, managed a slight nod, then died.

"He looks like a broken doll," said Brand. "How do you suppose he lived so long inside the creature's belly?"

331

"The Wee Folk are hard to kill," said Gudrin. "Interesting for one of his kind to have such a grand design. He was unusual for one of the Wee Ones."

She took out her Teret and made a sign over it and Dando's corpse. "I am saddened to see one who has lived so very long lying in death."

"The question now is, what do we do next?" asked Corbin.

"I think Tomkin has the Jewel," said Telyn.

Brand looked at her. "Yes, and we must follow him."

"But where would he go?" asked Telyn.

Brand knew in an instant. He believed that he now knew how the Wee Folk thought. It was always in terms of clever trickery. "Castle Rabing. Where Herla's huntsmen couldn't follow. I suggest we go there in any case, as we will be safe there to rest and think."

"But that's on the other side of the river," objected Gudrin. "He ran off into the swamp on this side."

"Never underestimate the trickery of the Wee Folk," said Brand. "I'd bet he's planning on doubling back on them like a fox and taking refuge in the castle."

Gudrin frowned at being lectured to by a stripling, but she nodded in agreement.

Myrrdin beamed at him proudly, slapping him on the back. "I never could have taught you so much in so few days. The world has done my work for me."

"Anything that involves a rest sounds like an excellent plan," said Corbin. "I, for one, could use a fully cooked meal."

As they all tumbled back into Myrrdin's magical craft to cross the river, Corbin approached Brand. "Tomkin? Castle Rabing? Clearly, we must have a talk, Brand."

Brand grinned. "We have much to discuss," he agreed.

Book III: SHADOW MAGIC

Translated from the *Teret,* the compendium of Kindred wisdom:

I will begin by pointing out that magic, in all its forms, is the greatest mover of land and folk alike in our world. The history of magic in Cymru, and in all of greater Albion, seems ever to twist and turn. But always it returns to the omnipresent themes of color and light. Digging deeper, the hooded scholarly Talespinners of Snowdon, Cardiff and Harlech come almost without fail to the bedrock legends of the Jewels of Power. Each of the Jewels harness a flavor of magic in a pure form, split apart from the others into the variety of hues that now exist.

Having established that most magic has at its source one or another of the colored Jewels, the next question is clear: From whence came the Jewels themselves? There are two legends that are most often quoted to answer this question. The version ascribed to by the Kindred, of course, involves the demise of the Sun Dragon. According to our legends, the Sun Dragon spawned nine lesser dragons which devoured their parent for the power the elder possessed. These young dragons fought for choice bits of the Sun Dragon, but each only managed to eat a portion, thus giving them specific powers. Over time, these foul dragons were each hunted down and slain by heroes of old. When their bodies rotted away, their bodies decomposed except for one jewel, the lens of each dragon's left eye. These came to be known as the Nine Eyes, or Nine Jewels, and each possesses the power of the original dragon.

The other often quoted story involves a Fallen Sunstone and its fragmenting. The River Folk claim that Cewri, the ancient Troll King of Gynwedd, broke the Sunstone into shards. Supposedly, Cewri struck the Sunstone asunder with a great blow from his hammer, the haft of which was made of a single whole trunk of a mighty oak and the head of which was forged from a mountain's heart. The place where this occurred, Cewri's home valley, is now known as the Vale of Flowers. According to the legend, the sundering of the Sunstone released a rainbow of colors onto the land that resulted in the lush growths of beautiful flowers that grow there in such profusion to this day. Some of these flowers were so pure of aspect, that when picked, they formed the Jewels as we now know them.

These topics might seem to young, yawning minds as worthy only of theological or theoretical debate. Others of a more fanatical bent might believe that seeking out answers to these questions is akin to blasphemy, and will result in the ruination of the Kindred through the awakening of sleeping enemies. I assure readers that neither of these proposals are fact! The Jewels exist and are physically evident, as are their effects upon our world and daily lives. Understanding the truth of their origins can only serve to better our lives through our increased wisdom.

—Jerd of the Talespinners, written circa the Third Era of the Earthlight

Chapter One
Twrog Returns

The giant known as Twrog had stolen four pigs on his first visit to the farm. But these had not sated him for long. He felt no more need for revenge, that particular thirst had been quenched by the blood of the farmer he had smashed flat with a single cast of his lucky club. All that drove him now was hunger. He had already devoured the last of the pigs days ago. He had skinned them, an extra effort he rarely bothered with, and roasted them to perfection on a spit over an open fire of elmwood. They had indeed filled his belly and provided excellent flavor. Rarely had he dined so well. He had finished off the last hogshead and forelegs for breakfast on the third morning.

They had been fine-flavored, but not *quite* as good as the ham hock he had tasted once, the taste he had slavered over all these long years. That flavor still evaded him, still haunted him. He dreamed of it, even as he gorged himself upon the fresh pigs. What was it that made the ham different? He could not say. But it was beyond his primitive cooking skills, which amounted to little more than searing flesh, to achieve. And so it was that when the last of the fresh pork was gone, his mind went back to the farm. Could there be, somewhere on that farm, a better flavor still?

Soon after having this thought he found himself under his favorite Rowan tree, eyeing the farm once more. His belly rumbled. Somehow, the game he trapped did not compare to the sweet meats that came from the farm. Those tame, farm fed pigs made his normal diet seem rough and dull. Worse still was the tormenting memory of those ham hocks. Another detail had brought him back as well: the loss of his lucky club seemed to be hampering his hunting. He had not found it so easy to feed himself. The game seemed more scarce, agile and wary.

The truly galling thing was the sight of his lucky club, sitting right there where it had come to rest in the middle of an open field. The club lay in the midst of a large area of disturbed earth. He wondered, vaguely, if his club could have possibly turned up so much dirt, or if perhaps the strange River Folk had buried the farmer right there. In any case, the fact that it lay in plain sight was goading him. If only he could retrieve it, he felt sure, his luck would return and his larder would be full again.

Still, he hesitated. He was not a genius, not even for one of his kind. But one thing he did know was that robbing the same folk many times was asking for trouble. They soon grew wise and tricksy.

Before midday, he had given up on subtleties and postponement. His stomach noise, once a gurgle, had become a full-throated growl. He marched downslope to the farm, determined to regain his club at the very least. And if one of those excellently flavored pigs happened by...well, a giant could not control his appetite forever.

The first minute or so of the raid went very well indeed. No one was in evidence, in fact, the farm looked deserted. Only a few pigs milled about in the damaged pens. Of the River Folk and their accursed crossbows he saw nothing.

Greed split his huge shaggy face with a grin. He had worried for nothing. He would get his club and have the run of the place. Clearly, the humans had been so terrorized by his first visit they had quit the farm and left it all to him!

He took another step, reaching his club. His hand never made it to his lucky weapon, however, because as soon as he stepped into the area of black disturbed earth, he fell. At first, he had no idea how this thing was possible. Had the land itself opened up some magical doorway to devour poor Twrog?

Then a stake shoved its way through his foot, and he unleashed a grating sound, a roar of pain. They had laid a trap for him! As if *he* were the game and *they* were the hunters! The wrongness of this crashed through to Twrog, who barely managed to keep from falling face-first into the trap. Had he done so, he realized, he might have been killed, for there were dozens of thick stakes planted down there.

Fortunately, the trap was only waist-deep. Possibly, they had not had time to finish it, or they had underestimated his size. In either case, his shock and hurt quickly turned to rage. He retrieved his club and heaved himself painfully out of the hole.

He pulled the stake out of his foot with another roar of pain. He threw it at the farmhouse, but it fell far short of the mark. Hefting his lucky club, he began to limp back toward the Deepwood.

Twrog stood, rubbing at his bloody foot. His brow furrowed. He couldn't simply slink away from these vicious farmers. He knew they might have other surprises awaiting him, oh yes, Twrog knew that very well. But he was hungry, and angry. This is not a safe combination when giants are involved.

So he limped not to the safety of the forest, but rather toward the pigpens and the farmhouse. First, he crashed in the roof of the pigpen just for spite. But he didn't tarry there, having other things in mind. He headed with a humping gait for the farmhouse. Sure enough, just as he suspected, several River Folk came out and pelted him with arrows. He grunted at their sting, but knowing he could not easily catch his tormentors when he had a bad foot, he focused on the house itself.

He smashed in the roof with a tremendous roaring swing. The chimney crumbled, and somewhere inside a high-pitched keening began. This brought a fresh grin of satisfaction to his face. He hoped he'd crushed another of the farmer's family members inside. People, including little ones, came running out the windows and doors. He raised his club to smash down a child as it wriggled out of a second story window, but a scent he caught then made him freeze.

Was it? Could it be? Yes! He smelled that which he had thought lost for all these long years. It could only be one thing, *ham hocks*. He paused, sniffing, idly swishing his club at men who got too close and thought to frighten him with pitchforks and torches.

His nose led him to limp over to the far side of the house. There, he found a small outbuilding with smoke trailing out of the roof. With a quick swipe, he removed the roof from the place. A smell of smoking wood and succulent pork met him. He reached inside and found the place full of hams.

Twrog had found his first smokehouse. He filled his game sack with all it would carry, while the River Folk tried to put out the fire that had erupted in the house and worked to save the children crawling out the windows.

Dragging the game sack behind him, he soon vanished into the cool gloom of the Deepwood. His club rode his shoulder again. His foot hurt badly, but he would wrap it in a poultice and eat well. Overall, he accounted the raid a grand success.

Chapter Two
Little Timmy Hoot

After Thilfox Drake had chased him from his freshly gained cradle, the changeling named Piskin fell into despondency. He had managed no better than a few hours with his pretty maid, and had gotten no more than a single meal at her breast before disaster had struck. How had the River Folk gotten wise to him so quickly?

There was only one likely reason, Piskin's eyes narrowed to slits as he whispered the name to himself as a witch might whisper a curse: *Dando*.

Bitter, bitter Piskin! Oh, how the fates had shifted against him! Oh, how he hated that little monster Dando. He still was not sure whether Dando had failed in his task of disposing of the babe, or if he had committed a base act of treachery. Was he a simpleton or a conniving devil? The results were the same in either case; the River Folk were wise to him now. His own folk, he reflected, made the very worst of friends and the most vicious of enemies.

He tried to sneak his way into more windows, of course. But every human in Riverton now scrambled to lock their doors and ward chimneys. He searched, but all the easy spots had been taken. Ever it was that when he finally found a tiny bed with a cooing infant ensconced, that prospective babe turned a leering eye and thumbed its nose at him when the mother's back was turned. Every cradle in town was strictly guarded, or had already been claimed by another changeling.

341

He was driven from the best houses down to the worst. Skinny brats with boils and bruises, their sort he found plentiful in stilted shacks that huddled around the fish-smelling docks. Their mothers were frazzle-haired and twisted of lip. Kind words were few, and buffets many. Still, he had to take what there was. Even a cold crib and a sneering mother was better than life in the woods.

And so it was that he managed to pluck a year-old child from a sour-smelling cradle. The mother's name was Beatrice Hoot, and she had a pack of seven older children to worry about. Stealing the babe, little Timmy Hoot, was likely the easiest job Piskin had ever bothered with. Wanting to make it quick—and since he was only half-hearted in the task at best—he simply launched the child out the nearest window. It fell like a stone into the Berrywine that flowed under the shack and floated away with all the other refuse.

Sighing with resignation, Piskin transformed into a vague semblance of the child he'd disposed of and winced in distaste as he pulled the stained bedclothes up to his neck.

Soon after, Beatrice Hoot slapped open the door and marched up, staring down at Piskin. So sour was her expression, Piskin felt sure at first that she had witnessed his abduction.

"Quiet today, ain't you Timmy?" she asked.

She dug at the foot of the bed and lifted aloft a stone ward. Piskin sucked in his breath at the sight of it, but realized almost instantly that the ward was a false one. It had been drilled through, and had no power. He almost snorted, but managed to hold back the un-babe like sound. Not all the River Folk were so wise yet!

Seeing that the ward was still there, Beatrice's face softened and she tucked it back into place. She gathered up Piskin to her breast. "There now, little Timmy, time for some lunch."

Piskin opened his mouth and smiled. At least, this was something.

His shock was unimaginable when a cold nasty substance was rammed into his open mouth on a hard spoon. He choked and sputtered. Fish-paste? What's more, it was *cold* fish-paste!

He spit it out, and she cuffed him. The second spoonful came, and he choked it down.

The door creaked open.

"Mama?" asked a boy at the door.

"What? Can't you see mama's busy? Go work the nets, boy."

"That's just it, mama! I've caught something special."

Beatrice cocked her head to look, as did Piskin.

The boy held aloft a dripping baby. "Look what came up in the net! It's brother Timmy! He must have fallen out the window."

After a stunned moment they both shared, Piskin felt Beatrice's fingers squeeze like iron bands into his flesh.

By the time Piskin had escaped that foul shack, Beatrice Hoot's fingers bled and his head had many lumps and bruises. He barely made it out with his life. Still spitting fish-paste, he was forced to leap out into the river itself and float away with the rest of the local waste.

When at last he managed to drag himself onto the shore like a half-drowned alley cat, he hung his head and fumed.

Not long after, when twilight came to the land, a flittering wisp came to whisper him a tale. He batted at her, not in the mood for gossip. But she was excited and insistent. Finally, heaving a sigh, he listened to her news.

As he listened, hearing of the great battle at the Merling stronghold, hearing of the Wee One who had stolen Lavatis from Oberon himself, he was impressed. There, he thought, was a kinsman who knew what he was about!

But, as the tale turned dark and full of woe, he learned that this fellow had wielded the Blue Jewel poorly, and had been devoured by the very Rainbow he had summoned. Lastly, he learned another of the Wee Folk had stolen the Jewel yet again. The entire story could scarcely be believed.

As he questioned the wisp, one final detail changed everything for Piskin. That detail was the name of the Wee One who had wielded the Jewel. The name was that of *Dando*.

Piskin bounced a foot into the air. The wisp backed away, her wings buzzing. Piskin breathed through clenched teeth. Something was up. Something big. Some *conspiracy* had brushed by him and he had been too thick, just as Dando had said, to even notice it. A conspiracy, perhaps, of impossible proportions.

He learned the name of the second Wee One, the barbaric one who now purportedly possessed the Jewel: *Tomkin*.

There were great plans afoot up in the north, in the marshes where dead things thrived. Piskin knew in an instant that all his misfortune was wrapped up in this tale somehow. He had been a dupe, a fool, the ignoramus of the story. He swore to himself by the silver light of the Moon that he would get to the bottom of all this. And when he did, there would be repayment.

He turned north and headed up the riverbank with great, determined strides. Each bounding step carried him further than any human had ever managed to leap.

Chapter Three
The Elf in the Wood

Mari Bowen never got the calico dress she had wanted for her birthday. She had, however, escaped the elf in the woods with her soul and her life, and she accounted this as an even better birthday gift.

After moping about her birthday disappointments, she considered telling her mother about the elf she'd met under the ash trees. The more she thought about it, the more convinced she became that telling mother would be a bad idea. Her parents were already rattled with gossipy stories about a giant killing a farmer up near the border of the Deepwood. And, of course, there were many claims of changeling children being discovered all over Riverton.

Mari thought that probably not all the stories were true, but she felt sure that *some* of them had to be. After having met an elf herself, she knew such creatures were real, and they were dangerous.

The elf. She couldn't stop thinking about him—that was the real truth. She had danced with him, he had touched her, and she had felt things awaken in her she had never known were there.

Oh certainly, she was not entirely innocent. She had known some boys. She had been kissed and chased. But the elf was different. She had felt real desire with him. She had wanted to give her virginity to him—he who was not even a man.

She was no fool. She knew that she had been in mortal danger. Quite possibly her encounter could have ended when her heart exploded in her chest, like that of a horse ridden to ground by a drunk rider who wields his whip with abandon. But maybe, just maybe, it would have ended differently. She might have lain with the elf sweetly, under the spreading branches of the silent ash trees.

Mari sighed. Her household chores seemed more stiflingly dull than usual. She felt like slumping over her broom. She tired at the very thought of churning milk. Morning dragged, turning into an eternity of folding bed sheets, hauling water and stacking firewood.

By the time she was freed for lunch, she had already made up her mind. She would head up the hill—but not to go into the forest. Elves liked the cover of trees too much. She would be safer in the open fields.

She went to her dresser and after a few quick glances about to make sure none of her siblings watched, she had pulled out the ash leaf ward she had found when she had first met the elf. She secreted it under her shawl and hurried out into the sunlight. She affixed the ward around her neck with a loop of braided yarn. The leaf fluttered against her chest and she felt braver knowing it was there.

When she found the spot where she had first met the elf, she stood in her father's field aghast. She put her hands to her face and stared in open-mouthed disbelief. Every stalk of the field was blackened and curled with blight. She had not a moment's doubt where this curse had come from.

Mari called to the elf, her anger growing. She knew how hard Father had worked to grow that grain. The elf had spoiled it, just for spite. Just because she had resisted him. She marched to the edge of the woods, and she called him. She demanded that he come forth.

There was no response. The slight breeze that ruffled her dress and her hair, but carried no music with it. She felt a pang of regret, even through her anger. Would she ever see her elf again? Had he found another girl to accost, at the next farm perhaps? For some reason she could not quite understand, this thought upset her. It caused her pain.

She called out again, stepping into the green cool gloom under the trees. There was no response.

She finally did what she knew she should not do. She called the elf by his true name. She walked deeper into the wood and called his true name, over and over.

"You?" said a soft voice from behind her. She turned, and saw him. Some of her anger evaporated. It was hard to stay angry with one who was so beautiful to gaze upon.

"Yes, me."

"Why do you shout my name as a bird might sing of worms in the Earth?" asked the elf, walking around her. He was clearly vexed. His manner was anything but seductive this time.

Mari turned to keep facing him. She held her ward tightly. She pointed to her father's blackened field. "You did this, didn't you?"

Half his mouth smirked. "You summoned me from my home to file a complaint, girl?"

"Why did you wreck our crops?"

The elf shrugged. "I owe you no explanations. My folk do as they will here. Our Pact is broken, remember?"

"You and I made a bargain. We danced. Both halves of the bargain were completed. You had no cause for spite."

The elf finally looked troubled. She knew that bargains and wagers were important points of honor for his folk.

"What will we eat when the snows come and there is nothing for the mill?" she said, scolding him as her mother might. She put her hands on her hips. "Had you thought of that?"

"Hardly," he said, "but you have a point concerning idle malice after a bargain is complete."

He gazed at her, bemused at her manner. He smiled. He began to circle her again, slowly.

She turned her head to watch him. "What are you thinking?" she asked.

"I'm thinking that you didn't come here to complain about a blighted field. I'm thinking that you came here to dance with me again."

347

Mari crossed her arms. "I came here to see if you still haunted these woods," she admitted, "but all such thoughts were driven from my mind when I found the sorry mess you made."

The elf had stepped behind her. Suddenly, his face and breath were at her shoulder, whispering hotly into her ear. "Let us make a new bargain," he said.

"What bargain?"

"I will repair your father's fields. The grain will wave yellow and pure again in the breezes. All you need to do is put aside that dirty leaf you wear."

She rolled her eyes and turned to him, shaking her head. She pushed her face almost into his, teasingly. "Not likely. Try again!"

He stepped back from her, surprised. She was glad to see him look surprised for a change. She felt a touch of pride, she had faced one of the Fair Folk and she could plainly see he was not her master.

"You intrigue me, child," he said, smiling anew, "I will offer you a fair bargain, something I've never done with one of your kind. Let us just dance together. That's all, just dance. And neither shall owe the other anything when the dance is done."

"With my ward on?"

"Naturally."

"And at a normal pace?"

He chuckled. "It will be most gentle and slow, I assure you. Stately, even."

And so she agreed and Puck did play his pipes, and they did dance together under the ash trees. Mari felt her heart quicken at his gentle touch. She had danced before, of course. But the thumping tread of boot-wearing farm boys was nothing like this.

The elf was gentle and seemed to be enjoying her company just for what it was. Neither of them had further designs, she felt. He played sweet music that did not intoxicate her mind, but simply made her happy with its clear sounds. They danced together, for the joy of it. His touch was light and kind, but it

348

did not make her burn. She could still think. She could still decide.

After they had danced to many songs, the elf finally stopped. Twilight had begun to fall over the land.

"Milady," he said, "I must take my leave of thee. It has been sweet, but time is pressing."

Mari felt a pang. She knew that he meant that it was the twilight hour, the time when his kind could most freely move about. He would seek out another to dance with. She knew this, as that was the way of his people.

"I have another bargain to suggest," she said quietly, coming to a decision. "I wish to lay with you. And neither shall owe the other anything when we are finished."

The elf looked very surprised indeed, and she was glad to see his expression. Perhaps no other had freely made such an offer to him. He recovered quickly, however, and began to circle her again. This time she let him step behind her, without turning to face him.

"Such unions are forbidden, for your people and for mine."

"I thought the Fair Folk did as they pleased."

"That's true," he said, and he stood still. He blinked at her, uncertain. It made her heart glad to see he felt conflicted.

She began to step around him, while he stood in thought.

"You will wear the ward?" he asked.

"Naturally."

He laughed, noticing her circling and the reversal of roles. It was clear to them both that he was now the hunted.

"And we will proceed at a normal pace?" he asked, eyes sparkling as he repeated the question she had asked earlier.

"It will be gentle and slow," she said laughing in return.

"Stately, even?"

"Yes."

And so it was that they both came to realize he was as entranced with her as she was with him. She let him lay her down. She felt the cool leaves on her back and in her hair. Events took their natural course, and she would never forget them.

When darkness had fully fallen over the land, Mari Bowen hurried home again, knowing her mother would be crying and her father would be looking for a switch. Behind her, the field of grain was whole and wholesome again. She sighed to see it and to see Puck, who stood at the very edge of the wood, his skin shining slightly with reflected moonlight. This time, she left Puck wistful and restless, rather than the other way around.

What she did not know was that she was already with child.

For, you see, surviving such close contact with one of the Fair Folk was exceedingly rare. But when both parties agreed to such a union, and both lived through the experience, there was *always* a half-fae child born. This fact had a great deal to do with why such willing unions were strictly forbidden by both peoples.

Chapter Four
Castle Rabing

"So this is the property of our ancestors?" asked Corbin incredulously. "Why have we never heard of it?"

Myrrdin looked troubled. "That omission from your education has much to do with me," he said.

Brand eyed the cloak of night that fell around them. He was worried about the redcap. He had warned the others about it, but none save perhaps Modi seemed concerned. All of them felt that the creature wouldn't dare attack with so many of them together, but Brand wasn't so sure.

Castle Rabing had once been a huge fortress, but now it lay in ruin. The outer walls, long since torn down, were now no more than a set of long low hills that drew lines around the region. But those low hills still held some power and could avert the Faerie, which was why the group had come here. Inside the fallen walls, there were towers at the four corners, each broken and toppled long since. The southern tower was near the river and it was there that Brand had met the redcap one night. Facing the East was the gatehouse, a structure that remained somewhat intact. In the middle of the fallen walls was the largest and most intact structure, the central keep. It still stood, but with many smashed in walls, fallen stairways and tumbled stones.

Instead of settling in the keep or one of the towers, they huddled around a too-small fire in the midst of the ruined gatehouse. It had four walls and only one entrance, as the inner gate had been filled with fallen debris. For a small group, it functioned as a fortress in miniature. Brand sat on a tumbled stone block from the damaged walls of the gatehouse around him. The firelight illuminated the rusted iron grille of a great portcullis that had once barred the outer entrance. Warped and hanging loosely, the portcullis was now easy to slip past. Diced by the grille, squares of orange firelight flickered on the landscape beyond.

They had debated camping in the ruins of the main keep, which was more intact and much larger, but had decided against it. Myrrdin assured them that the keep had no potable water, unlike the gatehouse, which had a spring-fed pool at its center. Brand suspected that there were darker reasons for avoiding the keep. He thought of the redcap in the southern tower, but said nothing to the others. Worse things still might haunt the keep.

"You were here when this castle was...alive?" asked Telyn, intrigued.

Myrrdin looked uncomfortable. "Normally, only the wisest few do I take into my council," he said. As he spoke, he fiddled with his staff, poking at the fire. He used the staff for everything from walking to stirring coals, but never did it seem to scratch or blemish. Brand wondered where within it the green Jewel Vaul resided. For he was quite certain now that the staff held Myrrdin's power.

"We aren't the wisest, perhaps," commented Corbin, eating an apple he had gotten from somewhere, "but we do have a need to understand these things."

Myrrdin nodded. He poked at the fire some more and tossed on a few more dead sticks before answering. "Yes," he sighed, "I was here when this castle was more than an abandoned pile of masonry."

"But why don't we know of these things? Why don't we have some memory of our people's lives before migrating to the Haven?" asked Telyn.

"Because your elders and I, at the time, felt that it would be best if history were forgotten. You see, people had had enough of war. Most of the warrior houses—you call yourselves clans, now—had been wiped out. People considered them largely the

352

reason for the devastating wars, and no one wanted to see them rise again to repeat past mistakes."

"So Clan Rabing was one of these warrior houses?" asked Telyn.

"Exactly so," said Myrrdin.

"They wanted to forget, so they didn't tell their children of the past," said Corbin, staring into the flames. "It sounds more like we were beaten then, and that the Pact was a surrender, a shunting aside of humanity to a wilderness that no one else wanted."

Myrrdin moved uncomfortably. "There is some truth in what you say. But recall that the Faerie were devastated and exhausted as well. They lost far fewer lives than the humans, but they can't replace them so quickly. A hundred warriors lost among the Faerie may take as many years to recover."

"That, of course," interjected Modi, "is one reason they used humans to produce rhinogs. They needed warriors that bred more quickly."

"Well," said Brand, speaking for the first time. He noted that they all turned their eyes to him and there seemed a new respect in their attitudes. It gratified him and made him a bit uncomfortable all at the same time. "Well, let's discuss our current situation. We have yet to see Tomkin, but he is of the Wee Folk and their stealth is legendary, so he could be anywhere. We haven't seen the Wild Hunt yet, but they too, could be hiding themselves. I don't think they can come across the outer walls without great effort, if at all, so we should have the warning we need."

Before continuing he glanced at Myrrdin, who nodded in agreement. "But we must assume that they will come and that they will work to break the ancient charms of this place," he said. "I suggest we finish our talk quickly and prepare to meet our enemies."

Modi grunted in agreement, but seemed disapproving of Brand's commanding tone.

"Agreed, Brand," said Corbin. "But I for one must know what happened to bring you all the way to the Merling stronghold."

Brand quickly related the events of the last several days, discussing Old Hob, the Will-O-Wisp, Tomkin and Voynod. He made sure to mention their deal with Tomkin, as he had promised. He hurried his tale, leaving out any mention of the axe's effects upon his thinking and emotions. Indeed, it seemed that the axe tugged at his mind even now, for he felt anxious about the redcap and the expected arrival of the Faerie.

Brand stood up at the end of his tale, but Telyn waved him back down. "Wait, Brand. I simply must know what happened to the rest of you while we wandered the marshes for days."

As no one else spoke first, Gudrin took up the tale. "The night of the Merling attack was a strange one. I can't account for the others, but it seemed to me that the wisps that you speak of so highly led me astray, although I'm loath to admit it.

"Separated from the rest of you, I soon found myself alone in the blackness of the marsh, in a darkness as complete as any I've ever known in the deeps of the Earthlight below Snowdon's frozen crown. I found to my despair that I'd left my knapsack behind. Only my Teret did I take with me, doubtless because I love it most," she said, thumping her leather bound tome affectionately.

"The Merlings fell upon me, and they netted and bound me. I managed to lay a few of them upon the mud, but it was not enough," said Gudrin, glowering into the fire at the memory. "I believe I would have wielded the axe that night had I been carrying it. I might well have gone feral then, and ruined everything. For this reason, I account us all lucky that Brand took it up that night and still bears it now."

"I too," said Corbin, "was captured in a similar fashion."

"Yes," said Gudrin, shooting a disapproving glance at Corbin for the interruption. "We were both taken, and brought together, being dragged in a most undignified fashion through the muck trussed up in nets like huge frogs. That's when Myrrdin and Modi appeared and raided the surprised Merlings."

"Indeed," smiled Myrrdin. "You did look like great netted frogs."

Gudrin snorted. "Anyway, they bashed and thrashed the Merlings that dragged us and we searched for you two until the sun rose, but found only a few mushy tracks leading off into the trackless regions of the marsh. We followed them until we found what must have been Old Hob's pond, although we didn't know it at the time and saw nothing of that evil being. After that, we lost your trail. We found the skiff and decided to continue our journey, since it seemed that your tracks led north as well."

"Also," said Corbin, "we didn't know that you had the axe and had reason to believe that some other party of Merlings had taken it back to their stronghold. We thought that way might lead to the axe as well."

Brand nodded and rubbed his hands together. He gazed out into the darkness of the gatehouse. He thought to see movement, but then figured he had been mistaken. He wanted to rub his eyes, but his gloves and his hands beneath them were too encrusted with filth from the hard trek across the swamp. He ground his teeth together instead.

"When we reached the Merling stronghold we came as guests," continued Gudrin. "The Merlings encircled us with armed fighters, but kept their distance. We met with their king and managed to find a means of communication. He related to us that he was essentially neutral, but was glad for the recognition of his people as worthy of notice. He spoke much of the unfairness and misunderstood status of his people amongst the other races."

"Never have I heard such a complainer!" said Modi unexpectedly. "Not even the Wee Folk can whine so interminably!"

Gudrin gave him a withering glance. "On the second day of our discussions with the king, we learned that Dando was already there, making deals with the Merling king on behalf of the Wee Folk."

Brand smiled despite his unease. The thought of the Wee Folk and the Merlings bitterly lamenting to one another of their misunderstood statuses as thieves, spies and prowlers amused him.

"Then the Wild Hunt came in search of Dando and Lavatis. Dando sought to wield Lavatis and turned feral, as you witnessed yourselves. Now, we find ourselves here, alone, and perhaps the target of the Wild Hunt as well."

A silence fell over all of them, but it was broken when a branch sailed down out of the darkness and landed neatly in the fire. The fire flared up a bit, eating the dry stick hungrily. Modi and Brand were the first up, and both reached for their weapons reflexively.

All of them looked up to the highest pile of stone that still stood in the ruined gatehouse. There, still wearing his fawnskin cap, sat Tomkin. Calmly, he hopped down to the ground and bounded forward to join them at the fire.

Brand sat back down, breathing deeply. The axe on his back shifted and he patted the knapsack absently to quiet it. "To what do we owe this pleasure?" he asked.

The manling warmed his fingers over the fire. "Tomkin is here to claim the promised boon."

Brand nodded. "Ah, the pouch!"

"Hast thou the craft to remove thy own curse, cheating witch?" asked Tomkin of Myrrdin in a conversational tone.

Myrrdin laughed off the insult. "For you, I would do so even without the bargain you made with Brand. For you have stolen that which Herla so greatly covets!"

Tomkin looked startled then suspicious at the idea of Myrrdin freely removing the pouch. He recovered quickly, however. "Wouldst thou then grant another boon?"

"Possibly," said Myrrdin in a tone that indicated he already regretted his rash words. "As long as it involves not one drop of my precious blood."

Tomkin shook his head. "No. Tomkin asks for something far more difficult to provide."

"What?" asked Brand, interested now.

"Sanctuary," said the manling. He nodded, indicating something beyond the twisted grille of the portcullis.

Brand turned and gazed out into the darkness.

"Music," said Telyn. Her voice was not elated this time however, but fearful.

Then the sounds came to Brand, the sounds of wind in trees and water running over stones. The music of earth, sky and water.

"The dark bard has come," said Telyn.

"Dost thou grant my boon?" demanded Tomkin.

Myrrdin appeared serious. "Yes. We will defend you to the best of our ability."

Tomkin nodded, satisfied. Then he produced the pouch from beneath his tunic. There was no sign of Lavatis, but Brand suspected it was in his bag or stashed beneath his cap.

"Removing the enchantment will take some time," said Myrrdin, tapping his bearded chin thoughtfully. "I'm not even sure I can find the required ingredients here on this damp ground. It will take an extensive search, at the very least."

Tomkin scowled and opened his mouth to speak, but Brand cut him off. "There is no more time for that, or any more chatter," said Brand, coming to his feet. "The dark bard can't pass the walls by himself, of this we are sure. About the others, and Herla's powers using Osang, I don't know. What do you know, Myrrdin?"

"He will be stopped, but only for a time. I don't know how long. There is no telling how the centuries might have eroded the charm that protects these walls. It was once quite strong, but now..." Myrrdin shrugged.

"Then we must assume we are about to be attacked," said Brand. "Let's man these old walls and get this grille back into place. This gatehouse and the main keep seem to be the most intact spots to defend. Telyn, would you be so good as to climb up that wall and keep watch for the enemy?"

Nodding and smiling, Telyn climbed nimbly up to the spot he indicated.

"Kills two Merlings and fancies himself a captain," muttered Modi, stumping off into the darkness.

"Modi?" Brand called. He frowned to himself. He needed the big warrior's cooperation.

Brand and Corbin set to work on putting the grille back into place. They soon found they could barely move it.

"Look at the blast marks on this thing," said Corbin as they grunted and heaved. The rusted metal creaked and grated against stone. "It appears as if the grille was blasted inward! I wonder what terrific force could have done such a thing."

"The Rainbow could have done it," said Brand.

357

Corbin looked at him. "You're right. Think of it, Brand, centuries ago our ancestors fought for their very lives on this very ground."

"Let's hope that we fare better than they did," replied Brand.

Chapter Five
Tomkin's Freedom

They toiled at the grille, but at first it would not budge. Then abruptly, they made progress. The grille gave a grinding screech and moved with a lurch. Stumbling, they looked up to find that Modi was at their side. He had a huge branch in his hands and was using it for a lever. All straining and working together, they managed to get the grille back into the archway. Using levers, they tumbled stones up against it to hold it in place.

"There!" said Brand, "that's something, anyway."

"Not if they jump the walls," said Modi, stumping away into the darkness again.

Brand and Corbin looked at one another, deflated. They had forgotten the way the huntsmen had so easily passed over the walls of the Merling town.

"Perhaps we should consider a retreat to the river," said Corbin. "We could use Myrrdin's craft again to escape them."

"But where would we go?" asked Brand.

"Back to the Haven?" suggested Corbin.

"It would be like the flight of the Rainbow all over again," said Brand, shaking his head, "they would eventually run us down and slay us all. At least here there is a charm and walls that might help us."

"Besides," said Corbin, eyeing him carefully, "you rather like making a stand here, in the ruins of our ancestral homeland."

Brand looked back at him and smiled. "You always know me best, Corbin. What better place is there for two river-boys of Clan Rabing to die?"

Still the music of the dark bard played in the distance. It made them want to sit and listen to it, to be lost in the beautiful sounds of the world around them, but they resisted the temptation.

"Hard physical work seems to help keep your mind clear," Brand told Corbin. "Let's shore up the walls where we can."

Tomkin perched atop the broken walls and watched them work. "We need more than stone and steel to hold out the huntsmen," he said.

"What do you suggest?" asked Corbin, leaning on a branch he'd been using as a lever.

"I could go for help."

Brand and Corbin looked at one another. "But if we lose the Jewel you bear, our whole purpose is lost."

Tomkin shrugged. "If we sit here and wait, all is lost anyway."

Brand discussed the matter with Myrrdin, who had just come up with more wood for the fire.

"My, but that infernal music is persistent, isn't it?" he asked the others. "Usually, it is quite compelling and all who hear it are soon dancing until their hearts burst. The charm on this place must be working still. Any sign of the other huntsmen, Telyn?"

"None, I can't even make out the dark bard. I wonder how long it will take him to realize we aren't being affected by his spell."

"Hopefully, a great while," said Myrrdin.

"What do you think of Tomkin's idea? He wishes to go for help."

"I will alert both the River Folk of North End and Riverton about our situation," said Tomkin.

"You would be willing to endanger yourself to save us?" asked Corbin in a somewhat incredulous voice.

"Certainly!" said Tomkin. "Thou hast no cause to call me a coward.

360

Brand and Corbin exchanged glances and pursed their lips, but said nothing.

"Well," sighed Myrrdin, "There's little else we can do, unless we try to flee. We can't last long in a siege, there is little food or water here. I agree, it is best that you go get help, Tomkin. None of the rest of us could slip past the Wild Hunt...but I would require that you leave the Jewel here with us."

"Mistrustful witch!" declared Tomkin.

Myrrdin held up his hand. "We need to be sure that the enemy doesn't get his hands on that which he has sought for so very long. You must leave the Jewel with us while you go to get help."

Tomkin pursed his lips. "That could be managed," he said with the air of one making a great concession. "I can promise that the Jewel won't leave these walls. If..."

Brand rolled his eyes. "Another boon?"

"Not a new one, but the fulfillment of an old one," said Tomkin. He produce the pouch again and waggled it at them.

"Right, go ahead and remove it, Myrrdin," said Brand.

Nodding in agreement, Myrrdin sat down and reached out with the tip of his staff. He lifted the burden from Tomkin's neck. With a deft flip of his wrist, he tossed the pouch into the fire. It snapped and crackled. A brief gout of green flame shot up in response.

"Done!" said Myrrdin, getting back to his feet.

"That's it?" sputtered Tomkin.

"You said it would take a great while," said Brand.

"Yes, I wanted to maintain our leash over this little gentleman for as long as possible..." said Myrrdin with a reluctant shrug.

Tomkin nodded slowly and narrowed his eyes. This bit of trickery was something that he understood. "Finally, thy behavior appears rational."

"And now," said Brand, holding out his hand. "Let us relieve you of Lavatis that you may complete your quest."

Tomkin hopped up and grinned at each of them in turn. Brand frowned and the axe twitched suggestively upon his back.

361

With a tremendous bound, the most amazing Brand had yet to see performed by one of the Wee Folk, Tomkin leapt up to the top of the damaged walls of the gatehouse. Taking great, springing leaps he commenced running along the walltops.

"Free! Free! At long last Tomkin knows freedom once again!"

The others watched him bemusedly. When he came to Telyn, sitting at her watchpost, he gave another great bound and cleared her head. She ducked reflexively, smiling. Brand noted that she was working at something up there, fashioning it with her hands. He was too distracted to be feel anything but a flash of curiosity about it.

"What treachery do you plot? Don't try to leave with the Jewel, Tomkin!" called Brand.

"There is no fear of that, river-boy!" Tomkin shouted back, laughing.

"Enough celebrating, Tomkin!" called Gudrin. "Time now to go get the help you promised."

Tomkin stopped his bounding and came back to the fireside with two startling hops. He sat near the blaze, once again warming his fingers.

"Well?" demanded Brand, increasingly impatient.

"It is done," said the manling.

"What do you mean?" demanded Gudrin.

Modi snorted, shook his head, and went back to work on shoring up the grille.

"It is done, the task is already complete," said Tomkin. He gave Brand a leering grin.

"Tell us how then!" demanded Brand.

"For another boon, perhaps," said Tomkin.

Brand stepped forward. The axe moved with excitement upon his back. "For the boon of not being sliced in twain, you—"

Corbin stopped Brand with a gentle hand laid on his shoulder. "Indeed, Tomkin, you surprised us all with your speedy execution. Forgive us if we are at a loss concerning how your task was completed. But before more boons will be forthcoming, including that of your protection, we must feel that you have been honest in your dealings with us."

362

"Right," said Brand, "tell us what you're talking about or Herla can have you right now."

Gudrin smiled at Brand's vehemence. "There is some of your brother Jak in you after all, Brand," she said.

Tomkin took it all quite well. Hopping up, he set his cap to a more rakish angle on his head and eyed them all. Clearly, he relished their lack of understanding. "Quite simply, I located the wisps that fled Old Hob's lantern several nights earlier. Distant cousins of mine are the wisps, as thee might not be aware."

Brand felt it unlikely that Tomkin was related to anything as delicate and beautiful as the flittering wisps, but said nothing.

"I told them of the situation here, and asked that they return your favor by flittering off to Riverton and North End to summon help," finished Tomkin.

"But they can't use our speech!" objected Brand, pacing now. "How will they communicate the message? Why would the Riverton council believe a creature such as a wisp in any regard?"

Tomkin shrugged. "This is none of my affair. My part of the bargain is already complete. Word has gone out."

Brand felt his anger rising, but Myrrdin tried to calm him. "It is no matter, Brand. There could be no faster way to get to your relations. A wisp could fly there in a single night. It might not work, but then again, it may."

Shaking his head, not trusting Tomkin an inch, Brand walked away to talk to Telyn. She still sat upon the wall top, fashioning something up there in the darkness.

"It looks like Tomkin has had the last laugh on us again," he called up to her. "What are you working on, Telyn?"

She made no reply for a moment, and then she lifted something white up in her hand. He frowned up at her, but before he could ask about it, she tossed it down to him. He fumbled with it for a moment, and then lifted it up into the light cast by the distant fire to examine the object. It was a candle, a rolled taper of white wax. It had an odd smell to it...then he knew.

"More witchery?" he hissed up at her. "Is this what you've been up to all this time?"

Her soft laughter came down from the darkness. "Oh Brand, you really must drop some of your prejudices. After all, you do bear a living axe on your back!"

Brand frowned at the thing and held it pinched between his thumb and forefinger as one might a dead rat. "What's it for?"

"It's a beacon," said Telyn. "The same as before. It's to guide the army of the Haven to us."

Brand snorted. "The army of the Haven? It doesn't exist."

"Well, I know of one of its best soldiers."

Brand smiled and tossed the candle back up to her. She caught it deftly. It felt good to be free of the thing. "But the last one called more than we bargained for. Might that not be the case here, too?"

"Possibly," admitted Telyn. "But Myrrdin and I have been working together on it. He's been teaching me things about the craft that should greatly improve the results."

Brand nodded, not liking the sound of it. He sighed. "I should go back to the others."

"Yes," she said. There was an awkward silence, and Brand felt the fool. He wanted to tell her all sorts of silly, emotional things, but he didn't.

"Take care," he said, turning to leave.

"Brand?"

"What?"

"I think of your kiss all the time."

"And I think of yours," he said, smiling in the dark. Then he left her and rejoined the others who argued over the best way to mount a defense of the ruins.

Chapter Six
Oberon's Daughter

"Let us assume that help is coming," said Corbin. "That means that we are under siege. The charm may or may not hold until our reinforcements arrive, so it makes sense to continue preparing for an assault."

"Exactly," said Myrrdin. "There are a few things I can do to aid us, but I need help."

"Name your needs, wizard," said Gudrin.

"I require many fresh shoots of hardy plants," said Myrrdin. "Sapling trees, young ferns and vines would do the best. I need all that we can gather."

"You plan to wield Vaul," said Brand. "We will gather all that we can, but it is dark and this land isn't terribly lush."

"Yes, you must carry torches and go in pairs," said Myrrdin. "Please don't stray far from our defensive position, such as it is, and come back at the first sign of trouble."

"I'll go with you, Brand," said Corbin. Brand nodded and smiled, it would be good to work alongside his favorite cousin once again.

"Hold, Brand," said Myrrdin, lightly touching his arm. "I have another task for you. One of greater import."

"What is it?" asked Brand.

Myrrdin waited for a moment as the others broke up and headed out into the darkness. Gudrin and Modi formed one team, while Corbin and Telyn formed the second. Tomkin remained to tend the fire. He cast occasional glances at them. The firelight reflected from his glass-like eyes.

"Even if I wield Vaul and our band stands together, I don't think we can face the Wild Hunt. In the coming hours you will have to wield the axe, Brand," Myrrdin told him. "You will go feral as surely as did Dando if you aren't properly attuned by then. Therefore, there is no greater need for us than that you gain mastery of the axe."

"How do I do this?"

"Unfortunately, it is the Faerie that will decide that."

"What!" said Brand loudly. He glanced toward Tomkin and found that he was staring back at him. He lowered his voice. "I'm lost then!"

"Not necessarily," said Myrrdin. "In any case, you must try."

"What do I do?"

"There is a Faerie mound within the walls of Castle Rabing. It is an ancient place, Cairn Browyyd, it is called. You must locate it, out to the west of the fallen keep. It is said that four great human kings lay dead beneath the earth there, and in their noble death they have opened a path for the Faerie. Like all the mounds, it is a spot they can gather when called and ignore the normal rules of movement—and the magic of wards."

"I must go there?"

"Yes," said Myrrdin. "You must walk nine times widdershins around the mound, following the path of the Faerie."

Brand blinked at Myrrdin. Part of him could not believe he was even contemplating such an act. To summon the Faerie, to invite them to join him at one of their mounds—this was a mad thing, sorcery. Only witches and short-lived fools attempted such nonsense.

"Am I to dance with them?" he asked, his voice querulous. "I—I am not like you, Myrrdin. I couldn't dance with the Faerie and survive."

"I don't know what will be required of you. It is never the same thing twice with the Shining Folk."

"Shouldn't I take a second? Isn't that what you said I should always do with the axe?" asked Brand.

"Normally, yes," said Myrrdin. He smiled. "I'm pleased that you have been heeding my words. But for this task, you should go alone. Your friends can't help you on this journey."

"What if Herla is summoned? Could he be the one that is called to the mound?"

Myrrdin frowned. "Possibly, I don't know. I doubt he would come. Things are going his way now, he has no need to take such risks. More likely, you will meet with the idle and curious among them. Hopefully, they will not be unpleasant..."

Brand thought to himself that this seemed a faint hope, but he said nothing. "I suppose I will set out, then."

"Yes, time is of the essence."

Their eyes met, and each knew that they may not survive the night. "Thanks for your help, Myrrdin," said Brand. He moved to walk past him.

"Often," Myrrdin said, grasping his arm one last time, "often, it is the way of the Faerie that a wager must be made. You must make the wager, and it must be made wisely, to achieve what you desire."

Brand slipped through the gap they had left in the archway where the grille didn't quite meet the stone and he found himself alone outside the walls of the gatehouse. The stench of the swamp wafted with the cool night breezes. Mists chased one another across the face of the gray-shrouded moon overhead.

He headed for the ruins of the main keep. To the westward side of the ruins he found Cairn Browyyd. The grassy mound was bare of trees, vines and shrubs, as always seemed to be the case with such places. He approached the place without hesitating and soon found the ring in the grass that circled the mound. He set his boots to the path and walked widdershins around the mound. On the fifth time around, it seemed to him that the moonlight had brightened. *The breezes are sweeping away the mists,* he thought.

As he completed the seventh circuit, the moon was brighter still, and he knew in his heart that he had never seen it so bright. All the world around him was lit by the silvery light. He didn't dare to look up at the swollen, gibbous moon that surely hung overhead. Like a great baleful eye in the heavens, it had taken notice of him, one particular insect crawling around this sensitive spot upon the night shrouded world. As he completed the eighth circuit, the breeze died and the world seemed to hold its breath.

As he walked the last circle around the mound, his head slowly filled with lovely sounds and smells. Hot, fresh honey and spices seemed to boil beneath his nostrils. Rippling music played in the distance. It grew harder to place one foot ahead of the next, but still his boots went on, seemingly of their own accord.

His gaze, fixed down upon his boots, fell upon shining cloth of a radiant garment. He looked up slowly to see who he had answered his call. He faltered and almost fell. It was the Shining Lady.

He opened his mouth to speak, but words were far beyond him. Hers was the unearthly beauty of the moon and the stars. Telyn was crude and simple beside her, flawed in a thousand ways. Compared to her ethereal beauty, all human women were as animals: gross and unrefined.

She smiled at him and her arms floated forward to poise, ready for his embrace. Brand's knees threatened to buckle, but he kept his feet. Hot desire flooded through him. He took a single step toward her.

Vaguely, he became aware of others that moved around him, but he had eyes only for the Shining Lady. Wisps flittered and swooped. Slit-eyed goblins scuttled about the crest of the mound. His back felt the prodding of what was perhaps one of the elfkin. It poked at him with its finger and doubtlessly laughed. He imagined that the elfkin joked with its fellows, but he didn't care. Nothing mattered but the cold beauty he reached for.

He took another step forward, and now he knew that he would embrace her, that he would lie with her. Her eyes told him that he wouldn't be refused, that he would know more pleasure than any man of the River Folk could ever comprehend. The fact that her embrace meant death was nothing.

368

The elfkin prodded him again, more insistently this time. He rolled his shoulders, trying to evade it. He didn't turn away, he remained fixated by his Lady. He took another step. He reached out with his hands and his fingertips almost met hers. An electric thrill ran through him. Sweat flowed from his hair down into his eyes and burned them.

The elfkin rapped upon his shoulder now, rudely. It all but drove its fist into his back. Brand snarled, but could not, would not turn from his Lady. When he had her in his grasp, he vowed, he would strike the blighter down with his axe.

His boot swept forward again. Now his fingers touched hers, and he knew expectation and tension that he had never felt before. Her lips curved to form the inviting shape of an open-mouthed kiss. He began to fall into her embrace.

The elfkin struck him. Hard. It rapped him on the skull so hard that for a moment, it seemed that his vision faded out. Purple splotches of color and pain marred the vision before him.

Enraged, he knew there was nothing for it but to act. Thinking not at all, he wheeled, snarling, and reached up to grab the haft of the axe. He lifted it out of the stifling knapsack and it flashed, shining brighter even than the giant moon overhead.

There was no elfkin there. A few wisps floated curiously about, but the nearest creature that could have struck him a blow seemed impossibly far from him. Confused, Brand turned back to the Shining Lady, who still rode foremost in his mind.

She too, was gone. This horrible fact all but broke his mind, then. Tears sprouted from his eyes. His knees gave out and he fell upon them, weeping.

He heard a twitter, then a giggle. "You stole her!" Brand screamed. Raving, he lurched up from the ground. He didn't need the axe to urge him into a lumbering charge.

The Faerie gave way before him as he reached the top of the mound. They circled him, dancing away as he came close and laughed at him in childish voices.

The manlings and wisps danced about him in a circle, dodging his rushes with glee. Spittle ran from Brand's mouth, his eyes bulged from his skull and only hoarse croaking sounds came from his throat. Fully in the grip of the berserkergang, he charged at first one flittering shape then another, axe upraised. He didn't slash and cut at them, but always kept the weapon high and ready.

Sure that no mortal man could catch them, the Faerie played the game, expecting him to collapse in a shivering heap. None accounted for Ambros. Perhaps they didn't truly know what it was that they faced.

The axe waited for its moment, and when it came, the Eye of Ambros winked, as brightly as a stroke of silent lightning. Blinded, one of the scattering figures dashed the wrong direction, and Brand struck. The axe cut the creature in twain. It tumbled to the grassy mound like a stricken child.

Gasping, Brand halted. The Faerie were gone.

He blinked at the dark world around him, uncomprehendingly. It took a hazy length of time for his eyes to fall down upon the small corpse at his feet. He gazed at it in growing horror.

It was an elfkin maiden. A beauty not so perfect as the Shining Lady, but much more innocent and child-like. Letting fall the axe, Brand gathered up the corpse and clutched it. He wept to see such a lovely creature in death and to know himself as her killer. He found that a lock of her spun-silver hair had been shorn off and lay in the grass. He grasped the lock, brought to his lips, and felt its light, feathery touch.

"Why?" asked a voice from behind him.

Brand cringed with guilt. "I lost my temper and my mind with it. One of them kept poking and prodding at me!" he said, hating the whining sound in his voice.

"None of my folk touched thy person."

"But, I felt..." Brand trailed off and realized the truth with new horror. It had been the axe itself. There had been no elfkin poking at him. The axe had prodded him and rapped his skull just as it had in the past, trying to warn him about the Shining Lady. In his charmed state he had become enraged and misdirected his wrath toward the Faerie.

"Thou hast taken from me Llewella, one of my own daughters. I request repayment of this debt," said the voice.

Without turning, Brand knew the voice to be Oberon's.

Unbidden, the image of Myrrdin came to his mind. He recalled Gudrin's story about Myrrdin's youth, so many centuries ago. He felt he understood the moment that Myrrdin had met with the farmer, bearing the man's dead daughter in his arms. He hung his head in shame. When he could speak, he nodded to acknowledge the debt. "Tell me what you want."

"The Axeman will grant my wish?"

Brand felt some of his composure return. He felt distant from himself. He touched the silvery lock of hair that reflected the liquid moonlight into his eyes. "Tell me what you want," he heard himself say.

"Thou art wiser than when last we met. I request a small thing."

"The return of Lavatis," said Brand.

"Wiser, indeed wiser," said Oberon, as if to himself.

"I need something as well," said Brand quietly. "I need to be attuned to my accursed, but beloved axe, so that I might never strike down another innocent."

Oberon laughed. He laughed long and loud, he laughed until tears burst from his eyes and the world rang with the sound, but there was no mirth in it. "One debt of blood is not enough!" he cried. "He commits murder upon my family, Llewella's body is not yet cold before him, but still he asks for a kindly boon!"

"I would not want to repeat tonight's mistake," replied Brand.

Abruptly, Oberon stopped laughing. "That is not a matter to be decided by me, Axeman, but rather by thee."

"Why do you call me Axeman?" asked Brand. Finally, he turned to face Oberon. He looked so marvelously young. He was the father perhaps of a hundred generations of his folk, but still his body was that of a young teen. The light of the overlarge moon reflected from him, so that his smooth skin seemed a luminescent white.

"Are you not the Axeman? Did you not wield Ambros tonight, and then set it aside unaided?" asked Oberon, almost in a whisper.

"Yes, but only after slaying with uncontrolled bloodlust," said Brand.

"There! The proof is in thy own words! Thou art the axe's master, child. For none, young Axeman, can set aside the axe unaided, save for its master."

Brand blinked at him. He looked down at the axe. His hand trembled as he reached out and grasped the haft of it. To his surprise, his mind did not leave him. His thoughts were rougher than before, but they were still his own.

* * *

Telyn had been restless in Brand's absence. None of the party had been idle, but Telyn found the waiting very hard indeed. She felt each hour tick by since Brand vanished upon the Faerie mound. The ticking was extremely difficult to endure. The pain of separation took her by surprise. She'd always been a free spirit, and was unaccustomed to pining away for anyone. She'd liked boys before, but had never felt great anguish at their absence. Out of sight, out of mind, that's how it had always been with her.

She had to admit to herself her feelings for Brand had grown curiously over these last weeks. She had not been an innocent before…but with Brand, matters had taken a more serious course. She even wondered at moments if they might marry one distant day—should they both survive this perilous time.

Overwhelmed by an urge to *do* something, she slipped out of the camp in the midst of the night when Brand had vanished upon the mound. She did not *intend* to follow him—to spy on him. But she had to admit to herself, she wanted to do precisely that. She kept thinking about what might have happened to him. That he was only a mooncalf river-boy, one who was even more sheltered in the ways of the world than was normal for citizens of the Haven. Could he really stand up to a pack of the Shining Folk, even with his fancy axe? What if he were lying upon the mound wounded, bleeding out his lifeblood into the grasses? No one would be there to hear his weak cries. They might come look in the morning to find his cold eyes staring into the bright sun, with dew droplets forming on his motionless lashes.

Telyn had to go look for him. She could not help herself. Confident in her own skills of stealth and flight, if not fighting, she slipped away over the crumbling walls and crept out of the circles of light formed by the fires. She ran lightly across wet grasses and did not halt until she stood at the foot of the mound.

It was bigger than it looked in the distance. Surely, it had to have been a great king they had buried here. Perhaps it was an entire family. She wondered briefly what they'd been like, and if their name had indeed been Rabing, as Myrrdin had suggested.

A soft sensation came to her as she eyed the quiet scene. Was it a sight or a sound? Oddly, she wasn't sure at first, thinking perhaps it was both. The moonlight seemed to brighten overhead as she stood there. Then the music came clear and swelled in volume, and she knew the truth. It was a lute, with a masterful player plucking the strings. The lute was her favorite, she thought. How had the player known?

"Step forward musician, that I may know you," she said. She hoped desperately it would not be the Dark Bard. She did not want to think for a second she had enjoyed the sweet music of a dead-thing.

A figure walked around the mound toward her. He was a glimmering figure—like a man, but smaller and more lithe. He looked both young and ancient at the same time. His face was full of cheer and sadness in equal measure. Seeing his fine features, Telyn's breath caught in her lungs and she had to tell herself to continue breathing. His strumming continued, and it filled the air with sweet music.

"Don't you like my playing, maiden of the River?" the elf asked her.

"Indeed I do," said Teyln, sighing the words. "I think, in fact, I like it overmuch."

"Good," said the elf. He walked closer until he stood a dozen steps from her. He smiled and tilted his head. "How is it I've been so fortunate this evening?"

"Fortunate? How so?"

373

"Why, to find a girl like you here in this lonely place."

Telyn eyed him warily. "I search for another."

"Indeed?" said the elf, stepping three paces closer. "Is he more fair than I?"

Telyn paused, but she forced herself to nod. "Yes. He is to me."

The elf stepped backward, as if injured by her words. "But he is not here, is he? He has perhaps, forsaken you for another? Will you not follow me, maiden? I will lead you to a place of—"

"No," she said, and she reached into her tunic and pulled out her ward, which was a river stone worn through naturally and looped with a thong. "This stone is not drilled. It is powerful enough to keep your kind at bay."

The elf's upper lip twitched. Was that a sneer? He recovered quickly, and turned the twitch into a fresh smile.

"Why would I need to be kept at bay?" he asked, and his voice was as smooth and soothing as his music. "Can we not just talk? You have nothing to fear from me while wearing your ward."

Telyn blinked at him. "I would know your name, elf."

"I will tell you, if you would only agree to walk with me. I'm so lonely this night. It is quiet here, and all the others have gone to play around mounds that do not reek of death."

Telyn's heart pounded at his words. What did this being know? Did he speak of Brand?

"I will walk with you," she said.

He turned, and offered her the crook of his elbow. It was a courtly gesture. Telyn took his arm without thinking and together they walked beside the mound.

"Now, tell me your name," she said.

"My," he chuckled, "you are a strong one. Most would have forgotten to insist. Wouldn't you like to know of other things? Such as what has become of your beloved?"

Telyn's worries resurfaced, but she regained her composure quickly. "One thing at a time. Tell me your name, elf. You have promised."

The elf gave a shuddering sigh. "I have promised," he echoed. "I am known as Puck."

Telyn almost ripped her arm from his, but controlled herself. She knew something of the lore of elves. This one was high indeed in their lineage. "Are you then...the son of Oberon?"

"The same," he said. "Would you like to dance? I sense you are an excellent dancer. And I am an excellent judge in these matters!"

Telyn, to her surprise, found she did *wanted* to dance with him. She imagined herself twirling and kicking while he smiled and both their eyes shone with shared moonlight. The strumming...but how could she be hearing his lute now, when he was no longer playing it?

She shook her head. "Not now," she said. "Let's just talk for a time."

Puck pouted. "Always is this the way of the maiden," he said. "They claim we influence them, but in truth, we males are always the ones that are manipulated! How many hours have I spent wooing softly for so few moments of bliss? The ledger is harshly in your kind's favor, I assure you."

Telyn laughed. Puck looked at her, and laughed with her. The two stepped along their way more lightly now. They were as two schoolchildren skipping down a road.

She smiled broadly and felt herself slightly drunk. Her feet were light beneath her, and they carried her effortlessly forward on the path. Looking down, she noted that there *was* a path beneath her feet. A shining path of silver grasses. She halted, swallowing a giggle that tried to burst from her throat.

"You've tricked me!"

Puck looked at her in mock horror. "How so?"

"This path! We walk beside the mound!" she said, ripping her arm loose from his. "How many times have we made the circuit? If I step from the silver grasses, will I be lost in-between?"

He cocked his head and gave her an appreciative nod. "You are no foolish stripling, are you? Rare it is I meet one of your age who knows of these things."

"Answer my questions, Puck," she said.

He shook his head, his face absurdly mournful. "Alas, I am not in your power, fine lady."

"I know your name."

"And thus, you can call upon me, and perhaps do me some small harm. But you can't command me, as I have made you no promises."

"I will walk with you no further."

"You make me sad," he said. "Are you certain?"

"Yes," she said firmly.

Shaking his head, the elf backed away from her, continuing on the path toward the Twilight Lands. He circled the mound and vanished from her sight ahead.

"Should you change your mind," he called, his voice sounding distant and echoing, as if he called up to her from the bottom of a dark well. "Come find me!"

And so Telyn found herself standing alone beside the mound. She knew a deeper terror then than she'd ever felt before. She tried to think, but it was difficult. She knew that if she had stepped too far along the path, she could not deviate from it or she would be lost forever between the world of the Fae and the world which was her home. On the other hand, if she continued on her way forward, she would arrive in a strange world where she had never been. She would surely be lost there, more surely than she was now.

Looking this way and that, she almost called for Puck to return and guide her. Perhaps she could survive his gentle touches and caresses at least long enough to return home.

Telyn opened her mouth, but no calls issued forth. She stopped herself. This was exactly what the elf wanted. This is why he had abandoned her. He was waiting. He would come back, after a frightening delay. He would wait until she sobbed for him, frozen with fear on this path of moonlight. He would wait until she offered to remove her ward…he would wait until she was his.

She made a decision. She turned around on the path, and took a step backward along it. She took another, and then a third. This was dangerous, she knew. Reversing oneself while circling a mound was possible, but increasingly difficult the further along one had gone. She was not sure how far she had come, but she felt certain that if she called for Puck's help, she would be lost forever. She would never have Brand—possibly, she would never see her world again.

Clearly envisioning Brand and clutching at her ward with both hands, she took six more steps along the path, then two dozen more.

The land wavered before her. Instead of silver, the grasses appeared coppery. At times, they bled until they became the color of a sunset over water. She took another step, and could no longer see the path at all. There was nowhere to go. Tears streamed from her face. She did not look back. She did not want to see if the rest of the world was gone behind her as well. She lifted her foot to take yet another step. There was nothing else to do. Perhaps she could still win through and find her way home, somehow.

A hand fell upon her shoulder. She jumped and put her foot back down without taking the step. She whirled her head around.

Puck stood there, very close to her. "Don't move," he said in a whisper.

"I don't want to go with you."

"You've made that abundantly clear, stubborn child," he said, but there was some gentleness in his voice. "Why won't you come with me? Would it be so unpleasant? Am I so unsightly?"

"You are beautiful, and I'm sure the experience would be glorious. But my heart belongs to another."

"Humph," said the elf. He reached up and took her chin very delicately. His touched had a burning coolness that was exciting and slightly painful at the same time. She allowed him to guide her with his touch, as she was desperate.

He turned her head, and pointed a long finger to her left. There, she saw the silver grasses. They were no more than three steps away.

"I see the way," she whispered. She turned to thank him, but there was no one there. She knew a new moment of panic. She turned her head slowly and found that only when it was directed precisely so, was she able to see the path. She aimed herself that way, and took three quick steps.

Telyn found herself on the path again. Her body was sheened with sweat, despite the coolness of the night air. She followed the path around the mound without further incident until her world was strong and vibrant around her.

It was just before dawn when she returned to her own world. It had taken half the night, she realized, to walk less than a mile. But that was no matter. All that mattered was that she *had* returned.

When she made her way back to the crumbling walls, she decided not to try to follow Brand into such places on her own again. She would make a guiding candle instead, a beacon to direct him home. Like the case of her own plight, in such places each person had to test their own resolve and could not rely on others to save them. Brand would make it home or he would not. It was his fate, and she did not have the craft to alter his destiny for him.

Chapter Seven
The Armory

Brand stood in a very different time and place than Telyn. He stared down at the axe in his hand. It was true; he was the axe's master. But was this yet another of Oberon's tricks? Had he been the axe's master all along, and simply not known it? Or had the wily old elf actually done him a service? It was difficult to tell. He had asked for the ancient Oberon's help in mastering the axe, and now he could not deny that he had mastered it. But the experience had not been as expected. It had been rather like asking a jailor to be freed and having him point out the prison door was unlocked. Brand felt the fool.

"Now, I require that my debt be paid," Oberon told him.

Brand narrowed his eyes. He realized that if he gave up Lavatis for his debt, he then would have nothing left to bargain with to rebuild the Pact. He thought of arguing that Oberon had done nothing to help him, but he could not do so in good conscious. Possibly, Oberon's words had served to *convince* him he had mastered the axe, and that was the key to it all. He doubted he would get any straight answers out of the elf concerning the matter, so he didn't try.

"I will wager with you," Brand said, his heart heavy as he spoke the words. "Double, or nothing at all."

"Double?" said Oberon, immediately intrigued. "Double meaning...?" He pointed a long finger in the direction of the axe.

"No," Brand snapped quickly. He knew he loved the axe too much now, despite what it had made him do. He could never give it up. He also knew that one couldn't hope to win a wager with the Faerie if it wasn't honestly made. He could never give up the axe, but....

"I will only wager what I can give," Brand said. "I will wager my head."

Oberon nodded, as if not in the least surprised. "Very good. And the wager itself?"

Brand thought hard. "I've chosen the items wagered, perhaps you could suggest an acceptable challenge," he said at last.

Oberon looked at him then, and smiled. "Wise again," he said. He thought for a quick moment. "I will wager that thou cannot strike through the central flagstone of this castle's southern tower."

"Strike through a flagstone? With the axe?" asked Brand, surprised. "I don't know if I can do it. Won't the axe shatter, or just bounce off?"

"That's what I'm wondering, Axeman!" Oberon laughed and circled Brand twice. He took out his pipes and played six thrilling notes. "Hence, the excitement of the wager!"

Brand opened his mouth then closed it. Words failed him. The Fae were so strange. One moment they might be your mortal enemies, the next they may appear to be blood-brothers. But then the third moment came, when they seemed completely mad. Their natural way was to treat all of life as a game—even death could be an amusement.

Oberon circled him again and came close, putting his lips near Brand's ear. The axe twitched at his presumption.

"Hast thou never a thought for the axe?" the elf lord whispered. "Does the mystery of it not burn thy very soul?"

"I think of little else," Brand admitted.

"Then we shall test its edge and your strength of mind together upon a single flagstone!" proclaimed Oberon. A cheer went up from the smaller ones, who had returned and now surrounded them. "The wager is spoken and it is done!"

"It is done," said Brand.

Oberon danced with excitement. His pipes traveled up and down the scale twice with impossible speed and precision. Brand wondered that Oberon could be so joyous while his dead daughter lay cooling at his feet. The Faerie were a strange folk, of that he was sure. Grief and joy, life and death, these things seemed so close together with them as to be one and the same.

Shouldering the axe, he followed the elf toward the southern tower. As he walked, he noted that he still held the silvery lock of the elfkin-maiden's hair, Llewella's hair, in his hand. Absently, he slipped it into his pocket.

Surrounded by the Shining Folk, he saw that they carried the dead body of the elfkin maiden, held high like a trophy. Of his own companions, he saw nothing. He wondered vaguely if they could see him. It was said in the old tales that those taken by the Faerie often saw the same world, but couldn't locate the people in it. To both the taken and their families, it forever seemed as if the others had vanished from the world.

Brand soon stood in the midst of the southernmost tower. It was the one where Telyn and he had spent the night when they met the redcap.

Oberon indicated the very flagstone upon which they had lit their fire. That night now seemed a very long time ago. It was here that the redcap had stained its cap with Telyn's blood. Brand eyed the top of the broken walls, but saw nothing of the creature. Shining Folk thronged the walls, however, reminding Brand of Riverton children watching the Harvest Moon races.

Brand eyed the flagstone and reached up to grasp the handle of the axe again. "Lavatis and my head are yours should I lose. Should I win, my debt is erased," he said to Oberon and half to himself.

Oberon just eyed him. He cocked his head, in what Brand had learned to be the manner of the Faerie when they were curious about River Folk. It seemed that for them, once something was said, there was no need to repeat it later.

Brand flexed his fingers and reached for the axe. Around him, the gathered Faerie fell silent. All their strange eyes glittered, focused upon him and the haft of the axe.

Brand raised the axe aloft. As if it had been awaiting this moment, the axe sent a surge of pleasure through him. His face split and his teeth revealed themselves. The axe rose overhead almost by itself. The Eye of Ambros burned brightly, outshining the moon that rode the heavens overhead. The warm amber light lit up the ruined tower and the encircling Faerie, and even the Shining Folk drew back from its glory. The manlings and wisps whispered in hushed tones, striking wagers of their own.

Brand no longer doubted himself or the axe. He stood squarely over the scorched flagstone and held the axe aloft in both hands. He brought it down with a single, crashing stroke.

The flagstone exploded into fragments and fell inward with a crash. A pall of dust exploded up into Brand's face. He realized that there was a hole there, that he had broken into a hidden chamber beneath the tower. The amber light of Ambros caused things to gleam with yellowy reflections. Golden motes of dust glittered and floated around him.

"What trick is this?" demanded Brand. As the dust cleared, he made out the shapes of weapons in the chamber. Swords, pikes and crossbows filled the space beneath the tower.

"An Armory?" asked Brand. "What are you playing at, Oberon? I've won our wager!"

"Almost," said Oberon quietly.

Brand looked at him then turned back to the broken flagstone. Yellow eyes glared up at him from the chamber. He knew in an instant the he was face to face with the redcap.

"Ah!" shouted Brand. "You want me to slay this foul bogey! I see your game now, and you won't be disappointed!"

He jumped down into the dusty blackness and the very stones of the castle seemed to swallow him up.

Brand stumbled, and felt a pain that should have crippled his ankle, but it was as nothing to him. He held the axe high to light up the scene. A great number of finely-made weapons met his eyes, and the sight of them brought him pleasure. Then he saw the redcap. It had retreated to one of the racks, where it took up an ornate sword and shield. Brand recognized the black diamond on its shield: it was the mark of his clan.

Without further hesitation, Brand strode forward to strike down the redcap. It was a menace and it had harmed Telyn. It was not fit to live.

The redcap hissed and made ready to meet him. There was a brief passage of arms. Brand was surprised when the redcap caught his axe upon his shield and turned it. He was even more surprised to find the other's sword poised at his throat.

For some reason, however, the creature paused in slaying him. Its yellow gaze met Brand's, and Brand knew he faced death a thousand times over in those ancient eyes.

Then he willed the axe to flash, and it did as he bid, filling the chamber with blinding Amber light. The redcap screeched and Brand beat its sword away from his throat. He struck again and again, knocking aside his foe's guard. When its breast lay open to a killing stroke, he raised the axe again.

Panting hard, he felt the exultation of victory. To slay his enemies and drink their small lives, that was his purpose now, it was clear in his mind.

Yet, something tugged at him, gnawed at his guts. It was the black diamond on the shield. The creature at his feet, he knew, was the last defender of Castle Rabing. It was related to him, somehow. It seemed wrong that its passing should be so ignoble.

"Know, last defender of Castle Rabing, that your task is at an end," he told it. "I, a Rabing by birth, am now the lord of this place. I release you from your duties."

For a frozen moment, the two regarded one another. Brand wondered if the thing could even understand his speech. Then it made an effort, although not a violent one, to rise. Moving with the painful efforts of an old man, the creature knelt before him, exposing its neck.

Brand knew immediately what it wanted, but despite the axe's urging, he resisted. "No," he said. "Perhaps you have had a hard path, but it is at an end. You are free to go."

The redcap said nothing. It removed its stained cap, clutching it to its breast. Brand wondered how many victims had been drained of their blood to feed this thing and soak its vile cap. His lip curled of its own accord.

Brand turned as if to go. The redcap's hand shot out and it grasped his ankle with steel fingers. "Release me, lord," it croaked.

Brand knew pity and disgust. He gave in to the urgings of the axe. With a single stroke, he chopped off its head.

The head rolled to a stop at his feet. The dead mouth smiled at him.

Brand grabbed up the shield and climbed his way back into the tower and the misty night outside. The Faerie were gone. There was no sign of them. Brand realized numbly that he had won the wager. His head was his to keep—for now. He felt alone and cold. He shivered in the darkness.

He walked back toward the tiny flame of what he suspected must be another of Telyn's beacons. Singular point of light burned steadily in the distance. Nothing else of the gatehouse could be seen in the darkness. Brand indeed felt drawn to that steady pinpoint of brightness. He wondered distantly if he could have seen it from leagues away. Had the axe changed him in some way, so as to make the beacon shine more clearly to him? Had he become a creature of the twilight? He was only a river-boy of the Haven, yet lately he had walked and dealt with the greatest of the Faerie. Could a man do such a thing without permanently changing his spirit?

As he walked onward over the dark landscape, thinking such weighty thoughts, he absently put the axe back into his knapsack.

It went without complaint. He stared down at the ice-white blades. His hand was free of it, without a struggle. It was as Oberon had said: he truly was its master.

* * *

"Brand!" cried Corbin. "Brand has returned!"

Brand made no response, but instead trudged up to the gatehouse's entrance with his head hung low.

"You've been gone for days, man!" said Corbin. "We worried you would never return!" He scrambled down from his watchman's post on the walls and strained at a lever. The grille shifted just enough to allow Brand to enter the gatehouse.

"Days?" asked Brand vaguely. "I recall only one night."

"Often," said Myrrdin, "people who walk with the Faerie find that time moves at a different pace with them."

Corbin came close to him now, and Brand heard him suck in his breath. "Are you hurt, cousin?" asked Corbin in concern. He took Brand's arm. "You're wet and sticky—" Corbin drew in his breath sharply. "Is that blood? Are you wounded?"

Brand shook his head. "It's not my blood," he said in a hollow voice.

Brand felt the others' hands lessen their grip then, as if they wanted to pull away from him. He felt a pang at this. He was a murderer, and none would want to stain themselves with the blood of his victims. He thought of Oberon's daughter and her silver locks. He recalled her name, *Llewella*, and felt a wave of sickness come over him. Would all others revile him from this day forward?

Corbin helped him to the fire, then drew away and tried to inconspicuously cleanse his hands. Brand felt tainted. He thought of the redcap, who also wore garments soaked in the blood of its victims. He crouched before the fire and stared into the dancing yellow tongues, oblivious to those around him.

Myrrdin approached him. He sighed as he seated himself on a fallen log they had pulled near the firepit to serve as a bench.

"A new dawn is only hours off and Herla has yet to break through the charm that protects this place," said Myrrdin. "Even the dark bard has given over his endless music as futile. It appears that we will pass another night safely."

Brand stuck out his hands to warm them. Then he saw they were stained and splotched with blood and drew them back into his cloak. In his pockets his hand felt the feathery touch of the elfkin-maiden's silvery hair. He rubbed it briefly between his bloodstained fingers. His eyes stung and he blinked back tears.

"I've looked often to the Faerie mound where I sent you," said Myrrdin gently. "Each night there have been dancing colored lights and signs of great activity. What has occurred, Brand?"

"I've slain innocence and evil both," said Brand. He stuck out his hands again and looked at them. He wondered at the price upon his soul that mastering the axe had taken. "I've slain them in the world and in myself, both together."

Myrrdin looked troubled, but he nodded. "Was there a wager to be reckoned?"

"Yes," said Brand.

"Have we lost—anything?"

"Oberon wanted Lavatis, but I wagered my head instead," said Brand in a dead voice.

Telyn sucked in her breath sharply in alarm. Modi gave a heavy grunt of approval. Brand realized for the first time the others were all listening intently.

"It seems to me that you must have won the wager, given the stakes," said Myrrdin.

Brand nodded.

"Who then was slain?" Myrrdin asked.

Brand eyed the blood on his hands and flexed them experimentally. For the first time, he considered washing them, but doubted he could ever fully remove the stain. "A daughter of Oberon. I cradled her severed head in my hands."

"Ah," said Myrrdin. He nodded in understanding. "It is a wicked feeling, is it not?"

"Yes, wicked," said Brand. He eyed Myrrdin, and the other looked to him like an ancient man, crooked and bent with years and hard times. Brand knew he thought of the farmer's daughter he had danced to death, or perhaps of worse things that he had known over his long life. "I also slew the redcap that guards this place," Brand added.

Myrrdin bounded up from the bench. He stood over Brand. "You have slain the redcap of Rabing Castle?" he demanded.

"Yes," said Brand, not looking up from his hands.

Myrrdin set to pacing then. He tugged at his beard ferociously as he circled the fire. "This event is three things at once," he said, "amazing, good for the future, and terrible in the present."

"What do you mean, wizard?" asked Gudrin. Brand noticed for the first time that Gudrin had been scribbling notes of this entire conversation. He snorted softly, wondering if he would be the subject of a story in the Teret some centuries from now.

"Amazing because the redcap is not easily overcome," explained Myrrdin. "It is the vengeful spirit of this place, made here long ago by great butchery and empowered by the rage of all the victims of that butchery. Good in the long run, because all this area shall return more quickly to purity and usefulness with the absence of such a creature. Terrible in the present, because I believe the redcap's presence kept alive the charm of warding upon this place."

"So," said Gudrin, "with the redcap dead, Herla should soon be able to cross the fallen walls. This siege may soon become a battle."

"Exactly," said Myrrdin, "we have little time left now, I should think."

Brand thought about Myrrdin's words, and soon came to better understand Oberon's choice of contest. He had caused Brand to slay the redcap, which would allow Herla to pass the walls. There would be a battle now for certain. Perhaps Oberon thought he might do better than to gain just one of the Jewels. Now there were many in play and there would be many chances for a wise player to snatch them up.

"I have some small good news," Brand said. He told them briefly of the armory he had found guarded by the redcap. They quickly agreed they should set out at first light to investigate the find and arm themselves for the coming conflict.

"Too bad we have no army to supply with these arms," said Modi regretfully.

Brand blinked as a pail of steaming water was placed before him. He looked up to see Telyn there, smiling at him worriedly. He nodded in gratitude and she touched his brow with her lips before going to gather more wood. Brand began to carefully wash his hands. The spot where she had kissed him still tingled and it warmed him somehow.

"What about all these green shoots you've had us gather for days, Myrrdin?" asked Corbin. "What will you make with these?"

Myrrdin smiled at that. "You'll see!" he said. "In the first light of morning, you'll see what!"

They talked for a while longer, but soon decided it was best to bed down again for whatever remained of the night. Modi was already snoring by this time. Corbin's watch continued on the walls, and even Brand lay down and closed his eyes. Sleep didn't come easily however, as each time his eyes shut he saw the child-like face of Oberon's daughter.

His eyes snapped open when the axe tapped his back some time later. He found that Tomkin crouched before him, head cocked to one side. He sat up and the manling hopped backward reflexively, then crouched again.

"What do you want?" hissed Brand. From the sounds the others were making, it was clear that they slept.

"Thy tale was woefully incomplete," said Tomkin.

Brand was irritated at having been awakened. He rested his head on his hand and laid down on his side. "You should have tagged along if you wanted to know more," he growled. "They are your people, after all. Why didn't you just join the throng that circled me?"

"And have it be *my* head that thee wrongfully severed?" chuckled the manling.

His words caused Brand a pang of guilt that the creature couldn't have understood.

Tomkin continued talking unconcernedly. "I would be hard put at any rate to fit in with Oberon's court. I've spent too much time with River Folk. Thy stink permeates my person. The others would have known."

Brand waved him away and tried to go back to sleep. This time, his axe gave him a sharp rap of warning. A sudden pressure on his ribs made his eyes snap open again. Tomkin now stood on his chest. The manling gazed down into his face like a presumptuous housecat.

"What are you doing?" Brand asked in amazement. Brand shook him off and sat up. Tomkin hopped down and smirked at him.

"Calm thy anger. We must speak plainly."

Brand was as surprised at the idea of one of the Wee Folk speaking plainly as he was to have been walked upon. He glared at the manling, but nodded for him to continue.

"Dando had a dream, and I think it was a good one," Tomkin said. "He wanted the Wee Folk to wield a Jewel and thus become more than sneer-worthy. I bear Lavatis, and thou art the wielder of Ambros. If we can strike a bargain of sorts, we shall be the ones to govern a new Pact and hold Herla at bay."

"But what of Oberon?"

Tomkin sniffed. "The elf lord has no basis for power left. It is best to deal with those who wield power."

"But you don't *wield* power," pointed out Brand. "Dando tried and went feral. Oberon is already attuned to the Jewel and would do the best to balance things between the Haven and Herla."

"Ah, but he is also likely to give the worst terms for just those reasons, is he not?"

Brand thought about it for a moment, recalling the Pact and the seemingly endless tribute of one seventh of their crops. At the time, such a bounty was unquestioned and reasonable, but now, with the expansion of possibilities, it did seem a lop-sided arrangement.

"If a deal was struck between the River Folk the Wee Folk—given that we could properly wield Lavatis—our terms would be nowhere near so harsh," said Tomkin.

"But you don't speak for your people," object Brand. "You are only a spy from the marshes."

At this, Tomkin grinned. "Thou art mistaken," he said. He turned, placed his fingers over his mouth in an odd configuration and performed a perfect imitation of the call of a night insect that infested this region of the swamp. An odd buzzing sound filled the gatehouse, but no one else took notice.

"I've brought a companion."

There was a blur of movement and a creature very much like Dando sprang over the gatehouse wall and scuttled forward to join Tomkin. The creature tipped his hat to Brand and bowed low so that his coattails flipped up.

"Piskin, at your service, sirrah," said Piskin. He flashed a winning smile. His accent and speech were quite different than Tomkin's, being both more modern and more eloquent.

"Huh! Another spy!" whispered Brand. It came to him Modi would have said exactly the same thing. Perhaps he was beginning to think like a warrior. The idea made him smile grimly.

Tomkin looked angry and opened his wide mouth to retort, but Piskin laid a hand on his shoulder and shook his head.

"Not at all, sirrah, not at all," said Piskin, taking Brand's comment in stride. He paused his strutting in front of Brand, and gazed up at him steadily. Brand thought that perhaps the creature recognized him, but he could not recall having met him.

"I'm an envoy in fact, for my people," continued Piskin. "The Wee Folk have lords of our own, you see."

"Are you a lord of the Wee Folk, then?" asked Brand, putting his head on his elbow. He recalled once having been greatly interested in the Wee Folk, but now he just wished he could get some sleep.

Piskin cleared his throat, touching a lacy handkerchief to his lips as he did so. "I am of noble birth, yes," he said, "but let us speak of more worthy things—"

"Are you from Herla's pack? Do you run before the coursers?"

"No! No! A thousand times no, sirrah!" said Piskin, horrified at the suggestion. "I've nothing to do with those hotheaded turncoats and runabouts. Not a brain between the lot of them, I've always said."

Brand smiled despite himself. He nodded to indicate that Piskin should continue.

"I represent the high-born and—" here he glanced sidelong at Tomkin, "—and the low-born amongst the Wee Folk. We feel that we've never been given a fair shake. We've never been taken seriously as a political force. This has changed, now that first Dando and now Tomkin have gained and maintained possession of the Blue Jewel. Clearly, although Dando wielded it prematurely in his own defense, the Wee Folk can and will defend their right to this source of power."

Brand yawned. Piskin reminded him of the lawyers that old man Silure had sent to try to argue them out of Rabing Isle. He was only two feet high, but he was clearly a stuffed shirt.

"So, I'm here to bargain on behalf of my Folk," Piskin continued. "We will soon be in the position to summon the Rainbow in our defense—and control it."

"But Lavatis is staying here for now," said Brand. "We made a deal to that effect with Tomkin, who possesses the Jewel."

Piskin cleared his throat again. He paced back and forth before Brand, twirling his walking stick with easy grace each time he turned around. "This is an unfortunate detail," he admitted. "Let me come to the crux of our offer. We wish to form a new Pact with the River Folk. The new Pact shall be one of mutual defense. You shall retain the axe and wield it in our joint effort at the head of a respectably-sized army. We shall provide information about the enemy and wield Lavatis as our part of the defensive effort."

Brand frowned in concentration. This was serious business, he realized. It sounded attractive, but he didn't like the idea of enraging Oberon, nor the idea of depending on the Wee Folk for the Haven's defense. Still, he was in need of whatever allies he could garner.

"In principle, we're in agreement," said Brand. "I would propose something perhaps less grand and more immediate."

Piskin leaned forward intently.

"We both need to survive this siege by the Wild Hunt. If we work together, I think the Wee Folk are more likely to retain control of Lavatis and we the axe."

Piskin paced a bit more. When he stopped, his eyes narrowed, and he took on the more cunning look that Brand had so often seen on the faces of his kind. "What is to keep us from taking the Jewel away to safety right now?"

Brand shrugged. "Tomkin has given his word. And as I understand it, any of the Fae would sooner die than break their word."

Piskin pretended to cough into his hanky. "Indeed," he said, "well, what if others, shall we say, decided that Tomkin wasn't the best guardian of Lavatis?"

"What are you getting at?" asked Brand. Tomkin too, seemed suddenly more interested.

"What if Tomkin were to ah—lose the Jewel?" asked Piskin. He gave a suggestive twirl of his cane, ending in a light rap upon his skull that dented his top hat.

"Thy hands would be severed first," growled Tomkin.

"I'm but one agent of the Wee Folk," admitted Piskin. "But as the River Folk say, where there is one Wee Folk in sight, in the brush there are another dozen."

Brand frowned and Tomkin glared, but both realized that he could be telling the truth. If any type of creature could slip into Rabing Castle unnoticed, it would be the Wee Folk. There could be a small army of them nearby and they would never know. Their presence standing in front of him showed that the charm that kept out the Wild Hunt had no effect upon them.

Tomkin snarled and crouched, eyeing the brush around him with sudden suspicion.

"Okay," said Brand, "you could take Lavatis away right now. That would help the Wee Folk. But still the Wild Hunt would be on your heels. And you would have abandoned us and all hope of a Pact with the Haven. Worse, Herla might well overcome us and the axe would be lost as well."

Piskin thoughtfully smoothed out the dent in his top hat. "Sirrah, you make a fine point."

"Will you work together with us, to gain our trust?" asked Brand.

Piskin pursed his lips and nodded. "Agreed," he said. He replaced his top hat upon his head and twirled his walking stick once. "There is much to be done."

"What exactly—" began Brand, but he was speaking to the night air. Piskin had bounded over the walls and away. Tomkin, running in a crouch, followed a moment later.

Brand lay under the stars and thought about how strange the world had become. Sleep soon overcame him, despite his worries.

Chapter Eight
The Living Wall

Tomkin sprang after Piskin and although the other was surprisingly spry, Tomkin managed to catch him as they passed over a thorny mass of blackberry bushes. He grabbed hold of the other's foot and they went rolling in a squabbling heap.

"I demand you unhand me, sirrah!" hissed Piskin when they were both standing again.

"What's all this then about my losing the Blue Jewel?" demanded Tomkin. He studied the other with narrowed eyes. He'd only just met him, and he had seemed a harmless, overly talkative sort. Now, after having listened to his proposals to Brand, Tomkin was not so sure Piskin was on the same side as the rest.

Piskin shrugged and straightened his top hat with excessive care. He pushed out each dent and smoothed the creases with rapid, irritated strokes of his fingers. "You can't be serious about wielding the Jewel yourself, can you?"

Tomkin's lips uncurled, showing rows of ice-white, triangular teeth. He was gratified to see mild alarm on Piskin's face at the sight of them. "I'm serious when I say thou shalt *not* wield it!"

Piskin tried to smile, but it was a flickering expression. "Let's not bicker, brother!" he said. "Now is not the time for squabbles. We shall stand united as a Folk. We shall hold onto this Jewel for all Wee Folk everywhere. Who wields it is immaterial. What matters is that we are now a force to be reckoned with. None shall sneer at the Wee Folk after this day!"

"I can hold with those words," Tomkin agreed cautiously.

Piskin's manner changed on the instant. He was again wreathed in smiles. He reached to clap Tomkin on the back, but at the other's snarling reaction, he withdrew his hand like a snapping turtle pulling its head into its shell.

"No matter!" he said. "No matter at all! Let us head onward now, we are late for the gathering."

"What gathering?"

"Why, have you not heard?" Piskin asked, incredulous. "I can't fathom it! And you being the guest of honor!"

"Speak plainly, fop."

Piskin's lips quivered again, but he regained his composure. "Such rough manners! I constantly find I must remind myself of your upbringing. No fault of your own, it was, I know, I know."

Tomkin glared at him suspiciously.

"Well, to continue: the gathering is in your honor, as the new bearer of the Jewel. As Dando sacrificed his whole being, we hope it won't be the same with you. The gathering is not far from here."

"Where is it?"

"Did I mention there will be ladies there?" asked Piskin turning suddenly with eyebrows riding high. "Yes, many lovely women of our kind are attending. Rare they are in these parts, I understand."

Tomkin licked his lips. In truth, he had not laid eyes upon a member of the opposite sex since Dando's party in the marshes long ago. He felt temptation tugging at him—but still, he was wary.

"Where is it?" he repeated.

Piskin sighed with a burst of exhalation. It was a sound of bemused exasperation. "Persistence is a virtue!" he said. "But in your case, you might be taking things too far! Allow me to give you a word of advice: don't inspect every gift given too closely—or you might find people stop giving them to you."

Tomkin blinked, then tilted his head. "Where...is...this...gathering?"

"Very well, if you must know, it is atop mount banning in the Red Rock range. We'll be there in a trice, if you would only follow along like a good fellow."

Piskin arranged his hat on his head, twirled his walking stick twice and hopped off into the night. Tomkin did not move. He stood staring downslope at the other's retreating back.

Finally, as Piskin reached the edge of the marshland, the border where the territory of Rabing Castle's walls once stood, he halted and looked back in surprise. "Hullo? What's the hold up?"

"I'm not going," said Tomkin.

"WHAT?" Piskin cried, and came hopping back up the slope. His hops were small, rapid and irritable. "How can this be? How can a bumpkin refuse the hand of a dozen maidens who might otherwise be unwilling to grace his lumpish face with their spittle? This is your hour, man! This is your moment. You simply have to make the most of it."

"No," said Tomkin.

"Why?" hissed Piskin in utter vexation.

"Because I will stand here with the River Folk. I trust them more than I trust the likes of thee."

"Fool!" said Piskin through clenched teeth. He hopped in spun in angry circles around Tomkin, who watched him closely all the while. "You will do no heroics. You will die here, as did Dando. You are even less attuned to the Jewel. You will be forced to use it, and you will die, and they will take it from us. Can you not see, brother?"

"Do not come near me again," Tomkin said.

"Why ever not?"

"Because I will remove thy head and thy limbs," said Tomkin in utter sincerity. "I will toast them over a peat fire and chew the meat from thy bones."

"Barbarian!" huffed Piskin, but he retreated a yard or more.

Tomkin turned away and headed toward the River Folk and their fire. He glanced over his shoulder several times as he went, but he saw no more of Piskin.

* * *

"Brand! Wake up, Brand! Look, it's wonderful!" said Telyn. Her hands shook him. Brand groaned aloud and opened one bleary eye. Instead of bright sunlight, he found himself bathed in a cool green gloom. He sat up blinking in astonishment.

Vines as thick as tree trunks plunged up from the ground, growing before his eyes. Trees and bushes rippled and thrust upward, reaching for the morning sun. Stone blocks heaved and were shouldered aside by living green spears. A tangle of tea roses battled a sapling tree, each climbing the other like bundles of twisting snakes. Even the grass rustled and groaned. At the edge of the wall, dancing with his staff upraised, Myrrdin coaxed each of the drooping shoots they had planted the night before into explosive growth.

The walls now completely surrounded them, but still Myrrdin worked. Sweat sprouted from his brow despite the chill morning air. He ran back to the center of the gatehouse and stood upon the cracked fountain. Spring water bubbled up into the bowl of the fountain and trickled away through the mossy cracks. He held his staff overhead with both hands. At his feet the moss rippled and grew up over his boots. Tiny purple flowers sprouted around the buckles and laces.

The walls continued to grow. Brand watched in amazement as the stone ruins of the gatehouse were overcome by towering walls of dense vegetation. As the plants surged ever taller they turned inward, bowing to form a dome. Rustling leaves knitted themselves together. Vines grew crosswise now, binding together the curving tree trunks like the poles of a river raft. As the vines thickened, they sprouted sharp thorns as long as daggers.

"And so we lose sight of the sun again," said Gudrin.

Brand looked at the others. Modi gaped upward and frowned. Telyn clapped her hands and laughed. Corbin sought for fruit amongst the brush near the entrance. Already he had an armload of what looked like peaches.

"Peaches in winter!" cried Brand. Corbin walked up to him with a grin and tossed him one. Brand caught it and bit into it. It was delicious. Both of them grinned at one another and the miracle that grew around them.

"So what if they can fly?" cried Corbin, gesturing at the dome overhead that now closed itself completely. They were enclosed in a cool green gloom. The plants continued to rustle and twist.

"So what?" echoed Brand. He laughed aloud and ate the rest of his peach. Corbin handed him a second.

"It's good to have you back again," Corbin said.

Brand looked at him. He nodded and sighed. "You too," he said.

Corbin nodded and ate yet another peach. He moved around to the others, handing out fruit. It was good to have clean, fresh food in this place. Everyone's spirits ran high.

Finally, when it seemed that the wall of greenery would swallow them whole, Myrrdin stopped his magic. He lowered his staff and stepped back. He turned to them, disheveled and bathed in sweat from his labors. His grin was wide and his eyes alight. "I've done it!" he cried. "I've not conjured such a thing since the dead kingdoms lived!"

"It's beautiful!" gasped Telyn. She rushed up to the leafy walls and ran her hands over the woven vines and thorns. She plucked a flower from a bed of ferns and held it out to Brand. He took it, smiling. Just to look at her radiant face seemed to lift more of his burden from his shoulders.

Myrrdin was eyeing them while he brewed a pot of tea over the breakfast fire. "It seems clear that you have two seconds, Brand," he said. "Such a thing isn't unprecedented."

"Will it last, Myrrdin?" asked Telyn. "Is it truly alive? Will it fade soon?"

"It is a living wall," said Myrrdin. "The best that I could make it. The wall will live, yes. A very long time I should think. Especially if it is cared for and provided sufficient water."

"Brand!" said Telyn, whirling on him. "If we survive this, we should make this all part of the Haven! People should live here again and see this wonder!"

"Ha! Next, you'll be planning to raise these old walls again!" said Gudrin.

"And why not?" asked Telyn. "The old pact is finished, anything is possible. Who knows what new provisions the next pact will hold?"

Telyn turned a sly glance to Brand then, and gave him a sidelong smile. Brand stiffened, suddenly wondering if she had overheard some of last night's talk with the Wee Folk.

"Um," said Brand. He cleared his throat. "I have some news in that area."

Everyone turned to him.

"I spoke with Tomkin and another of his kind, Piskin. We came to an agreement of sorts."

"What!" shouted Gudrin. "You've been negotiating with the enemy without our knowledge? First, I hear that the walls of Castle Rabing are being raised again, and now this!"

"I – I didn't plan it that way," said Brand. He looked to Myrrdin from support, but he seemed more interested in his tea than the conversation. "They just came to me and wanted to talk."

"I see," said Modi coming forward for the first time. "Now that the Kindred have given over the axe to the River Folk, no one is concerned with their fate. Their opinions amount to nothing."

"No, no," said Brand, "it's nothing like that. They just woke me up and we decided that it would be in both our interests if neither the axe nor Lavatis fell into Herla's hands."

The two Battleaxe Folk grumbled something to one another and crossed their arms.

"Continue," said Gudrin.

"That was it, really. That's all I committed to, mutual defense in this place."

Nodding, the two Kindred stumped toward the entrance. The grille that covered the entrance was now all but buried in a mass of fern fronds and woven thickly with thorny vines. They stopped there and began a heated discussion of their own, in their own tongue.

Corbin and Telyn came close to Brand. Corbin put a hand on his shoulder and whispered in his ear. "It seems that the

398

Battleaxe Folk aren't pleased. Perhaps events haven't proceeded quite according to their plans."

"But what did they want?" asked Brand. "They gave us the axe to defend the Haven and eventually to come and aid them at Snowdon, I suppose."

"Perhaps you weren't supposed to negotiate a new peace with the Wee Folk and set about refortifying Rabing Castle along the way," replied Corbin.

"Yes," said Telyn in his other ear, "and perhaps they realize that you left out much of last night's conversation."

Brand looked at her, startled. If she knew that, then perhaps they did as well, hence their distrust. "But I wasn't trying to hold out information on them, I just wanted to make things seem innocent, which they were," sputtered Brand.

Their conversation was interrupted by a squeak and a sudden thrashing about in the thorny wall Myrrdin had created. They broke apart and lifted their weapons, approaching the living wall with caution. There they found Tomkin, arguing with a thorn. It was determined to hold on to his deerskin tunic.

"Ah, another spy!" said Modi. Brand smiled, thinking of his own words last night. Modi reached up and released the struggling manling with his powerful hands. He was careful, but even so, Brand noted a trickle of blood running down into his sleeve. Brand's respect for the wall rose a few notches, it seemed to work like a living guardian to prevent intruders.

Tomkin hopped down into the green gloom that enclosed them all and rearranged his torn clothing. "Never in all my days have I struggled with such a beastly growth," he complained. He hopped close to Myrrdin. "Thy doing, I suppose, cheating witch?"

Myrrdin ignored him. He seemed to be busy now with his staff, whittling and trimming it. Brand blinked in surprise. The staff seemed to have grown, at least a foot. Several leaves sprouted from it now as well. He resolved to question Myrrdin about it later.

"What have you to report?" he asked Tomkin.

"Report?" sniffed Tomkin. "Humph. I bring thee tidings from the Wee Folk."

"Very well," growled Modi, "Speak! Can we expect an army of little bounders to help us?"

"Hardly!" snorted Tomkin. He laughed aloud. "Clearly, thy misunderstanding of my folk runs deep. No, our army consists of many scouts and envoys. Even now they approach every power in reach of here for help."

"Ha!" shouted Modi. "Spies and foppish liars!"

"Tell us of what's happening!" urged Brand. "Where is Herla? Did the wisp you sent out get through to Riverton?"

Tomkin grinned, showing his sharp white teeth. "Herla circles these very walls, just beyond thy senses. Every puff of white mist hides the shadows of a dozen Huntsmen. We've tried to lure them off, but we have not the craft to fool Osang, which rules any illusion or image we can conjure up. Six of the Wee Folk lie trampled in the mud around this place, having tried to fool him."

"What of the Wee Folk that are loyal to him?" asked Corbin.

Tomkin looked disgusted. "He trusts none of them. He has leashed them like dogs. They bound about on long leads before his coursers, those that haven't deserted him."

"That's good then!" said Corbin. Tomkin glared at him. "I only mean that they can't spy on us if they are bound."

Tomkin nodded, but kept a slitted eye on Corbin. "The wisp made it to North End and Riverton. The word from that way is that a flotilla of River Folk are even now poling their way through the swamp to our aid."

The River Folk cheered at this. Modi looked sour.

"The wisp, however, was captured upon her return to the swamp. Old Hob caught her like a firefly in June while she slept on a leaf, exhausted from her trip."

Brand drew his lips tight. "Poor thing," said Telyn.

Tomkin grinned at Brand. "Already, thy reputation grows, Axeman. Thou art now the man who turned Old Hob's lantern yellow, rather than its ancient green! Every kind of folk whispers of it and laughs, as Old Hob has few friends."

"What news of Snowdon do you have, manling?" demanded Modi.

"Thy folk too, have benefited," said Tomkin, clearly displeased, "but for those tidings, I shall require a boon."

Modi roared with disgust, and Brand believed for a moment that Tomkin had forfeited his life. Sensing conflict, the axe twitched and lifted the flap of the knapsack of its own accord.

"Speak, manling!" boomed Modi. "Thy boon is thy continued life!"

Tomkin smiled and bounded away. In a thrice he crouched upon the broken fountain. "My boon only grows with threats!" he cried.

Enraged, Modi stumped after him. Tomkin loosed long ringing laughter as he bounded about the gatehouse, easily evading the warrior. Modi stooped to grab up a rock and hurled it. Tomkin dodged offhandedly.

Brand ran forward, feeling the axe's excitement grow. He grabbed Modi's arm as he went to hurl another chunk of masonry. "We must cooperate!" he shouted.

Modi moved to shake him off, but Brand held fast to his arm with both of his. Modi roared and threw him backward. Brand lost his feet and fell. Tomkin's laughter rang in his ears.

Brand leapt back to his feet and reached back for the axe. The haft of it came easily into his hand. Vitality surged through him. Tomkin's laugh became shrill and tinged with insanity. Brand opened his mouth and loosed a battle cry that burned his throat and made his lips run with spittle and blood.

Modi, transformed before him from an ally to a savage enemy. Brand realized then and there with perfect clarity that Modi had always desired the axe, that he coveted it, that he had never meant anything less than to take it. It was a filthy thief that stood before him, a liar and traitor who had posed as a friend just to come close to his beloved Ambros.

Brand lifted Ambros high, planning to will the Jewel to flash and blind the thief. Then he would rush in and end it.

Then the world turned green. He himself was blinded. He blinked and staggered back, wondering what trick had overcome him. He heard heavy tread before him and he struck blindly before him. He chopped into something hard. There was a grunt and a clattering sound. Then a new set of lights went off in his head.

He crumpled into the grass and broken stone. As he lost consciousness, he willed the axe to flash. He thought it did so, but it might have just been Modi's heavy boot, slamming into his head.

He knew no more.

Chapter Nine
Story of the Jewels

"It's obvious," said a heavy voice. "A stripling river-boy can't be our champion."

Brand's eyes fluttered open. Overhead, the green of the living wall filled his vision.

"Ah, the champion awakens," said Modi, for now Brand knew it to be his voice. Modi's huge features came into view. He stood over him, grinning. One of his eyes was closed. He put a gloved finger to the closed one. "You only blinded one of my eyes. I was ready for the sole trick you've learned," he said with a rumbling laugh.

Brand tried to rise. He winced and grabbed his head. Lights flashed and played inside his skull.

"Never," said Corbin, "has there been any doubt that you are the superior warrior, Modi. That was never the question. The question has always been one of control."

"Ah, and I'm not worthy on that account, is it?" asked Modi. "I think I showed great restraint in not killing the fool."

"You goaded him!" shouted Telyn. "You lost your temper first, going after Tomkin with stones! If you'd had the axe, you'd have gone feral and tried to kill us all!"

Brand struggled to rise again. This time, he made it to his elbow. His first thought was of the axe. He couldn't see it or feel it. It had been taken from him. His heart despaired. He got to his feet with a groan.

Everyone stood near, save for Tomkin, who was nowhere in sight. They all stood around him, arguing, except for Myrrdin who huddled by the fire. Brand saw his knapsack there and headed toward it.

"When it comes time to face Herla," said Modi behind him, "you will all wish that I were wielding the axe, feral or not."

Myrrdin stood and shouted at them. "Enough bickering! We need to get the arms from the south tower stored here in case the Riverton forces arrive before the charm fails us!"

The others looked at him, and then reluctantly separated. Soon the two Battleaxe Folk headed out of the entrance, talking in their own speech. Corbin and Telyn soon followed.

Rubbing his head, Brand sat down beside Myrrdin. His eyes were on the knapsack. He thought to see it twitch. Perhaps it could sense the nearness of its master.

"I'm sorry, Myrrdin," said Brand. "I lost control again."

"But you didn't kill him," said Myrrdin.

Brand blinked. "I thought I was the lucky one."

Myrrdin shook his head. "You are the axe's master. Had you truly wanted to kill Modi, things might have gone differently."

"Was it you who caused the green flash?"

Myrrdin held up his staff as an answer. He had carved it down considerably, to where the green Jewel Vaul could be seen. Still half-covered in fresh wet wood, the Jewel glittered in the cool gloom of the gatehouse.

"Does the wood always grow over it that way?" asked Brand, fascinated by its beauty.

"Yes. I first found it in the Vale of Twrog, a troublesome giant that lives in the Deepwood. The Green Jewel stood in the heart of a stout oak tree. The leafy tops of the tree rose a hundred feet or more. Never had I seen such a tree, and in my heart I knew what had been lost lay inside."

"You had to cut to the heart of a great oak to find it?" asked Brand, amazed. "In comparison my efforts seem minor."

Myrrdin shook his head. "No less than mine. The Jewels are different, that's all. Vaul is no less capricious in its own way. For you see, as I cut into the great trunk, I found the bones of Vaul's former master, embedded in the living wood. I had to cut away many finger bones to pry the Jewel from its former master's dead grip."

"How did you defeat the giant?" asked Brand feeling like a child listening to the wild tales of a drunk oldster by a tavern fire.

"I didn't. I made a bargain with Twrog. I fashioned him a club from the stoutest limb of the oak. I told him it was magic, and it would bring him luck, and it did. He helped me take the tree down, in fact."

"So you got a Jewel of Power and he got a big magic stick, eh?" asked Brand. "That sounds like a deal one of the Shining Folk would make."

Myrrdin didn't answer that, so Brand hurried on, not wanting to offend him. The wizard was reputedly of Fae blood, after all. "Can all of the Jewels flash to blind people?" he asked.

"Those of light and fire can, such as the Jewel of Flame," said Myrrdin, cutting away a bit more wood with deft strokes. About half of Vaul's green surface was revealed now. Several strips of white wood still enclosed it, however. Brand was reminded of fingerbones, clutching at something beloved. He shivered, wondering if the axe would someday have to be pried from his dead fingers.

"Tell me of each of the Jewels," asked Brand. "It seems that I must know what I'm dealing with. I've heard nothing but childhood tales."

"There is much in those tales," said Myrrdin. "There are various theories as to the origin of the Jewels, but in all the legends, the Sunstone or the Sun Dragon was split into the nine known colors, which when mixed or shown apart in their pure form represent all the forms of magic. This process works in a similar fashion to the human eye. Everything that can be seen is represented to the eye as a combination of colors and light. Just so, all magic is some mixture of the various varieties of magic of which the Jewels are capable.

"The three primary Jewels: Crimson, Blue and Amber, are often judged more powerful than the three secondary stones of Green, Lavender and Orange. The three less known, but no less important stones are called collectively the Dark Jewels. They are those of Quick-silver, White, and Black.

"Of such great power were the Shards of the Sunstone that many duels and even battles were fought over the possession of each. In olden times Pyros the Orange – as the Jewel had been named after one of its earliest and cruelest possessors – was perhaps the most destructive and well known. Pyros was infamous for the burning of the six villages of the lake peoples many generations ago. The sorcerer and tyrant Pyros had fashioned the Jewel into the crest of his silver crown and enjoyed lancing anyone or thing who stood up to him with a fiery beam of pure heat. After a time this habit led to a bald, scarred head and a terrifying countenance and reputation, which seemed to suit the tyrant's tastes. Eventually, he was brought down, but not soon enough to save the lake people, who afterward retreated into the cool gloom of the forests and rivers and never seemed to regain their former numbers nor their trust of Men. They are now known to you as Merlings, I believe."

Brand looked up in surprise at this. Could Merlings and their deep hatred of men have stemmed from such a time? It seemed very plausible at the moment. He gazed at the fire again. It crackled and popped as it ate the dry wood.

"The Orange Jewel is the heart of fire," continued Myrrdin, "Legend has it that after Pyros was killed, an ancient wurm devoured the Orange to make his fire hotter, and managed to make his fire so hot he could burn his way into solid rock. So doing, he burned himself an endless labyrinth of trackless tunnels beneath the Black Mountains. It was a labyrinth so immense that the wurm has for centuries been lost to the light of the sun. To this day, the Battleaxe Folk attribute the wurm with the creation of their home, the Earthlight, beneath Snowdon."

"I've never heard that story from Gudrin."

Myrrdin smiled. "Not all the Kindred agree with that version of history. They like to claim that they created the Earthlight themselves."

"Pray continue. What of the other stones?" asked Brand, putting his chin in his palm.

"In the present age of Albion, many of the Jewels are lost," continued Myrrdin. "Others are hidden, to be used only in secret. Few even among the wisest of folk know where more than one or two of the Jewels might lay, and none know the whereabouts of them all."

"What of our enemy of the moment?" asked Brand.

"Herla wields Osang, the Lavender Jewel. Osang rules magic of sight, sound and movement. His coursers can ride over water, over or even *through* obstacles, silently, invisibly. At times they can even fly for short distances or seem to teleport."

"Are we safe inside your living wall, then?"

Myrrdin snorted. "By no means! –but, we are less vulnerable than we would be in the open."

"What of Vaul?"

"Ah! My favorite! Glad I am that I was fortunate enough to become its master. The Vaul, the Green Jewel, is the most creative of the bunch. It gives me power over earth, plants and growth...or rot, poison and spoilage. Its wielder is a shaper of nature, for good or for ill."

"And Lavatis?"

"As you know, it has the power to summon the Rainbow. It rules the rain, wind and is powerful upon the sea. Lightning can strike those near it when it is wielded."

"What of the other colors?"

"Sange, the Red Jewel, wields blood magic. It possesses power over flesh and blood, allowing the wielder to heal wounds...or do other, terrible things. It was lost in the same great war that brought down these walls. Ambros, as you've already learned, is the Jewel of combat, bloodlust. It's able to drive men wild in battle. It can put fear into the hearts of enemies as well. It's perhaps the most emotional of the Jewels.... The one who wields it can inflame the hearts of an army."

Brand was silent for a moment, mulling over this. He wondered if he would ever lead an army into battle. Somehow, the berry patches of Rabing Isle seemed more distant than ever.

"Those are the six colors of the rainbow," said Brand. "What of the others?"

Myrrdin glanced at him, then continued. "The Dark Jewels are less known, and were lost in the distant past. If they exist today, we have only legends that hint about their nature. The White Shard was the creator, the basis of all the others that split apart and is now gone from the Earth. The Quicksilver was the molten reflective lump left behind by the White after all the color had been drain of it. It is the Jewel of null-magic. It removes color and life and magic from the world, rather than adding it. The Onyx is the Black Jewel of death and decay. Darkness, vile evil and unspeakable spawnlings come from it. All true evil powers seek Necron, the Onyx Jewel."

Brand fell silent for a minute or two, contemplating all the Jewels. He held up his hand then, although he would have loved to hear more of Myrrdin's tale. "What's that? I hear something."

Myrrdin halted his tale and blinked. "Drums," he said after a moment. "Wardrums, I should say."

There was a creaking, scraping sound as someone struggled with the grille at the entrance. Both of them stood and Brand shouldered his knapsack. The axe inside quivered excitedly.

Telyn's face came into view. She struggled with a load of full quivers. "Rhinogs!" she cried. "I see a band of them, they must be scouts. They're coming down from the northwest!"

Chapter Ten
Battle

Everyone ran to the walls and looked out to see the rhinogs, but none had eyes as keen as Telyn. After a while, they thought they saw a few black-furred backs moving over the downs a mile or more off.

"I see many men on rafts as well!" cried Telyn excitedly, pointing in the opposite direction.

"Can you see whose side they're on?" shouted Brand.

Telyn leaned out farther, poking her head through the opening Myrrdin had made in the living wall with a single wave of Vaul. As the lightest and most agile, she had been elected to climb the thorny mass to the top of the dome overhead. "Ouch! Damn these thorns. Yes, I see the blue and white livery of the Riverton Constabulary. They must be ours!"

"Will they reach us before the rhinogs?" asked Corbin.

"They come by water while the rhinogs march through mud. They should be faster," said Modi.

"There are others with the men," called down Telyn. "Wee Folk bound ahead of them on the shores and I think some of the Battleaxe Folk are weighing down the rafts as well."

"Huh," grunted Modi. "It would be good to have some true warriors at my side."

Brand ignored the jibe and went back to work, storing arms the others had carried up from the redcap's armory inside the dome. "We must work fast. We can't be sure that the charm will hold Herla until help arrives. Already, his coursers test the boundaries."

"Already the place abounds with Wee Folk spies," complained Modi, moving an armload of crossbows to the walls where loopholes had been set up.

Tomkin put in an appearance then, using the front entrance this time. He watched Modi warily as he entered, but the big warrior just ignored him. He approached Brand with a toothy grin.

"It appears that help is on the way," he said.

"I doubt your word no longer," said Brand, grunting as he helped Corbin roll a fallen stone back into place on the wall.

He looked down at the armor he had gotten from the red cap's horde. Most of it he had not bothered to put on yet. The breastplate and greaves lay in a heap, but he wore a chain shirt over his homespun tunic. The rings jingled and clinked against the stone as he heaved stones with Corbin. He wasn't sure if all their efforts would help in the coming fight, but it was easier on the mind than just sitting around waiting.

"Thou art clad in armor," said the manling, watching him. He looked Brand up and down with a discerning eye. "Add the breastplate and some leggings...a full-fledged Rabing knight you would be! To the untrained eye, that is."

Brand tried to think of something useful that the manling could do, but he was so small that nothing came immediately to mind. "What tidings do you bring?" he asked.

Tomkin grinned. "Popular, we are. Three armies march to meet us. And a likely Fourth might appear."

"Three? Four?" demanded Brand, almost letting go of his end of the block.

"Watch what you're doing, Brand!" cried Corbin. They both had to shuffle under the block's weight to prevent smashed fingers and toes. Grunting and heaving, they worked the block into its place, and slumped against it, panting.

"What are you talking about, manling?" demanded Brand. He was wishing he had removed his chain shirt now, as Corbin had. The extra weight was tiring. But he couldn't help thinking that a pile of armor lying on the ground would do him little good if the enemy were to suddenly appear.

"Army one, the rhinogs who follow their goblin sires, who in turn follow their sire Old Hob," began Tomkin, ticking them off on his thin fingers. "Two, the Merlings that churn the river to boiling mud as they come down from their village bent on vengeance, no doubt. Third is the possible—and quite likely— appearance of Oberon with a host of his kind."

"You said four armies. Was that just big talk?"

"Four would be the River Folk coming to help. But, as you suggest, they hardly count as an army."

"That wasn't what I meant, you—" snarled Brand.

"What of the Wild Hunt?" interrupted Corbin.

Tomkin shrugged. "Good point, but I account them as one with the rhinogs."

"Merlings and Oberon," muttered Brand. "Who will they side with?"

"Themselves, of course," said Tomkin.

"I think Tomkin's right," said Corbin. "We ourselves aren't the reason they come, it's the concentration of power that we represent. They aren't interested in us, just the three Jewels that we bear."

Tomkin nodded. "The Wild Hunt has treed us, but has taken too long to finish the prey. Now others have taken an interest."

"Hmm," said Corbin, rubbing his chin. He walked over to his own chain shirt and began to struggle it down over his form. It clinked and rasped as he fought with it. A shirt of chain is much harder to put on than a normal shirt of wool or leather. Metal links do not give and stretch like cloth.

"What is it?" asked Brand, looking around the green dome. Everything seemed deceptively calm and normal.

"It occurs to me," said Corbin through the clinking links, "that the Merlings aren't likely to be stopped by the charm. I doubt the rhinogs are ghostly enough to be halted, either. Could you give me a hand, here?"

Brand helped him tugging the chain shirt down over his barrel-chested form. He then eyed his own pile of armor. "I think you're right. The time is past for shoring up our walls. We must prepare ourselves for battle."

411

Tomkin hopped after him as he began to don his armor. The metal pieces had been well cared for. Wearing his regular clothing for padding, Brand pulled on a chain shirt and worked to buckle on a breastplate. Corbin helped him don the unfamiliar armor. Modi had suggested that they only wear a few key pieces as they were unaccustomed to it and that full armor would be as likely to kill them as save them in battle. As he buckled on the breastplate Brand realized with a shiver that the leather straps should have long ago fallen to dust. They felt supple and fresh, however.

He looked up to see that Corbin was looking at him in concern. As had so often happened in their youth, they were thinking along the same lines.

"How is it that these straps and buckles are so fresh and new?" asked Brand, his lips curled.

"I think we both know," said Corbin, eyeing the straps in his hands as if he held a fistful of worms.

"The redcap?"

Corbin nodded.

"But what kind of leather, then...?" asked Brand. He dropped the breastplate and wiped sweat from his brow. "It's human, isn't it? What else would the redcap use for leather?"

"I don't know," said Corbin, examining the straps, "he could have used Merlings, or animals...I doubt too many of the marshmen would have ventured this far north, so far past the borders of the Haven."

"Right," said Brand, grabbing at this straw to keep his stomach steady, "right! Just Merling skin at worst, perhaps even something more wholesome."

Not speaking, they buckled the rest of their partial armor into place. Still, each time his hands had to touch the supple leather of the straps, Brand's finger tingled and his stomach churned. He had touched Merling skin before, and this felt different, and the tone of it was much too light.

"How are our junior warriors?" asked Modi, coming up to them. He wore a breastplate and a giant shirt of chain that hung down almost to the ground.

412

"We stand ready to fight for the Haven," said Brand, reciting a line he had heard from the Riverton Constabulary weekly meetings.

Modi nodded at this answer. "Good," he said. He paused for a moment, thumbing his axe. "There are things..." he said, and then faltered.

The two river-boys watched him, their faces expressionless.

"There are things that warriors must say to one another before entering battle together," said Modi at last. "Our personal differences we must set aside. Often, warriors in the very act of a duel will quit their struggles and fight together as brothers against a common enemy. Sometimes, after the battle is done, the duel resumes. Other times, it does not."

Brand and Corbin looked at one another, and each knew what the other thought. It wasn't exactly an apology, but it would have to do. "We will fight at your side, Modi," said Brand.

Modi nodded. He opened his mouth as if to speak again, but nothing came out. He nodded again and turned to stump away.

Brand and Corbin each carried shields now. Brand had given the sword he had found in the armory to Myrrdin, who refused to wear armor. Corbin had a real battleaxe now, to go with his shield. Even Gudrin had armed herself with a jacket of woven steel scales and a heavy crossbow. Telyn kept her familiar bow, but chose a long slim dagger with a very keen edge and attached the sheath to her belt.

Brand, having found no better storage for the axe than the knapsack, kept it there still, riding on his back. It seemed less troublesome when it was kept covered, like a horse that is quieted by wearing blinders.

Telyn shouted down a warning that none of them understood.

"What?" shouted back Brand. She poked her head down from the leafy dome and Brand's heart was gladdened by the image of her face, surrounded by her dark hanging hair.

"The Riverton Constabulary! They've made landfall at the ruins of the southern tower!"

"Perfect!" shouted Brand back. "We must meet them and show them the arms there!"

It was quickly decided that he and Corbin should go and greet the newcomers. They marched proudly out into the daylight. Brand felt glad to be free of the oppressive green gloom of the domed gatehouse. The axe was particularly pleased, it sensed battle was imminent.

"I wonder if your father leads them," said Brand, puffing a bit as he hurried in the heavy armor. He wondered too, if he could last a whole day's march in such gear.

"I hope Tylag is with them," agreed Corbin. "He will be proud to see us armored like lords."

"Do you think he knows of Clan Rabing's real history?" asked Brand.

"He might. I find it difficult to believe that the Clan Elders don't know the truth behind these secrets."

Brand nodded and was about to say more when a shape bounded up from behind them. He reached for his axe reflexively.

"It's only Tomkin," said Corbin, putting a hand on his elbow.

"And a good second you make," replied Brand quietly. He turned to the manling. "Are you joining us to greet your fellows, Tomkin?"

"My fellows are knaves," said Tomkin, "I am to bring two wet-nosed warriors back to the gatehouse."

"Why?" demanded Brand.

"The wench lookout has spied a conflict. The Merlings have met with thy army before it could reach safe land. The river is filling with blood even now. I suggest you forget about them and retreat."

Brand and Corbin looked at one another. They both knew there was only one thing to do. They took off toward the southern tower at a run. As he ran, Brand pulled the anxious axe into the light. It gave him a surge of strength and soon he had outdistanced Corbin. The other shouted to him, but Brand neither heard, nor cared to hear, his words.

Tomkin kept up with him, however.

"Thy feet are like the pounding hooves of a charger," he remarked.

Brand made no reply.

"Thy pace is a killing one. I wonder at the endurance of thy heart. Will it explode, or simply stop of its own accord?"

Brand felt a flash of irritation. He made a sudden sweep with the axe, and clove Tomkin's soft fawnskin cap from his head. Tomkin made a squeak of surprise and missed the next log he was bounding over. He tumbled through the air and landed in a heap.

Corbin puffed by a few moments later, hooting at the Tomkin, who growled back at him. Corbin's chain shirt jingled madly as he followed Brand, hopelessly trying to keep up.

Brand reached the southern tower and paused there. All along the shore raged the first true battle he had ever set eyes upon.

About half the rafts and boats had reached the shoreline. A line of blue and white clad men, armed with every manner of makeshift weapon, faced the swarming Merlings. On the land they had the advantage, but in the brown, churning water the Merlings roped and plucked them one a time from their boats. Once in the river, the men were made quick work of.

In the center of the conflict a large raft worked its way toward the shore. A banner of blue and white flew from its mast. The men aboard cast lines to the men on the shore, but as often as not the Merlings intercepted the casts and yanked the boatsmen into the muddy water. Brand's eyes fixed upon a large figure at the center of the raft. It was his uncle Tylag, Corbin's father.

Vaguely, he knew he should wait for Corbin, his second. But the desires of the axe, never greater than when in the face of battle, were too much. He raised both his shield and Ambros high over his head and charged. As he charged he screamed like a madman. Flecks of spittle showered his new grown beard and his eyes all but started from their sockets. Far more noticeable to the combatants, however, were the brilliant flashes of light that Ambros loosed. It was as if lightning struck in their midst. Merlings and men alike were blinded and many were struck dead on both sides after a slight lull in the fighting.

The Merlings got the worst of it, as they liked bright light less than men and seemed to recover more slowly from the dazzling effects.

As he charged, his scream was drowned out by the rumble of the skies overhead. Thunderclouds billowed and darkened the skies with unnatural speed. Brand knew in his heart that the thunderclouds gathered for the axe and would follow it to the ends of the Earth if battle could be found there.

The men of the Haven, turning to see this armored madman charging their flank, fell back before him. They opened a hole in their lines, and he plunged through it. He splashed into the river and lay about him with the axe, slaying Merlings with each stroke. Often, the axe flashed, and the heat of it caused the bloody water to boil away upon its bright surface. The Merlings sought to slip close and jab at his legs under the water, but the flashes revealed them and he slew them with swift strokes that threw up clouds of steam and spray. They tried to cast their barbed grapples, but he severed them in midair so that they splashed down harmlessly.

Around him, the men of the Haven took heart. They didn't know who this knight of olden times was, but they realized he was fighting for their lives and they joined him. They took up bows and boathooks, using both to keep the Merlings at bay while they drew in the rafts to shore. Brand's lips stopped screaming and instead he broke into song. It was a song that he had never heard before, nor could he later recall the words, but he knew it was a battle song, one that Ambros had perhaps heard centuries before.

Soon, the men of the Haven around him had taken up the song as well. Brand noted with frustration that he could only rarely find a Merling now to slay.

"Cowards!" he raged at them, seeing them flip and slither through the water upstream. He shook the axe at them, and the men who had gathered around him quailed at his fury.

"They are gone, Brand," said a voice at his side, "but we have more enemies now."

Brand whirled to see Corbin, who pointed back up the rise that led to the southern tower. There, gathering silently from the white mists, were the mounted coursers of the Wild Hunt.

416

A dozen, then two dozen, then three dozen appeared. They seemed to take form out of the mist itself, as if mothered by it.

Chapter Eleven
Voynod's Challenge

"Brand? Corbin, my son?" roared a familiar voice.

They turned to see Tylag, wading in from his raft, which had all but reached the shores by now. "Could it be that two Rabing boys have become knights of old?" he asked, incredulous.

Brand smiled to see his Uncle safe, and in that instant, he felt much of his sense return. He could think clearly again, even with the axe in his hand and blood coating his face. "We must get everyone into the ruins, Uncle," he said, "we have a great store of arms in that tower, and a strongpoint built further back."

"But we have defeated the Merlings!" said Tylag, raising his hands high. "I had thought us betrayed by the Wee Folk when they attacked, but now I see that those we came to rescue turned and saved us first!"

Brand pointed up to the rise where the horsemen gathered. "Now we face the Wild Hunt."

Tylag's face darkened and fell from elation to dread. "The Wild Hunt," he said in a haunted voice. "I had hoped they were only horsemen from the north. I had told myself and my men they were nothing more for days now. But how can I doubt you two, who wield such power? Truly, it is a dark day for the Haven when we must face fell legends that should have long since passed on."

"We are beyond the borders of the Haven, father," said Corbin. "And I doubt our borders would now provide any barrier to these foul things, in any case."

Tylag nodded, gazing up the slope with haunted eyes. A subtle piping began then, slipping into their thoughts insidiously. Brand became aware of it and knew it to be the work of the dark bard. It was the song of the dead, the dead that still walked and acted as if they lived. He wondered how long it had been playing.

"You bear the standard of Riverton on your raft, father," said Corbin. "Does this mean you are their leader?"

Tylag looked startled, as if he had been sleeping. "Yes, yes! I...I was once Chief of the Riverton Constabulary. No one else on the Council had the training to lead the army....I am the general of this army," he finished vaguely, as if just realizing the truth of his words. He turned to his captains, who had come up around them. Everyone but them seemed to be gazing up the slope, as if sleeping on their feet.

"What are we doing standing in the bloody river!" roared Tylag in sudden rage and disbelief. He slapped the lieutenant nearest him and cuffed a soldier who had sat down in the shallow water and closed his eyes. "Up men! Secure the boats! Form up ranks on the shore!"

While Tylag and his lieutenants spread out, waking up their troops, Corbin and Brand made their way to shore.

"That was frightening," said Corbin. "I had no idea that the enemy could stop an army with a song."

"The Dark Bard is entrancing," agreed Brand, although his voice sounded not in the least entranced. "There must be justice meted out here," he said. "These cursed creatures used up their lives long ago, and if they won't die of their own accord, I shall personally finish the lot of them."

Corbin looked at him in surprise and uneasily eyed the axe that rode Brand's shoulder. "We should break past them, Brand," he urged. "We should break through their line and get the army into the protective region of the ruins. There, we can give them better arms and positions."

Brand paid him no heed. Sloshing out of the river and onto the muddy shore, Brand raised his axe in challenge to the

419

enemy. A scattering of those that sat their dead horses on the rise lifted their weapons in answer.

"We should kill them all now," he said, "while we have the numbers. Soon the rhinogs that follow their goblin sires will tip the balance in their favor. That is why they wait to attack us! They fear us!"

"I don't think so, Brand—" began Corbin.

Brand whirled on him and for a moment seemed about to raise the axe to him. He contained himself with visible effort. "They hope we will quail and become weak under the force of the bard's music!"

"Yes, but look!" said Corbin, pointing. "They are gathering their strength even as we gather ours. More of them appear out of the mist with each passing minute! This must be the work of Herla wielding Osang."

Brand looked and glowered to see that Corbin was right. He looked back at the army that surrounded him. Already, he had begun to think of it as *his* army. "They are gathering strength more quickly than we are. Our men are slowed by that irritating piping. I don't even see Herla yet, nor the bard, but I shall put a stop to that damned piping!"

Brand slowly lifted the axe high into the air. A liquid amber light poured from it, not a single blinding flash as before, but a river of light that reached out to touch every soldier that struggled on the muddy shoreline. He began to march up the slope with long strides.

Corbin followed him, calling to Tylag, who quickly ordered his men to advance. Many of the Riverton troops, seeing the champion who had forced back the Merlings advancing on this new threat, had already fallen in behind him. To everyone, especially Brand, this seemed the natural order of things.

"Voynod!" he bellowed, "cease your infernal piping, man! I would rather hear the sounds of a tavern hound sicking up the putrid contents of its stomach!"

At his words, as if a spell had been broken, the piping stopped. A familiar figure pressed its way through the coursers to the fore. It was Voynod upon his unbreathing horse.

"We meet again, river-boy," said the bard. "This time, you are on the wrong side of these charmed walls. There is nothing to save you."

Unbidden, the image of Oberon's daughter came into Brand's mind. Once again, he cradled her severed head in his arms. He could see the life drain from her whitening face. Rage filled him.

"You face the Axeman now, piper!" he roared. He began to trot forward, getting ahead of his men on the difficult slope. "Where is your master? I wish to slay all your company at once! I will slay each of you in turn!"

At this, Voynod lifted a black-gloved hand. The coursers, who had been readying to charge Brand and the men advancing behind him, halted.

"You seek to challenge me?" hissed Voynod.

"*I DO!*" Brand shouted back without hesitation. Still climbing the slope steadily, he paused only to sweep the popping sweat from his brow. "As a lord of Rabing Castle, I challenge thee!"

"I accept your challenge, child," hissed Voynod.

"Brand, no!" cried Corbin from behind him. "Wait for us!"

"Stay back!" roared Brand over his shoulder. "All of you, stay back!"

Tylag had no need to repeat the order. All along the advancing line of men, they halted and watched quietly. None shouted encouragement, nor did any man make a wager. Not even the darkest heart among them could face the Dead with a smile or a thought for anything other than destroying these foul creatures.

Brand, however, was wreathed with smiles. He tossed aside his shield and took up Ambros with both hands as the bard began his charge. He set his feet flat upon the earth and crouched. He planned a low sweep to cut the horse's legs from beneath it. All he had to do was bring the bard to the ground so that the good sweet earth might finish its long overdue work.

The bard thundered down the slope at a gallop, heedless of the rough terrain or the treacherously wet slope. His horse's hooves pounded and tossed up great clots of black dirt behind it, but it didn't snort, nor make any sound of fear or effort.

Despite its charge, the horse's great, dead lungs were as still as the grave.

Brand swung his blade in a low sweeping cut. The bard was right there, on top of him. He caught sight of malicious lavender eyes, like those he had seen within Herla's stag head. Brand was shocked when the galloping stopped and became silent at the last instant. His axe cut through nothing. He could only think that the horse had taken flight. Then a great shock went through him, and he was knocked backward with terrific force. He rolled down the slope head over heels. He regained his feet, but slipped in the mud. He looked down to see a great dent struck in his breastplate. The blow would have cut him from belly to throat if he had been unarmored. Behind him, the line of men set up a ragged cheer to see their champion back on his feet.

The axe! The thought was a scream in his mind. Without it he was just Brand, not the Axeman. Without it, everything hurt: his breastplate pressed against his sternum, his legs trembled with the strain of running in heavy armor. He saw Voynod wheel and come around for another charge. His horse tossed its head in a horrible parody of life. If anything, the dead animal was more horrifying than its rider.

Even as Voynod raised his silvery sword and charged again, Brand spotted the axe. It was nearby, lying beside the blackened corpse of a tree that long since given up the struggle to survive in the swamp's evil soil. Brand scrambled toward it, and a polyp exploded under his feet. He grimaced as a thick acidic liquid sprayed him. His eyes blinked and teared.

His breath came in hoarse gasps as he reached the axe. Behind him the thunder of hooves grew. He turned and raised Ambros even as Voynod's blade swung for his head. He blocked the cut with the axe and it flashed when the two weapons met. Voynod hissed and the foul smelling vapor that issued from his lungs was like a cold wind in Brand's face. Walking his horse around Brand in a circle, Voynod rained blows down upon him. Brand managed to block them, staggering under the assault. Each blow caused the axe to flash. Overhead the thunderclouds boiled and rumbled. To the men at the foot of the slope it was as if a dozen strokes of lightning struck the combatants in quick succession.

"Know, river-boy, that I myself slew your cousin Sam," Voynod told him mockingly.

"Ambros!" cried Brand, blocking another blow. "Know, piper, that I wield Ambros the Golden!"

"When Herla learns of your death, I will be granted a boon," hissed back the other. "As my boon, I will ask for a steaming draught of your lifeblood, river-boy!"

Brand caught another blow with the axe and this time he slid the edge of it down to the base of the other's sword. He managed to slip the blade over the sword's hilt. Three black-gloved fingers fell into the muck and squirmed there for a moment before falling to dust.

Losing only a moment's focus, Voynod switched the sword to his left hand and wheeled the horse so that he could still strike down at Brand. Brand jumped back and hacked at the horse's legs. Hamstrung, the dead thing staggered, but didn't fall. Urging his crippled horse to retreat, Voynod headed back up the slope.

Brand gave chase, crying out as he leapt after the rider and wrestled him from his failing mount. In a last vile act, the bard sank his teeth into Brand's gauntleted hand. Brand yelled in pain, so great was the power of the bite that it crushed his finger right through the steel mesh. Then the flesh fell away to dust and only a skull still remained, its teeth clamped upon his hand. He tore it away and tossed the crumbling skull from him. The horse, riderless, soon staggered and fell apart.

"Victory!" shouted Brand, holding Ambros high. The golden eye winked, and the army of the Haven came upslope, cheering. Brand noticed that only the dark bard's sword and pipes remained behind to show that he had ever existed.

"Let no man touch these accursed things!" he commanded them as they swarmed around him. "We'll carry them with sticks and bury them in the deepest sinkhole of the marsh." There was no argument from the troops.

Brand led them in the final charge upslope, but the coursers just sat upon their horses, waiting. As the men came close, the white mists that had birthed them closed around them and the

Wild Hunt vanished from view. Reaching the spot where they had stood, Brand would have believed them all to have been ghosts except for the hoofprints that marked every inch of the muddy ground.

"Where have they gone?" he snarled.

"Herla has pulled them back," replied Corbin, gasping as he topped the slope. "Perhaps he awaits the rhinogs—or the darkness."

Brand nodded. "He won't wait long. But it matters nothing! We shall be victorious in every instance!"

Corbin nodded and slapped his back. "You fought well, cousin. I did fear for your life."

Brand tolerated his touch with difficulty. "I fought poorly, but I will do better next time."

Corbin handed him his shield. "Here. You forgot this."

Brand took the shield and thanked him. "It seems so much less important than the axe, but thank you."

"Perhaps it could have taken that blow that so mars the beauty of your breastplate, Brand!" said Tylag, finally huffing up to the top of the slope.

To Brand, his Uncle's words burned like base insults. He glared at him, and the bloodlust that still gripped his mind caused him to see a mocking smile on Tylag's face.

"Shut up, fool!" Brand muttered. It was hard for him not to shout at his Uncle. He even thought of shoving the old man back down the slope to see how far he would roll.... *That would be good sport!*

He reminded himself with an effort that such thoughts must be spawned by the axe, and that he was its master. To demonstrate the truth of this to himself, if no one else, he put the axe back into his knapsack and pried his fingers loose from its haft.

A wave of fatigue and even vertigo passed through him. He swayed on his feet and Corbin slipped a supportive arm around his shoulders. Corbin and Tylag exchanged relieved looks, which Brand noticed and felt embarrassed by. He thought of the things he had said and done and his face flushed redder.

"I'm sorry," he said to his relatives, almost in a whisper. Tylag came up and hugged him.

"There's no need, Brand," said Tylag, gripping his shoulder. "You saved us all! We can take a harsh word from the champion of the Haven!"

Then they all marched to the gatehouse. It had begun to rain, but for most of the men the day had just gotten started. All the supplies needed to be unloaded from their boats and the craft needed to be secured. Tylag himself supervised the unloading and the distribution of the arms found beneath the southern tower.

All that afternoon they worked until, just as dusk reddened the skies, the rhinogs arrived and surrounded the ruins.

Chapter Twelve
Strange Leathers

All the way back to the gatehouse, Brand thought of Voynod's words. Could the bard truly have been the one who executed Sam in the barn at Froghollow? It seemed so long ago and far away. Should he tell Corbin of it?

"What is it?" asked Corbin, following his thoughts and feelings as usual.

"I—just something that the bard said to me before falling to dust."

"He was a foul dead-thing, Brand. Nothing he could say would bring anything but pain to the listener."

"True," said Brand. They went on several steps in a growing silence.

"So what did the monster say?" burst out Corbin at last.

Brand would have laughed, had the news not been so grim. Instead, he only glowered at his feet, which felt too tired to keep going. Somehow, he managed to force them to keep plodding on.

"Something bad, then," said Corbin, filling in the silence. "Something about the Haven, about our people there...."

Brand sighed. "What's the use? If I wait long enough, I suppose you'll just figure it out in that clockwork mind of yours. The bard claimed that he, himself, slayed Sam."

Corbin stiffened, and Brand bit his lower lip, feeling his cousin's pain. Ever since they had spilled Sam's body from the cliffs into the flood of the Berrywine, Corbin had not been as light of spirit. "I'm sorry to tell you. Who even knows if it's true, Corbin? We have no way of knowing."

Corbin nodded grimly. "He could have just been trying to unnerve you," he said, "but I think not. It makes too much sense. The blow was a clean, single sweep, which Voynod could have managed with his sword. Things were more likely to have been drawn out and messy if the rhinogs had been involved."

Brand winced at the image that came to mind at Corbin's words, but he couldn't refute the other's logic.

"You yourself had sighted the bard over several days prior to Sam's death," continued Corbin. "No, it makes sense. I believe it, and I must say I'm greatly relieved."

Brand looked at him in surprise. Corbin looked haggard, his eyes dark in their sockets. He seemed anything but relieved.

"No, really," said Corbin. They halted and Corbin grabbed both of Brand's shoulders and held him at arm's length. "I'm indebted to you, Brand. I would never have known if Sam's death had gone unavenged. It would have always haunted me."

Brand smiled then, but it was a grim thing, with no mirth in it. His smile turned to a humorless grin. He felt a wave of pleasure that he couldn't understand, and then he realized that it perhaps had something to do with the axe. It was pleased, pleased that a wrong had been violently righted. Harsh justice had been meted out, and nothing gratified it more.

Corbin looked at him oddly. "The axe?" he asked.

Brand nodded, his odd expression fading.

"I wonder what motivates it," said Corbin.

"I do too, sometimes. It seems like a strange spirit."

"I mean," said Corbin, groping for words, "does it think? If so, what does it think about? Is it just reacting to things or does it make plans and execute them?"

Brand shook his head. He had no answers. Both brooded over this for a time. The two marched the rest of the way to the gatehouse in silence. When they arrived the grille was levered back to allow them to enter.

Modi clapped a heavy hand onto Brand's shoulder the moment he appeared inside the green dome. "Well done!" he said with more feeling than Brand had ever heard in his voice. "Well done indeed!"

Brand smiled tiredly. "Thanks," he said, thinking that perhaps Modi wasn't such a dark-hearted bully after all. It seemed that he could admit when he was wrong, which counted for a lot in Brand's book.

"What happened, Brand?" called down Telyn. She still maintained her post at the top of the dome. She hung upside-down with her knees crooked over a thick branch. Brand marveled at her lithe form.

"We won!" he shouted up to her, knowing that would please her. "But looking at you hanging up there, I know the battle was nothing next to your acrobatics. I thought I was reckless!"

She laughed and their eyes met. Brand felt a thrill go through him. She swung down a vine that Myrrdin had conveniently grown from the top of the dome to allow her easy access to her perch. She ran to him and kissed him, and Brand learned the best time to greet one's love was after facing death.

"I feared for you," she whispered, her head on his chest.

He stroked her head awkwardly, trying not to catch her hair with his gauntlets. He shook them off when he realized there was Merling blood and the dust crumbling dead-things on them.

"I need to clean up," he said in her ear.

She nodded, but didn't let go. She hugged him and he could almost feel her squeezing even through the armor that encased his chest. Then she pulled away and examined the dent in his breastplate.

"You were nearly killed," she said matter-of-factly.

Unable to deny it, he said nothing. Corbin came up to say it all for him. "Brand here is indeed the Axeman, the Champion of the Haven," he began. In glowing terms, he detailed the events of the battle. Everyone hung on his words, save for Brand, who tried to shed his dented armor, and Myrrdin, who brooded near the broken fountain.

He went to rest with Myrrdin. Moodily, Myrrdin scratched at the soil between his feet with the freshly-carven tip of his staff.

428

"Did you enjoy it, Axeman?" he asked after a time.

"No, and yes," said Brand.

"What do you mean?"

"It was like smashing your hand on a table after drinking too much in the tavern. It feels good at the time…."

"But afterward, when the glow fades, you're left picking splinters from your bruised palm?"

"Exactly," agreed Brand.

Myrrdin nodded. "I'm glad to see that the glow has faded."

"So am I."

"You will have to wield the axe again, Axeman. Very soon, I should think."

"I know," said Brand, rubbing his sore arms and legs. The armor he had shed had bruised him.

"Soon the sun will set, and all through the night, the goblins will not let us rest," said Myrrdin in a faraway voice. Brand felt that he wasn't predicting the future so much as describing a painful memory. "In the last hour of night, when humanity is at its lowest ebb and the Shining Folk at their peak fervor, they shall flail and torment their brutish offspring into a frenzy great enough to overcome their natural cowardice. At that hour they shall attack us."

Myrrdin dipped his head back down and continued to scrawl shapes and lines in the soil at his feet. Brand looked at them for a moment, but found them disturbing to the eye and quickly looked way. He gave an involuntary shudder as he rose and left Myrrdin to his sorcery.

He looked up into the dome of greenery and thought he could make out the steady glow of Telyn's unnatural beacon. It burned still, although there had been many gusts of wind that should have blown it out and it should have long ago exhausted the tallow coating its wick. It made his mouth go dry to think that Myrrdin was teaching his arts to Telyn. Could he truly marry and bed a witch? He made an effort not to cast his eyes to where she now built a fire. After pondering it, he concluded that if she could stand living with a moody, murderous Champion of Ambros, he could learn to tolerate her witchery. He sighed and once again longed for the simple life of the Haven. It seemed all but lost to him now.

Some hours later Tylag and his lieutenants came to inspect the domed gatehouse and the defenses they had put up. Brand was gratified to see that they now wore proper armor and bore real weapons of the sort that normally only hung over the mantles in most of the Haven. Tylag carried a fine broadsword, its shine and luster showing a keen edge.

"What I can't understand," Tylag told him after he had gotten over his initial amazement and distrust of the unnatural dome, "is how this weaponry was so well cared for! It must have been a dozen centuries since our clan manned these walls in whatever great battle brought them down."

"Nine centuries, to be exact," said Gudrin.

Tylag shot her an odd glance, and then turned back to Brand again. "How is it possible? If I didn't know better, I'd say that this sword had been freshly oiled within the last month!"

"Most likely," said Brand, "it has."

"And the oils and the leathers used," marveled Tylag. "I've never seen their like! Could it be Merling skin?"

"There are many wonders here beyond the borders of the Haven, Uncle. Some are best left unquestioned."

He gave Brand a hard look, and Brand returned it. Tylag nodded as if in understanding, and eyed the blade speculatively. He took Brand's hint and asked no more on the subject. They needed the weapons, and perhaps even more they needed the morale that the weapons gave his ragtag army of farmers.

"There isn't enough room in here for our whole force," said Tylag, switching subjects. "Not even for half of us. But, it will make an excellent headquarters and bulwark for our troops to rally around. Crossbowmen can man the loopholes you've been setting up and easily shoot over the heads of the footmen outside. We can maintain a shelter in here for the wounded, as well."

The wounded. Those words echoed in his mind. He had marched on ahead, still wrapped in the glow of the axe after the last battle. He had thought only of his own killing, but had little considered the number of Haven people who must have died in

430

the fighting. He felt a pang in his gut. Which of his childhood friends had already fallen unnoticed into the mud behind him?

Soon after that thought, the wounded began to arrive. Borne on palettes and makeshift stretchers from the shoreline, tired and muddy troops began to carry them into the cool gloom of the gatehouse. Outside the sounds of digging could be heard as fresh, shallow graves were being dug. The dead of the Haven were buried outside the borders of their homeland where they had spent their entire lives up until this very day.

"Here," said a bass voice behind him. Brand turned to see Modi, thrusting his breastplate at him. Brand took it, and saw immediately that the dent had been hammered out. He smiled at him and Modi looked uncomfortable.

"Here, wear a helmet this time, or the rhinogs will shoot your fool eyes out," said Modi gruffly. He extended his other thick-fingered hand and gave Brand a steel helmet with a neck guard of fine mesh hanging from it. The helmet was brightly polished to a mirror-like surface. A single spike protruded from the top of it.

Brand took both the breastplate and the helmet with a nod. "Thanks," he said, "those of the Haven say that there are no finer arms or armor than that made by the Kindred."

Modi smiled briefly. "Then they are right. I chose this helm from the pile because it is indeed from the forges of the Kindred. The cursive mark of the forges beneath Snowdon decorates the spike."

Brand nodded, examining it. Fortunately, Modi had left before Brand went to put the helm on his head experimentally. Inside the helm, the protective sheath of leather padding had that same disturbing softness to the touch that so much of the other gear from the redcap's horde had. Brand rubbed his fingers together as if to rid himself of the feel of it. Was it Merling, or human? He wondered what marshman had never returned to his humble hut after perhaps hunting for Merlings in the far north....

Gritting his teeth, he forced himself to place the helm upon his head. If one of his fellows had given his life to help arm the army of the Haven now, in its hour of need, he told himself he

431

must accept the gift and hope the man's spirit would be forgiving.

"Rhinogs!" came a shout from above. Others had taken over Telyn's post among the leaves now, giving her a rest. A red-faced man with long, skinny limbs had clambered up the rope and now shouted the alarm to those below. Even as he cried his warning, the man fell from his perch. He crashed down onto the stone fountain that stood in the center of the gatehouse. A huge shaft, perhaps an inch thick, had pierced his skull. The black tail feathers of a raven fletched the heavy bolt. Blood filled the fountain where once sweet water had flowed.

Even as the warning shout came, Brand realized that he could hear something in the distance. It was the beat of the rhinog wardrums. This time, however, there wasn't just a few of them, hammering out messages from scout band to scout band. This time, there were hundreds of drums – maybe thousands, all pounding at once, all in unison.

As the next few hours passed, the noise grew and grew. By nightfall, the sound was that of an army of ogres hammering on the door at midnight.

Chapter Thirteen
Hilltop Meeting

Brand and Corbin stood together on the top wall of the old keep, one of the few structures that remained relatively intact. The night had closed around them and everywhere was the noise of the rhinog army. Brand turned his eyes to the west, where three great catapults had been dragged through the muck and into a ragged line. Riding upon each of the catapults were five or six goblins, their eyes slitted and their thin long whips flicking out viciously. Scores of rhinogs strained in the mud to drag the catapults closer to the ruined castle. When they staggered or fell, the goblins whipped their offspring furiously.

"What do you think they're loading into those catapults?" asked Brand, watching. "There is little stone over that way, they would have to drag each load up from the river."

Corbin eyed him sidelong. "I can barely make out the silhouettes of the catapults themselves, much less what they are loading into them!"

Brand glanced at him, and then peered out into the darkness. He watched as a rhinog fled from his task, dropping the heavy rope and dashing toward the trees. A goblin sprang after him and ran him down quickly. The rhinog, although he was twice the size of his sire, fell to the ground in submission. The beating was lengthy and wickedly thorough. Brand watched the brute thrash in agony and felt some small remorse for the creature.

"What about those two?" he asked Corbin. "Surely, you can see that devil of a goblin beating his own offspring so viciously."

"What are you talking about?" responded Corbin. "Brand, it's dark out. Night fell an hour ago! These creatures need neither torches nor lanterns, it seems. I can't see a thing out there."

Brand felt a cold hand squeeze his insides as he realized the truth of Corbin's words. It *was* dark out. The enemy only had a few fires going here and there. But somehow, he could still see them.

Corbin turned to him. Brand kept watching the goblin beat his offspring, refusing to look at Corbin. He could all but hear his cousin's mind working.

"You can see in the dark, can't you?" asked Corbin simply.

Brand nodded. He continued to watch the goblin. The creature's thin arms lifted the whip again and again. The whip was slick with blood now. The rhinog only quivered as each blow fell upon it.

"You're glad you can't see it," he said quietly.

Corbin continued to stare at him. "It's the axe. Ambros has worked a change upon you," he said.

Brand breathed deeply, but said nothing. The goblin halted its punishment and now kicked the rhinog repeatedly until it heaved itself up and staggered back to the rope it had dropped.

"What if you become something...else?" asked Corbin. "Maybe you should put aside the axe while you can, Brand."

"You know I can't," answered Brand. "The Haven needs me as a champion. I've borne the axe for days now. I can bear it one more day. I only pray to the River that I never become something wicked."

"I think we should talk to Myrrdin about this," suggested Corbin. "I don't recall him mentioning any such changes coming over the bearer of Ambros."

Then Brand told him of what Myrrdin had said, about finding Vaul in the center of a great oak tree that had encased within it the bones of its previous owner.

Corbin's eyes were haunted as he envisioned it. "It consumed its master," he said. "Just as Lavatis went feral and

434

consumed Dando. Just as perhaps Osang has taken the human heart from Herla and turned him into a wraith of the night."

Brand nodded. "I wonder how Myrrdin has managed to keep Vaul at bay, supposedly for centuries."

Together, they returned to the gatehouse of rustling greenery and sought out Myrrdin. They learned from the others there that Myrrdin had left, heading out on an unexplained errand to the east.

Brand and Corbin looked at one another. "That's where the Faerie mound is," said Brand. Concerned, the two headed out with more urgency into the night again. As they trekked toward the mound, they heard an odd sound. A tremendous cracking sound rang out across the ruins. Then a brilliant ball of flame arced through the night sky. It made an eerie, whooshing sound like the flaring of a smithy's forge when it is being stoked when it passed overhead.

"Burning pitch!" cried Brand, halting. "They are going to fire our camp!"

"Should we turn back?" asked Corbin.

Brand looked at him for a second, then snapped his head back up to the sky as another great crack was heard and the catapults launched another crackling fireball at the army of the Haven. He realized that the decision was his, as the Champion of the Haven. He had become a leader and even Corbin reflexively turned to him for guidance. He didn't like it, but there it was. He had to decide.

"No. We'll find Myrrdin. He said they would harass us all night until just before daybreak when the real attack would come."

"Let's pray that he's right," said Corbin, following his lead. Soon they reached the Faerie mound, and Brand could tell in an instant that something was happening. The mound seemed brighter than it should be, as if the moon shined down upon it, although there was no moon overhead. The silvery light that he had seen while summoning Oberon was growing upon the mound.

"There he is!" shouted Brand pointing toward the ghostly image of Myrrdin, who was just rounding the mound. "He's walking the mound!"

"What? I don't see him," replied Corbin, peering into the darkness. He took a step in the direction that Brand had indicated.

As Brand watched, he saw Myrrdin fade in and out of his vision. A shiver ran through him. It was as if he saw a ghost walking the circle of fallen grass around the mound. "No, we must follow his path. Widdershins, we must walk, nine times around the mound."

He set off, and after a moment's hesitation, Corbin followed him. As they marched around the mound, it seemed that the fireballs quieted and dimmed as they burned wide swathes across the sky. The flaming explosions they made as they struck the gatehouse and the encampment around it seemed dream-like and distant.

"How many times have we walked the circle, Brand?" asked Corbin behind him. His voice seemed a trifle faint.

"Three times," he said.

"The mound seems brighter each time we circle it."

"Yes," said Brand.

"But," said Corbin, "there is no moon tonight, Brand."

"I know."

They marched in silence. Three more times they saw the keep, the catapults and the burning camp.

"Is this how the night world looks to you now, Brand?" asked Corbin, his voice a wavering echo. "This silvery brightness that turns everything into colorless shadows.... Is this what you see without sun, moon nor torch?"

"Yes, it is like this—but not as intense."

They fell silent until they had rounded the mound eight times. Corbin halted as they began the ninth. They could no longer see much of the world around the mound. Only the burning camp was recognizable, now a silent yellow shimmer on the horizon.

"I—I think maybe we should stop," said Corbin.

Brand turned back and looked at him. "I don't think we can. It would break the spell."

"Can't we just—" said Corbin. "Can't we just step off and get back to the camp? They must need us there."

"We're entering Oberon's realm now," said Brand. "If we stop between realms, we may never find our way back."

"I'm afraid, Brand."

"I know."

They completed the ninth circuit, and as they did so music came to their ears. It was sweet music, beautiful music. It wasn't the same as the deep earth sounds that the dark bard had played, but rather the lively tunes of the elves.

Several figures stood at the top of the mound. Brand made them out, marching toward the top, although it seemed a long way. He passed the spot where he had slain Oberon's innocent daughter the night before. The grass was withered and blighted where her blood had stained it.

Myrrdin was there, speaking with the others in low tones. Beside him stood Oberon. It was he who played sweet music. Towering over them all was the unmistakable figure of Old Hob. Wisps no longer circled the eldest goblin, but he had one in his lantern again. By her yellow glimmer, Brand knew it to be the wisp he had returned to her people days earlier. He recalled that the Wee Folk had told him of her recapture after she had spread the word that they needed aid around the Haven.

Corbin's labored breathing behind him told him that his cousin still followed despite his fears. Brand wondered at his own lack of fear and could only attribute it to the events of the past several days. Had he become accustomed to contact with the Faerie? Or was the axe somehow filling him with courage and a level head? He didn't know the answer.

The conversation was held in low tones, but it was clearly heated. Frequently, Myrrdin gesticulated with his arms and robes flaring, while Old Hob made violent gestures with equal emotion. Only Oberon seemed to be keeping out of it, content to play his pipes and listen.

"Hail!" called Brand to them, making his way to the top of the mound.

The three turned to face him, and only Oberon seemed unsurprised.

"What are you doing here, Brand?" demanded Myrrdin.

437

"Ho, Ho!" roared Old Hob. He took a step back and raised his lantern, peering with its shimmering light. "A Knight? What treachery is this, witch? You plan to slaughter us while we parlay, is that it?"

Brand wondered why Old Hob didn't recognize him, but then realized that he must look quite a bit different in his armor and wearing his spiked helm. He drew himself up a few paces from the three and stood as tall as he could. If he was to be cursed with bearing the axe, then so be it. He would act as the Axeman.

"I am Brand, the Champion of the Haven, the wielder of Ambros the Golden," he said.

"Ah!" said Old Hob in recognition. "The snot-nose that lost me my pets! And who is the ragamuffin that struggles up the slope behind you?"

Brand glanced back at Corbin, who returned Brand's supportive smile with a wan one of his own. "He is my second."

"You should not be here, Brand!" called Myrrdin.

"Ah, but he *is* here," said Old Hob. He stepped forward, causing Oberon to hop nimbly from his path. The yellow circle of light cast by the last wisp in his lantern pooled about Brand's feet. "You've changed, man-child."

"You, on the other hand, have not," replied Brand evenly. Just the presence of Old Hob, so near, set the axe on Brand's back to quivering. It was all he could do to keep his lips from curling into a snarl. "Myrrdin," he called. "What are you doing here? Are you parlaying with the Faerie?"

Myrrdin came close and hissed in his ear. "Yes! I work to arrange a new Pact, but it hinges upon us being victorious over Herla in the coming battle."

"What is the nature of this new Pact?" asked Brand.

"There is no time to explain!" said Myrrdin. "You must return to the camp, where you are needed! Dawn is coming very soon!"

"First tell me of this new Pact. Dawn is many hours off."

"No, it's not," replied Myrrdin. "Day-break is almost upon us. Time works in tricksy ways when one walks in Faerie light.

Do you remember tales of people being lost for a year and a day, but not having aged but a few hours?"

Brand nodded, but he grabbed Myrrdin's arm as the other turned to walk away. Myrrdin gave him a dark look. Brand removed his gauntleted hand.

"Have a care," said Myrrdin.

"Tell me what you have wrought here in this devilish place."

"I seek to rebuild the Pact, to restore what was."

Brand turned hard eyes upon Myrrdin. "You would have us tithe again? You would have the Haven give tribute to the Faerie in turn for their protection?"

"What other arrangement could there be?" interrupted Old Hob, looming near. Brand looked up into the hideous face of the eldest goblin. He backed away and reached back for Ambros. Old Hob lifted his lantern high overhead and cackled. Brand grasped the haft of Ambros and stood his ground.

"You! Are you a traitor to everyone?" demanded Brand, pointing the head of the axe at Old Hob's chest. "You plot peace with us even while your goblins fight the Haven!"

Old Hob hissed at Brand, causing a fog of cold breath to descend and cling to his face. "Right now my goblins will not follow me, their own sire. I plot for the future, manling."

"Brand!" pleaded Myrrdin. "There is no time! Whatever the future, in the present the Haven needs you! Dawn approaches!"

"Then I will go," said Brand. "But know this, Myrrdin: Things have forever changed. The River Folk will not bow down to the Faerie again. We will not give tribute, nor restrict ourselves to our native lands. We will live again within the walls of Castle Rabing!"

"Impudent spratling!" shouted Old Hob.

Brand ignored him. "Oberon!" he called, looking past Old Hob's leering bulk. "I must go, but when we meet again, we will wager once more!"

Oberon merely nodded to him.

Brand retreated down the slope. Behind him, he could hear Old Hob's continuous, bitter complaints.

After Brand left them, Myrrdin could barely meet the eyes of Oberon or Old Hob. He'd promised the boy would be reasonable, but he'd *changed*. Perhaps it was the influence of that accursed axe. Whatever the cause, it was unforeseen and unfortunate.

"You'd better get the leash back on that barking dog of yours, Myrrdin," said Old Hob.

Myrrdin glared at him, but did not respond.

"Stuff and nonsense!" Old Hob proclaimed. He shuffled away, still shouting to the others over his shoulder. "I've better things to do than whisper on this mound. One way or another, things are in flux. Mark my words! Goblins will have their due yet!"

Myrrdin watched the misshapen figure retreat downslope. Oberon, Myrrdin's sire, sat upon the grasses at the very crest of the enchanted hill and took out his pipes. He did not play them, however.

Myrrdin wondered what his father was thinking. He thought perhaps he knew. "You believe this to be a grand error in judgment? Is that it?"

Oberon smiled and shrugged. "What is done is done. The question is: can matters be repaired?"

"That's what I want!" Myrrdin exclaimed. "We've had two centuries of easy times since we've last faced one another in battle. What good can come of returning to armed conflict now? Have we not learned the benefits of peace?"

"The goblins certainly have not," Oberon laughed.

His father's laugh did not fool Myrrdin. He was not piping or dancing. He was displeased, despite his easy manner.

"This all started with the Wee Folk, of all creatures to launch a war!" Myrrdin said in frustration. "They have played their grandest trick of all this time! They broken the world around them wide open, and now the blood will be flowing on all sides."

"Don't forget the Kindred," said Oberon. "They were not innocent. They recklessly released the axe into the hands of the

440

River Folk. They have irresponsibly unbalanced the natural order of both worlds."

"But it all goes back to the Wee Folk stealing Lavatis," said Myrrdin. "The Kindred knew the Pact would fail when you had no power to control the Fae. They moved to aid the River Folk and forge a new alliance. The Wild Hunt saw their chance and moved in to scoop up more Jewels. It's a disaster all the way around."

Oberon looked at Myrrdin's staff speculatively. "Where shall thy Jewel stand on the fateful day?"

Myrrdin sputtered. "With the River Folk, as I have pledged," he cried, scandalized at what his father subtly suggested.

"Even if the River Folk become the central cause of this bloodshed?"

"It is a maelstrom. No one party is to blame. I can't say Brand is wrong to demand new terms for peace—no more than I can blame you for letting the Blue slip from your fingers."

Oberon gave him a dark look. He stood and put away his pipes. He touched his forehead with a single long finger of salute. He did not embrace his son before he vanished from the hilltop. Myrrdin did not expect it. They had been no more than civil to each other for years.

Chapter Fourteen
The Keep

Telyn had never been one to sit still for long. The siege of the crumbling castle wore on her nerves. In the night, as the enemy arranged their catapults and formed ranks, she slipped between walls of the stronghold and glided away into the darkness.

She'd seen something out in the fields southward. Something that reflected moonlight. It was small, but did not resemble a goblin. When the small figure took a great leap from a tumbled pile of boulders and sailed over a briar patch, she knew what it must be.

Telyn was fast, but few were as fast as one of the Wee Folk. She was forced to call out to the other to hold and let her catch up. The figure vanished when she called to it. She knew it had gone to ground. She accounted this as a good thing. If the manling had sprung away and run off at full speed, she would never have caught up.

She trotted forward to where she'd seen the other disappear. She crouched in the grasses, breathing hard. "Tomkin?" she hissed.

Unexpectedly, another of the Wee Folk popped up to greet her. "Madam," he said with a sweeping bow. He removed his hat as he bowed and then returned it with a flourish, tossing it into the air so that it landed at a perfect cant upon his pate. He smiled at her, and his teeth seemed overlong.

"Who are you?" she asked.

"The name's Piskin, pretty maid!" he said. He ran his eyes over her in a somewhat predatory fashion. "Might you not have strapping a baby at home? You do appear to be of age…."

"Ah, no," said Telyn, taken aback by the odd question. "I am not married."

"A pity. Well, soon enough that will change, I'm sure. Don't say no when your young man comes knocking, now! We would not want your best breeding years to pass you by, would we?"

Telyn blinked at him. She was on the verge of becoming angry, but decided to mark down the matter as one more odd interaction with the Fae. "On another matter, Piskin: have you seen Tomkin?"

Piskin cleared his throat. "Indeed," he said. "He's not the most gentile of my folk is he?"

"I suppose not," she said. "Would you happen to know where he is?"

"Chasing a rabbit down its hole I suppose, to eat its kits raw."

"Oh, I should hope not. That sounds vile."

Piskin hopped two steps closer to her, and leered upward into her face. She recoiled from him slightly. She hoped her reaction was not obvious and rude. Piskin seemed to take no notice of her retreat.

"I will confide in you, and you alone, milady," he said in a conspiratorial whisper. "He is a vile one, that Tomkin. *Bumpkin*, that should be his name, I say!"

Telyn blinked at him and laughed. "I have to admit, he is ill-mannered at times. But his heart is in the right place."

Piskin harrumphed and tsked. "As to that, I cannot say. He is not here, however, and I would urge you to avoid him. But something else comes to mind: I had thought he would be hiding with soiled trousers behind your ramshackle walls. Your inquiry, however, indicates he has been absent for quite some time, am I correct?"

Telyn blinked in annoyance. Moment by moment, she continually found herself liking Piskin less. "Yes," she said, wondering if she should offer this ill-mannered manling any information at all. "I don't know where he is, but he's not behind our walls."

Nodding, Piskin tipped his hat to her. "Good luck with your hunt then, milady. I must be off. Remember what I said when this is all over: don't let yourself become barren and old! It would be a grand injustice for all!"

"Um, right," she said, and watched him bounce away. She frowned after him, marveling at his rudeness and single-mindedness. What business was it of his when she wedded and had children?

She returned to the stronghold certain of only one new thing: she did *not* like Piskin.

* * *

As Brand and Corbin rounded the mound for the last time and returned to their version of the world, they realized that much time had indeed passed. The sky was not yet pink, but neither was it black. The bluish twilight heralded the coming of dawn. They walked away from the mound and toward the camp, which was nothing but smoldering embers now.

"There!" hissed Brand, grabbing Corbin's arm and pointing with the axe into a nearby thicket. "Rhinogs are inside the perimeter and inching closer to the camp."

"I don't see them, but I no longer doubt your night vision," replied Corbin in his ear. "They must not be affected by the charmed walls."

"Either that, or the charm has lost its potency. Myrrdin said it was only a matter of time."

The two hurried toward the camp. Brand found there was no point in trying to be discreet while wearing metal armor. He strode proudly, almost wanting the rhinogs to attack. It would feel good to cut some of them down. Very good. Somewhere, in the back of his mind, he knew that what he felt was the bloodlust of the axe, but that didn't seem to matter. He saw no way to avoid killing this day.

As they neared the burnt camp, he saw that it had been all but abandoned. Burnt corpses marked where some of the

Haven troops had met with grim ends, immolated by burning tar.

"Here, look!" said Brand. A sick feeling ran through him. "This is the body of Pompolo! The hetman of North End! There will be no more good ale left in his town after this."

"Pompolo? No! Could it be someone else?" Corbin asked as he came to gaze upon the corpse for a moment. A dozen days ago they had supped at Pompolo's table. His hook, which he had ever claimed helped him take up even more empty ale jacks, made his corpse unmistakable.

"It seems worse somehow," said Brand, "to look upon the body of a friend. It makes me think that everyone of these dead men had loved ones, people who would be shattered and weeping to see this."

"So many of us have been killed already," agreed Corbin. "But I fear that many more will fall before the battle is done."

"This body has been beheaded!" said Brand moving on across the battlefield. "Could we be too late? Has the battle already been waged and lost?"

"No, I don't think so," said Corbin, eyeing the corpse he indicated. "The head is nowhere near. The bodies are all soaked in the muck of the swamp as well, as if dragged through it."

"But no fire has touched it," protested Brand. "If the rhinogs haven't yet attacked, how did it get hacked apart?"

"Over there is another, and it is more completely dismembered," said Corbin. "I see no signs of rhinog dead, however. I must admit I'm at a loss."

"Let's move on to the dome," said Brand. "I'm wondering how it has fared through this fiery night."

As they approached the entrance, they were halted and challenged. Brand lifted the axe and let it wink its golden eye once, to identify himself. A ragged cheer went up from the men in the gatehouse when they entered.

"Where is Tylag?" demanded Brand.

The men at the gate ushered him through and into the gatehouse. There he met Modi.

"Tylag has left me in command here. He has taken most of the militia to the keep. They have concealed themselves in the crumbling walls and the thick brush there. The rhinogs have been dropping flaming pitch on the camp all night, although we left it hours ago."

"Is Telyn still here?"

"The girl? No."

"Have the rhinogs attacked yet?" asked Corbin anxiously.

"No," replied Modi. "Not in strength. Just fireballs and raven-fletched crossbow bolts. They will attack soon though, just as Myrrdin said. They have waited the night to harass us and keep us from sleeping. At our lowest ebb, they will attack. Their ways redefine cowardice."

"But what of the bodies outside?" asked Brand. He explained about the dismembered corpses that littered the area.

"They are from the river, from the battle with the Merlings. Every tenth volley or so from the catapults launch bodies, rather than fireballs," said Modi. "The fighting has slowed of late. I think they prepare for a new stage of battle."

Brand eyed the smoldering keep grimly. He felt the axe urging him to charge, to take matters to the enemy, but he fought to think clearly. Perhaps his companions were right. Brand looked down at the axe. The haft of it was still in his grasp, despite the fact that the last attack had long since been beaten off. With a concentrated effort he placed the axe back in his backpack. A wave of fatigue swept over him and threatened to turn the world black.

"I think I must take this pause in the fighting to rest," he said. For a time, he knew no more.

* * *

Telyn sought Tomkin in the ruined castle. Moving about in the fortress was difficult. The stone was old and had been weakened in unknown battles centuries earlier. A granite bridge between battlements might be as solid as bedrock or as treacherous as a muddy cliff in a storm. Often, as she climbed between broken towers and crumbling parapets, she was forced to take leaps to cross yawning expanses and thus avoid a fall. All the while the slow, steady bombardment continued. Stone

446

balls, the heads of slain River Folk and occasional clumps of burning pitch flew and crashed all around.

She found Tomkin at last in a dark chamber in the back of the castle. It was a protected area at least, and the bombarding stones had not yet managed to penetrate the old walls this deeply. Tomkin was alone in the chamber and stood at the rearmost window, gazing out toward the Black Mountains.

Sensing something odd about his manner, and the manner of those who stood guard outside, Telyn approached him quietly. Her padding feet made little sound on the rough flagstone floor. Each flagstone, mortared together in a perfect mosaic a thousand years earlier, was emblazoned with a painted symbol. Glancing down at the faded paint she thought she recognized the symbol. The writing was ancient in style, and the script was hard to read, but it had to be the cursive form of the letter "R".

"Yes," Tomkin said. "They painted each stone the same. Clan Rabing always was a prideful bunch."

Telyn's eyes flicked up toward Tomkin, but he still stood gazing out the window. How had he seen what she saw?

She knew the answer the moment he turned to face her. He was wearing the Blue Jewel. Lavatis glimmered on his chest, hung there by a light chain of silver. The Jewel brightened as she gazed at it, almost as if it greeted her. Could it be winking in acknowledgement of her gaze? How strange was the Blue! She knew only a little of its history. Long in the possession of the Faerie, tales of the Blue were wild and fanciful.

"It's beautiful," she said.

Tomkin stared at her. His odd, black-glass eyes reflected the light of the Jewel on his breast. When he drew breath, she saw now, the Jewel brightened, ever so slightly, as if it drew breath with him.

"Indeed it 'tis, girl. Its beauty corrupts my mind. I can feel it."

Telyn stared at the Jewel. "It's different than Ambros," she said. "I know a little of the Jewel's history. It is a long story of bizarre behavior—and frequent death. It is known to some as the Jewel of Madness. Only Oberon has been able to hold it at bay for long."

Tomkin's nose lifted. He stood proudly on the window sill. "Much of that history was due to the odd habits of those who possessed it, not due to the nature of the Jewel itself!"

Telyn nodded in understanding. "You love it dearly now, don't you? You can't bear to hear even a bad word spoken of the Blue."

Tomkin nodded, and his prideful gaze dimmed somewhat. "There is a grain of truth in thy words."

"Are you going to wield it, Tomkin?"

"I have donned it, and I have attuned myself to it. The Blue stands ready should the need come."

Telyn licked her lips. She moved to stand next to him in the arched window. There was no glass there, if there ever had been. Winds puffed in through the window into her face, lifting her hair up so it flew about her in a wild pattern. "I fear for thee, Wee One, should you need to wield this glowing thing on your breast. Some say you will fail."

"Who speaks so?" Tomkin growled. His teeth bared themselves, and if anything, she thought they were a shade brighter than before.

Telyn slowly turned her head, eyes wide, to gaze down at Tomkin. There was an odd look on his face. "Piskin showed great concern," she said, "he told me—"

"That vicious little fop!" Tomkin shouted with sudden feeling. Then he laughed wildly. His head opened wide so his teeth, gums, flaring lips and flapping tongue were all revealed at once. "He plays every game at once, and invents two more besides!"

She knew a sudden rush of fear as she gazed into his face. She saw a fresh, frightening madness there. Was it the Jewel's influence, or was it Tomkin's natural personality coming to the fore? She could not be sure. Brand changed when he took hold of the axe. She had expected some variety of change in Tomkin, but she had not expected this. She did not see bloodlust in the manling's eyes, but rather a new light that did not come from a sane, healthy mind. She was not sure which was worse. She thought about her task as Brand's Second. Could she perform such a service for Tomkin? She doubted it. Things could not be the same, as Tomkin had no love for her, and she would not even be able to catch him, should he spring out this window and race away.

Tomkin stopped laughing, and Telyn realized it was raining outside now. A gentle sprinkle at first, which quickened into a steady tapping.

Telyn stared outside, not daring to look at the madness in Tomkin's face. "Tomkin," she said in a whisper, "did you call this rain?"

"It will come from there, when it is born upon this land," said Tomkin, as if he had not heard her. He pointed out the window into the hazy distance past the limits of the silvery rain drops.

"What will come, Tomkin?" she asked in a whisper. "Do you call the Rainbow?"

Tomkin did not answer. It was as if he dreamed, or hallucinated with a fever. She was sure he was seeing and hearing things her mind had no hint of. The rains paused outside, but these skies did not clear. Clouds shifted and roiled up there, hanging over the castle walls.

"Will thy hand reach to mine, should I fall?" asked Tomkin suddenly.

Telyn looked at him in surprise. There was a new expression there upon his waxy skin, one she had never seen before upon the face of a Wee One. It took her a moment to recognize it as a look of fear.

"Yes," she told him gently. It seemed to her as if her voice came down from miles above them both. She almost could not credit herself with saying the words. "I will stand with you— whatever comes to greet us."

The two gazed out the window together, side by side, tiny manling and human maiden. Neither knew what was coming, but both understood they would at least not face it alone.

Chapter Fifteen
Brand's Gamble

Brand awakened in confusion. He had just put the axe down, hadn't he? Wielding the weapon was exhausting. Had he truly slept long? He checked the sun in the sky, noting it had moved further to the west, but he could not have slept for more than an hour. His mind dulled again and his chin sagged down again to touch his breastplate. He forced his eyes to open fully and snapped his head back up. He blinked at Corbin in confusion. "I must have nodded off for a moment."

"Indeed you did," said Corbin.

"You should not have let me sleep."

"You needed it."

"I must admit I'm unsure what to do," said Brand, climbing wearily to his feet. "If we hold, can we truly kill all the rhinogs ever spawned that are sent against us? And then the Wild Hunt after that?"

"I can't answer such a question, I'm sorry, cousin," said Corbin.

Brand looked at the men around him. They seemed a frightened lot of farmers, which was exactly what they were. They were tired and scared and dirty and cold. Soot-streaks, burns and bandaged limbs were everywhere. He felt all the worse for having abandoned them, but at least he had stopped Myrrdin from reforging a Pact that would put them under the yoke again for another century. He wondered how the day would end.

Inside, he knew what he must do. He needed the axe to uplift him, and he called upon it to do so.

"Take heart, River Folk!" he shouted and grinned at them, and let the axe surge heat down his arm and into his body. He held it aloft and the Golden Eye winked brightly, blinding everyone present. "The Axeman is among you! The rhinogs are cunning and vicious, but they are cowardly by nature. They are no more than Merlings bearing fur and you all saw how the Merlings fared against the axe! The rhinogs will do no better!"

The men cheered and wiped at their tearing, dazzled eyes. Their cheers turned to cries of fear as a fireball whooshed down and landed upon the dome. A smattering of liquid flame dripped down into the enclosure, but somehow it held up. Brand could see now that many burnt spots decorated the once leafy dome. It was still solid however, and nowhere had it been burnt completely through.

There came a keening sound from outside, and a dozen low horns blared at once. The men inside the dome scrambled back to their positions without having to be told. The attack was on.

Brand and Corbin rushed after Modi to the entrance where they looked out into the dimly lit landscape. Dark figures ran forward in crouched positions, hurrying from one scrap of cover to the next. Suddenly, a great flight of black-fletched arrows and bolts clattered against the walls. One bowman of the Haven fell back, clutching at his chest. They returned fire and Brand saw several rhinogs fall.

"There!" he told Modi. "Tell them to concentrate their fire to the west. That brush is hiding a dense pack of the enemy, massing up for a charge. I think the goblins themselves may be in there."

Modi gave him a quizzical look, but relayed his orders to the crossbowmen, who fired with good results. A number of rhinogs and several goblins fled the thicket. Those that ran in the wrong direction were shot down as they came out into the open.

In the meantime, a large number of enemy had reached the walls. Even as the Haven archers trained their weapons down upon them, several new companies of enemy bowmen appeared as if melting into being from the landscape itself and pelted the Haven troops with arrows to keep them ducking. Thusly covered by their archers, the assaulting rhinogs threw up grapples and clambered up the crumbling walls. Wielding a knife in each hand, they fought viciously with the men on the walls. But the thorn-laden vines and the longer weapons of the River Folk tore them apart. Brand and Corbin moved from spot to spot and hacked down any of the enemy that managed to wriggle their way into the gatehouse before they could stab men in the back.

Suddenly, the rhinogs fell back and retreated. The River Folk cheered and drilled arrows into the humping furred backs. The assault only lasted minutes, but they all felt exhausted. A few rhinog injured still wriggled amongst the vines, skewered by thorns and arrows.

"We showed them something of the Haven!" shouted Brand, elated to see their enemy fleeing.

"Your cheek is torn," said Corbin.

"It's nothing. I would love to pursue them and cut them down, but even the axe couldn't protect me from so many arrows," said Brand. "Here, man! What are you doing?"

"I'm bandaging your cheek. It's bleeding."

"Nonsense! It's nothing but a scratch! Leave it, man!"

Corbin gave up, throwing his hands up. "Okay. You're the Axeman. I'm sure you can't be bled to death."

Brand sighed and closed his eyes to think. "Yes, all right cousin. Fix my wound."

Even as Corbin finished his work, not ten minutes later, the goblins managed to whip their offspring enough to launch another assault. This time, they focused on the entrance, sending dozens of fresh troops against the makeshift barrier that the old, twisted portcullis provided. Again, the enemy archers pelted the walls heavily with black-fletched bolts. Modi, Brand and Corbin ran to the entrance. A desperate struggle commenced. The sheer force of their stinking, struggling bodies forced open the portcullis. Modi threw his weight and strength against it, along with the two strong river-boys. For a moment, they held. Grunting and sweating, the struggling knot of soldiers on both sides filled the air with foul stenches. Finally, their sheer numbers overwhelmed the defenders and the rhinogs forced their way inside.

"Brand! Behind you!" cried Corbin as he battled a furiously screeching rhinog that thrust and slashed like an ape with arms made of leather ropes. Brand whirled and split the skull of rhinog that sought to ram a long knife into his back. He turned back to the flood of rhinogs that were pouring into the breach and raised aloft the axe.

"Ambros!" he cried aloud.

It flashed with the brilliance of a lightning stroke. Those rhinogs that were immediately before him fell back, screeching. Smoke rose from their fur and their eyes had been turned to steaming, boiled eggs in their sockets. Brand realized with a mild shock that they had been struck blind. He strode forward into the reeling mass of them, laying about with the axe. Each stroke stilled another wriggling form.

Two goblins, brave enough to follow at the rear of their broods, met him at the fallen gate. They hissed at him in hatred. Their whips lashed the air like leather snakes. He caught and severed one lash with Ambros, but the other slipped into the protective shell of his helmet and laid open his cheek where Corbin had just closed it. That goblin he cut down, while the other made good his escape. The dozen or so surviving rhinogs chased after their fleeing sire. Another assault had been broken.

"Oh, by the River," said Corbin in a weak voice.

Brand turned to him, suddenly concerned. His own eyes were streaming tears of pain. "What is it, cousin? Are you injured?"

Corbin made no reply. He laid about him with his sword, butchering the blind and injured rhinogs. Their quivering, stinking mass of bodies choked the entrance. Corbin hewed twice more, then fell to his knees and vomited.

Brand walked back to him, his footing made uncertain by the shifting soft backs of the dead. "Are you injured?" he repeated.

Corbin looked up at him gasping. He shook his head. "No, I'm just sickened by the slaughter. Aren't you?"

Brand blinked at him, and realized with a shock that he wasn't. The coppery smell of blood and the roasted-meat smell of burnt flesh did nothing to turn his stomach. Vaguely, he wondered at what he had become. After a time, Corbin regained his feet and went to rest by the fountain. Someone had removed the body of the lookout that had died the day before at this very spot, but his blood still stained the bowl of the fountain.

"Am I unnatural, Corbin?" asked Brand.

Corbin looked up at him and shook his head. "No more so than Modi. Look at him. He is a veteran of many wars, I suppose. He is no more concerned by the dead than we would be for a pile of fresh-picked broadleaf melons that leaked their sap upon our cart."

After they had cleared the dead from the entrance and replaced the gate, no more attacks came. Dawn finally arrived, and the cold light of early morning lit up the awful scene of carnage. Brand thought that it had been better left hidden by darkness. They watched the battle that progressed some distance away at the main keep. At first, Tylag and his men had surprised some of the rhinogs, having dug into hiding places amongst the brush surrounding the crumbling keep. Soon, however, the enemy had encircled them and hemmed them in. The catapults had been concentrated there as well.

As they watched the battle rage, they ate salted beef and swallowed their rations of water. Corbin worked at not sicking up all that he ate. Brand ate steadily, without sickness or gusto.

"Somewhere, in the middle of all that, is Telyn," said Brand in a distant voice.

"Tylag, too," echoed Corbin.

"Had I known she'd left, I wouldn't have come here first."

"Then all might have been lost for these men," Corbin sighed. "Besides, we had no way of knowing."

"We should go to their aid."

"How can we? If we leave here alone, entire companies of rhinogs will fall upon us."

"We need not go alone. We can lead the men on a charge. They won't suspect such a thing."

454

"Of course they don't expect that! It would be suicide! Even your axe can't stop a storm of arrows, Brand. Our armor might see the two of us through, but we would be killing our fellows, as surely as if we had swung the blades ourselves."

"We shall go alone, then," said Brand.

"You shall do no such thing," said a bass voice.

Brand turned from eyeing the keep to see Modi looming over them. He turned back to the keep. Another fireball arced high and belched more smoke and flame from the crumbling battlements. Distant screams could be heard.

"I shall do as I will, warrior," said Brand.

"Then you are a fool."

"Have a care."

"You are the one without a care. Haven't you noticed the conspicuous absence of Herla? Do you not wonder why he lets the children of goblins do all his work and waits to launch his huntsmen?"

"He's right, Brand," said Corbin, "he's right. Herla is only interested in the Jewels, naught else. Rhinogs will die and more will be spawned, the same can be said of River Folk. True power lies in the Jewels. In a way, this battle is just a distraction for us."

"What are you talking about?" asked Brand.

"Don't you see?" responded Corbin. "Herla's just waiting for a chance to come out of hiding and sweep down on you. He wants nothing but the axe. We can't just give it to him."

Even as Corbin spoke, thunder rumbled in the North. Brand followed the sound and turned toward the Faerie mound.

"What I want to know is what happened to Myrrdin," said Corbin. "Perhaps we were wrong to stop him from arranging a renewal of the Pact with Oberon. Right now he could be bringing his archers to our aid. Surely, that would rout the enemy."

Brand turned on him. "We weren't wrong. Is that all we of the Haven have died for here today? To return to serving tribute to the Faerie? Perhaps you would have us wash their feet for them as well."

455

Corbin made no answer. The thunder in the North rumbled again, and the sky seemed to darken a bit as clouds rolled in from that direction.

"Another storm?" asked Modi with a grunt. Brand could see that his military mind was factoring that into the situation. "We could use the water. I'll have the men set up buckets to catch the run-off," he said, stumping off to shout orders to the weary troops. Many of them slept now, slumped over their weapons and using cold stone blocks for pillows.

Brand stared northward.

Corbin followed his gaze, and then looked at him. "What is it?"

Brand just stared. He reached back and pulled the axe from his pack. "I'm only glad it was not I who had to decide how things would go this day," he said.

"What are you talking about, Brand?" asked Corbin, sounding alarmed.

Brand stood up. He planted his feet and set his spiked helm upon his head. To Corbin he said: "Follow me, my cousin, or follow me not, as you will."

With that, he paid no more heed to those around him. A feral grin split his features as he felt the joy of wielding the axe once more. With three deft strokes he cut a path through the thick blackened vines. Sap ran and bubbled like blood from the damaged growths. They parted and fell away from the incredible sharpness of the axe, vines that had withstood fire, knives, axes and arrows.

Brand kicked out the vines that choked the opening and tensed himself to jump through. He felt hands upon him, and had he not known them to be Corbin's, he might have severed them at the wrists. Instead, he used the strength of arm that the axe lent him to throw his cousin to the ground. Gathering himself, he crashed through the living barrier, which already crackled as it sought to knit itself back together.

He hit the ground hard and grunted heavily. He climbed quickly to his feet and set off at a trot toward the main keep. He never looked back to see if Corbin followed, nor did he watch for rhinogs or the Wild Hunt. His eyes stayed upon his

456

destination, only glancing now and then to the north and the growing storm that brewed there.

The rain began to spatter down and the sky darkened rapidly. The morning sun had long since vanished. Clouds of steam rose up from the smoldering encampment and the burning keep ahead. The thunderclaps to the north became more regular and louder.

Brand heard another, running beside him. He knew without turning that it was Corbin.

"The thunderclaps," gasped Corbin. "They're footfalls, aren't they?"

"Yes."

"It must be Tomkin, then! He's summoned the Rainbow, even as Dando did before!"

Brand didn't answer. He didn't have to. Even as Corbin shouted the words in the growing wind and lashing rain, the shimmer of the Rainbow was clear in the north.

They topped a low rise and looked down into a gully. The gully was filled by a dozen or so huddling rhinogs. A single goblin walked among them, administering salves to the wounded among his brood and lashes to those that irked him. Brand hesitated only a moment. With a wild howl of ferocity, he jumped down amongst them. Ambros winked of its own accord, bringing shrieks of terror from the huddled enemy. Corbin plunged down the slope after Brand.

The rhinogs scattered in all directions as would rabbits discovered at midnight in a farmer's garden. Even the goblin scrambled to get away, perhaps believing that these two armored soldiers were but the point men of a company of attackers. Brand strode after this last and ended its long life with a single stroke. The head he grabbed up and hurled after the fleeing backs of its offspring.

"That one will never spawn another monster!" he roared. He grinned at Corbin, who panted and stared at him as if he stared at a stranger. "Thanks for following me, my cousin! Are there any others behind us?"

Corbin shook his head. He was gasping for air, beyond speech. He leaned forward and put his hands on his knees. His sides heaved.

"So be it," said Brand. "We shall win through alone. These foes have no stomach for a fight unless they have carefully planned every detail. We will baffle them by assaulting them single-handedly!"

As he climbed the far side of the gully, Brand heard Corbin mutter after him, "the River save us if they lose their bafflement."

When they gained the far side of the gully and set off for the keep, they were buffeted by powerful winds. The shimmering colored lights of the Rainbow grew in the north. The huge feet and legs were almost visible in the pouring rain. With each fantastic footfall, a deafening clap of thunder rang out over the landscape.

"Fool Tomkin! You are the greatest of fools!" screamed Brand. The storm tore the words from his mouth. Blood, sweat and rainwater trickled down his cheek into his beard and his mouth. He tasted the salty mixture and it was sweet to his tongue.

As they ran, they saw the Rainbow reach the three catapults that sat at the edge of the dank swampland. Great shimmering hands descended from the skies and picked up one of the war engines as a child might pick up a toy. The catapult was raised up, up, out of sight, then came crashing down upon the second engine. Both smashed apart and burst into flames as their loads of hot oil and pitch ignited. The third catapult crew, under the harsh lashes of their masters, bravely worked to turn and aim at the monster. Even as the Rainbow took a step forward, the catapult snapped one final time and sent its fiery load into the shimmering mass of the Rainbow's shoulder. A wad of gauzy, insubstantial flesh was ripped loose from the creature. It loosed a deep otherworldly cry of pain that caused agony in the ears of all that heard it. The catapult crew cheered and the Rainbow staggered, but didn't fall. Moments later the last catapult was crushed beneath the heavy tread of glimmering feet.

Most on the battlefield had their heads turned to watch this struggle of titans. Brand and Corbin used the valuable time to run up undetected behind another band of rhinogs. Brand saw they were archers, and he felt a hot hatred for their black-fletched bolts. Ambros cut down several in a flurry and then they were through the enemy lines and running toward the keep. They ran right past a knot of struggling men and rhinogs.

"We should help!" cried Corbin.

Brand shook his head. "Can't. If the Rainbow reaches the keep, Herla could at last gain Lavatis. We must be there."

"Brand, look!" cried Corbin, pointing to the east.

Brand turned and saw the Wild Hunt. Following their bounding vanguard of Wee Folk were the Huntsmen, the unmistakable stag head of Herla among them. They were hellbent for the keep as well, and were moving much more rapidly than Brand and Corbin could on foot. Brand watched as Osang was raised to the stag head's mouth and a long, low, mournful note was winded that rolled over the land.

"The charm has failed!" shouted Corbin in despair. "We can never beat them! Perhaps not even the Rainbow can reach Tomkin first!"

Brand cursed and wished for a horse, although he was no master rider. He was a man at home riding the ripples of the Berrywine, not the undulating back of a warhorse.

As it was, both the Rainbow and Wild Hunt beat him to the keep. A terrific struggle ensued: men, rhinogs, coursers and the great feet of the Rainbow all met and slew one another. The first gate they met as they panted up to the top of the rise was only a ruin of stone and twisted metal. Brand cursed as he saw the tunnel behind it had fallen.

"Must we climb the walls themselves?" he demanded aloud.

"Here!" cried Corbin. "The side door! It has been smashed in! Perhaps we can get into the tower!"

Brand followed him at a dead run and soon passed his exhausted cousin. He shouldered aside the last remnants of a once stout door whose ancient timbers crumbled to the touch. Into unexpected blackness they stumbled, groping their way over bodies and fallen bricks to a spiral staircase of cut stone. They quickly wound their way up the steps, ducking their heads and scrambling over yet more bodies.

"There are many more rhinog dead than human," said Brand. "But we can ill afford the losses anyway."

"I can't but think of how many firesides will go without family members after this business is finished," said Corbin. "I believe I just climbed over the fat body of Osho, the grocer from Riverton. Remember him, Brand? He used to give us barrel-apples for free when we were kids."

"I can't but think that there will be no firesides for any of us to go back to, should we lose this day," replied Brand grimly. He continued to climb over the warm, sticky bodies to the top, ignoring the smells and the textures. Behind him, Corbin followed, making gagging sounds. Brand wondered that he had anything left in his stomach to sick up. For once he was glad for the axe and the callous courage it seemed to give him.

Up ahead the din of battle and the pink light of dawn filtered down. They tumbled out onto the crumbling battlements of the keep and almost immediately were spotted by a bounding figure. It gave a strange, warbling cry and pointed at them as if accusing them of a most heinous crime. Brand stepped forward, snarling at the Wee One.

"It's one of Herla's foul little jackrabbits!" he roared as he swung.

Bursting out with laughter, the Wee One launched into the air, doing a flip before it came back down in the same spot. It waited for Brand's next move, its legs tense. Brand grinned grimly and took a half-step forward. The Wee One crouched, watching closely, clearly confident and enjoying the sport. Behind them, Corbin averted his eyes as he knew what would come next.

Ambros flashed then, even as Brand stepped up to swing again. Startled, the Wee One's desperate leap took it right over the side of the battlements. Brand laughed as it blindly tumbled down to smash upon the rocks far below. Corbin shook his head and wondered if even one of the Wee Folk could survive such a fall.

They heard a sound behind them then, the sound a gusting wind whipped around great exposed stones might make. They turned back to see a courser land beside them upon the battlements. Another arrived a moment later, landing its horse as a man would taking a great leap over a fallen tree. Brand hadn't until this moment really seen them fly, but now he had no further doubts.

"Retreat down the stairs, Corbin!" shouted Brand. "They can't get off their horses, they won't be able to follow."

Corbin dove for the steps, even as the coursers began their approach. They ignored him and were intent solely on Brand.

"Come with me!" demanded Corbin.

"No!" shouted Brand. "Telyn and Tomkin are somewhere in this keep. I'll not be driven from it."

"Then I will stand with you," said Corbin, coming up behind him.

Brand frowned, but felt a twinge of gratitude. He hadn't relished facing two specters alone. The coursers came at them, and Ambros flashed, but seemingly without effect upon the enemy. Perhaps their eyes were too old, too fleshless, to be pained by light, no matter how bright.

"Look, Brand!" shouted Corbin. "The Rainbow!"

All of them looked, even the coursers. An astounding figure of beauty rose up and rounded the towers of the keep to stand beside them. Up close, Brand saw the pure colors that striped its body, each hue more brilliant than the last. Its head was on a level with them, and Brand looked into its dancing eyes made of blue flames. The otherworldly eyes regarded him and the others, each in turn. Even the coursers seemed at a loss in the face of such fantastic beauty.

A great hand rose up. With a deliberate, swift motion, the Rainbow swept the coursers from the battlement. They fell away into the wind without a cry. Brand saw one horseman's claw-like hand of white bone clutch at the edge, and then it was gone. Brand and Corbin raced for the nearest doorway that led into the keep, lest the Rainbow change its mind about whom it favored.

"Well," said Corbin as they huffed down another hall of fallen walls and bodies. "At least we know that Tomkin is still in command of his creature."

"But for how long?" asked Brand aloud.

They continued through the keep in silence. Ever it seemed that the battle had escaped them. In the distance they heard the

461

shouts and screams of dying men and rhinogs, but around them was only the aftermath of battle, never the event.

After mounting another set of steps, however, they came upon a knot of soldiers in the ragged, stained, blue livery of Riverton. As one, they raised their weapons at the sight of Brand and Corbin, and then lowered them in relief and recognition. They set up a ragged cheer as Brand lofted Ambros and commanded it to wink at them.

"Brand! Corbin, my son!" shouted Tylag, coming forward with his arms spread. "How glad I am to see your young faces!"

"How goes the battle, father?" asked Corbin anxiously.

Tylag's face faltered. "Not well," he said, his voice hushed. "We are reduced to small pockets like this." He indicated the score of men who stood with him in the shadowy halls. "Our forces are scattered about the keep. I've dispatched messengers to try to gather them together, but as yet, none have returned."

"What of Telyn and Tomkin?" asked Brand.

"They are both here," said Tylag, nodding toward another chamber.

Brand noticed that Tylag and the other men of the Haven shunned that chamber. All of them stood far from the entrance. But his heart leapt at the news that Telyn still lived. Without waiting to hear more he strode into the chamber and found her crouched over the tiny figure of Tomkin. Tomkin lay beneath a pile of what looked like sackcloth. She looked up and briefly smiled.

"I'm glad that you live, Brand," she said.

"I too, am uplifted," he said. They came together and quickly embraced. Brand smelled her hair, and his chest seemed to expand with well-being.

"How is Tomkin?" asked Brand in a whisper. "Has he gone feral yet?"

"No, but I fear that is not far off. He has been calling for you."

"How soon thy Folk forget the quality of good hearing," chuckled a voice from beneath the sackcloth. There was a sudden flurry of movement under the material, and it was thrown back. "Ah! There, I can breathe! I'm not a sick child, woman!" shouted Tomkin irritably.

Brand's mouth hung open to see him. The whole of the dark chamber throbbed with the light from Lavatis, which hung as an impossibly huge weight around his tiny neck. After a moment, Brand recognized the pulse of the light. It matched the beating of the Wee One's heart. His face was pale, drawn and sickly-looking in the blue light. He struggled up to a sitting position, but then sagged back down with a sigh and closed his eyes.

"Another gang of rhinogs!" he screeched. "The coursers cut at me!"

Brand and Telyn knelt beside the dying manling.

"He's torn between two worlds," said Telyn.

"He's strong, but it's only a matter of time until he becomes one with the Rainbow and goes feral," said Brand.

"Do not talk as if Tomkin were already dead!" shouted Tomkin, his eyes fluttering open. His great mouth split wide in a familiar grin. "Saved thy arse, I did, river-boy!"

"Indeed, Tomkin. You did that," said Brand.

Shouts erupted from the larger chamber outside. Brand jumped up, expecting a flood of rhinogs and coursers. Perhaps Herla himself was making his final move to claim a second and third Jewel.

Instead, a bounding figure came into the room and pounced upon the prone form of Tomkin. Brand lifted the axe, suspecting it was another of Herla's turncoat runners. But after a moment, he recognized the intruder. It was Piskin, the one who had made deals with him on the part of the Wee Folk just a few nights ago.

"Fool!" screamed Piskin, shaking Tomkin's fallen body. "You've ruined the chance of a millennium! Never shall our people again be so close to grasping true power!"

"Have a care, changeling," said Tomkin's weak, but dangerous voice.

Brand and Telyn looked at one another. Brand realized then where he had heard Piskin's voice before. It was that of the false infant they had chased from Lanet Drake's apartments.

He took a breath and took a single step toward the two Wee Folk.

Telyn laid a hand upon him. "Perhaps we shouldn't interfere. This is their business."

"I'll have the Jewel instead!" shouted Piskin, "Dando was in my debt, he did me a great harm, and I'll take the Jewel as my repayment."

Brand thought to see him lay hands upon Lavatis. Tiny hands grappled and teeth flashed white. Brand was reminded of two tomcats as a flurry of a struggle ensued, the action too fast to follow. Before Brand could reach out to restrain Piskin, the manling leapt up and ran away, shrieking. His eyes bulged, his face was white. He held his right arm curled against his chest. Dark blood stained his fine waistcoat. Brand saw that his hand had been bitten off, leaving only a stump at the wrist.

Brand knelt again beside Tomkin, and the dying manling flashed him a smile full of blood-circled teeth.

"Told him I would have his foul hand!" chuckled Tomkin. He made no move to spit out the severed hand. Brand reflected that the Wee Folk were a strange lot.

The pulsing Jewel on the manling's chest beat faster now, and it seemed less regular.

"Should we take the Jewel from him?" asked Telyn in alarm.

"Try it!" said Tomkin. "My hunger has yet to be sated!"

"Would it kill him to remove it? What would the Rainbow do?" asked Telyn. Even as she spoke, Brand knelt beside the manling. He reached out his hand tentatively, wondering if he would fare better than had Piskin, should he try to snatch it.

Tomkin made a choking cry. "The ants cut at me!" he cried. Brand's eyes widened as he watched rips appear on the thin flesh of the manling's shins and ankles. Blood welled up from the cuts. Tomkin writhed in agony. The blue pulses filled the chamber with rapid, flashing light.

"Brand! The monster is coming!" cried Tylag from the hall. Even as he spoke, Brand felt the stone beneath his knees shiver. The ancient timbers creaked and groaned. A great crash sounded out in the main chamber and men screamed. Daylight and clouds of choking dust flooded into the room.

464

"We must get out, Brand!" cried Telyn, tugging at him.

"Tomkin!" shouted Brand, and for a second the manling's eyes fluttered open. "You have earned my friendship. Have I earned yours?"

Tomkin's grin resembled a snarl. He nodded weakly.

"Then Tomkin, allow me to take the Jewel from you. Let me take up this burden, that you might live to see another day."

Tomkin didn't reply. His eyes were closed and his breathing was ragged.

Brand reached down and gingerly took the Jewel Lavatis from his neck, expecting at any moment to see those sharp ice-white teeth snap shut upon his fingers like a poacher's trap. But although Tomkin's body shuddered when the Jewel was lifted from his breast, he allowed it.

Brand staggered to his feet. The wall before him gave way, and he felt the terror of facing the Rainbow once again. A great shimmering hand forced its way into the chamber and began to grope for the Jewel. The Rainbow loosed an odd, insane howl that shook the flagstones.

Brand looked down and saw Telyn take up Tomkin's limp form and hold it to her chest as one would a child. She fled the chamber with Tomkin's body flopping loosely against her.

The Rainbow, now freed of any master and full of madness, reached for him and the Jewel. Brand cried out and hacked at the brilliant fingers. Chopping into the hand felt odd, almost as if he were cutting at a bag of soft cotton. A shimmering finger fell to the floor of the chamber and flailed there. The great hand was snatched back. The flagstones ran with liquid colors and outside, the creature loosed another howl. Its huge face came near the opening and a single, mad eye of blue flame regarded Brand.

He wasted no more time. He ran into the hallway after Telyn. Behind them there was a terrific sound as the Rainbow ripped away the wall of the keep. Those of the men who had not already fled in terror joined them, including Tylag and Corbin. As they ran they could hear the thunder and the smashing blows of the Rainbow as it followed them unerringly.

"It's no good, Brand!" shouted Telyn. "The Rainbow can sense the Jewel! It is drawn to it the way things are drawn to my beacons!"

Brand stopped and eyed her, knowing the truth of her words. He put away his axe and lifted the chain from which Lavatis hung and looked into the depths of the stone. It seemed to him that something there regarded him in return. He felt a shiver chase through his body. He kissed Telyn's head, and then pushed her away.

"Run," he told her. He glanced at Tomkin's still form, which Telyn still carried, and wondered if he yet lived. Telyn looked at him in surprise, and she searched his face for a brief moment.

"You mean to wield the Jewel," she said, her eyes filling with an expression of horror. She opened her mouth to beseech him. He shook his head, kissed her mouth and lifted up the chain and the brilliant Blue Jewel again, gazing into it.

"Good luck, cousin," said Corbin. He pulled at Telyn's shoulder and together they fled with the rest of the troops down a stairway that still remained whole.

Left alone in the shaking keep, Brand stood to face the Rainbow. It shook the walls and stove in the ceiling. Insane eyes burned down upon him.

Brand slid the chain amulet that contained the Jewel Lavatis over his head, and he took it for his own.

He fell to the dust-laden flagstones and began to rave.

Chapter Sixteen
The Bloodhound

Brand awoke groggily with great pain in his legs and side. He was surprised to find that he was outside, lying across something large and hard. Disoriented, he looked around. In the west, the sun was dying, already half-hidden by the crooked dead trees. He was vaguely surprised to realize that the battle had lasted a night and a day. Then he rose up on one elbow, and saw that the thing pressing against his belly was the wall of the keep. Then he saw his belly, and he screamed.

His scream came out as an odd, warbling howl. His belly was a vast shimmering spanse of brilliant hues. He was the Rainbow.

Tiny things pained his feet and side. He turned ponderously to see that rhinogs were hacking and cutting chunks of the vaporous stuff of his body from him. He swatted at them and they died. He stood up, then staggered, unsteady on his injured feet. He fell to his knees again...

...and was back in the keep. His mouth was encrusted with centuries-old dust. He choked on it, and tried to rise. He sensed something near him, something bad...

...he was the Rainbow again, but now he had lost his balance and was falling. It seemed that he had been falling for a long time, as if it took quite some time to reach the distant ground with its tiny, fuzz-like grass and pebble-like boulders. He wondered if it would hurt when he hit, and it did...

467

...in the keep again. This time he tried to rise quickly. The thing that approached him, the bad thing, was very near now. He felt for Ambros, and it slapped itself into his hand eagerly. A shock ran through him as the two Jewels sensed one another, and declared war upon one another. The battlefield was his mind, and as the two siblings charged one another, it seemed like great wet clumps of brain were torn up and tossed about in his skull. He groaned...

...and found himself floundering outside the keep again. The ants were back at it, chopping at him, hacking the stuff of his body loose in cotton-like chunks. Determined to stop switching bodies, he fought to hang onto being the Rainbow. He rose ponderously up into a sitting position and crushed a band of rhinogs in the process. He recalled the bad thing in the hall, stalking his prone form. He turned to look into the keep, and saw himself, lying prone on the flagstones. An antlered figure rode a tall dead horse forward. It carried a boarspear with a broad gleaming head. A small dog rode with it on its unbreathing steed.

Not knowing what else to do, Brand reached down with his shimmering hand and placed his palm gently over his prone body. He took care not to crush himself accidentally. Some dark part of his mind wondered what would happen to his soul if he did die while in the body of the Rainbow. Would he become one with the wind and rain forever? Or would it be much worse than that?

Herla thrust the boarspear into the gauzy flesh of the great hand, and Brand worried for a moment that he might drive it all the way through the hand and slay him. He swept the hand toward the horseman, who backed away and then leapt into the air itself.

He saw more coursers and rhinogs approaching the spot, from all over the keep. Clearly, they had taken the fortress by storm, despite all that the Haven troops had done. Not knowing what else to do, he decided to pick up his own body and bear it to safety. Perhaps then, as the Rainbow, he could yet turn the tide of the battle.

He gently picked himself up and lifted his body high into the air. It was an odd experience, and his greatest fear was of

468

losing control while transporting himself. He didn't relish awakening as himself in the midst of a hundred-foot fall. Not knowing where to head, he turned toward the Faerie mound. The sun was almost gone and the twilight after dusk was falling over the land. Soon, he would be able to walk the path around the mound. Perhaps he could find Myrrdin.

It was exhilarating to be the Rainbow. He was a giant, a vast shimmering creature that could march where he would and do as he willed. None could oppose him. He felt now and understood the intoxication that had gripped both Tomkin and Dando. How could they, as the smallest of Folk, resist the allure of being an all-powerful giant?

And still, the ants bit his ankles. He looked down and behind him, and knew fear again. Wee Folk bounded like fleas about his feet. Coursers raced after him by the dozens. Herla himself trailed him, boarspear leveled. He saw Herla lift Osang and wind it. More coursers appeared from hidden spots all around and converged upon him. The Wild Hunt was in full pursuit, and he was the prey.

He ran for the mound now, and the coursers trailed him. Osang sounded again and the Wee Folk bounded about at his feet like hopping fleas. He soon outdistanced them, but he knew that he couldn't outrun them forever. They would trail him to the very foot of Snowdon and beyond, to the distant shores of the sea itself. When he reached the mound he placed his human body gently upon the grass and let the body of the Rainbow lean back, back—back further still...

...he awakened as a great crash resounded behind him. The Rainbow had toppled. Wee Folk and coursers raced up to it and hacked at it. He climbed to his feet and began to circle the mound, widdershins.

Before he was around twice, the coursers had noticed him and came up to where he walked the path around the mound. They hacked at him, but to no effect. They were like ghosts to him. Their blades flickered and flashed, but could only make him shy away. As he continued to circle the mound the coursers faded until he could no longer make them out at all. Only the twilight land of the Faerie seemed real. He was relieved to find that the Rainbow no longer pulled at his mind.

Somehow, by circling the mound, he had left it behind in that other place, and had freed himself of it.

But there was someone trailing him. He never doubted who it was. He glimpsed the other now and then, each time he circled the mound. As he rounded the mound the fourth time, he glanced back to see the antlers of his enemy as the other walked his horse on the path behind him. Herla was gaining on him. Brand turned back to the crushed grass of the Faerie path and tried to walk faster. It was difficult, like wading in sucking mud.

Clopping hoofbeats echoed strangely in his ears. He sensed his enemy coming closer. It was all he could do to resist the urge to look back. He lowered his head and pressed forward, putting one foot before the other, plodding steadily. It seemed that the more he tried to hurry, the more resistance he felt. It was as if unseen veils pressed against him, as if he fought the current of an invisible river.

He made another circuit, the fifth? Or was it the sixth? He could no longer recall. He sweated and strained with the effort. Slow hoofbeats sounded in his skull like the clanging of church bells. Unable to resist the urge any further, he looked back over his shoulder. His heart jumped in his chest. Herla was only a dozen paces behind him. He saw the Jewel Osang embedded in the great horn. Its deep, violet hue glowed in the Faerie half-light. The red staring eyes of the bloodhound matched it.

He halted and twisted his body to half-face his enemy. He dared not take his feet from the path. His sides heaved and sweat ran from his neck and burned his eyes.

The other halted his horse, and they regarded one another. A long moment passed, during which neither spoke.

"I require the Jewel, Lavatis," said Herla. His voice was odd. It made Brand think of gravel rasping down a mountain face.

"It is not mine to give."

"Do you serve the elfkin, then?"

"I am the Axeman of the River Haven," said Brand. "I serve the River Folk."

"Then Axeman, as your King, I command it," said the other.

470

"You are not my King."

"I am the last Human King. None other lives."

"You are not my King," repeated Brand stubbornly. He felt a pang as he said it, however. Did this thing really believe itself to still be the King of humanity? Was it possibly correct? He felt lost for a moment. He realized that he faced a being that had once been human, and who had once ruled among the Dead Kingdoms...when they had still thrived. He wondered what lost histories could be learned from its eldritch mind.

"I see that you do not understand," rasped the strange voice. "You and I are not truly enemies. We have the same goals. I am still human, despite my great age."

Brand felt an odd twinge of disbelief come over him that threatened to cloud his mind. Could he truly be having this conversation with King Herla himself?

"I ask a final time, Axeman of the House of Rabing. Yield to me, and join me to rule and empower all humanity. All the wrongs done to our people shall then be avenged."

Brand took a moment to marshal his thoughts. It was difficult. "We aren't the same. There is a great gulf between us."

"What gulf? We stand in limbo, half-way between worlds, but only a few paces apart."

"I speak of the gulf that stretches between the living and the dead. Whatever you were in life, I can't accept the rule of the dead."

"You sadden me, Axeman. Nothing has saddened me for centuries. Know that you cannot oppose me here."

"If you close with me, I will chop the legs from your horse. You will fall to dust as you should have nine centuries ago."

The other laughed. It was an odd, lonely sound with no joy in it. "If my end would come so easily, Axeman, why has it not happened for fifty generations? With my long weapon, all I need to do is knock you from the path, and you will be lost forever in the twilight lands of the Faerie."

"Then the Jewels you crave will be lost with me."

"Well said, but a small matter of sorcery will recover them."

While speaking with Herla, Brand had been edging away down the path. Now, he willed the axe to flash and he turned to continue his march around the mound. He only had a few more circuits to make and he would have reached his goal. Perhaps he could somehow win this race.

Behind him, the odd laugh sounded again. "My eyes are old leather! My skin has long since been leeched from my skull! A bolt of lightning could not blind your King now, Axeman!"

Brand made no reply. Instead he saved his strength for wading ahead around the mound. He heard the slow clopping of the dead horse begin anew behind him. Dread ran cold fingers down his back. He wondered which would be worse, to die with a boarspear in his guts or to step off the path into the nothingness between worlds.

He made the seventh circuit, and began the eighth. But Herla was closer than ever now, and Brand knew he could never finish the ninth. His mind raced, trying to come up with a plan.

Halfway through the eighth, he stopped and turned. Herla was only a few paces behind him.

"You must decide what you value more, my death or the Jewel! I'll not give you both!" Brand said. As he spoke he pulled Lavatis from around his neck and flung it by the chain into the air.

Before it could vanish into the netherworld of the Faerie twilight, however, Herla leaned forward with great speed and thrust his spear into the glittering chain. It snagged on the broad point and rang there with the sound of metal clattering upon metal. Herla pulled it back, making his odd sounds of laughter.

"No!" shouted Brand, aghast at the speed and accuracy of the creature. Why had it not slain him with a cast, if its skill were so great? He could only think that it had not dared to disarm itself. The spear would surely have vanished into twilight if the cast had missed. Not knowing what else to do, Brand swung Ambros at the spearhead. The axe flashed as it clove the head from the shaft of the spear. The broad killing point fell with Lavatis. It lay at the edge of the path, and Brand knelt to reach for it.

He was buffeted by the shaft and nearly knocked from the path. Herla swung it like a club and beat at him. Only one of Brand's knees remained on the path, and he knew terror as he had never known it before. The numbing cold of the void ate into that part of his flesh that had strayed from the circle of beaten grass. Not even the depths of the Berrywine, running silently beneath a surface of ice, could have been so cold.

He struck with the axe again, but at the horse's legs this time, as it had stepped closer. Ambros sheared off the right foreleg at the ankle, and the dead horse stumbled, but did not go down. It tossed its head and made an odd, rattling sound. Brand was sickened to think that it could still somehow feel pain.

Scrambling to regain the path and his feet, Brand dragged the chain behind him with Lavatis still dangling from it. Fighting to manage his crippled steed, Herla followed him. His progress had been greatly slowed, however, and now Brand was leaving the horseman behind. As he began the ninth circuit, he looked back to see that the horseman carried the shorn-off horse hoof in one black-gloved hand. He was still coming, although slowly.

Brand thought to hear the last human king say something as he left him behind on the path. "Axeman, you sadden me...."

Shivering, Brand pressed ahead into the unnatural land he sought. He yearned to see the sweet golden sun overhead again.

He finished the ninth circuit and stepped upon the mound in the silvery light of the full moon that always seemed to shine here. He walked slowly up the mound, tired from his struggles and bothered somewhat by his leg, which hadn't fully regained feeling after touching the void. He could see a circle of figures that stood at the crest of the mound. They worked together to play a quiet doleful tune.

"Oberon!" called Brand to the tallest of them.

The figure rose up and lifted its lantern. Inside the iron cage, a lone Wisp shone her wan light. Brand's heart fell as he saw he had been tricked. It wasn't Oberon, but Old Hob who sat atop the mound. Around him capered a dozen or so goblins. They chortled obscenely among themselves as they came to encircle him.

473

"Ah, the river-boy returns!" said Hob. "I've been waiting for thee, there is a debt yet to be paid!"

"Hob, I've had a very long day," said Brand, feeling his exhaustion and rising anger. "You'd best leave me, lest your spratlings be left without a sire."

"Ho! The river-boy has teeth and dares to shake its axe at the great Hob!" rumbled Hob. Brand noticed that Hob's advance did stop, despite his words. Around them the furtive pack of goblins shifted their feet.

"Six wisps, doest thou owe me, mortal child," hissed Old Hob as he shuffled a step or two closer. His long knobby hand snaked out from his stinking robes and moved toward Brand. "For payment, I'll relieve thee of Ambros the Golden."

Brand ducked, for even as he watched Hob's long, snake-like arm reaching forward, the other swept the lantern around in a low arc, aiming for his head. Brand stumbled and rolled once downhill. All around him the goblins rushed in, like jackals closing on a faltering beast. Brand caught himself and rose, however, Ambros still in hand.

The goblins leapt back, chittering in disappointment. Brand caused the axe to flash and cut at them. They fell back in alarm. Then he faced Old Hob, who now towered above him.

"I'll have your head!" he cried, attacking Hob. Hob parried the slashing axe with his lantern and a great clang rang out across the silvery landscape. The last yellow wisp, released, flittered away into the darkness.

The goblins had scattered. Taking long strides, Hob retreated down the slope. He paused before vanishing into the void. "That's seven! Seven Wisps doest thou owe me! I have a long memory when it comes to debts, Axeman!" hissed Hob.

Brand was left alone on the hilltop. His head turned toward the distant sound of slowly clopping hooves. As he watched, Herla came into being at the bottom of the hill on the opposite side from Hob. He saw with relief that the horse was having difficulty mounting the slope with a shorn-off hoof.

"Old Hob, heed me," he shouted. "I would parlay with you."

Old hob was only half-visible in the twilight, having nearly reached the bottom of the mound.

474

Herla paused in his efforts. He was busy with his horse and his hound. Could it be he painted the shorn hoof with blood from the hound's bowl? That is how it looked to Brand, and he sickened at the sight of it.

"What is it, river-boy? Thou owes me a debt."

"I acknowledge this debt, and I wish to arrange repayment," said Brand. "I would offer you a Jewel to help me defeat Herla," said Brand.

"That is an interesting proposal," said Hob. He took several strides back up the mound and became more fully visible. "Thou hast my attention fully."

"I would, of course, require a boon," said Brand. Old Hob had spotted Herla now, and they both eyed the dead king warily.

"Ha! As I suspected, of course! Nothing but base trickery. A boon? The debtor requests a boon? Nonsense," sputtered Hob.

"Well, if you have no interest in the Goblin Folk acquiring a Jewel of power, our discussion is at an end." Brand made an easy gesture of dismissal.

Hob shuffled two more half strides up the mound toward Brand. He eyed Brand with slitted eyes. "What would be the nature of this boon? And what would be the nature of my repayment?"

"Osang. If I defeat Herla, and you have given me material aid to do so, I will grant you possession of the Huntsman's horn."

"The horn Osang?" asked Hob, almost as if he could not believe his ears.

"It would be fitting, don't you think, for the lord of goblins to possess such a thing? It contains within it the Lavender Jewel of Shadow magic. Is it not the goblin way to have dominion over sight, sound and stealth?"

"What must I do?" asked Hob in a harsh whisper, taking yet another half-stride.

"You must help me defeat Herla. You must stand with me and fight, or help in some other way."

Hob laughed at this. He did, however, take another few strides up the mound. He was now better than half-way up the slope. "Despite the fact that we have clashed at arms twice, such behavior is not the normal goblin way. We do not stand and fight face-to-face with anyone. We prefer subtler methods."

"I care not what your methods might be, only that they are effective."

"Osang should belong to the goblin folk. Long have I said it," whispered Old Hob, half to himself, "I agree to your terms, Axeman."

Hob took another stride upslope.

"All right then, if you will not be a comrade at my side, then give me a trick to help me defeat Herla. And hurry, he has finished repairing his horse with blood from his wooden bowl. Surely, you must know some weakness I can exploit."

The huge goblin shuffled another step closer. Brand felt the axe twitch at the nearness of Hob. It wanted nothing more than to cleave the monster's head from its grotesque body, and for once Brand agreed with it. But he held it in check nonetheless, for Herla was moving again.

Herla became more distinct, his outline fully formed at the bottom of the mound. He was in the same world as those who stood conspiring on the hilltop. The Huntsman cast aside the wood shaft of his boarspear and drew his sword.

Brand snapped his head back to Hob, who had taken the moment of his distraction to creep another shuffling step closer. Brand looked high, fully expecting to see Hob's lantern coming down to dash his brains out of his helmet.

But Hob didn't attack him. Instead, he leaned down, stooping over Brand. His noisome breath washed over Brand as he spoke in a hushed voice.

"One thing I do know."

"Speak!" Brand commanded.

"I know the true name of the hound that has ridden with Herla for all the long, long years."

"Tell me."

And so Hob whispered the true name of the hound in Brand's ear, and Brand shuddered to hear it. For it was a vile and evil name, a unique name that none other on Earth nor in Twilight had ever shared with it.

"I understand now," said Brand. "Herla is the one haunted."

Hob nodded and retreated.

Herla lifted his sword in challenge. "Have you changed your mind, boy?" asked Herla. "As perhaps the only kinsman I recognize in this world, I offer you another chance before I must slay you."

"I will not yield," said Brand.

Herla nodded, having expected nothing less. "Know that after you die, I would shed a tear for thy passing, if only my eyes were capable of it."

Brand held his axe aloft, and knowing that battle was near, it gave him strength. "I will not shed one for you, Herla. You and your hound have drunk the blood of too many. Come, meet the Axeman."

And so with a ghastly cry of challenge, Herla charged up. The steep slope caused the charge to slow. Osang did not provide him speed or flight in this place, Brand was relieved to see.

Brand managed to sidestep the charge, but it was a close thing.

They came to blows. The fight was terribly uneven. Brand knew himself to be little more than an untrained farm boy. It was one thing to chop at rhinogs that were little more than hairy beasts. It was quite another to face a true lord of battle, who had fought for nearly a millennium from horseback, and who had slain thousands of men before Brand.

The only thing that kept Brand alive at all was the flashing axe and the guidance and strength of arm it gave him. And so he managed to meet the blade that licked out in silver flashes from Herla's arm.

The stag antlers of Herla's headpiece blackened out the stars from his vision. The Lavender Jewel Osang didn't flash or blind him, but it did pulse with each stroke of Herla's sword.

Brand backed away, panting, beating down the other's faster, lighter blade. He tried to circle in front of the horse to get a low cut where Herla could not parry. But his opponent would have none of that and kept circling the horse to match him. Brand caught the other's attacks, but just barely. Any lesser weapon would have failed him miserably. An axe was not meant for this sort of thing. Any axe is a weapon designed to bash down the enemy weapon, to knock it aside. One could not stand and parry and thrust with an axe. An axeman had to be on the attack, his only defense was to weave an attack such that any enemy coming close would be cloven in two.

But Herla knew of such tactics. He knew when to give ground and when to advance. And he controlled his horse with such precision that it was as if he had four legs himself. He knew how to get around an axeman's guard, the moment to step in, when the axe had made its cut and was on a downward path. Before Brand could turn it and cut a new arc in the reverse direction, his sword would lash out, forcing Brand to stumble back or catch the sword with the haft of his weapon.

Judging he was close enough, Brand called to the dog. He did call it by its true name.

The dog reacted, lifting its evil head to eye Brand curiously. Herla and his horse cantered back a step, surprised.

The bloodhound met Brand's eye, and Brand knew then that the thing was something more than a dog. It was something else entirely.

"You call my pet?" asked Herla, chuckling. "Do you perhaps think she will turn on her master? Maybe bite my hand?"

Herla stepped close to attack again, and such was the ferocity of the attack that Brand knew then he was lost. Before, the huntsman must have been holding back, testing him. But now he came on with a violence that no mortal could withstand. The blade flickered faster than the eye could follow. Brand wove his axe in a defensive pattern, but the tip of the sword slipped past and pierced his mail at the shoulder. His left arm hung limp and bleeding.

Brand called the dog's name again.

The horse reacted as if stricken and threw its head. Herla struggled to turn it back to press his advantage. He lifted Osang to his lips and blew a single clear note. At the bottom of the mound, dark figures on horseback began to slowly appear out of the mist. Herla had summoned his coursers.

Brand raised the axe, willing it to flash its most brilliant. Ambros did as he bid, and a blazing light shone forth that would have burned away the flesh and eyes of any normal man. Even Herla was affected. He cursed and threw a black-gloved fist over his face. Then he recovered and moved forward, holding his sword out for a killing thrust.

"Sange!" cried Brand, speaking the dog's true name a third time. Hearing it, the dog did alight, hopping from Herla's saddle for the first time after nine centuries of riding.

Chapter Seventeen
Osang

The bloodhound landed on the ground between them. It looked from one to the other, and it lifted its lips from its sharp fangs and grinned at them. Brand saw something in its eyes. He saw the red glimmer of ruby light. Then it ran away down the slope.

"Blood magic," said Brand, staring at it. He understood then, seeing the thing run from them, that it had long been Herla's master, not the other way around.

Herla stared with him after the retreating bloodhound. He let his sword arm drop to his side. The coursers, who had been advancing up the slope, held their ground in a great circle around them.

"You have not defeated me, Axeman," said Herla.

"No."

"You have, however, freed me at long last."

"So I had hoped," Brand said.

"You are truly of the Clan Rabing, Axeman. I, as your King, wish to return you a favor for having freed me of the bloodhound."

"Speak."

"I grant you title to these lands, to these kingdoms of the Dead. I will tell you that if you drive out the evil that sleeps here, these lands can flourish again and times can be good for our people. There is a power here that has turned this place foul. A power like the bloodhound that was my master for all these long years, even as I dreamed that I was its master."

Herla's dead eyes looked down at the ground, and he pondered the earth which had awaited him patiently for centuries. Finally, the earth would feel the touch of his feet. "Do you know from whence came this mound?" he asked Brand.

Brand shook his head.

"It is a burial spot for our people. Here are buried all the kings that built these castles. To this place all our kings eventually come to rest," Herla said. He lifted Osang then and winded it for a final time. The coursers moved uneasily in their saddles. Their steeds stamped, but blew no pluming breath. Each of them raised a weapon in salute of their king.

"Know thee all that Brand is now the lord of this land. The last living lord. The hound has jumped from my horse and our curse is finally lifted. We can step down from our mounts and rest our weary bones. I command you all to do so."

After he finished speaking, Herla and all the Wild Hunt stepped down from their horses. The horses stepped lightly, feeling no burden for the first time in their memories. The horses melted first, then their riders. Herla still stood, however, after the others had faded to dust and black smoke.

"You are free, but your bones will still dissolve?" asked Brand.

"This is as it must be," Herla said, nodding. "We have lived on in death for far too long. I thank you, Axeman."

He raised his sword in one hand and held it high. In the other hand he held high Osang, the horn of Shadow magic, and he sank down into the mound. After a moment, only the horn and the sword remained lying at Brand's feet.

Brand put his axe away on his back again.

He shed a single tear, not for Herla, but for the passing of the last king of humanity. He had been a force of evil, but even the Faerie had feared him, and it was hard not to be prideful of that fact. Possibly, for many centuries, Herla had been the only human they had not dared to mock or scorn.

Then Brand heard a raspy throat being cleared. He didn't need to turn to know that Old Hob crept closer up the slope out of the shadows.

"Excuse me, lord Axeman," said Old Hob. The huge goblin's eyes were fixated upon the bejeweled horn which now lay upon the grass before Brand.

Brand nodded. With his gauntleted hand, he pointed at the horn. "I give you Osang, goblin, as was our bargain. But know this: the axe is a greater power than the horn, and the humans will ever defeat the goblins should you choose to wield it against us."

Old Hob took several half-strides closer, knobby hands working together. A single long string of liquid dripped from beneath his cowl.

When towering goblin had dared come close, Brand brandished the axe and let it glow in Old Hob's face.

"Treachery!" wailed Hob.

"No," said Brand. "A clarification only. This is the boon I ask: You must marshal your goblins and their rhinog offspring and quit the field. You must withdraw and allow your goblins to make no more rhinog offspring with human women."

"As thou wishes," said Hob.

Brand nodded and stepped back.

A vastly long arm with a twisted hand and six long fingers stretched forward. With wickedly-curved nails at the end of each finger, the hand snatched the horn from where it rested on the grass.

Brand allowed it. He had no desire to touch Osang. He had already dealt with two of the Jewels at once. The very idea of placing his hand upon a third Jewel was unthinkable. He was certain that the burden of it would break his mind completely.

Hob took a huge breath and slowly let it out. He clutched Osang tightly to his chest. "Ah, the power of it," said Hob. "It throbs and trembles against my breast, as warm as a fresh-caught maiden. Your debt is forgotten, Axeman. My wisps are freed, but I no longer hold you accountable for their loss. I will marshal my goblins and their children and march them from this place."

Shuddering from the power of Osang and salivating with the joy of holding it in his lumpy green hands, Hob hurried downhill. He vanished when he reached the misty bottom of the mound.

Brand sighed, finding himself all alone in the silvery lands of the Faerie. "I suppose I must circle this mound nine times more to get back to my land," he said aloud to no one.

A flittering golden ball of light came up to him then, and he recognized the wisp whom he had released for a second time this night. He smiled at her exquisite beauty and she lit up his face with her yellow glow. She blushed and curtsied in the air.

"I will lead thee," she said, her tiny voice squeaking in his ear.

He startled to hear her, and she flittered backward in concern. "You can speak?" he asked.

She nodded. "My voice is too faint for a human ear in thy lands."

Brand nodded in return. He followed the floating golden mote that was the wisp down the slope.

* * *

While Brand walked the Twilight Lands, Telyn again found herself feeling restless. The battle was over, her young man was gone to places unknown and the combination was too much to be borne. She helped with the wounded for a full day, every few minutes gazing out toward the mound where Brand had vanished. Was he alive or dead? Did he lie in silver grasses, wondering if he would ever see her again?

Telyn took to heading out to the mound at odd hours, usually at dawn and twilight. He was most likely to return then. Sometimes, wisps appeared and twittered at her. She ignored them, not impressed by their ethereal beauty. Somehow, when one was truly worried and heartsick, the wisps were less enchanting to gaze upon.

On the second night of waiting and checking for Brand, she heard a strumming lute. She stiffened, but kept walking. The chords were lovely, and the sound filled the night air with a warmth that was unnatural for this time of year. Her head filled with the scents of lilac and honeysuckle. She knew of these tricks, however, and did not falter in her step. She turned away from the mound and headed back toward the ruined castle with an even stride. She promised herself she would not stop walking, nor would she deviate from the path until she reached safety.

The lute and presumably the player followed her. She did not look around over her shoulder, although she burned to do so. Every dozen steps she reached up and touched her ward—making sure she had not somehow lost it. The grasses beneath her feet took on the silvery quality of the Twilight Lands, and she looked up to see the moon was riding high and was no long obscured by clouds.

The player came to walk with her across the lonely field.

"Lovely night, is it not, darling?" asked Puck.

"It is cold and the air smells like stumpwater," she replied. She was lying, but she did not want to give him the pleasure of knowing his enchantments were working.

The elf chuckled. She still did not look at him, but she could see out of the corner of her eye that he was living up to the name of the Shining Folk. He glimmered brightly in the moonlight as if filled with soft radiance.

"You are a stubborn one!" he said.

"If you must talk, tell me something useful," she answered. "Tell me of Brand."

"Must we discuss a boring river-boy?"

"You could leave me in peace instead."

"Ah, but I sense you came here for love! If Brand does not return, will you not dance with me? I could make you forget him."

Telyn broke her vow to keep walking. She stopped and drew her knife. She raised it to the elf, and he backed away, throwing himself down upon his knees.

"Oh please!" Puck said mockingly. "Put away your blade! Do not sever my head from my shoulders. I will make amends."

Telyn huffed and began walking again. Suddenly, the elf was at her other side, whispering in her ear. "I can tell you about Brand, if you will tell me something first."

She stopped again and looked at him. He was lovely to look upon. The very opposite of crude, craggy-faced river-boys. He was refined and sculpted and—almost perfect.

"What do you want to know?" she asked.

"Tell me of the Blue Jewel. What will be done with it?"

Telyn nodded slowly. "Ah, I see now why you have come. You are your father's lackey. You are here to wheedle and plead for his foolishly lost bauble. Well, I don't have it, and I'm not in charge of its keeping, either."

For a fraction of a second, the elf registered anger on his face. He stared at her, and his lips twitched as if they wished to pull into a tight snarl. She tightened her grip upon her knife. At his side, she noted now, he did carry a rapier. If he drew it and lunged, she was not sure she could defend herself.

Puck watched her closely. After a moment, he regained his composure and went back to pleading. "Lovely lady, you wound me with your scornful words."

Telling herself to stay more civil, Telyn began walking toward the castle once more. It was difficult to turn away from him, to force her feet to begin moving again. Hadn't she made a pledge to herself? Ah yes, she recalled it now. She was not going to speak to the elf. She was not going to pause in her journey or be turned to another path. So far, she had not kept her pledge. Her jaw set itself, jutting forward, and she forced her feet to move. Once she was walking again, each step became easier. She wondered at the elf's power. Surely, without her ward, she would have been swept away and become his plaything. She shivered, although the night air was not truly cold.

Puck followed, pacing alongside her again. "My offer stands," he said. "Tell me something of the Jewel, and I will tell you something of Brand."

"I don't know anything special," she said. "Tomkin wielded the Blue and called the Rainbow. When he lost control of it, he handed it over to Brand, who commanded the Rainbow, as I'm sure you witnessed.

"Did the Wee One die?"

"No, he had a hard time of it, but he managed to survive."

"Interesting. Did he hand over the Jewel willingly, or was it taken by force?"

"He was very weak at the time, but he did not fight."

"Hmm," said Puck. He did not sound happy with her answer. "And what of Brand?"

"He wielded the Jewel in Tomkin's stead. Have your people no eyes? I would think you knew this story by now."

"We have eyes everywhere," said Puck, smiling oddly. "Sometimes, we even share your own with you."

Telyn shuddered, and again had to force herself to start walking. She had unaccountably stopped.

"What I want to know," said Puck, "is whether Brand wielded the Jewels both together?"

Telyn considered it. "Yes, I would say he did. But not quite at the same time, since he could only see out the Rainbow's eyes or his own at one time, not both together. Still, they were both actively affecting him."

"Very interesting. Now, I see the hour is late, and we are near your encampment. I will take my leave now, pretty maiden—"

"No," she said. "I will not permit it. You will tell me of Brand, as you promised."

Puck's answering smile was wide, but insincere. "Of course," he said, speaking through two rows of perfect teeth.

"Where is Brand?"

"In the Twilight Lands."

"Has he been wounded?"

"Several times."

Telyn sucked in her breath. "Is he mortally wounded?"

"I should think not."

She sighed in relief. "What of Herla?"

"That creature has sadly passed on."

She cocked her head and regarded the elf. "You feel sadness at the passing of such a monster?"

Puck drew himself up. "The Dead are merely in another state of being. We among the Faerie do not judge them as harshly as your folk tend to."

Telyn shook her head and laughed. "We find bloodthirsty Dead to be unredeemable and thoroughly evil."

"Nonsense!" said Puck, and she thought there was a ring of honest outrage to his words now. Perhaps with this topic she had somehow struck past his fawning façade. "There is no true *evil*—only the pleasant and the unpleasant."

"Well then, I would most definitely say the Wild Hunt qualified as unpleasant."

"A difficult point to argue," he conceded.

The two walked together until they'd reached the foot of the crumbling walls.

"Good bye then," she said as the elf lingered.

"Can I not be rewarded with token of affection?" asked Puck.

Telyn looked at him and shook her head. The elf was positively incorrigible. He stood expectantly, hopefully, and she found herself weakening. She straightened her back and thought of Brand's face.

"No," she said.

"Not even a single, chaste kiss?"

"Never," she said, but she smiled at him as she left him at the walls and walked back into the encampment.

Chapter Eighteen
Homeward

When Brand left the world of twilight and returned to the world of sun and stars he found the area around the Faerie mound deserted. It was morning, as best he could tell from the bluish cast to the sunlight. How long could he have spent in that other place, he wondered? Perhaps, he thought to himself with a chill, it had been much longer than a single night.

There were a few rhinog bodies laying about, stinking in the sun. He thought they had a great stench about them, living or dead, but that in death they were probably worse.

He trudged wearily, wounded and sore, toward the damaged keep. The bright sun and his fatigue caused his eyes to squint. But even with his eyes half-open, he kept them sliding from side to side warily. Who knew how things had gone during his absence? Hob had promised to withdraw, and Herla had fallen, but there were still the Merlings and the Faerie who might attack him.

After he had gone no more than a dozen heavy steps and had begun to consider removing at least some of his armor, someone hailed him.

"Oh hey! Brand!" shouted Corbin. He came up behind him and clapped him upon the shoulder.

Brand turned him a tired smile. "I'm very glad to see you made it."

"I feel the same. I've camped upon that hill, waiting for two days now. The nights were hectic, let me say."

"Thanks for waiting for me. Had it been a century, I would hope you would have given up."

"Never!" beamed Corbin, "but seriously now, you must tell me how things went. We know that the Wild Hunt vanished. Soon after that the rhinogs withdrew, marching in the direction of the Black Mountains. They flew a white ribbon, so we let them go. I hope this was the right move."

Brand nodded. "It was indeed." He told Corbin the details of his adventures in the twilight lands.

"So, you gave Old Hob the Horn of Shadow?" he asked, worriedly.

"I know, not the best of enemies to empower. But I needed his help to beat a greater evil and we struck a bargain. If you don't keep your word with these creatures, there is little basis for ever achieving peace."

Corbin nodded, for once he kept quiet about his own opinions. He turned to helping Brand remove his armor and bandage his wounds. None were life-threatening. Brand reflected that he made an excellent second. There was nothing the axe needed more to help balance a man than a trusted, cooler head.

Brand enquired about Myrrdin and of course Telyn. Myrrdin had never returned from the Faerie mound after the night Brand had told him he would not remake the Pact. None had seen him or Oberon from that day to this. Telyn had been sick with worry about him and had taken shifts upon the mound, as well attended Corbin's. She had kept busy helping the wounded, hunting for food and scouting for the army.

Others of the River Folk army soon joined them as they marched to the ruins. The news of Herla's destruction spread quickly. When Brand arrived at the encampment, the army was in fact packing up to march homeward. They had lost nearly a third of their number, but at least some kind of happy news was theirs to report.

"We will return here one day," Brand told the assembled men when they had finally stopped cheering him. "We will make this place green again, and it will be part of the lands of men."

The cheering was muted and more ragged as he talked of returning. Many of the men looked as if they would rather never leave the Haven again. Some, however, roared approval for his fighting spirit.

"I will say this last," said Brand, pulling out the axe again. It provided him a burst of energy and good spirit. "We will not have the Faerie or any other folk as our masters again. The Pact was an arrangement of tribute. It was a servile, pathetic state for the River Folk. We will not buy peace that way again. By the Golden Eye of Ambros I do swear this!"

He lofted the axe and it flashed. Everyone there felt a ferocity of spirit overtake them, and their voices rose up to a roaring shout. They cheered and slammed their palms together until they stung. The walls of the ruins rang with the sound.

Brand marched to the boats and the army followed him. Brand saw Tylag and Corbin exchange glances, but he didn't care. Not one whit. For he meant his words, Axeman or not, he would live and die by them.

They sailed home and none dared to delay them.

Brand's heart grew heavy, however, as they approached Riverton. He feared, somehow, that the town would have been fired and ruined in his absence. Perhaps everyone he knew, save those on the boats with him, had perished in some attack while the army was away.

Corbin and Telyn had asked him about his dark mood, but he didn't tell them what he was thinking. Best to let them enjoy the feeling of victory for as long as possible, should despair be waiting for them at home.

So it was, when Stone Island hove into view and everything looked right about it, his face split into a grin. Only Corbin caught on.

"You thought perhaps we were coming home to something awful, didn't you?" he asked quietly as the boats all jockeyed to be first to the docks. The River Folk on the docks cheered to see the returning army. Soon half the town turned out, fluttering handkerchiefs and colored ribbons at them.

Brand shrugged. He knew there was no dodging Corbin's mind. "Oberon and Hob were missing from the battlefield. Not to mention the Merlings. Our army wasn't home to protect our people and I didn't know where the enemy might be."

"You feared they may have attacked here," said Corbin, nodding, "now that I think about it, the thought makes me shudder. Do you really think that our enemies might have fallen upon our civilians out of spite?"

Brand snorted. "How do you think the Dead Kingdoms came to have their name?"

Corbin nodded gravely but clapped Brand upon the back. Brand winced from the wound Herla had given him. Somehow, it seemed to hurt more as the days passed and it began to heal.

"Forget all those worries! They must have feared our vengeance too much to dare it!"

Brand thought about that as the celebrations began. As usual, there was wisdom in Corbin's words.

After the celebrations, however, certain key questions remained. Everyone wanted to know the answers. Chief among them was the question of what was going to be done with the Blue Jewel. People seemed to accept that he was the Axeman now, that the Amber Jewel should be Brand's to keep. But the second one, no one knew what to do with it. They all seemed to want to talk about the subject, however.

One night in a remote parlor of Drake manor, Tylag and Corbin discussed it with Brand. Tylag was of the opinion that it should be taken to the Riverton Council and there a decision could be made properly, in accordance with Haven law. Brand rejected this idea.

"I'll not give it to a crowd of River Folk elders. No offense, Uncle, but they wouldn't know what they were dealing with. Can you imagine Old Tad Silure with a Jewel of power? He'd drill a hole in it and sell it as a ward."

Tylag had to laugh at that, but his manner was uneasy. Brand could tell his Uncle was handling him delicately, so as to not set him off. Ironically, just the thought of his Uncle having to dance around with words like that made him angry. He fought to control his temper, and the axe rolled around on his back restlessly. He had, by now, gotten a much heavier pack of thick black leather and metal studs to stow it in. He dared not carry it on his belt, it was just too dangerous. If even a child walked up and ran a finger down the blade, well, that would be a nine-fingered boy who went home that day.

"They all have read and heard of the Jewels," said Corbin, supporting his father.

Brand laughed. "That's nothing. Hold one in your hand and let it burn a hole in your mind. Walk as the Rainbow. Then face down the Faerie in their own lands. At that point, you will know what you are talking about."

"No need for disdain, Brand," said Tylag.

Brand took a deep breath, but he made no apology. "I'll not leave the choice up to them. I know Uncle, this is hard to take from a youth, but I don't think they can make this decision. They would want to keep it and would fight over who should try to wield it. Any of them that did might well end up like Dando. Either that, or they would want to trade it back to Oberon for a renewal of the Pact. I find both of these choices unacceptable."

Corbin nodded approvingly. "Your logic is accurate. I can't see another result from the council."

Tylag shot his son a look of annoyance. He continued talking, but Brand could not do more than appear to listen. He tried hard to think about his uncle's words calmly. He knew he was a wise man, but he also knew that Tylag really didn't understand what the Jewels could do to a person. He understood his uncle's point of view, but the argument remained.

"You don't want to try to use the Lavatis again yourself, do you Brand?" asked Tylag gently.

Brand looked up. His uncle and cousin were leaning forward over the table, looking at him. He realized they knew he hadn't even been listening.

He shook his head. "No. Absolutely not," Brand said. His voice lowered, and sounded almost haunted. "I never want to be the Rainbow again. There is madness in its eyes. And if you walk as the Rainbow, I think you lose a tiny bit of your sanity, permanently."

The others looked relieved and haunted by his words at the same time. Brand told them he had decided to leave Riverton and return to his own Isle.

In truth, Riverton seemed oppressive to him now. He needed room and time to think.

Chapter Nineteen
Parlay

When he finally did make it home, Jak welcomed him, but looked at him as if he didn't know where his little brother had gone. He kept giving him sidelong, worried glances. Brand knew what was wrong. Brand Rabing wasn't the same man at all.

For a day or so, he knew relative peace. He had grown up, and the world had changed around him as much as he had. His home wasn't the same as before, but it was still good. He felt he could breathe easily again, and that was a good thing. But this breathing space didn't last long. Very soon, visitors began popping up. Brand would soon find there was no end to them and that as the Axeman, he was never going to have much peace in his life.

Among the first visitors, and the most insistent, was Tomkin. Telyn had told Brand that after the Rainbow faded away and the rhinogs had retreated, Tomkin had recovered quickly. In typical Wee Folk fashion, however, he had not focused on gratitude for his life. Instead, he had fixated on the idea that Brand had made off with his Blue Jewel into limbo. Never mind that the Jewel had almost killed him and that if it hadn't then the Rainbow, when it went mad, would surely have finished the job. What Tomkin wanted to know was where his Jewel was, and when Brand was going to hand it over.

Not knowing what to do, he put off Tomkin, asking him to return at the end of the week. Hopping mad, quite literally, the

494

wild little fellow had run out of the place in a huff. Brand didn't blame him. But he just didn't feel he could hand over Lavatis to the folk who had so recently run with Herla as the vanguard of his coursers. At least not without thinking about it.

Before the week ended, he had several other visitors. Gudrin came next to the Isle and stumped up to his door. Brand threw it open before she could raise a fist to knock. He smiled at her and threw his arms wide for a hug. She blinked, slightly shocked, but allowed him do to it. He gathered that hugging wasn't something the Kindred did often, but he didn't care.

"I'm very glad you came, Gudrin. I need advice as never before."

Gudrin nodded and sighed once they were seated comfortably. Jak withdrew to the kitchen and busied himself with mugs of coffee.

"I'm not surprised," she said, "when one has wealth or power, that is when the decisions become the most difficult."

"Why is that?" Brand asked. He didn't doubt her, but truly wanted to know her reasoning.

"You see, when you truly have wealth, everyone needs you. That is when relatives come out of the stone itself needing a loan. This places the rich woman in the position of having to decide who gets help and who does not. She must decide who pays the rent, who eats and who starves. A poor woman has no such worries. Power of any kind works the same way. The more you have, the more others will seek it, and you must then decide how to distribute what you have."

Brand nodded, seeing her point. As a lowly river-boy no one had much cared about his opinion, and the good part of that was they weren't angry with him if he didn't agree with them. But now that his opinion carried such weight, everyone around him was anxious.

"I'm finding new friends at my door every day," he said.

Gudrin chuckled. "I'm sure they are very friendly until you tell them 'no'."

"Exactly," said Brand. "But what I need help with today is what to do with the Blue Jewel. I'm assuming, of course, you are an impartial party in this matter."

"No, I'm not," said Gudrin, shaking her head sadly. "I can make no such claim and I doubt few can. But at least I can tell you that the Kindred are not seeking ownership of the Blue Jewel. But neutrality? Of course we are not neutral! We are very interested in who gets the Jewel."

"All right then, I can accept your honest answer. Who do you wish to see with the Jewel after the dust settles?"

Gudrin frowned into the fire. She did not answer immediately. Jak brought out two steaming mugs of coffee, and Brand thanked him. Brand asked him to sit and listen to their talk, but Jak begged off, saying there was work to be done on the east side of the island.

Gudrin and Brand looked after him as he left. "It is the same way with Modi. They have strong opinions, and don't trust themselves not to blurt out their thoughts at such a meeting."

"Where is Modi?"

"Outside, watching the river for trespassers."

Brand nodded. He was quite used to Modi's paranoia by now, and he had learned to approve of it. "You still have not answered my question."

"True," said Gudrin, sighing. She fumbled with her Teret, but then put it aside again. "I can't think of a single passage that would help in making this decision. Let's list the possibilities. You could keep the Jewel, or give it to another of the River Folk. This would make you strong, but also create new enemies, namely the Faerie and the Wee Folk."

"Exactly my thinking."

"You could return it to Oberon, asking to remake the Pact in a new form. This restores the balance of power to what it once was, and has the benefit of stability."

"I'm sure that is what Myrrdin wishes me to do."

Gudrin nodded. "Besides that? I'm not sure. Find a neutral party you trust? I'm not sure I know of any."

"What if I gave you the Jewel, Gudrin?" asked Brand, eyeing her intensely.

She looked surprised. She laughed and sputtered. "I can hardly think of a worse fit for one of our breed than that of Sky

Magic! Imagine! A creature that lived fully forty years before she first felt a raindrop trying to master the Rainbow!"

"I think you have the strength of spirit. Commanding the Rainbow isn't like mastering the axe, it doesn't drive you mad with bloodlust."

"Perhaps not. You aren't overcome with the *berserkergang*, that's true, but you are quite easily driven insane by it. In case you hadn't noticed, Brand, all of the Jewels are somewhat mad. Possessing any of them inevitably affects the mind of the bearer."

Brand nodded, admitting what she said was true. Twice, the Wee Folk had tried to wield the Blue Jewel and had been overcome by Sky Magic. Dando had died, and Tomkin would have died as well had Brand not been there to interfere.

"So," he said, "you don't desire the Jewel."

She sighed. "I'm too old. The burden would be too great."

"There is one other option you have not mentioned...."

"What? Do you think to buy off the Merlings and end your conflict with them with this gift? I don't think they have the strength to wield a Jewel, Brand. They would only lose it to the first one strong enough to come and take it."

"No, no," Brand said, shaking his head. "Not the Merlings. I'm thinking of the Wee Folk. Tomkin, most likely. He gave it to me as a matter of trust. And he survived his first attempt with the Jewel."

Gudrin looked at him as if he had gone quite mad. "The Wee Folk? And a wild one at that? Brand, I can hardly think of a more chaotic bunch. The Merlings are organized in comparison!"

Brand nodded, frowning deeply.

"I can see this decision weighs heavily upon you. But I'm afraid I'm here to make matters worse, and worse still after that."

Brand looked at her unhappily and gestured for her to get on with her news.

"First of all, the Riverton council asked me to tell you they have officially declared you to be the Champion of the Haven. This is a new title, and makes you a lord. In fact, you are now the only lord of the River Folk."

497

"A lord?" asked Brand, aghast, "we have no lords in the Haven. We swore off such things...long ago."

She nodded and sighed. "Nevertheless, you are now a titled lord."

"No, that simply won't do. Do they plan to provide me lands and a tower and retainers? That is simply not the way of the River Folk. I'm not even a clan leader."

"It hasn't been your way for many years," Gudrin conceded, "but you have to understand that everyone will feel better about your possession of the axe if you are a lord. You can't be a person of great personal power and refuse the title of lordship. People expect it, they desire it. They want you to be a personage of greatness, so that there is an easy, understandable reason for why you are special."

"Fine," Brand grunted. "You can tell them I'm Lord Rabing, and I'll take as my land the ruined Castle Rabing. That, at least, I feel I've earned."

"Good enough," she said, and then she gave him a hard look. "Have you already decided who will have the Jewel?"

"No. Not yet."

Brand studied his mug of coffee. He didn't like this title, it sounded more like a job than an honor. "They mean to send me hither and yon seeking out evil, don't they?"

"You are indeed getting wiser," she chuckled.

"In a way, that is probably a good thing," he said. She watched him, not offering any comment. After a moment, he continued. "It's the axe. This thing doesn't want to sit still. Never. It craves adventure, and if I ever sit still, as I've been doing these last few days, it grows ever more concerned about every fly that taps at my window. Every deer seen nibbling at the melon leaves causes the axe to jump about in paranoia."

Gudrin snorted. "I'm not surprised. We had the axe for a long while in our keeping, and we kept it far from any of our hands. All our folk who wielded it managed to slay great evils, but ever would they turn back upon our own people and slay them as well until brought down. Many eventually took their own heads with the axe."

"Ah," Brand said wryly, "I see now why you brought it to Riverton. Dupes abound here."

She laughed, but turned serious soon after. "Lord Rabing," she said, using his title for the first time and smiling at his alarmed reaction, "there is one last thing the Kindred would ask of you out of friendship."

"We have no greater friends than your people. Ask," he said.

"The goblins and their rhinogs have withdrawn from our mountains. But our problems are far from at an end. If you find you have a peaceful moment here, and the axe desires adventure, please come help us beneath our mountains."

Brand nodded without hesitation. He felt the axe shift excitedly on his back.

"I will most certainly do so."

Chapter Twenty
Telyn's Kiss

Gudrin didn't stay the night, but rather returned with Modi, who tirelessly rowed her back to Riverton. She said she planned to return to Snowdon with the good tidings of Brand's victories and his plans to come aid them in the future. She bade him not to wait too long.

The axe, for its part, was enthusiastic about the idea. It wanted nothing more than to head off for a new adventure in a new part of the world. The more enemies encountered on the way, the better.

Brand quelled it and his own wanderlust with some difficulty. He still had not decided what he would do with the Lavatis, and the end of the week was approaching. He felt determined to give Tomkin an honest answer by then. He felt he owed the Wee One that much at least. But by midweek, he had still come to no decision, and the stress of it combined with the restlessness of the axe had put him in a foul mood.

Telyn showed up at the door as darkness fell over the island. A light dusting of snow came down behind her as he opened the front door and smiled to see her. She had a shawl wrapped tightly around her head, showing only her smiling face. The knife she had found back in the redcap's armory was still ready at her belt.

Brand let her in and took the liberty of brushing the snow from her shoulders. Once the door was shut with a grinding of frost, she leaned close. "Are we alone?"

He shrugged and smiled. "Jak is about, but he is probably reading upstairs in his room."

She looked scandalized. "Corbin isn't here? I thought he was supposed to be your faithful second!"

"I didn't think that meant he should follow me about like a hound," said Brand shrugging and smiling at the idea, "he's back with his parents in Riverton. Aunt Suzenna needs more looking after than I do. Her grief is all the worse with winter falling around us."

She looked somewhat upset still, but the expression quickly dropped. She grabbed his tunic and kissed him by surprise. It was a hard, full kiss and his pulse quickened at the feel of her lips.

The axe interrupted by rustling and thumping his skull lightly. All but snarling, he pulled the pack from his back and tossed it onto a waiting easy chair by the fire.

Telyn cocked her head at him. "Is that axe a she? I sense jealousy."

Brand laughed. "The axe is upset by squirrels in trees. Jealous yes, but I don't think of it as female."

"Does it move while it's alone?" she asked, eyeing the pack on the easy chair, "can it move by itself?"

Brand shook his head and rubbed his chin, looking at the thing. When it was further from his body, he felt less irritable, but even so he was annoyed that Telyn had halted kissing and started talking about the axe. Perhaps, he thought, this was the thing's evil plan all along. Perhaps, it had gotten what it wanted by distracting her.

"Now, where were we?" he asked, pulling her close.

They kissed for several minutes longer. Brand reflected that he had never had time like this to really be close and alone with Telyn. He enjoyed it thoroughly.

Finally, she stopped him with a soft hand to the chest. Brand looked down at the gently pushing hand with disappointment.

"Brand Rabing!" she said, laughing quietly, "You have changed! I recall being the one who chased harder."

Brand smirked. He had his hands on her elbows.

"I have a confession to make," she said, "I didn't come here just for this."

"No?" Brand tried to keep the disappointment out of his voice.

"I am enjoying it, don't get me wrong. But there is something bad going on, down south along the Deepwood border. There's a giant, Brand."

Brand pulled her a fraction closer. He shrugged. "There are always giants in the Deepwood."

"Of course, but this one has been raiding a pig farm in the Haven."

"A pig farm?" snorted Brand. He managed to sneak in another kiss and she responded briefly.

"Yes. A farm owned by my cousins. A Fob farm."

Brand sighed and let go of her. He put his hand to his face.

"What is it?"

Shaking his head, he walked over to his pack and strapped the axe to his back again. It shifted about excitedly. "Fine," he said, "if that's your purpose, I'll be off. Just tell me where it is, and I'll bring you this giant's head for your father's mantle down in Riverton."

She pouted. "You are mad at me?"

"Not at all."

"Liar."

"Did you even want to kiss me?" he asked, suddenly feeling a pit of depression coming over him. All everyone wanted was his service. He had become the rich man Gudrin had described. Even his love wanted something for every favor.

"Oh, Brand," she said, sensing his mood, "of course I did. Don't be upset. We can go in the morning. Just because I came to you for help doesn't mean I don't really care about you."

Brand thought about that, and took a breath. Perhaps the axe heightened every emotion, not just anger.

There were two easy chairs in front of the fire. The axe soon occupied one, while they occupied the other.

Chapter Twenty-One
Twrog's Hunger

Twrog was back, barely a week after the second raid on the farm to ponder his third. He had his club, but he had run out of ham hocks. He had promised himself this wouldn't happen. He had counted the hams several times, each time resulting in a different total, as often happened to him. But he was fairly sure he had about a dozen of them. This should have lasted him nearly two weeks, if he had only stuck to his promise to himself. He had sternly resolved to eat no more than one a night.

The very first night, of course, he had broken the promise by consuming two. He forgave himself this weakness. After all, it had been the very first time he'd tasted ham in so many years. Could he really blame himself for his lack of control?

The second day had gone poorly, however. He had consumed one ham for breakfast, figuring that after all it was indeed a new day. This left him starving by lunchtime of course, but he had managed to sate himself with a rather stringy black bear that he had dug out of its lair where it tried to hibernate. By evening, he lost control and gorged himself on the fourth and fifth hams.

And so it went throughout the week. He had miscounted, fortunately, and had several more than the dozen he had estimated. But they were all gone far too quickly. It was with great sadness that he gnawed on the heavy bone of the last one.

He cracked the bone and used the shards to pick at his teeth dismally.

Within a few days he found himself eyeing the farm again. His foot hadn't even healed over, and there had been no less than seven arrows and bolts he'd had to pluck from his hide. What horrors would he find waiting for him if he raided the farm a third time? He felt a new sensation as he eyed the farm this time. Twrog felt afraid of the River Folk and their wrath. Singly, they were helpless against him. But they were tricksy, and working together as a pack, they were dangerous and could cause him a great deal of hurt.

But his hunger would not leave him alone. The hams were forever in his mind now, his memory of their flavor sharper than before. He dreamt of them. Standing under the Rowan tree, he slavered over the heavy smells of the last pigs that still milled about the pens. He had to have them.

If only he could come up with a plan. He spent the night with his great arms wrapped around his knees, staring downhill at the farm.

The next morning at dawn he woke with a start. Birds scolded him from their safe perches. Squirrels cast sticks down at him. He considered uprooting their trees and giving them the surprise of their tiny lives—he had done such things before— but it was simply too much effort today. Besides, he was hungry. He had been here many times, looking down on the farm, while he was hungry. But today was different. Today, he felt he could do something about it. Today, he knew where they kept the hams. And so he stood and stretched, reaching for his club.

And he froze. Down in the yard around the farmhouse, something was happening. There were people down there. Four of them. They marched out toward Twrog. One of them looked shiny and glinted in the sun. Twrog had to search his hazy memories, but he felt sure that the man wore armor. He had not seen a man in armor in many, many years. He could not recall the last time, in fact. But he knew that a man in armor was dangerous. Such men knew weapons, and knew how to hurt a harmless fellow like Twrog.

Twrog growled and slammed his club idly into the trunk of the Rowan tree. It shuddered and burst with fleeing birds and at least one shocked squirrel. Twrog paid no heed to these tiny creatures. His eyes were fixed upon the man in armor. Had the farmers brought him to protect their hams? Just how many hams did they have left?

Twrog's eyes narrowed in calculation. They would not have brought a man in armor for just their last broken buildings and a scattering few hams. They probably had to pay the armored man in hams, what else did they have? He nodded to himself with a growing certainty. They had more hams, somewhere. Plenty of them. Scores of them. Perhaps down in the basement. He might have to dig them out, and he vowed to do it. He would tear that house apart this time. They had unfairly hidden their meats from him, and made a fool of him. He would not leave again without having them all.

The man in armor walked closer. A few others with bows ready walked with him. He seemed to be heading toward the very spot Twrog stood. Could he have seen him? Or perhaps they had noticed the burst of birds? Twrog wasn't certain, but he hunkered down and moved away from the hill, circling the farm in the forest. He would wait until the armored man was gone, then he would find those hidden hams.

Twrog managed to stick to his plan for many long minutes. He hunched in the trees, at the very border of the farm that was closest to the farmhouse. He would begin his search at the house, for he could not figure any other spot they might be keeping their horde of fresh hams. He was quite convinced by now they had a great number of hams. Probably in the basement. It would be cool and dark there, like a cave. They must have stacked them down there. Stacked them like cordwood.

After the armored man had long since vanished into the trees, Twrog made his move. He felt he was quite clever, actually. They had gone to the spot where they had twice seen him exit the forest. Now, he would surprise *them* with a trick! He was coming at them from a completely different part of the forest. They would have nothing planned to stop him now, he felt certain of it.

He gripped his club and regripped it. Slaver ran from his chin. The farm was quiet, and he couldn't stand to wait any longer. He stood tall and marched out into the open fields.

At first, everything went very smoothly. He was wary, however. His foot had not yet healed, and it still pained him and caused him to walk with a limp. But as he approached the farmhouse and heard the whoops of the surprised humans inside, he began to run in a stumbling gait, dragging his bad foot behind. The thatch roof had not been completely repaired since his last visit, but they had done some work on it. Timbers shored up the beams, but it still sagged down deeply in the midsection.

He dug into the smokehouse first, of course. He was horrified to find it empty. He could have sworn that he had left a few hams behind in his rush to escape last time.

He roared in disappointment. It was so *wrong!* So *unfair!* They had taken their meats and hidden them. They wanted them all for themselves, these greedy little creatures. He swung his club with a heavy grunt and demolished the smokehouse once and for all. Splinters and smoldering bits flew everywhere.

He stepped up to the farmhouse next, and small screaming figures fled in all directions.

* * *

Brand was in a foul mood. Telyn had brought him here, and he had expected a fight. Instead, he'd found a lot of stinking pigs and a cold trail. She had neglected to mention the giant hadn't been seen in a week. The thing could have been anywhere by now. He had no desire to trudge about in the Deepwood on the barest hope they might encounter the creature again. He was no tracker, no huntsman. He (and the axe, very definitely) preferred a stand-up fight. Brand found himself nostalgic for the circumstances of his earlier battles. Rhinogs didn't make you go hunting for them! They came up and did their business and died where they stood, at least you could say that for them.

506

He walked with Telyn and her two cousins, glowering fiercely. His chainmail, the same shirt he had taken from the redcap's armory, glinted and jingled as he walked. The Fobs all exchanged worried glances, eyeing him in concern. He tried not to notice this, as it would only irritate him further.

They led him up to a spot under a rowan tree and showed him where the earth was trampled down. They explained the giant had often watched them from this spot. They figured that he might just come back at any time.

In fact, they stared at the trees around them and gripped their bows tensely, as if they thought the monster might burst out upon them any second. Brand snorted. They weren't cowards, not exactly. Cowards would not have come out to a giant's favorite spot in the first place. But they were a nervous bunch of farm folk. Telyn nosed around in the trees, showing more bravery than her cousins.

"Come out! Come out! Come on, worthless, fat oaf of a giant!" shouted Brand at the trees. The Fobs looked at him, startled. He grinned at them. He thought suddenly, strangely, how easy it would be to pull out the axe and slay them both. He would make quick work of it, that was for sure.

He shook his head and took a deep breath, trying to settle himself down. His mood dampened somewhat. He told himself that was the axe talking. It was bored, and had been promised a fight, and now it wanted blood. Any source would do.

The Fobs were staring now. They weren't staring into his eyes, but rather.... He looked down and noticed he had the axe in his hand. He could not quite recall having pulled it out of his pack.

Even the axe made him angry. He gave it a good shaking, cutting about at the air with it. His throat burned with a growl.

"Brand?" asked Telyn from behind him. He almost whirled, but caught himself. He didn't want to face Telyn like that, with the axe in his hand and having a good grip on his mind. Lavatis, which still rode in his pocket, wasn't helping. The Blue Jewel was not in contact with his skin, but his mind was affect just by carrying it. His mind, for its own part, squirmed.

"Brand, I don't see the giant. Why don't you put that away for now?"

507

Brand took another breath and nodded. He put the axe away, slowly.

"Sorry," he said briskly, "the axe is just bored, that's all."

He noticed the Fobs were all a fair distance from him. This made him grin. They were afraid of him. Telyn blinked and smiled in return, hesitantly. She took a step forward, but only a single step. Brand figured there must be a wolfish quality to his grin.

He threw his hands up and laughed a true laugh, shaking his head. "It does that sometimes," he explained, "if I become moody, just back away. Telyn will handle such moments, she's very good at it, as you have just witnessed."

Before any of the Fobs could speak, however, a great *cracking* sound came to their ears. The sound was rather like that of a tree being felled in a forest. It came from the direction of the farm, behind them.

"The giant!" said Brand, and the grin slashed open his face again. He showed all his teeth and flashed out the axe.

"Brand?" said Telyn at his back, but he didn't stop. He was running and the axe was out, and life was good again. The others ran after him. Let the fools follow. Let them play with their bows. He would give them a show.

When he came out of the forest and first saw the giant he felt surprise. Not shock, but surprise. It was bigger than he had imagined. Its head rode even with treetops, as high as any farmhouse chimney. The legs would be all he could reach, most likely, the belly being too high, about ten feet up.

He ran faster.

The giant, having finished with the smokehouse, advanced upon the sagging farmhouse. Children and oldsters ran from the windows and doors.

Brand gritted his teeth and ran hard, wishing he had a horse. He had less than a quarter mile to go when the giant took hold of the roof. The giant's arms bunched, then relaxed as the roof came away. Brick walls shivered and fell partly to rubble. A plume of smoke and dust curled around the huge head as the giant dipped its face down into the interior, looking for something.

"What do you hope to find, monster?" roared Brand, hoping the challenge would slow it. The monster showed no sign of hearing. Taking up its great club again it beat down the walls with methodical swings. Brand was surprised at its power, but didn't slow his step or feel even a thread of fear.

The giant was digging now, tearing into the floors. The second floor pancaked down onto the first. The giant smashed its way further in, standing fully in the house's remaining walls. Suddenly, it went down to one knee. Brand realized that it must have driven a leg down into the basement.

Roaring, the thing continued to smash downward with its club, widening the hole.

Brand raised the axe, he was near the monster now. He commanded the axe to flash, and was gratified to see the great head wince. A thick-fingered hand came up to shield a misshapen face.

Brand was winded, but cared not one whit about it. He began slashing. A huge hand batted at him, as if he were an insect to be shooed away. The ends of two great fingers fell into the barnyard. A great gout of blood burst from the severed fingers and the giant loosed a howl of pain.

The giant threw handfuls of bloody bricks at him. One struck his head and his skull rang inside as might a bell. He saw arrows sprout from the giant's face and chest, but both of them knew arrows were insignificant.

The giant had its foot free of the cellar. With its good hand, it lofted a massive club.

Twrog turned to face the Axeman, and the Axeman did what he had to do. He did not step back, he did not quail in fear, he did not worry about the brick that had that left one eye shut and swollen. He charged in close. The club whistled down, striking explosively where he had stood a moment before.

Brand came close enough to slash at the legs, making the giant back up. It smelled of sweat, blood and crushed leaves.

The giant's leg slipped into the hole it had made so recently. Brand swept with the axe once more, slashing open the great belly which was now within reach.

An ear-breaking roar sounded. The great oaken club swung and Brand's axe flashed to intercept it. Brand was shocked that club didn't give way to the sharpness of the axe. Any normal wood should have parted, but the club was not a normal club. It caught Brand and sent him sprawling. Only the giant's awkward position kept Brand from being dashed to death upon the ground.

Struggling to rise, Brand wondered if he lived his last moments. One more swing and the giant would have him. But the giant had other concerns. Holding his slashed open belly up with one hand and dragging his club with the other, he yanked loose his foot and ran for the Deepwood with a rolling gait. As he ran, he gave great honking cries, like blasts of a huntsman's horn.

Brand judged the giant's pace, and decided he could never hope to keep up. He thought vaguely that he needed to get a horse for these adventures.

He let himself sag down in the dust. Bricks pressed against his back, but he didn't care.

Telyn came to him and ran soft light fingers over his face. The fingers felt nice and he smiled with bloody teeth at her. She was saying something, but he didn't know what it was.

Chapter Twenty-Two
Tree-bones

When his eyes fluttered open again, he saw a different face looming over him. It was Myrrdin. He struggled and sat up, grunting. Telyn and her cousins had dressed his wounds. He found himself leaning against the side of the barn in the shade. They must have dragged him here.

With a sudden jolt of worry, Brand looked for his axe. He found it still in his white knuckled grip. He had not released it, even when his mind had left his body behind. He sighed and put the axe into its sack and rubbed his face. The axe did not complain, as it had let blood flow today.

"Welcome back, Myrrdin," he said, trying to sound cheery and failing.

Myrrdin chuckled and pulled a kitchen chair with a missing leg from the demolished remains of the farmhouse. He propped the broken chair against the barn and sat beside Brand. "I came to see how you were doing as the bearer of two great burdens. Not so well, it appears."

"I'm doing quite well! You should have seen it. Did the others tell you? The thing was huge. Not as huge as the Rainbow, of course, but bigger than anything else I've ever faced."

"I'm told that before you caught up with that unfortunate giant, you nearly turned the axe on the Fobs."

Brand growled. "That's gratitude for you!"

"Oh, they are thankful. But they are still afraid. Of both you and what may come out of the Deepwood next."

"Afraid of me?"

"Brand, you are not acting as your normal self. You are bearing two Jewels. Many minds would break under the weight of just one."

"I only wield the axe. I never touch Lavatis."

"Yes, that is wise. But the Blue Jewel is still affecting you. It magnifies the fury of the other. It makes it harder for you to resist. You must give it up."

"The Fobs all live and the giant is gone," complained Brand. "What more do people want?"

Myrrdin shook his head sadly. "They want peace, not vengeance. None of this had to happen. Many have died here."

Brand eyed Myrrdin coldly. His eyes were slits. "So, what do you really want, wizard?"

Myrrdin took a deep breath, but Brand put his hand up to stop him from answering. He struggled to his feet. "Don't speak, for I know the answer. It is plain on your face. You want the Blue Jewel for your own."

"No Brand," said Myrrdin gently, as if he were addled. "I want to return it to Oberon, who has wielded it for so many years. He kept creatures like this out of the Haven for two centuries."

"I think we can handle our own affairs now. As should be self-evident from the state of that giant."

"Oh yes, he was mortally wounded, of that I have no doubt. But it's a sad thing to be forced to take a life, Brand. Oberon kept this tragedy from occurring without killing anyone. He could have kept the giant in the Deepwood, where it has dwelt for so long. Even I took pity upon Twrog long ago when I found him there."

"So, you once took pity upon that giant?" asked Brand becoming furious. Every time a story of Myrrdin and the Faerie came to his ears, the tale ended in deep sorrow and death for the River Folk. The pity was always bestowed upon some other creature. "You admit yet another mistake that has caused my people yet more grief. Come with me, we will find the truth behind this giant."

512

Brand stood up and didn't want to listen to any more nonsense from the Fobs or the meddling wizard. He marched into the Deepwood following the blood trail. Myrrdin followed him quietly.

They marched for hours, until at last the shadows stretched long between the trees. Night fell, and still they kept marching. Brand's axe lit the way, showing the giant's trail clearly. Brand marveled at the giant's vitality. A man would have succumbed to death miles earlier. It was early morning the next day when the two of them finally came to an open glade surrounded by vast thickets of spiny vines. The giant had run through these, blazing a trail through the twisted morass of wild growth. In the center of the glade was a massive oak tree. The giant's corpse rested against the trunk amongst the black, snake-like roots. So large was the oak that it dwarfed even the giant's body. The tree itself had been broken, the top half having long ago been torn away. Like a broken black tower, the trunk stood alone in the center of the glade.

Brand stepped out into the glade and eyed the giant. The slack face drooped down upon the chest. Somehow, seeing the great being in death caused him to feel a twinge of pity for it. There were so few of its kind, and he could see that in many ways it was like a huge lonely child.

"Why did he come here?" he asked aloud as the Myrrdin came out of the forest behind him. He turned to Myrrdin. "Why did Twrog come here to die?

"I've told you about this spot before. Recall the story of Vaul. This is the spot where I came to possess the Green Jewel."

Brand marveled at the tree, circling it. He remembered the tale well. Myrrdin had told him that he had found it inside a huge tree in the Deepwood. He had dug it out of the tree with the help of a giant. Brand nodded slowly, understanding now. Twrog was the giant who had helped Myrrdin dig the Green Jewel from its living encasement.

"And the club? It is a piece of this great oak, isn't it? That is why it didn't shatter when I struck it with the axe. It was enchanted by your Jewel."

Brand mounted the tree, climbing up some fallen limbs.

"Sometimes Brand," said the wizard, "it's best not to look too closely at the past."

Brand ignored him. He climbed up until he could see into the rotted core of the huge trunk. He saw where the Green Jewel must have been discovered. Encased inside the core of the trunk were white bones.

But the bones enveloped in six feet of solid oak did not surprise him. He had known that the previous owner of the Green Jewel had been overcome by it, and had been consumed by it. The power of the Jewel was the creation of huge, roiling growth, and that was also the danger of it. Unless one mastered the Green Jewel fully, the wielder could become one with the greenery it so loved to create.

So, what surprised him was not the presence of the bones, but their *size*. The finger bones, each as thick as his own arm, were upraised from the core of the trunk upon a wrist of even thicker bones. Clearly, he looked upon the entombed skeleton of a giant, a giant that was even larger than Twrog. The upraised hand had once held Vaul and in a final act, had lifted the Jewel up to keep it from being consumed by the uncontrollable growths. The love the owner had for Vaul was beyond all else in the world. Even as Vaul killed her, the giant had reached up to ensure that the Green Jewel was the last thing to be consumed by the great tree's trunk.

"She loved the Jewel more than even her own life, didn't she?" asked Brand.

Myrrdin looked troubled. He had come to stand near Twrog's foot, which was still caked with black forest earth and dried blood.

"The hand is here, Myrrdin, just as you said," Brand said, "but you left out a critical detail. The hand is that of a giant. One even larger than Twrog here."

"Yes," said Myrrdin. He did not raise his eyes to meet Brand's.

"She was his mother, wasn't she? The giant you slayed to take the Green Jewel."

Myrrdin sighed. "It was a very long time ago, Brand."

Brand laughed. "You lied! No wonder you took pity upon Twrog. Compared to you, this creature was an innocent."

"The Jewel consumed the she-giant. I didn't slay her."

"Nonsense. Come clean, man! Don't you have enough riding on your conscience without more pretentions and deceptions? You did something. Something that caused her to wield the Jewel before she had mastered it, perhaps."

"Brand, you have to understand the times. I was much like you. Young and new to battle. The last armies of your people were following me. They needed strength to stop Oberon."

"Something vile. That's what you did," said Brand. He hopped and slid down the branches of the great oak to look up at Twrog's corpse.

"Brand, you should understand better than anyone. What would you have done to save your people when we faced Herla in the Dead Kingdoms? Or, to put it more clearly, what would you *not* have done?"

Brand rubbed his chin with the attitude of one that was puzzling something out. "Oh, I'm not saying I'm better than you, wizard. Not that at all. I'm not saying I would have done anything different. But I am enjoying your discomfort. Let's have it all out now, the truth."

Myrrdin sighed and shook his head.

"None of that now. I'm going to get to the bottom of this. Corbin could do it, and so will I. First, there was how you found the place. The Deepwood has a thicker, more lush growth of trees and brush than anywhere else known to us. That's what attracted you here, to search for the Jewel. You knew it must be here somewhere."

Myrrdin flashed him a look of sheepish annoyance and did not answer.

"Ah-ha!" shouted Brand. "I can see I'm on the right track. Let's see, you figured out the she-giant had the Jewel. But giants are a simple folk, probably it would be difficult for her to master Vaul. Apparently, she knew this and you had to force her to do use Vaul's power. So you...you went after her child, didn't you? You captured him, tormented him perhaps. And so she used the only power she had, the Jewel, and it consumed her. After that, all you had to do was dig it out of the trunk. Am I missing any important bits?"

Myrrdin glared at him. "Let's talk of other things."

"Let's finish the tale. Out of pity for the giant child, you cut him a great branch from this trunk and fashioned him a club from it, so he could survive alone in the wilds."

Myrrdin looked up, thrusting his chin high. "Your deductions are close enough. But let us finally talk of current events. That's what matters now. What do you plan to do with the Blue Jewel?"

"Oh, that? I'm supposed to hand it over to you. Perhaps you would be so good as to transport it for me to Oberon."

Myrrdin shrugged. "You can walk the mound in Riverton and give it to him yourself, if you like."

"No. No, I will not."

"And why not Brand? Why not return it to the rightful owner and cause ruffled feathers to lie flat again? You might achieve another century of peace for your people."

"What will Oberon trade me for the Jewel?"

"What do you suggest?"

Brand smiled widely. "I suggest an offering. Let them toil all year long, every year, and then bring to us the results of their labors. Magical cloths, rare gems and delicacies such as the fruits from their fantastic orchards."

Myrrdin sputtered. "What nonsense! None of Faerie would toil for an instant to give their goods to the River Folk! Your demands border on the insane, Brand. The sibling Jewels have addled your mind."

"Nevertheless, that is my price. Humanity has two Jewels, the Faerie, so far as I know, have none. If they want parity with our strength, they must face reality. They are no longer our overlords."

"What you speak of is unthinkable. I would not even dare discuss it with Oberon, for fear of losing my head."

Brand shrugged. "You wield the Green Jewel, you have nothing to fear from them."

Myrrdin peered at him closely. "You have no intention of returning the Jewel to Oberon, do you? This is not a serious offer."

Brand peered back. He advanced a step and then stood close, facing the wizard. "Every story involving the Faerie and humanity is one of woe. Almost always, the sorrow has been

516

upon the human side. This will not continue to be the way of things."

Myrrdin nodded slowly. "I understand now how my sire felt when I abandoned him. He raged and he wept. He felt I was a traitor for a long while, that which he had raised as his own son had turned upon him. The same has happened to me this day."

Brand nodded in return. The axe wanted him to draw it. The desire was sharp in his mind. But he resisted the urge. "You have guided us for very long, Myrrdin, and we are grateful. But those times have come to an end. I will not return the Haven to the quiet servitude of the past. We will not bend a knee to any other folk."

"Oberon will not be pleased."

"If Oberon has more to say on the subject, he is welcome to come and discuss it in person."

Myrrdin walked away from him then, as darkness fell over the Deepwood.

Brand was left pondering the dead giant, the broken trunk of the oak, and the huge skeleton that lay entombed within it.

Chapter Twenty-Three
Brand's Decision

On the seventh morning, Tomkin showed up promptly at dawn. He rapped upon the door of the Rabing house with great tenacity until it was opened.

"'Tis the end of the week," said Tomkin, glaring up at Jak, who nodded and let him in.

Tomkin stood upon the table between the two easy chairs. Brand came in with two mugs of steaming broadleaf tea. He offered one to Tomkin who took it and drank greedily.

They eyed one another for a moment.

"You have made your decision," said Tomkin, "I can only assume you've decided to swindle me, as there is no welcome in your eyes."

"Perhaps you are right, Tomkin my friend."

"Friend?" spat the manling. "You dare use that word? It was through the power of that word that you first robbed me of Lavatis! Do you know what they say—my folk?"

Brand smiled thinly, amused by the Wee One's manner. Tomkin had begun to strut back and forth upon the table, gesturing with long-fingered hands. He reminded Brand of a rooster putting on a display for a flock of gullible hens.

"Tomkin the fool, Tomkin the mooncalf. That's what they say. My own relatives snortle behind their palms. Taken by a river-boy, he who has prided himself for decades—"

"Tomkin," interrupted Brand, "I'm giving the Jewel back to you."

The manling froze with both hands waggling every finger high over his head. He cocked his head at Brand and for once in his long life he was struck speechless.

"That's why my heart is heavy. You are a friend, and I fear that the Jewel will be your undoing, as it has been for so many others."

Brand produced the Blue Jewel, which did flash like the brightest summer sky as it came out of his pocket. He tossed it, rattling on its chain, to Tomkin. The manling snatched it out of the air and held it tightly to his chest, as a mother might hug her long lost babe.

"I—" said Tomkin, halting for a moment. Brand could tell that he was almost unable to speak. The Jewel reflected in his obsidian eyes. "I can't believe it. I know now that the Wee Folk can truly call you friend. None other has made a gift to us, other than the tip of a boot or the spittle flying from their lips."

"I only hope the River Folk and the Wee Folk can work together now. All changelings must be removed."

"Of course," said Tomkin quickly. "We will guard your borders as scouts. Not a rabid squirrel will set foot in the Haven without a prompt report being made to Riverton."

"Great," said Brand, smiling. It was true, now that the Blue Jewel was gone from him he did feel more at ease. "Tomkin?"

"Yes, *friend?*"

"Just don't lose it."

End of *Shadow Magic*

Fantasy Books by B. V. Larson

THE HAVEN SERIES
Volume I: Haven Magic
(First three books: Amber Magic, Sky Magic, Shadow Magic)
Volume II: Dark Magic
(Books 4 thru 6: Dragon Magic, Blood Magic, Death Magic)
Volume III: Dream Magic (Series finish)

Visit BVLarson.com for more information.

8740793R00290

Printed in Great Britain
by Amazon.co.uk, Ltd.,
Marston Gate.